D1743554

THE PUPPET MASTER

Jess Sturman-Coombs is a writer of fiction to include, but not limited to, sci-fi, romance and thrillers. Her debut novel, Poker Face, has received glowing reviews and many requests for more. The Puppet Master is the second instalment in this legal thriller series. So, if you like what you find in the following pages, please keep a look out for the next instalment of gritty storytelling. There's definitely more to come from Ruby Palmer!

Jess graduated from The University of Northampton with a degree in law and lives in Northamptonshire with her son, daughter and husband. More details can be found about the author of this book on her official website jesssturman.wix.com/jess-sturman-coombs. You can also connect and interact with her via her blog 'Lock, stock and barrel', by clicking the link on the home page.

THE PUPPET MASTER
Book two in the Poker Face series...

Jess Sturman-Coombs

jesssturman.wix.com/jess-sturman-coombs

2

Printed and bound in the UK. First edition December 2012
Published by Jess Sturman-Coombs
ISBN 978-0-9571012-2-7

A CIP record for this book is available from the British Library

Cover design: Ivan Waldock

Dedications

I believe it is only fitting to dedicate your proud and finished work to those that have helped you to create it, whether that be by way of support, services, advice, assistance or love and faith. So, to all of those people who have helped to edge The Puppet Master that bit closer to the big wide world of publishing, I dedicate this story to you. You know who you are and I do too. Thank you so much.

I would also particularly like to thank my family and close friends. Thank you to my two beautifully creative children, Ollie and Madeline, for knowing all there is to know about the Poker Face series (save for the actual story because it's a 15+) and taking a huge interest in what their mummy does. You make the world so bright and I love you with all my heart.

Thank you also to my awesome husband, Robin, who hasn't changed a bit since we met. I have nothing but thanks for all you have done to help me achieve my ambitions in life. I love you.

And a final thank you to Ivan Waldock for another beautiful, elegant and striking cover design. They say you can't judge a book by its cover, and we all know this to be true, but an awesome cover certainly helps to get that book the attention it so desperately wants and needs. Thank you.

CONTENTS

1
Back off!

Ruby stopped reading through the Notice of Appeal on the Rossi file and smiled at the young man who'd just stepped onto the landing. She glanced at Danny, who was paying no attention as he poured through yet another stack of witness statements.

"Hi, is that for us?" she asked, eyeing the parcel he was holding in his hands. He looked smartly dressed from his nodding head to his steel toe capped boots.

He smiled, flashing a cute little dimple. "A Mr...Alessi?" he asked her, checking on his paperwork again.

"Yeah he's here but he's a bit busy right now," she explained, standing and making her way towards him. "I'll take it...Todd," she offered, pulling the lid off her pen with her teeth. He chuckled, his fingers instinctively moving to play with his name badge as he turned the clipboard towards her.

"Signature there, print there and mobile number there, please," he requested. She did as he asked only stopping after the first two numbers of her mobile. Danny was already watching with interest.

"Nice move," he mumbled under his breath. Ruby glanced at him and then back to the delivery driver before frowning sweetly. He grinned back, having the cheek to push it.

"Right there," he pointed out simply. "Just your usual mobile number will do."

She shook her head as her face began to flush. "I'm not giving you my mobile number," she told him in a whisper. She was cringing with embarrassment, knowing Danny was now utterly engrossed and keen to see how she would handle the unwanted attention. She was never going to live this one down!

"Why not?" he asked her innocently. "I don't bite, although I do like to go out and eat. I'm assuming you must eat sometimes too?" He gave her a brief checking out. She was small and he concluded that a good meal certainly wouldn't do her any harm. "Perhaps we could go out and eat...*together?*" he smiled. She laughed, surprised.

"I'm sorry...I can't," she told him straight, but unfortunately this delivery driver was persistent.

"Why? You got a boyfriend?" he asked her and she squirmed.

"Hmmm...I suppose...I...kind of." She didn't sound convinced and now Danny was leaning forward on his elbows, his mouth slightly open in astonishment. Her face felt very hot. How the hell was she going to get out of this!

"What does that mean?" the driver asked her, genuinely bewildered. "Is it serious?"

"Yeah come on, Ruby, is it serious?" Danny goaded. "You've got two guys very keen to find out what you'd consider your relationship status to be."

She looked torn and nervous. "I...I'm not sure..." she informed their visitor, resisting another look at Danny. The driver glanced between the two, sensing some issue between them and then turned to Ruby.

"OK...well...if you decide it's *not* serious then here's my mobile number." He jotted it across the top of the parcel and pushed it onto her desk. "Nice to meet you...Ruby," he smirked. She rolled her eyes at him like he'd just caused her a hell of a lot of trouble.

As soon as Todd had left to make his descent down the stairs Ruby took a deep breath and faced the gorgeous young man sitting across the room from her, the gorgeous young man who was now waiting for some answers. He was still leaning onto his desk looking exquisite, as usual.

"I'm sorry," she defended. "But he put me on the spot and I didn't know what to say."

"How about 'I have a boyfriend and he's sitting right here listening to this very awkward conversation we're having...*Todd?*' How about that?" he suggested, like it was that easy. She huffed at him like he was being ever so slightly unreasonable.

"I was embarrassed!" She dropped her hands to her sides wearily. "He asked me if we were serious and...I'm sorry...but I just don't know."

"Oh great," he snorted like it was funny, though she could tell from his dark expression that it wasn't.

"Other girls have had so much more from you than I have, Danny, it's hard to know whether you see this...thing...we have going on here as serious, as serious as your *other* relationships. I mean you say you're my boyfriend..."

"Correction, I *am* your boyfriend," he exclaimed using his pen to point at her, but she held up her palm to stop him.

"Yeah, but is that just because we've been through so much together and now you feel like you owe me? Are you just looking out for me like you would a sister? Is that all I am to you, Danny, a sister?" she accused and he pulled an utterly grossed out face and threw his pen down onto the desk.

"Oh my god, Ruby, if only you knew how much I do not see you as a sister! And, for your information, I do not feel like I owe you either. This isn't a sympathy thing we've got going on here, Ruby," he argued resentfully.

"What's going on?" Alessi interrupted, stepping out of his office to see what the raised voices were all about.

"Ask Ruby," Danny grumbled, picking his pen back up and turning his attention to his paperwork. "We've got the very important Rossi appeal coming up but apparently Ruby still has time to arrange a romantic dinner for two."

Alessi looked at her and she glared back at him, slinging the carbon copy receipt for the parcel in the direction of her desk. It missed and drifted to the floor and she shrugged like she couldn't care less. She knew that would hack off the disciplined, Mr Alessi. He would be keen to get it into a file marked 'Carbon Copy Delivery Receipts. Ones That Have Been On The Floor'.

9

"Oh I don't know, Alessi," she fumed looking up to meet his eyes. "How about you two dictating my sex life?" She was hoping to make him uncomfortable by using the word 'sex' but he didn't flinch or bite, making her all the more frustrated. "Just out of interest, Alessi, when will you stop messing with my personal life and get your own?" she asked him rudely.

He narrowed his eyes and tried to keep from smirking. "Are you suggesting I'm gate crashing your love life, Ruby, because I don't have one of my own to keep me occupied?"

"Yes!" she nodded firmly and he tilted his head back and laughed, highly amused by her.

"I'm not telling you when you can and cannot do it, Ruby," he told her coolly. "You're over sixteen, you're old enough and it's your life," he shrugged like she had his permission but she knew him too well. He was clever, he was sneaky and he was the biggest pain in the arse she'd ever come across.

"Don't give me that! You're my boyfriend's father and you've told him to keep his hands off me so YES you're interfering," she argued. "What's the point in giving me your blessing when you've told the only guy I want to be with that he can't be with me like that?"

"He's my son, it's my duty to make sure he does the right thing by his girlfriends," he smiled smugly. "It's not my fault his girlfriend happens to be you now, Ruby Palmer, is it? In fairness, I did tell you not to go there. I did tell you that I wasn't happy about you two getting together. You only have yourselves to blame."

It was all going his way and Ruby growled at him furiously before storming off to go get some air.

2
Walk Out

Ruby had walked out of work the day before, half an hour early, and left Danny and Alessi wondering where the hell she'd gone. They had searched the building high and low, tried her mobile and then happened to ask Amanda on reception if she'd seen her. Although there was no way Amanda couldn't have known they were looking for the feisty young teenager, who also happened to be Mr Alessi's most controversial employee, she'd chosen not to share her knowledge about Ruby's whereabouts with them. Ruby had told her to inform Mr Alessi that she was going home but, thanks to Amanda, everyone was late leaving the building.

Alessi was furious with the protracted and difficult receptionist for wasting everybody's time, especially his, and instead of staying late like he often did, he went straight home to shout at Ruby for being immature, hotheaded and disrespectful. He had to do it through her bedroom door though, because as soon as Ruby realised he was in a foul mood she'd run up to her room and point blank refused to come out again. She wouldn't even come down for dinner. The evening had been volatile and Danny had done his best to try and talk Ruby round, but she wouldn't speak to him either.

When she eventually emerged dressed for work the following morning, she couldn't find Alessi anywhere. He would normally have been perched on a stool in the kitchen, drinking his coffee and reading his newspaper, but today the coffee in the machine was untouched and Alessi's paper was still folded on the breakfast bar. It wasn't until she went to look for him, to ensure her usual lift in to work, that she noticed his car was gone too. She left the house and descended the front steps, completely astounded. He always waited for her!

Danny stepped out of the shower and into his suit before making his way to the kitchen just in time to spot Ruby slipping through the front door. He grabbed a coffee from the machine and scooped up Alessi's morning paper before following Ruby into the garden. He knew that Alessi had already left for work. He had been so bad tempered first thing that morning that Danny had told him he would follow him in. He wanted to make sure Ruby didn't get left behind. Ever since she'd spent a nightmarish journey on a hijacked double-decker bus he tried to save her from public transport whenever he could, ferrying her about when Alessi was either too busy or too grumpy to do it himself. His bare feet crunched over the gravel drive and he leaned against his own car as he studied Ruby's perfect rear profile. She was gorgeous and irresistibly hot-tempered. He wouldn't change her for the world.

"He said, and I quote, 'If she doesn't have the decency to come out of her room and talk to me like a grown up then she can damn well get the bus like a child.'" He smiled upon seeing her deep intake of breath. The slow rise and fall of her shoulders told him she was desperately trying to stay calm.

"The bus?" she asked through gritted teeth.

"Yup," he grinned, tilting his head to the side to check her out from another angle. She was seriously hot! "He said he's pretty sure with the attitude you've got you could still get on and ride at the reduced 'juvenile rate'. He left you £2.40 on the breakfast bar," he added on with a smirk. She suddenly spun round to glare at him and he tried to drop the amusement but it was too late, she'd spotted it. Just like that, Ruby was on one of her rants again.

"Ugh he infuriates me!" she fumed and he nodded.

"I'm pretty sure the feeling's mutual. Look, Ruby, chill out yeah? You are blowing this out of all proportion. It's not how you think it is, you're taking it all so...personally."

"Personally? I saved your arses from Mickey and helped to take his men out, Danny!" she yelled at him, her forehead creased with angry lines. "What do I have to do to be accepted around here?" she demanded bitterly.

"Not sleep with me that's for sure!" he frowned, hoping that would be obvious. "Look, Rubes, you *are* accepted around here! We know what you did for us and it took some serious courage. You have no idea how proud I am of you..."

"But not proud enough to commit to a relationship with me?" she interrupted firmly, her face showing signs of true Ruby fury, the kind that could make a grown man shake. Danny wasn't shaking, but only because he had a history of not very nice run-ins with people. He might get hit accidently by one of Ruby's flailing arms, but that was a totally different story to having been tied, gagged and beaten by Mickey and his men when they took over Alessi's house in search of the very incriminating Rossi appeal file. Mickey got much more than he bargained for; he got a lethal bullet. Ruby foiled his plans, helping to take them all out one by one and now the Rossi appeal could go ahead in a few months as re-scheduled.

Danny tried desperately to negotiate with Ruby's volatile temper. "Look, just because I won't sleep with you it doesn't mean that I'm not committed to you. I respect you..."

"Huh so all the girls you didn't respect get to have you like that and I get what?" She folded her arms defensively, her mouth pressed into a hard line.

"*You* get my heart, Ruby, is that not enough?" he asked her sincerely. She looked down at the floor and dug the toe of her sandal into the gravel, looking for a moment like she might be verging on reasonable. He waited patiently, watching the dark curls in the end of her hair move in the breeze, touching her waist as she sulked. "We agreed to wait until you were eighteen, remember?"

"To keep Alessi happy," she reminded him. "I don't actually want to wait until I'm eighteen, that's months away!"

"Look I'm older than you and I have more experience than you do. I'd just feel better not rushing it. It's not that long, Ruby, and you only recently found out that our scary mafia client, Johnny Giavani, is Alessi's father and that Alessi is mine. That's a pretty big deal, Rubes. You need to be sure that I'm what you really want. I will wait forever for you but you're potentially risking your whole life and safety, a life caught up rubbing shoulders with members of an organised crime group, for me. I'm not going anywhere so there's no rush, eighteen, nineteen, twenty, what does it matter? We're still with each other. I'm still committed to you, and only you."

"Twenty! Are you kidding me?" she exclaimed her eyes wide, her mouth open. He grinned at her. He hadn't meant that they had to wait till she was twenty, just that it didn't matter if they did.

"Ruby you were shot last year and you lost your dad that same night. Just before that you were held prisoner by Mickey and his men while they took you on a petrifying journey on a hijacked bus. You were harassed, roughed up and dumped in a bin on the order of Carlito's brother and that was all *before* being shot! After, you were held hostage by Mickey and treated horrendously. It's not like we've been sitting around here twiddling our thumbs avoiding sex. We have had a lot on, Ruby!"

"Ugh this isn't just about sex, Danny! This is about what you *not* doing it with me means."

"I don't understand," he confessed. "What does it mean?" He reached forward to touch her elbow briefly and she pushed her hands into her back pockets, a move clearly designed to make it impossible for him to touch her there again. He smiled slightly. Her stubbornness, although a living nightmare, was one of the things he loved about her. "Alessi just cares about you and I care about his wishes. He's my father, Ruby, and I should at least try and respect his authority on this. You live here, with him, and he just wants to look out for you. He worries we will rush into something and that I will then move on to someone else, or that we'll fall out over some *other* thing and won't be able to face each other."

"He's worried he will end up having to choose between you and me when it all goes wrong, Danny," she set him straight. "And we both know *who* he'd choose, don't we?" she grumbled feeling sorry for herself.

"I'm his son, Ruby, he can't very well turn his back on me, but equally he doesn't want to turn his back on you either. The situation really worries him."

"Well maybe if he hadn't shot and killed my dad he wouldn't have to worry quite so much. Thanks to him I'm trapped now. It's either Alessi's way or the highway!" she argued.

14

"I'm sorry, Ruby, I know it was a hard thing to do to you. But I can see why he did it, can't you? When I heard the way your father treated you, when I saw it for myself! The drunken ranting, the verbal abuse and the way he raised his fists to you and hurt you, I have to say that shooting him crossed my mind."

"Yeah and I appreciate that and all of this." She spread her hands wide to take in the mansion of a home and the vast established gardens and then she looked down at herself and dropped her arms helplessly. Even the clothes she wore were courtesy of him. "Danny, I feel like a pet, you know, one of those poodles that people dress up and give nice rooms and pretty beds to and all that...stuff!"

"You look great," he told her raising his eyebrows sexily and topping it off with an irresistible grin.

"That's not the point!" she snapped. "The point is that when my dad was around, OK, I accept that life was hell most of the time, but I always had somewhere I could go."

"Except when he chucked you out," he pointed out under his breath.

"Yeah but that was only ever for a couple of hours," she defended like that made it all okay. "I would go to Matthew's house and wait it out there. My dad would cool off and I would go home. But the point is that those couple of hours at Matthew's house were always conditional, there was always a deal. He gave me a place to stay and I gave him...I mean...he would want to..." She stopped, her eyes wide like she'd said too much already.

"What?"

"Erm...you know...cosy up and that," she cringed painfully and he frowned.

"Why don't you just say it how it is, Ruby?" he grumbled. He didn't like the fact that she and Matthew had spent so much time together. He really didn't like Matthew at all. The bloke was a creep and a user and he made Ruby feel like she was stupid and capable of nothing more than the gang lifestyle and the depressed housing estate in which she'd grown up. Matthew wanted to box her and keep her for himself. To do that to a wild

15

thing like Ruby was criminal, as bad as caging a bird and clipping its wings.

"We would make out in his bedroom, Danny!" she told him defiantly and he choked on his coffee.

"You and...Matthew?" he confirmed, fanning himself with the folded up paper.

"Yeah, that's what Alessi was talking about after that very first time he planted a bug on me, remember, after I accidently saw his private clients and looked at their file?" Danny nodded. He remembered that awkward conversation very well. Ruby had been mortified to discover that she'd been bugged and tracked and that Alessi had listened in on her evening with Matthew. He then insisted on giving her a sex talk. Ruby had never been so embarrassed! "He heard me arguing with my dad that night, my dad chucked me out and I went to Matthew's. I told Matthew about the argument and he took me in, like he always did. We watched a film and then we mucked about, nothing serious, but he wanted to take it further. He told me it was time we did it. He went on at me for ages; it was exhausting and I argued with him. He pushed it too far and I hit him with a metal tray and made his nose bleed. That passed a few hours and then I went home.

That's why I got 'the talk!' Alessi knew what my life was like but now I can't go back to my dad's and I can't stay indefinitely at Matthew's either. So when it all hits the fan, Danny, where do I go?" Before he could think of an answer she continued. "I'll tell you where I go...on the streets, that's where I go! I have no money and I work for Alessi, so that means I'll have no job either. How long till I'm finding money other ways, spending time with strangers like I spent time with Matthew...but without the tray for self defence?"

"No way - that's not going to happen!" he protested firmly. He couldn't believe what he was hearing and now he could see that her eyes had filled with tears. The unruffled Ruby was really scared. He had no idea she felt so vulnerable and alone. He tried to reach out to her but she pulled away. "Ruby, I would *never* let that happen. If you couldn't live here then you could live with me, in my apartment. I would never see you out on the streets like that, being exploited by men, probably married and twice your age." He cringed and tried to drive the disturbing thoughts from his head.

"But if we fell out over something, if you hated me, then you wouldn't say 'Come live with me, Ruby' you'd turn your back on me. If Alessi told you to you'd turn your back on me, in the same way that Alessi has told you not to sleep with me and you won't. He's the boss! I'm just here till he decides he's had enough of me and I'm sick of feeling like that, like he calls all the shots, like he has all the control. You refusing to sleep with me just proves my point. He barks the orders, you obey, and I keep my fingers crossed that he doesn't grow tired of his little charity case and cut me off completely, throw me out, wash his bloody hands of me! Do you have any idea how that feels?" she cried, her face flushed with anger. "He took my dad from me and he let me borrow all of this," she told him, spreading her arms wide again. "It's on loan, Danny, for just as long as I can keep him happy. He hasn't given me anything - all he's done is take away."

"Ruby, baby, I can see why you're scared but you're worrying over something that *isn't* going to happen. You could burn the house down and Alessi might shout a lot, might unleash some of his random lessons on you." She remembered those well, like being made to shred five boxes of brand new copier paper with a hangover from hell! Danny looked sorry for her now. "He would never actually kick you out, Ruby," he promised.

"Well maybe he won't need to because maybe I'm fed up with waiting for it to happen."

He didn't like the determination in her eyes. A determination he'd seen all too often before. "What's that supposed to mean, Ruby?" he asked her nervously.

"I'm bound to upset him sooner or later. I always end up disappointing..."

"No, that's not true, don't say..."

"Yes, Danny!" she interrupted stubbornly. "It is true and I'm not doing this anymore. He's going to have to get himself a new pet!"

She spun round and slipped into the house, locking the door behind her so he couldn't follow. He hammered against the wood with his fists while shouting out her name but she was already halfway up the stairs, climbing two at a time. She grabbed her mobile phone and shoved some things into a bag. She took one last look at the pink bedroom, wondering whether she was doing the right thing and then, before coming to a well reasoned decision, turned and ran back down the stairs.

Reaching the front door she looked out of the window but Danny wasn't there. She guessed he'd done exactly what she would do if she'd been locked out - he'd gone round the back. She took her chance, opened the front door, and made a beeline for the gates.

By the time Danny had managed to get into the house and realised she wasn't in her room packing, she was already on the street, walking.

3
Finding Ruby

Danny slammed the front door as he entered the house and Alessi looked up at Bardo with hesitantly. Bardo had been desperate to show his loyalty after briefly appearing to take Mickey's side in the storming of Alessi's property. He had been left little choice but to go along with it when the surprise attack came. He couldn't handle the situation alone; his mobile phone had been taken and his family had been threatened in return for his co-operation. With Ruby's bravery, and a decent dose of deception, they escaped with their lives.

Bardo now spent most of his time with Alessi on matters of security and he'd become a regular face around the place. Alessi folded the piece of paper in his hand and pushed it back into the A5 envelope in which it had arrived, just as Danny came into the dining room and pulled out a chair. His whole demeanour shouted 'pissed off', from the clenching of his jaw and the way he slumped back in his seat, to the way he glared at Alessi as he spoke.

"Any news?"

She'd been gone for weeks, with not a trace or a word, and the unknown was driving him insane. He'd spent hours driving around looking for her, especially at night. The stress was mounting and he'd started being rude and dismissive to clients and staff at Tangle and Alessi Solicitors, the firm owned by his father. Alessi sighed and tapped one corner of the envelope on the table as he studied the young man in front of him, wondering if he could handle it. Danny rested his ankle on his knee and folded his arms across his chest. "What?" he asked slowly.

"This came," Alessi told him as he placed the envelope down on the polished table and slid it towards him. Danny picked it up and looked it over.

"Another complaint from a client?" he asked casually. "What have I done now, told someone if they don't want to get done for speeding they should take their foot off the bloody accelerator?" Alessi shook his head.

"No, Danny, it's not from a client...this time."

Danny checked out the scrawled address, taking up most of the front of the envelope, and then opened it and unfolded the letter inside. He read it over, looking first at Alessi and then at Bardo. "So she's with Marlon?" he asked, astonished. Both nodded back solemnly.

"He sent the letter," Alessi explained. "It arrived this morning. Apparently he picked her up just outside here on the day she walked. She's been there the whole time. He recognised her as the infamous Ruby, who helped to take out Carlito and his brother, getting a bullet in the shoulder for her efforts. He also knows about how she played a major part in taking out Mickey and all of his men too.

"So what does he want with her?" Danny asked, having a good idea already but not wanting to admit it to himself. Marlon was a pusher who took in young girls with the promise of bigger and better things, right before introducing them to the immoral reality of strip clubs, brothels, drug pushing and trafficking. Even his home had a basement club for his most loyal and valued employees. His business was in the movement and exploitation of goods, be it girls, drugs, people's possessions or warehouse stock. If it wasn't bolted down it risked being acquired by Marlon and exchanged for the dirty money that lined his pockets and built his massive home. Alessi ran his hand over his mouth thoughtfully.

"He's making out he's looking after her, that he's taken her in because she had nowhere else to go. He says she's free to leave whenever she wants and that she misses you, Danny. He's invited us both to go see her and try and get her to come home."

"Well what are we waiting for? We go and get her back," Danny concluded.

"You're set for disappointment, Danny. He wouldn't have invited us to try if he thought she was going to leave. He's playing games and I'm not quite sure what he's up to. Perhaps I should just go by myself," Alessi suggested and Bardo nodded like it might be for the best. The last thing they wanted was for Danny to show any signs of weakness in front of Marlon. He'd pounce on it and use it against them. Alessi sighed, still thinking through the situation as he spoke. "Or we could wait it out for a bit. If we go now he's going to know we're eager."

"Well we are eager, so let's go now! How's she going to feel if we don't turn up?" Danny exclaimed. "She's going to think we've washed our hands of her and I promised we'd never do that. I promised her she wouldn't end up in exactly the position she's in now! She was petrified of this happening to her, Alessi, that's what all the arguing and tantrums were about. She was confused and insecure and I don't blame her either. Life has been really hard for her and she's constantly waiting for us to chuck her out. She expects us to give up on her because that's what people have always done with Ruby. We can't just wait it out, she'll be devastated."

"I know, Danny, I know," Alessi soothed, feeling his son's desperation. "But we need to be careful too. It's not always such a good idea to follow what your heart says, it can be dangerous," he warned.

"One visit wouldn't hurt though would it, Alessi?" Bardo chipped in, much to Danny's relief. "You know, just to reassure yourself that she doesn't seem hurt. Just see her, play it cool, ask her if she wants to come home," he trailed off as he looked over at Danny. "And expect her to say no."

A few days later they were sitting in Marlon's huge home. They had been taken to the 'seminar' room, a large space with a centrally positioned desk and chair, surrounded by lots of other seats. They took their places near to the desk and a short time later Marlon arrived. He made his way into the middle of the room in his khaki trousers and tight white t-shirt. His large muscles stretched the cotton fabric to near bursting as it clung like skin to his upper arms and broad chest. His feet were bare and wide and around his neck he sported a beaded necklace. An unlit rolled cigarette hung from his mouth, the moistness of his lips causing the paper to stick and stay in place as he spoke. He leaned back onto the desk and grinned sadistically.

"So, you came then?" He stated the obvious, looking very pleased with himself. "You needn't have worried, she's quite happy here. I'm looking after her *very* well. In fact I give her everything a girl could possibly need but still she pines over you, Danny. I hate to see her so sad so I told her I would arrange a little visit. She'll be here in a minute." He glanced at his watch and pulled a face. "She's probably just slipping into something irresistible for you," he guessed, looking Danny full in the eye, eager for a reaction. The young man ignored him, fighting to stay calm. Marlon frowned and sighed, they clearly weren't willing to be drawn in. "So, how's business?" he asked Alessi conversationally. "It's booming my end, let me tell you!" he bragged. Alessi remained concrete in his demeanour as he looked boldly into Marlon's deep, dark eyes.

"All ticking along nicely thank you...as always. Glad to hear the recession hasn't had too much of an impact on trafficking."

Marlon threw his head back and laughed out. "That's what I love about you, Alessi, the poker face. You're impossible to read, do you know that?" he continued to chuckle. "Of course, I also love the fact that my men are all so much more attentive now we have a little lady with us, you know, full time? It's amazing the impact a young woman can have on morale. A beautiful girl, a bit of skirt, a nice pair of..." he laughed again, watching Danny's expression crack slightly. "I was going to say eyes," he lied with no attempt to hide his amusement. "I can read you like a book, son. Don't worry I'm just playing with you. They've had their orders to keep their hands off else I'll shoot them off. I've proved my word already," he shrugged. "I can assure you that nobody else has gone near her since." Now Danny's mind was reeling, wondering what one of Marlon's men had done to her *before* he was shot. "Of course I can't stop them looking can I?" he went on and Danny fidgeted in his seat. He was feeling seriously agitated and he was hot too. The room had windows all along one wall and the sun was pouring straight in. Marlon removed the cigarette from his mouth and placed it behind his ear as he continued to watch them intently.

A slight tap at the door had all three's attention. "Come in, sweetheart," Marlon called out and the door opened slowly. Ruby made her appearance, looking gorgeous and very well too in her pretty pink skirt, flip flops and fitted white t-shirt. Her hair hung long and shiny and her skin looked bronzed. Danny just wanted to throw her over his shoulder and storm out but she seemed nervous. She couldn't look either him or Alessi in the eye as she walked over to Marlon's side and fidgeted like she was shy. She certainly wasn't the bolshie Ruby they knew and adored as she hovered at the edge of the desk, waiting for his instructions.

"You asked for me to come down," she reminded him like Alessi and Danny weren't even there. He smiled and nodded towards the other two men.

"You have guests my dear," he told her. She stayed rooted to the spot, unwilling to face them, and Marlon narrowed his eyes as if urging her to behave. "Don't be rude, Ruby, or they might not want to visit again," he warned firmly.

"I don't really want visitors anyway," she whispered, trying to look brave. He raised his eyebrows as if slightly taken aback.

"Ruby," he called to her and she was compelled to look up into his eyes. Suddenly, as if he had a spell over her, she turned to Alessi and Danny. She smiled fleetingly before looking at her feet.

"Sorry, I just feel a bit weird what with walking out on you guys and then you coming here. I didn't mean to upset anyone. It's really good to see you both and I've missed you." She glanced at Alessi. He was sitting back in his chair, his fingers linking both hands together, his thumbs pushing hard against each other as he watched her with interest. He seemed as intrigued by her now as he had been the first day she blagged herself an interview at his firm. She had talked herself right past Amanda, the snotty receptionist, and into a meeting with the office manager. Unwittingly she had done it all in front of Alessi, mistakenly believing him to be a client.

She was only sixteen at the time, fresh from school, but she'd landed herself a job...just like that. It was one of the things he admired about her: her grit, her determination, her courage.

She looked him directly in the eye without looking away, the first time she'd managed to since entering the room, but he also noticed that she had to take a deep breath before addressing him.

"Alessi, I would like you to know that I feel really bad for walking out without saying anything to you first. I should have said goodbye and at least thank you for...well...for everything really. I am eternally grateful for the roof you put over my head, the care you gave me after I was shot, the job at your firm, the private tuition and, of course, all the other things that you've done for me. Thank you, Alessi." She concluded her speech and he nodded.

"And the job, do you still want it?" he asked her gently, not taking his eyes off her for a minute. She could feel herself sweating under the pressure and she looked to Marlon for help.

"It's up to you," he shrugged.

"Erm...thanks, Alessi, but it's a bit far," she explained tactfully.

"I can arrange for you to be dropped off and picked up," Marlon told her helpfully and her jaw hardened like she didn't appreciate the offer.

"Conflict of interest then," she suggested quickly. "I'm not sure me living with Marlon and working for you would be such a good idea, Alessi. I'm sorry," she apologised and Alessi inclined his head in acknowledgement.

"Very well, Ruby, I'll sort out a replacement for you. Danny can't do it all by himself. He smiled at her and she felt a pang of regret. She looked at Danny, her eyes sad, but she couldn't maintain the connection, it was too hard. She looked away quickly feeling her heartstrings stretched to breaking point. If Alessi employed someone else they would be sitting across the room from Danny, her Danny. She could imagine what that would look like. How long till he was totally in love with that new girl and completely forgotten about her? She turned her attention to Marlon.

"Is it OK if I go now? I think I'm pretty much done here," she asked hopefully, her eyes threatening tears.

"Are you sure?" Marlon asked her with a frown. "You definitely don't want to go home? I'm sure Alessi and Danny would love to have you back." If he had a knife he'd turn it, she was sure. "You and Alessi can sort out your differences, can't you?" he persisted like he cared, and she looked from Alessi, choosing not to look at Danny this time, and back to Marlon.

"You don't want me here?" she asked him, sounding slightly concerned. He snorted as if surprised by her question.

"Ruby, you're welcome here as long as you want, you know that, but you're also welcome to leave whenever you want, you know that too, right?" he reminded her and she nodded.

"I want to stay," she told him firmly. "May I go to my room now? I'm not feeling very well," she asked again, and he huffed like he was exasperated with her.

"Teenagers eh, Alessi, sometimes there's just no talking to them! The grass always looks greener on the other side when you're young doesn't it, especially if someone offers you a better allowance, nicer clothes, a bigger bedroom...unlimited access to your boyfriend?" he tacked on with a smug grin and Ruby looked annoyed. "Oh by the way, Danny, you can visit here whenever you like," he went on. "I'm sure Ruby would be more than happy to see *you*."

Alessi's face was a little less poker and a bit more agitated now. His authority had just been undermined and he didn't appreciate it one bit. "If you don't mind, Marlon," he reeled him back in, only just resisting the urge to knock him right off his desk.

"Oh, of course, perhaps you'd better just clear that with Mr Alessi first," Marlon chuckled, looking at Danny. "I understand from Ruby that he's quite strict, a traditionalist, but a girl has needs too doesn't she?" Ruby dropped her eyes to the floor and sighed deeply. Marlon laughed at her affectionately, "Isn't that right, Ruby?" he tortured. "Would you like Danny to come visit...if that's OK with Alessi?" She clearly didn't want to answer and when she looked up into Marlon's eyes hers were pleading for him to stop, but he smiled and waited it out. He knew she would break, eventually.

"He can come if he wants," she replied, turning swiftly and leaving the room without seeking Marlon's permission again.

"My, she's a difficult one isn't she? I can see why you had problems with her, Alessi," he sympathised, a little too jovially for his words to be in any way genuine.

"I can handle Ruby, Marlon, don't you worry about that," Alessi assured him with confidence. "I'm pretty sure she will be back with me in time, where she belongs." He pushed his chair back as he stood, smoothing his tie against his shirt.

Marlon grinned and looked towards Danny who was clearly not ready to go. "You're very welcome to go up and see her before you leave, young man. I'm sure she'd be happy to see you alone. Of course, that's if it's ok with Mr Alessi here?"

Alessi spread his hands wide and shrugged. "I don't have a problem with it, but if you don't mind I think I'll wait in the car. I have some phone calls to make, so, please excuse me." Alessi made his way to the door and Marlon slipped off the desk, beckoning for Danny to follow him. He led him to the foot of the stairs.

"Up the stairs, third door on your left...take as long as you like," he grinned, slapping Danny on the shoulder. Danny frowned but hesitated no longer as he climbed quickly, desperate to see her again. He reached the third door on the left and knocked lightly.

"Come in," she invited softly and he was surprised to find that the door wasn't locked. She was sitting on the bed, her back to him, staring out of an *open* window. "I'm sorry but I don't think I was ready. It's so soon and it's...complicated. I'm trying. I swear I am, but..." She turned and looked over her shoulder to see Danny. He ran his hand through his hair, looking well and truly confused.

"Trying to do what?" he asked her and she swiftly looked away, thinking wildly about how she was going to handle him and his questions.

"I thought you were Marlon," she mumbled, her eyes wide, her head spinning.

"Ruby, I just wanted to see you on your own. Marlon said it would be fine to come right up."

"Well maybe Marlon should have asked me first. It seems nobody cares what I want," she sulked.

"Ruby! I care what you want. Why do you think I'm here?" he argued but she shrugged and didn't bother to turn back. He made his way round to the window to get into her line of vision. "Ruby, what the hell is going on here? Just come home now," he demanded and she frowned and shook her head at him. "I have a good mind to drag you out of here kicking and screaming," he threatened.

"Then what are you going to do with me, Danny?" she asked him with a hint of antagonism, leaning back onto her hands and crossing her legs like she was daring him to try it.

"Lock you in your bedroom if I have to!"

"Hmmm, very cave man of you. And what are you going to do with me then I wonder," she smiled wickedly and he huffed at her.

"Pack it in, Ruby, just come home...please?" he'd resorted to pleading, placing his hands on the bed so he could meet her at eye level. He didn't have long. He wanted to change her mind quickly and take her to the car that was already waiting outside.

"Look, Danny, I'm really pleased to see you and all that, and I'd love to come home with you, but Marlon gives me everything I need now. If you care about me, like I care about you, then please do something for me."

"Anything," he offered, before thinking it through first.

"Leave me alone, Danny, and don't come back here...ever!

A knock at the door suddenly took both of them by surprise and Marlon walked in. Ruby spun round on the bed, rising up onto her knees. She was immediately attentive, like a puppy that had just seen her master. Danny didn't like it one bit. "Marlon," she greeted him, her voice slightly higher than usual and with a hint of urgency about it.

"I'm sorry to disturb you, sweetheart. I don't want Danny to feel rushed but I just thought I'd better let you know that it's 6.30 already..."

"And?" Danny interrupted, feeling frustrated. He wanted Marlon to go away.

"And dinner is at 7pm. I'm sure Ruby must be starving. I worry about these young girls, desperately trying to stay thin and all that. They're always too busy to think about food aren't they? I just thought I'd let her know. Dinner is always at 7pm, we like to eat then. You are welcome to come after dinner, isn't that right, Ruby?" Ruby looked distracted as she fiddled with her watch like suddenly she was hungry and unable to think of anything else. "Ruby, is Danny welcome to come back later?" he persisted. She turned to Danny and looked deep into his eyes as she answered.

"I would love for you to come back later, Danny. I really miss you." Danny frowned, wondering why she playing such a cruel game. She slipped off the bed to get closer, moving in to push her hands inside his blazer and over his shirt. She nestled her head into his shoulder and hugged him tightly. He wasn't sure what to do. She'd just told him to go away and never come back and now she was holding him like she never wanted him to leave. He dithered for a fraction of a second before placing one hand on her hair and the other on her back to pull her in more firmly. She felt so good, so warm, and he desperately wanted to keep her. He already knew that he had strong feelings for her but suddenly his feelings were so intense he could cry, and he *never* cried. He wanted her back home and the last place he wanted to leave her was with Marlon. They stood for ages, neither wanting to let the other go, while Marlon watched on in silence.

Danny felt Ruby dig her nails through his shirt just before pulling away and glancing at her watch. "I'd better go and get something now," she told him sadly and he nodded. After one agonising and lingering kiss on the forehead he turned and left her, with a man he despised more than any other.

She looked up at Marlon almost in tears and he smiled back at her. "You did well Ruby...*eventually*. I'm very proud of you, my little Marionette," he praised and she perked up slightly.

"Really? So I did good then?" she asked, sounding insecure and desperately eager to please. He grinned, tugging on a tress of her long dark hair and walking her backwards towards the king size bed.

"It's nearly 7pm," he reminded her, looking very pleased, and her eyes widened in anticipation.

"Lock the door, Marlon," she whispered "I don't want Danny to come back and walk in on us."

4
A date at Marlon's

"Well, that was...weird!" Danny breathed as he climbed into the car. Alessi had been sitting with his eyes closed, head back, face pointed towards the roof. He immediately started the engine without a word. He stayed that way until they'd left the long, sweeping drive and were out on the open road.

"I was thinking exactly the same thing myself. There's something not right. I was watching her like a hawk, and although she was very hard to read, she did slip a few times. She said she wanted to stay confidently enough but she looked scared to me. It doesn't make sense because if she's scared of him then she could have just asked us to take her home. Maybe it's not scared, maybe it's something else. What else looks like scared?" he asked distantly. Danny shrugged and stayed silent. Unfortunately, nothing about what they had witnessed was obvious.

When they got home Danny explained to Alessi and Bardo about how she'd blown cold and then hot in the bedroom.

"I'm not so sure you should go back there, Danny," Bardo advised. "I know she means a lot to you and I'm not saying wash your hands of her, far from it, but I do think Marlon's eagerness to have you there is a bit...suspect...don't you?" He folded his strong arms across his broad chest. "He's definitely up to something and you need to be careful."

"But she said she wanted me to go back there tonight," Danny protested.

"She also said that she never wanted to see you again," Alessi pointed out, siding with Bardo. "If Marlon has any influence over her, which I'm pretty sure he does, then I'd say the last request was for Marlon's benefit and the first request, when you were alone and she asked you not to come back, was for her benefit...or yours."

"And if I go?" Danny asked, concerned that he might be on his own.

"Then we will support you, of course," Alessi confirmed. "I know how you feel about her and I'm not about to let Marlon divide us, and neither am I going to abandon Ruby, but I would ask you to be very cautious. Don't let your guard down, Danny. Don't slip into giving her anything of yourself, not until she's home and safe. While you're there, you're on Marlon's turf, do you understand me? You must remember her first request was 'don't come back'. She struggled to look at you at all in there and she only looked at me because she had to. I do believe that she's trying to protect you."

By 8pm Ruby had showered and curled the length of her hair. She applied makeup and then returned to the bedroom to find Marlon waiting for her. A big white box sat open on the bed and she looked over it with trepidation.

"A little gift...to help things along," he informed her with a smirk and a click of his tongue. "It's very...hmmm...exciting," he concluded. She approached the bed cautiously, despair creasing her forehead as she peered into the box. She reached down and lifted out the dress folded inside. It was very pretty - cream with a lace ruffled skirt and button front detail - but it was also very short, very low and *very* fitted around the bust. She cringed, letting it fall back into its container like it had dirtied her fingers.

"He's not going to go for this. It's not him," she explained, her eyes pleading for Marlon to understand.

"Why, what's wrong with him?" he asked her, looking like he'd just smelt something bad.

"Nothing," she protested, offended.

"Well then he'll love it. If he's a man, which as far as I know he is, and he likes girls, which I've heard that he does," he laughed, while she tried not to think about that "he'll be desperate for it. Now put it on, Ruby, and stop mucking me about. One minute I think I'm getting somewhere with you and the next...I'm wondering whether I'm trying to feed and clothe a lost cause." Her eyes suddenly became frightened and she conceded immediately.

"OK, Marlon, I'm sorry. I'll try...but I can't make him..." she panicked.

"Oh, Ruby, yes you can," he told her firmly. "The way I see it you don't have much choice *but* to make him, my little Marionette. You have both Alessi and Danny eating out of your hands so bloody get on with it. NOW!" he bellowed making her jump. She picked the dress out of the box as he leaned back in his chair and flicked open the viewing screen on his camcorder. The red light flashed and she turned away, knowing better than to argue with him now. She removed her t-shirt with her back to him and pulled the dress over her head. She smoothed it down, wishing it would go down further. She took time doing up the buttons on the front, desperately trying to think of a way out of it, but there was no other way, there was no 'out of it'.

Finally, she loosened the clip on the side of her skirt and let it fall to her feet, stepping out and turning to face him. His face lit up as he admired her in all her uncomfortable glory. There was no question about it, she was beautiful. "Very good, Ruby, and you managed to do it all without showing me a thing of yourself, even your hair covered your back most of the time. Very clever girl, but if it's going to get in the way perhaps we should get rid of the mane," he suggested, flipping his camcorder shut angrily. She reached up to grasp her hair in her hands. "Hmmm, if I didn't think Danny was so attached to it I'd cut it off right now just for messing with me, young lady. I can do that. You know that don't you?" he asked her and she nodded sadly. Marlon started filming again. "I think you should dance for me, Ruby," he told her in a low, smooth voice and her eyes flashed back up at him.

"Marlon, no, please I..."

"Ruby, you're arguing again," he pointed out, checking on his viewing screen to make sure he was still getting her in. He was. "I think we need to get you warmed up. We don't want you cold when Danny gets here do we?" he grinned, taking her by the hand and leading her to the basement, and his very own built in nightclub. The basement was where he took all his girls and where his men spent most of their free time enjoying their company. Ruby, so far, had been saved the humiliation of being thrown to Marlon's men and he'd promised not to let them touch her, and that included watching her, but *he* watched her and filmed her all the time. She desperately wanted to go home as the tears of desperation spilt and streaked her face. But tears wouldn't help her now. She should know - in the last few weeks she'd shed enough of them.

When Danny arrived at 10pm she was back in her room seeming much more relaxed and, this time, pleased to see him. She looked very hot and he was feeling it so he immediately took her hand and led her outside onto the balcony. He talked and she giggled, just like old times. She asked if he wanted a glass of wine but as much as he did he declined, concerned that it might be spiked. He was determined to keep in mind Alessi and Bardo's warnings. She shrugged and poured one for herself, which she then drank, very quickly.

"I thought we talked about you drinking," he warned her semi-seriously and she smiled a cute, and now slightly flushed, smile.

"I'm nearly eighteen, Danny, remember? Anyway Marlon allows me to drink," she told him. "In fact he positively encourages it," she whispered into her glass before turning away to pour and down another.

"He what?" Danny asked her but she shook her head and looked at him wide eyed, the epitome of innocence.

"Marlon doesn't mind as long as I drink...responsibly," she chose her word carefully. "He doesn't mind me doing other things either," she teased rolling her lips like she'd just applied gloss. Danny had his feet up on the balcony wall and he leaned onto the two back legs of his chair, already feeling out of his depth. She reached out and placed her hand on his knee, squeezing tightly, before running it up his leg. He jumped up before she got too far, acting like he'd just been burnt.

"Whoa, Ruby. OK, perhaps the wine wasn't such a great idea."

"Oh come on, Danny," she cooed, and he laughed nervously.

"I tell you what, why don't you come home with me and I'll think about it?" he reasoned.

"Huh, like I believe that! Alessi would never allow it. But you're not under Alessi's roof now you're under Marlon's, right?" He stepped backwards away from her and into the bedroom, quickly putting the bed between them. She giggled. He was so cute.

"Danny, are you scared of me?" she laughed.

"Yes. Yes I am!" he admitted shamelessly. "Look, Rubes, perhaps you could come home and we could talk about...this..." he suggested gesturing towards her and the bed.

"No, why don't we stay here, not talk, and *do* this?" she asked crawling up onto the mattress and making her way towards him. "Unless of course you really don't want me?" She stopped, suddenly looking sad and pouty and turning him to putty in her hands.

"Oh, Ruby, come on, you know that's not true. Don't be like that and don't look at me like that either," he begged, really struggling now. As soon as she was close enough she reached out to him and stood to undo his shirt, running her hands inside. He tilted his head back and took a deep breath before looking at her again. "It just can't happen here," he told her, firmly taking her wrists in his hands to stop them moving. While her hands moved he couldn't think straight. She huffed furiously at him.

"Why are you even here, Danny? If you're not going to give me what I want then you may as well just go...like I bloody told you to in the first place!" She yanked her hands away from him. "Stop playing games with me! Either give me what I want or go away...for good!" she snapped. He was momentarily stunned and she pounced on his hesitation. "What's wrong," she goaded. "Aren't you man enough?" He pushed her backwards onto the bed to get her out of his space.

"Why are you so nasty, Ruby?" he asked her angrily, placing his hands on his hips and trying to work her out; the dress, the make-up, the hair, the wine, *the blatant invitation*. He was piecing it all together and coming to a pretty good conclusion.

"Why am I so nasty?" she mocked. "Because, Danny, I'm fed up with waiting for you! If you don't want me I'm sure I can get what I want from one of Marlon's men. All you have to do is tell me it's over. Go on, Danny, say it and go!" she shouted, really wishing that he would. If only she could get him to see that leaving her was a good thing. If only she could turn him against her.

5
Hook, line and sinker

"So this is what you want is it, Ruby?" Danny asked bitterly, towering above her and placing his hands on her shoulders to pin her down flat. She hadn't expected him to do that, she thought he'd just walk out. She nodded slightly, looking straight into his eyes. The pain in them was clear, as clear as the crystal glass that she'd not long downed the contents of. He was close enough now to smell the deep red liquid on her breath. "You're sure about that are you?" he asked her flatly. He was furious. The weeks of waiting to find out if she was ok or lying in a ditch somewhere had taken their toll. Now he'd finally found her and she wouldn't come home! She was continuing to play with him and he didn't appreciate it one bit.

"Yes," she mouthed softly.

"Right, let's get on with it then shall we? I'll give you what you want, Ruby, save Marlon's men the bother!" he ranted, beginning to undo her dress as he worked himself closer to her. She bit on her bottom lip so hard he thought she might draw blood. "This is definitely all you want from me, like this? At Marlon's?" he persisted, undoing another button. She turned angry with him; anger always brought out her stubborn streak.

"Yes, Danny, this is all I want from you," she told him hatefully. "It's all I've ever wanted from you and it's the only reason I've stayed as long as I have because I thought, maybe one day, I might actually get something out of you! I thought maybe one day you might quit with the flirting and get on with it but, no. Alessi is always there telling you what to do and you are too weak to go against him! You're a coward, Danny! I bet the mafia hate you - the one that can't think for himself! Perhaps you should double check the blood line because I'm not sure you're even Alessi's. I'd bet money on it that someone got switched at birth!"

He shook his head slowly at her; she could be such a cow sometimes. His fingers were furious, his blood boiling, and when one button was too fiddly he resorted to ripping it right off and throwing it across the room. The dress was stupid and she wasn't; the two didn't go together. He wanted her out of it. She gasped out in shock and he paused, concerned that he'd gone too far when all he actually wanted was answers. She jumped on his indecision spitefully.

"That's not very respectful is it, Danny, what *would* Daddy say?" She laughed like someone had told her the funniest joke ever. But while he continued to hold her steady, the hysterics quickly turned to tears. They filled her eyes in desperation and spilled over as a huge sob wracked at her body. He pressed his mouth to hers and then moved his lips to her ear and whispered.

"Does Marlon think I was born yesterday?"

"What?" she breathed back, still shaking beneath him.

"Did he think I wouldn't know that you'd been dressed to hook me? You're bait aren't you, Ruby? He's told you to do this hasn't he?" She never replied but he felt another sob from beneath him and he knew he was right. "Ruby, I know you and I know you would never let any man treat you like this. I bet you want to kill me right now don't you?"

"Yes," she nodded her lungs breathless with anger. "But killing you wouldn't be good enough! I'd torture you first and, for the record, I couldn't give a toss about the stupid dress - you can burn it for all I care. I never want to see it again!"

"I want you to talk and I want you to talk NOW, Ruby," he told her firmly. She might hate him but at least he was getting somewhere, finally. It certainly wouldn't be the first time she'd wanted to cause him physical pain. "I can't help you if you don't talk to me."

"Please, Danny, how hard can it be? If you love me like you say you do, then why not, you never know, you might even enjoy it," she told him, verging on sarcastic.

"Why?" he asked her. "Give me one good reason why I should when you won't even come home with me?" Either she couldn't answer or she wouldn't answer. "Don't clam up on me now, Ruby," he urged her desperately, but she wouldn't open her mouth. Her lips were pressed so tightly he could see the tension in her jaw. "Has he threatened you?" It seemed the most obvious conclusion but she shook her head.

"No," she squeaked as the tears streamed from the corners of her eyes. "But if we don't do this I'm going to die," she told him, looking like she truly believed it.

"So he has threatened you? He's threatened to kill you?" he demanded to know but she shook her head again, confusing the hell out of him. "I don't understand, Ruby, can't you just tell me?" Another unhelpful shake and more tears.

"Please, Danny, you're making my life impossible. Choose, for god's sake, choose! It's either me, here, like this, or not at all. It has to be one or the other!"

"I'm not doing it," he told her defiantly and she began a new wave of hysterics, fighting to try and get away from him. His hold over her had slackened and she was almost out from under him as she begged.

"Then just leave me alone! Please, just leave me alone!" Her face and hair were soaked with tears and he wanted to let her go but he was running out of time and he couldn't stay all night. If she was going to be pushed for answers he was going to have to push her now, despite the distress and the heartbreaking sobs. He caught her and pulled her back, pinning her again but much more gently this time.

"Wait, listen, why don't you just say we did what you're asking of me? I'm guessing he can't prove it, can he?"

"No but he *will* ask you. What will you say?"

"I'll tell him I just had the most amazing evening of my life, this little dress did wonders, and I can't wait to come back for more..." He stopped suddenly and frowned. "Is that what this is about, getting me to come back for more?"

"Yes," she finally gave in. She couldn't take any more. "He wants to drive a wedge between you and Alessi and he thinks I'm the one who can do that. He's working for Officer Killen." Danny's adrenalin had started to pump, this was even more serious than he'd first thought! Officer Killen was the whole reason their client, Rossi, had been imprisoned. He'd been incarcerated for the last five years, serving a sentence for a murder he hadn't committed, a murder that Killen was responsible for. "*He* wants to turn you against Alessi and Johnny Giavani so they can use you as a bargaining tool to fix the Rossi appeal."

"How do you know all this?" Danny interrogated. He didn't have much time and he needed as many of the facts as he could possibly squeeze out of her.

"I overheard him talking to Killen in his private suite. It's just along the hall from my room. I went down there one afternoon when I was bored, just to check the place out. I heard talking and I thought I heard Marlon use Killen's name so I listened in. Killen told Marlon he needed to keep me here and then you would undoubtedly follow like a love sick puppy. If they wanted you back then Alessi and Giavani would have to agree to drop the appeal."

"What's in it for Marlon?"

"Plenty! Killen has agreed to get his force to look the other way so that Marlon can continue to do what Marlon does best, traffic, deal, steal, you name it, he'll have the freedom to do it. But please don't tell him I told you - he will kill me, just like that. I will suffer. Please don't tell him I told you, Danny," she pleaded.

"And you would have let me take advantage of you to help Marlon seal the deal? "You'd have gone that far, Ruby, even though it would mean losing the Rossi appeal when you know he's innocent?" he asked in disbelief and she nodded. He'd never understand in a million years. "Why wouldn't you just let me take you home instead?"

"You don't understand, Danny, I can't," she cried out bitterly. "We can lie to him about what we did here but there's no happy ending for us. We either have to keep on lying and carrying on like this or you have to agree to turn your back on me. You should just leave me here and get out while you can, Danny. That's what I want you to do, please." She was desperate but he shook his head at her.

"No way. If lying is the only way then lying is what we do. I *will* get you out of here, Ruby, trust me."

"That's not possible," she told him in a whisper. "If you take me from here, I'll die."

The door suddenly knocked once and opened. It was Marlon and he leaned through the gap to peer into the room. Danny quickly grabbed up a quilted throw from the foot of the bed and Ruby pulled it eagerly to her body; holding it tightly to her chest as her eyes filled with apprehensive tears. Her face had turned pale, wondering if Marlon could possibly know that she'd spoken out against him?

"Hi," Marlon greeted cautiously. "Sorry to burst in, Danny, but I thought I heard crying. Ruby sounded distressed, is everything OK?"

"Yeah everything's fine. I don't think she quite realised the impact her pretty little dress would have on me," he lied, concentrating on doing up the buttons on his shirt and hating having to pretend that he'd gone through with it. Marlon struggled not to show how pleased he was that his plan was taking shape.

"Ahhh poor little, Ruby," he cooed, taking in her distressed and tear stained face. He was heartless and sick and Ruby hated him so much; just his voice set her on edge. He looked back to Danny, satisfied that Ruby had done her job properly, at last. "You are welcome here whenever you want, son. Ruby might have opted to be under my roof but, as far as I'm concerned, she's your girl. She's kept separately from my other girls. She has her own space right here along the hall from my private suite and my men aren't even allowed on this floor. She's perfectly safe and she's all yours, so, what you say goes," he told him.

"In that case, in future, I would like Ruby to dress more like Ruby." Marlon frowned, confused. "If you don't know what that looks like, Marlon, then the way she arrived here is how *I* like to see her," he confirmed, eager for her to be more clothed around Marlon and his men.

"Of course," he agreed hesitantly. "If you want Ruby dressed head to toe in white or barely covered in black then that's your call. It's unusual I have to say, I mean, if you offered most young men the option of a real life doll they'd have her dressed, well, probably in next to..."

"How she was dressed when she arrived," Danny repeated flatly, interrupting him.

"Of course, you're the boss."

"Good - Ruby, go get changed," he ordered, practically pushing her, quilt and all, across the bed and towards the wardrobe. He continued to watch as she gratefully rifled through the hangers for something less humiliating. "Do you mind, Marlon?" he asked him with a frown, running his hands through his messed up hair and round the back of his neck.

Marlon hadn't realised he'd been watching her too. It was habit, but not one he intended to admit to her very protective boyfriend. He turned to sit on the bed with his back to her, while she grabbed out a pretty vest top and a pair of jeans. Letting the quilt fall to the floor she undid the two remaining buttons on the front of her dress and wriggled out of it, exposing a mark on her right thigh, so high up it reached her bottom. Marlon was still rambling about Danny being in control, in charge, the boss, all the things that Marlon figured he would be eager to boast. But Danny's mind was only partially there, the rest of it was wondering whether Marlon was hurting her physically.

She dressed quickly and spun round, coming to an abrupt halt when she realised Danny had been watching her. She looked petrified and her eyes flickered towards Marlon. If Danny blew her secret confession by losing his cool he could cause her unbelievable suffering. Yet, he was completely oblivious to the danger he posed just by being there. He smiled like he could read her mind and moved across the room to kiss her.

"I'll be back tomorrow," he promised before leaving the room and obliterating every energy reserve in his body resisting the urge to knock Marlon out.

6
The shocking truth

Danny climbed into the car waiting for him outside Marlon's place. He sat unable to answer Alessi and Bardo's questions, opening the window wide to get some air. He looked and felt ready to explode so they settled for letting him sit in silence. As soon as he was inside the house he made his way straight for the dining room and collapsed onto a chair. When Alessi and Bardo followed him, looking for an explanation, he leaned forward and rested his head in his hands.

"Danny, you need to tell us what happened," Alessi encouraged, waiting in the doorway. Bardo made his way to the other side of the room and now Danny was between the both of them. Laying his hands flat on the table and letting out a breath to steady himself first, he went on to explain about the way Ruby was dressed and how he got angry and scared her. He told of the fear he'd seen in her eyes and the confident words that didn't match her petrified performance. He explained how she told him she was expected to hook him, that Marlon was involved with the very corrupt and dangerous Officer Killen, and that if she didn't do as she was told she would die. What didn't make sense was that she was adamant that she hadn't been threatened by either of them.

"I think maybe Marlon's beating her or something," he eventually managed to confess, hating every second that she was still with him. He couldn't help but wonder whether she was being hurt at that very moment.

"Why would you say that? She looked fine didn't she?" Bardo asked.

"She looked more than fine to me," Alessi nodded and Danny had to agree but, after rubbing his face in his hands, he finally opened up.

"I told her to go get something else to wear and while she was changing I saw this mark...it looked like she'd been hit with something."

"Like what?" Bardo asked with a slow frown.

"Like where?" Alessi demanded, sounding mad already.

"It was on her right outer thigh, almost reaching her bottom. It looked liked she'd been hit with like...I don't know...like...one of those old fashioned hairbrushes, I suppose. One of those big oval ones, you know? It was like this oval type cluster of puncture marks, like the bristles were sharp and had pierced her skin. But I didn't see any other marks on her. Maybe that was a taste of what was to come if she didn't do as she was told. But that alone wouldn't make someone like Ruby so...compliant...would it? That's just not her...is it?" He wasn't sure about anything anymore but he noticed that Bardo's face had dropped and the lines of concern had smoothed. It had suddenly transformed to stone. He was now hard, pale and impossible to read. Alessi's had done the same and they were looking at each other.

"Why didn't I think of it sooner?" Bardo whispered almost to himself. "It makes perfect sense." Danny narrowed his eyes looking handsome yet exhausted.

"What, that she's being punished with a hairbrush?"

"No, Danny, your girlfriend...Ruby...she's..."

"What? What is she?" he asked looking from Alessi to Bardo.

"She's...an addict, Danny." Danny stared at Bardo for a long moment before shaking his head in disbelief.

"No, no she's not!" he argued, refusing to accept it.

"Yes, Danny, I think she is. The marks you saw, like her skin had been punctured by something sharp, high up on her thigh and perfectly concealed? They were needle marks, Danny. That's why she's so agreeable and I think I know exactly what drug he'll have her on too - it explains everything."

Danny pushed his chair out loudly and left the table, making his way to the bathroom where he was immediately sick. He sat on the floor and rested his head against a towel feeling nausea like he'd never felt before. Eventually his head stopped spinning and his stomach calmed. He splashed some water on his face, took a couple of breaths of fresh air from the open window and returned to the dining room where Alessi and Bardo were waiting patiently for him.

"OK, what are we looking at?" he asked solemnly as he returned to his seat, turning the glass of water he'd grabbed on his way back in a monotonous clockwise motion.

"OK, it's called Paradise, nice name but not so nice substance," Bardo informed them both. "It's relatively new and very sought after. It's frighteningly addictive too. Marlon will have been able to get his hands on more than usual because Mickey, Carlito and his brother are now off the scene, there will be less competition. It's hugely expensive but Marlon has the monopoly when it comes to drugs. Paradise gives the person who provides the first shot, also known as the feeder, complete control over the user. The user either doesn't know that's what's going to happen, doesn't believe it will happen to them, or is given the first shot against their will. The first shot is huge and it gives the biggest high imaginable. Imagine the best feeling ever and times it by a million, that's how good it feels," he nodded knowingly. "The drug takes over everything, nothing else matters. Girls experiment with it because it pretty much provides everything your body needs and suppresses all other urges. There is no such thing as hunger if the drug is maintained well.

"How does it work?" Alessi asked, lowering himself into a chair beside Danny, eager to learn all about it.

"The level of the initial dose is divided into two separate doses which are administered daily, exactly twelve hours apart. If the feeder knows what they're doing, and is committed, he will make sure the doses are managed with precision. They will be administered on time and at the correct level so that the user never feels like they're suffering or in need. The user will feel a constant tie to the person feeding them because they hold all the strings. Marlon can either make Ruby feel fantastic or make her suffer like you wouldn't believe." He paused and fidgeted uncomfortably before delivering the final blow. "He could also let her die."

"Die?" Danny exclaimed, feeling another wave of nausea coming on. They had to get her out of there!

"Paradise is lethal, Danny, unless you maintain the doses. If you keep the levels right then an addict can still live a long and healthy, although very indebted life. If you stop it outright the user suffers a massive heart attack."

"Is there no other way?" Alessi asked, pressing his steepled fingers to his mouth and glancing at Danny with concern. He now wished they'd had this conversation in private and found some other way of breaking the news to his son. "I mean cold turkey is clearly out of the window but what about gradual withdrawal, Bardo? Surely if maintaining the levels is so important then over time you could reduce the levels and wean someone off, yes?"

"It's possible...and also highly dangerous. You'd need to monitor their heart regularly. It depends how strong they are and how well they can adjust. Paradise significantly raises the heart rate when it's first used and the split doses keep it at that level. If you withdraw completely the heart rate drops and stops, a bit like pulling the plug on something. If you give too much in a dose then the heart can't take the added pressure. It can be done but the biggest hurdle will be convincing Ruby that you can look after her. She won't leave Marlon unless you can give her exactly what Marlon gives her. It's the Paradise that keeps her there. She stays of her own free will because staying literally means staying alive, and leaving means a painful death."

"How long would she have if we removed her?" Danny just about managed to pluck up the courage to ask.

"If she misses the first dose, Danny, the next twelve hours will be hell. Sickness, pain, sweats and hallucinations are just some of the early side effects. If she were to miss the next one she would die before the third one was even due. If you make it the full twenty-four hours you're lucky...or unlucky, whichever way you want to look at it."

"Can we get hold of it, Bardo? Enough to keep her going?" Danny asked desperately, daring to feel just a sliver of optimism.

"I can get it, yes. It's very expensive, which is why feeders like Marlon are so important. They provide it for free in return for whatever it is they want. We're now assuming that what Marlon wants is you, Danny, and for Rossi to stay in prison so Killen can continue to get away with murder. Without Marlon, who knows what Ruby would be doing to get the money to fund her extortionate habit?" Danny ignored that comment; it wasn't helpful to his stomach or his concentration. Instead he turned his attention to his father.

"Alessi?" he questioned hopefully, praying he wouldn't turn his back on her now.

Alessi thought long and hard, the silence intense. They watched as he ran circles around his eyes and over the bridge of his nose with the tips of his fingers. He had promised he would look after her but now she was addicted to an illegal substance. He wanted her back but he knew full well that what he would be getting back wouldn't be Ruby. She would be a different person, willing to do anything to get what she wanted and needed, despite the pain and suffering that might cause. He had seen people slip into drug dependency before, watched as they slid the slippery slope into manipulation and deceit, all just to score another hit. He couldn't bear to think of her like that, but what if they couldn't get her off the Paradise? She could potentially destroy everything he had - his reputation, his home, his son and, ultimately, herself. He shook his head trying to rid it of the distressing images and Danny frowned, his heart rate kicking up a notch. He was going to say no! Bardo was also concerned as Alessi finally looked up at him.

"Can we get it by tomorrow morning, Bardo?" he asked and Danny began to breathe again.

"I know I can get it," Bardo assured him. "It just depends if I can physically get it that quickly. She will want to see it to believe it."

7
A bug from hell

The next morning, while Alessi had a house meeting with Johnny Giavani to discuss Killen's attempt to fix the Rossi trial, Bardo arrived with the goods. It took all Danny had to keep from kissing him. He and Danny drove to Marlon's place but the man on the gates told Danny that Ruby had already rung down and said she didn't want to see him. The guy had a greasy biker look about him as he sat in his leather trousers, his foot propped up on the windowsill. His pathetic castle was a little cabin situated at the front gate but, while he was on duty, he was king of security and loving every minute of it. He didn't even bother to come out as he looked Danny up and down, getting off on the power of keeping him out.

"Don't worry, I'll see that she gets a visit," he sniggered running a dirty nailed hand over his greying beard and moustache. "She won't get lonely - I'll make sure of that." He widened his eyes like he couldn't wait. Danny just about kept his cool and asked to see Marlon instead but he was told that Marlon was engaged in a meeting and he wasn't to be disturbed. Danny agreed to leave it for another day. He was seriously frustrated but unperturbed. He was going to get in one way or another.

At 5pm they returned and Danny approached the gates again. This time he was faced with a different member of Marlon's group, a younger and much friendlier chap. Danny introduced himself and was met with a hand in greeting. He reached through the railings and shook it.

"Hey there, so you're Danny then?" he smiled, taking one last drag on his cigarette and flicking it onto the gravel at his feet. "Nice to meet you, I'm Smithy. Have you come to visit Ruby?" he asked, breathing the smoke out of the side of his mouth and away from Danny's face. "I hope she's feeling better..."

"Better?" Danny asked concerned that Marlon had hurt her.

"Yeah she's been pretty sick by all accounts, and all day too. Perhaps she's got a virus or something. I don't know how though, she never goes anywhere. Sometimes she comes to talk to me, she's a little sweetie. She shouldn't be here, Danny. Well, I'm sure you know that already and what's it to me? I just do my job, which is pretty much do as I'm told, turn a blind eye and ask no questions..."

"Can I come in and see her, Smithy?" Danny interrupted him calmly. He was still waiting for him to open the gate. Smithy suddenly realised he'd been rambling.

"Sorry, man, yeah of course you can. It gets well boring up at the front gates. You don't see people for hours so when someone comes along you find yourself...sorry...yeah...I'm doing it again." He'd noted Danny's discreet sigh and also that he'd grasped the railing standing between them, his grip so tight his knuckles were turning white. "In you go," he told him eagerly. "You know where she is I'm assuming?"

Danny nodded but didn't stop to chat any longer as he made his way straight for the front door. He hoped he wouldn't bump into the first guy he'd seen that day, the one who had turned him away, but he passed through the open reception area without being challenged.

The place was quiet and he made his way up the stairs to Ruby's bedroom. She wasn't there and her quilts were all over the floor. He slipped inside and tried to work out what had happened. He then noticed the light under the bathroom door and tapped lightly. There was no answer. He put his ear to it but there was no movement either, just silence. He pushed it open and there was Ruby, on the floor, pale and deathly looking. He grabbed a flannel from the shelf and soaked it before dropping to his knees and wiping it over her face and neck and whispering into her ear. She was non-responsive as he listened to her chest and felt for a pulse, both frighteningly fast. He started to dig in his pockets for his phone but she opened her eyes and panicked, trying to get away from him.

"Don't...don't," she protested and he held his phone up to show her it wasn't dangerous.

"Ruby, I was just going to phone for help, that's all," he explained but she seemed to be seeing something else.

"I don't like them...don't come near me. You're covered in them!" she told him.

"What? What am I covered in?" he asked holding his hands out and looking himself over.

"Spiders. I don't like them, they're everywhere! Go away! Go away!" she screamed, beating at her body and trying to kick Danny away with her bare feet. She moved like she could see millions of creatures all crawling towards her.

Once up against the radiator, Ruby was as far as she could go and she closed her eyes tightly and gritted her teeth as she waited for the eight-legged beasts to catch her up. They moved over her body from her toes to her face and then into her ears, which she was trying to cover with her hands. She slid down onto the floor and began to convulse, beads of sweat forming on her forehead and chest. Suddenly she fell quiet and limp and Danny scooped her head onto his lap and whispered again.

"Ruby it's me, baby, please wake up." She didn't respond. If he couldn't feel her heart pounding under his hand he would have sworn she was dead. "I have the drug," he tried to tempt her. "I have the Paradise, enough to keep you going. I have it here. We have a whole lot of it back at Alessi's place. Do you want to see?" She opened her eyes, slowly this time, and struggled to sit up. He helped her and now her eyes were wide and keen.

"Where?" she whispered back and he pulled the small vial from his inside pocket. She snatched at it like a starving child, turning it in her fingers and holding it up to the light. She looked like she'd just won the lottery.

"So I can come home?" she asked in disbelief, and he reached out and hugged her. She felt so fragile in his hands.

"Yes, Ruby, you can come home," he reassured, pressing his mouth to her forehead.

"I didn't want you to get dragged into all of this. I didn't want Rossi to stay in prison for something he didn't do and I didn't want to work against Alessi and Johnny Giavani. I refused to play Marlon's games and as much as I wanted it I turned down this morning's dose. It made me sick. I've been so ill today but he won't come see me. I begged him earlier. I actually rang him from my bedroom but he refused to help me. He told me I'd made up my mind. I knew I was going to get worse so I told the guy on the gate that I didn't want to see you anymore. I didn't want you to watch me die but it's too late now, Danny, I've missed a dose and Paradise kills people. It's killing me now - I can feel it. I want to come home but I don't think I'll make it."

"Listen to me, he's testing you. Marlon is trying to break your stubbornness by making you scared. If he really wants me that much he will be back in here at 7pm to give you the dose you need to keep you alive. You're valuable to him, Ruby. You are the only thing that might turn me against Alessi and he knows it. He wants you to suffer enough that you'll know he means business and quit messing him about. He won't let you die, you're too much of a loss, and you *are* going to feel better. Your body is just craving and that's why you're so sick. At the moment it needs Paradise to survive." She began to cry, feeling frightened.

"Danny, I'm not going to make it and I'm scared. I'm too young to die," she exclaimed. He held her shoulders and forced her to look at him.

"Ruby, missing one dose won't kill you. Bardo knows all about this drug and he said you will be OK. You feel like you're dying but you're not." Hope filled her eyes, quickly followed by more tears.

"Are you sure?"

"Yes," he confirmed sincerely, cupping her little tired face in his hands. "Right, here's what you need to do. I can't get you out of here like this so you need to wait for him to come at 7pm. Apologise to him, Ruby, and agree to never go against him again. Tell him that you will do whatever it takes to draw me in. Happily accept the second dose and let it do its stuff. When you're up to it take a shower, get changed and ask if you can go for a walk to clear your head. All he needs to know is that I'm coming to visit later and you can't wait. Make your way to the front gate and chat up Smithy so he'll let you out. I think he likes you so that shouldn't be too hard," he told her raising his eyebrows. "We will pick you up on the road outside and take you home. We will look after you. Do you understand?"

48

She nodded and snuggled into his chest. He could feel her body shuddering and she pulled her knees in tightly, still keeping an eye on the spiders that were now arching onto their back legs ready to attack. He tilted her head back against the radiator and ran his fingers along the dark hollows under her eyes. Now she looked like an addict. He washed her face again and took her to bed, tucking her in tightly. "When he comes tell him I've already been and I looked after you. I told you that you had a bug and to sleep it off. Tell him I said I will call in later and you think that I might even stay the night. He will think I'm easy game. Can you do that do you think?" he asked her and she gritted her teeth against another wave of pain and clenched her eyes shut as snakes slipped in underneath her bedroom door. They hissed and writhed under her bed, causing it to move and jar violently and she gripped the mattress tightly to keep from rolling off. She just about managed to give Danny a nod and then, after a painful convulsion, slipped into unconsciousness again, completely exhausted. It was only another half hour to wait and then, Danny prayed, she would receive her next dose of Paradise courtesy of Marlon. He kissed her head and left the building.

At 9pm she was only just reaching the front gate. She'd been ready for an hour but couldn't bring herself to leave the confines of her bedroom. Marlon had come and given her the next dose, just as Danny had said he would. Now she knew it was a simple case of doing as Marlon said and the Paradise would be guaranteed. She didn't want to live like that, but she did want to live. Danny had shown her a vial of the drug but what if that was just a lure? One vial wouldn't be enough and then she'd suffer all over again. The last thing she ever wanted to experience was a repeat of the last twelve hours. It was petrifying and she felt older for having been through it. Surely Danny, Alessi and Bardo knew what they were dealing with. If she stayed Marlon might actually manage to turn Danny against Alessi and it would be all her fault. Either way he might then ask her to do other things. Were there worse things than deceiving and trapping her boyfriend, turning him against his father and putting an innocent man behind bars? When it came to Marlon she would believe anything possible, no matter how grotesque, no matter how painful. She decided there was only one choice and she had to trust that Alessi had enough Paradise to keep her alive.

Her dilemma had been time consuming and now she was standing in front of Smithy sure of only one thing, it was late. She had no idea whether Danny had waited or given up. If she left and he wasn't there she would have no choice but to come back to Marlon and face a sullied future with him. There was no chance of running away and she'd never survive the next twenty-four hours. She had such desperate needs that whoever took her in she would belong to completely.

"Hey, gorgeous, you look like you're feeling much better!" Smithy grinned at her. Ruby smiled back at him shyly and nodded.

"Just a bug, I guess. It seems to be out of my system now." She rolled her eyes like it was a whole lot of drama. "Hey, Smithy, can I go out for a bit please?" she asked sweetly, pushing her hands into her back pockets and looking up at him through big blue eyes.

"I'd love to say yes, Ruby, you know that but I'd need to clear it with the boss first. It's his call and more than my life's worth to go opening the gate on you. You're obviously very important to him. I've never known him to accommodate any other girl on the first floor right near his own suite." Damn it! She was stuck and now panic was setting in. If Danny was still there, on the other side, he would be wondering where she was by now. Why had she wasted so much time even considering staying with Marlon? If she couldn't get out and Danny visited again she would be faced with either having to try and persuade him to go through with Marlon's request or lying to Marlon again. How long until Marlon found out about her deceit and punished her for it?

"Well?" Smithy asked breaking her concentration.

"Well what?" she frowned back at him. She'd lost track and he held up his mobile.

"Want me to ask?" He looked doubtful and she worried that even bothering Marlon might be enough to push him over the edge. She clenched her jaw and he saw the tension flex. She took a deep breath.

"Yes please," she nodded bravely and Smithy dialled, then waited. Ruby listened intently to his side of the conversation when Marlon *eventually* answered.

"No, there's no problem, boss. I've got Ruby keeping me company here. She looks much better...in fact she looks great. She wants to know if she can go out for a bit?" he asked and then paused, cringed, and answered again. "Sure boss." He held the mobile out towards Ruby and whispered. "He wants to talk to you." She took the phone gingerly, indecision now flooding her face. She paused for strength before putting it to her ear.

"Hello," she greeted, trying not to sound too scared.

"What are you playing at, Ruby?" Marlon barked at her and she pulled the phone away from her ear. He was loud!

"Nothing, I just wanted a change of scenery that's all," she explained, her voice soft but unwavering. She couldn't afford to flake in front of Marlon.

"Where?"

"Just up the road, maybe round the block. It's a warm evening and I desperately want to stretch my legs. I have been on the bathroom floor all day," she reminded him.

"Are you being funny?"

"No! Marlon, honestly," she defended quickly. "It's just that my whole body feels stiff and I ache. I thought...I thought a walk might help." This was her lifeline and his initial fury, rather than scare her into submission, actually spurred her on. She didn't want to stay with Marlon, she wanted out. There was a long pause and she watched as Smithy dragged his teeth over his bottom lip. He glanced at the gate as if willing her a yes. Marlon sighed and Ruby braced herself.

"You mess with me, Ruby Palmer, and you're going to be one very sorry little girl, do you know that? I will stop at nothing to ruin you. One way or another you *will* pay!" She felt her legs buckle a little and reached

51

out to steady herself using the railings. Could she do it? He was going to be furious but, hopefully, Danny was waiting for her and the pull of that was stronger than Marlon's threats. She took another deep breath.

"I understand, Marlon. It's just a walk, I swear. I've not once tried to get away from you have I?" he never answered. "I'll come right back. You give me everything I need. I'm not stupid. I know what you do for me..."

"Give me back to Smithy," he demanded, cutting her off and without giving her an answer. She handed the phone over, sure that she'd blown it.

"Yes, boss," he greeted and then listened before speaking again. "Well Danny told me before he left that he'd be back here at 10pm. Yup I understand." The waiting was killing Ruby. "And if she's not?" he asked pausing again for Marlon's orders. Smithy looked into her eyes sadly. Ruby felt sick and her head felt hot. Had he said no? She bit on her finger nails, desperately holding onto Smithy's every word. "Got it." He flipped the cover on his phone shut. "The boss says you've got half an hour, Ruby," he informed her.

"Half an hour," she confirmed with a nod and he unlocked the gate.

"Why did he call you Marionette?" he asked, pausing before he let her out onto the street. She frowned at him uncomfortably and he mistook it for confusion. "On the phone he said 'Put my Marionette on. I want to talk to her.' Why did he call you Marionette - is it your middle name?" he queried, thinking it sounded like quite a pretty name for a girl. She shook her head.

"It's another word for a puppet, Smithy," she explained. "He calls me his puppet...and I don't like it," she confessed. He looked suddenly awkward.

"I'm sorry," he apologised sincerely and then he leaned in close to whisper into her ear. "I hope you know what you're doing, Ruby, I'm going to really miss you around here."

8
A scary story

Alessi was waiting in the kitchen when the three made their way into the house. Ruby seemed shy and awkward as she leaned back against the work surface waiting for him to lose it with her. He was just finishing off making four coffees and he turned when she entered the room. After a few seconds of painful silence, other than the sound of the spoon swirling in the cup, he made his way over and stopped in front of her, sighing deeply. She was trembling with fear but instead of hollering and throwing his hands into the air, like she thought he was going to, he leaned forward and kissed her on the forehead and both cheeks gently. She looked confused, her blue eyes unable to focus on his as she crossed her arms and settled her gaze on her feet. Suddenly she was surprised when a pair of strong hands grasped her forearms, pulling her in for a firm cuddle. She wasn't sure where it came from but instinctively she began to cry, the unexpected affection both shocked and weakened her and he held her to his chest while she sobbed.

"I'm so sorry," she whispered into his now damp shirt. "I didn't think you'd take me back, Alessi. I was so worried you'd hate me."

He lifted her chin so he could run his fingers over the dark marks under her eyes and then placed his hands either side of her on the surface. She was now free from his warm embrace, where she would really rather have stayed, and trapped by his towering frame. "What happened, Ruby?" It was interrogation time and she wiped her tears on the back of her hands. Danny grabbed some tissues before jumping up to sit on the work surface next to her. Alessi glanced at him, unimpressed with his choice of seating but willing to let it go...just this once.

"We had an argument, me and Danny..." she began shamefully.

"I know all about the argument, Ruby. I want to know what happened *after* the argument. You know, when you drove us all nearly insane with worry." She nodded, feeling awful and trembled as she went on. Alessi could be really scary sometimes.

"I walked out and was just reaching the bottom of the road when a car pulled up. It was Marlon and he was really nice to me. I didn't know who he was but he said he was a friend of yours and that he was just about to pay you a visit. He knew who I was, said you'd told him all about me and that you'd taken me in after my dad was..." She couldn't bring herself to say the words and Alessi nodded and moved her on.

"And then what did he say, how did you get from that to this?" he asked, reaching forward and taking each of her arms in turn to look them over. Her face turned hot when she realised he was looking for needle marks. She pulled her arms away self consciously.

"Alessi, please," she protested indignantly, "I don't inject, it's not like that!" She couldn't bring herself to look at any of them now. He had searched her for signs of drug abuse right in front of Danny and Bardo and she had tried to defend herself, convince them that she wasn't a druggie...except she was. She was hooked on an illegal substance, a substance she would do anything for, and it shamed her just to think of it. "Marlon could see I was upset and he asked if I'd fallen out with you," she went on quietly. "He said you were hot headed and could be difficult but that you and he went back a long way."

"Yes and for all the wrong reasons, Ruby. My knowing him has not been through choice, let me tell you. Marlon, and many guys like him, are just one of the unfortunate side effects of my work and lifestyle."

"Well he made out you were friends. He said that he could put me up for a few days and that it was the least he could do."

"So you got into a car with a complete stranger?" Alessi asked, thereby pointing out what a complete idiot she really was. "How old are you, Ruby?"

"I wasn't thinking straight," she tried to defend herself.

"I'm not sure you ever do!"

She knew it wasn't going to be as easy as walking straight back in and starting where they'd left off; a lot had happened since then. "Marlon's place was really nice but there were loads of men there and I was frightened. He said that he wouldn't let any of them hurt me. He gave me his word and promised that he wanted nothing from me and then he gave me a room upstairs on the same floor as his private suite. Not long after I arrived one of his guys tried it on but Marlon caught him. He shot him in both hands just like that...right in front of me. One minute his hands were on me and the next, well, they were all over everything else." She shuddered as the tears spilled again. "I was petrified, Alessi. It was awful but it made me feel like maybe I could trust him. I mean he did that to one of his own men...to protect me." Alessi snorted and raised his eyebrows at her.

"But I shoot your dad after he beats you and I'm the baddie," he exclaimed. She shrugged uncomfortably.

"He was my dad, Alessi! Do you really not understand that? He was all I had. He wasn't great but he was mine. I was part of him and now...I'm part of nobody. I have no brothers and sisters, no dad, no mum, no family. I feel lonely, Alessi. It might have been a hole where I grew up but it was my hole," she told him pressing her index finger against her chest. "It was where I called home all my life," she pleaded with him as the tears rolled freely. She was fretting now, worried that he might actually turn her away, but instead he raised her chin with his hand as he spoke sternly.

"I do understand, Ruby. I'm sorry I hurt you but I was worried he might put his hands on you..."

"That's sick, Alessi! He was my dad!" she fumed attempting to push him away but Alessi was well balanced and strong. If she needed space she wasn't going to get it that way. She pulled herself tall, her chin defiant, her teeth clenched. "He was my father and he would *never* do anything like that. I wouldn't have let him!" She had always protested against there being anything like that, she was stubborn and too ashamed to even contemplate it. Alessi understood completely, but the man was far from innocent and his behaviour was leading to bigger and nastier things.

"Ruby, I'd been keeping a careful eye on the situation and I didn't make the decision I made lightly. In the very last fight you had with your dad he made you feel not just frightened but uncomfortable too, and you know it. The boundaries were all wrong, Ruby. He talked like he owned you, in the

55

same way as he spoke about his wife, your mother. I'm sorry, Ruby, but I wasn't going to wait around for him to take it further. You are safe here for as long as you want to be here. I will never ask you to leave - this is your home." She took a deep breath and smiled a shaky brave smile for him. Now go on," he urged. "What happened at Marlon's?"

"On the third day he came into my bedroom with another man. He was carrying a briefcase. He introduced himself and said he was a doctor. I told them I wasn't sick. They both thought that was funny. Marlon said he got private medical care, or something, and that while I was in his care he wanted me included on the policy. I wasn't happy about it but I was frightened of Marlon and so I let the other man examine me."

"Examine?" Danny queried, shifting on the sideboard. She looked up at him.

"Nothing heavy it was just my temperature, height and weight." She looked back to Alessi. "He also listened to my heart and read my pulse. It seemed innocent enough so I thought I was OK. When the exam was done the doctor worked something out on a piece of paper and told Marlon I should be given 10mls. I was confused but Marlon ordered him to prepare it for me. I was getting scared and Marlon was talking over me like I wasn't even there. He confirmed the time as approaching 7pm and the doctor recorded it, along with everything else, in a little black book. Marlon told me to lie on the bed, face down, but I refused. I told him I wanted to go home and I tried to leave but he wouldn't let me. It got really rough and he locked the door and kept the key. He told me we could do it the easy way or the hard way." She paused and bit her lip, her face showing how painful it had been. "We did it the hard way, Alessi," she confessed, sounding desperate. "It was horrible."

"You must have been petrified," he sympathised and she nodded and wiped at the tears, but they just kept coming.

"He injected me with 10mls of Paradise at 7pm on that third day and my whole life changed forever. When I finished enjoying the feeling of complete ecstasy he told me I would need a smaller dose of 5mls at 7am in the morning and then another at 7pm. He said it would continue like that. I

56

told him I didn't want to be on it but he said to give it a few days and see how I felt then. He introduced me to a girl called Sammy, said he didn't want me to be lonely. She was allowed to stay in my room with me. She was so nice, my age, pretty and really funny." Ruby smiled, losing herself in a happy place for just a few minutes.

"Ruby," Alessi encouraged and she came back again.

"Sorry, I'm just so tired," she confessed, her face pale. "Sammy was lovely and she spent the next three days with me, chatting, watching TV and just...hanging out. It was nice to have a friend. I've really missed Sasha, she's my best friend," she told Danny and he nodded. He remembered her best friend from school very well. "It was nice having another girl to share stuff with, you know? Sammy told me that Marlon had spotted her shopping in town one day and told her he could take photos of her and send them to a modelling agency. She was very pretty," she smiled, looking up at Danny. He ran a finger under her chin as he stared back into her eyes.

"You are very pretty too," he confirmed sincerely. A beautiful gesture but she felt far from pretty.

"Thank you," she smiled back politely. "Marlon promised to make Sammy's dreams come true. There wasn't anything she couldn't do. Her hair was really blonde, long and shiny and she could sing like you wouldn't believe. She did really well in her exams too, a straight 'A' student!" Alessi smiled and nodded like that was very good to hear. "But then she told me she was on Paradise as well and I was totally shocked. She told me it was good for keeping her slim and that she needed to be slim to get famous, Marlon had told her that. She'd been on it a while but she'd decided that she could stay slim without it. She told me it was easy and all she needed to do was be realistic, eat healthy and exercise. That's what all the magazines said. She didn't want faddy drugs to rule her life. She told me that she'd asked Marlon to get her off it before I arrived and he'd agreed to withdraw the doses." Ruby stopped like she couldn't go on and Danny ran his hand through her hair, hooking it behind her ear so he could see her face.

"We're here, Ruby, you can do this, honey," he reassured her.

"Well one night I was given my 7pm shot but she wasn't given hers. She was really excited about coming off it, wouldn't stop going on about it..." She paused again, rolling her lips like she didn't want to confess. "But then...she got sick...in my room. I called Marlon and he took her away, said he would look after her but he just shut her in another room. He took me to see her six hours later and she was dragging her finger nails through her skin. She was saying she was on fire. She was sweating and throwing up, she was really sick. At 7am he gave me my next shot and then took me to see Sammy again. She was screaming and begging him to help her but he refused to give her any more Paradise. She'd been due her shots a couple of hours before mine. She was due 5am and 5pm shots so she'd missed her second shot by the time I saw her and was already two hours into the next period of withdrawal." Ruby looked up from Alessi to Bardo and then to Danny, her eyes big and full of sadness and regret. "She died in front of us," she whispered. "She grabbed at her chest and arm and she couldn't breathe," Ruby choked out, grief stricken.

"She had a heart attack?" Bardo asked her softly and Ruby nodded, trying to stop the damn tears that just wouldn't let up.

"Right in front of us, Bardo, and none of us did a thing to help her. She was young and all alone when she left the world forever. When Sammy died so did her dreams, her beautiful voice and her beautiful hair too. I was devastated and petrified of going that way. I was so mad at Marlon and I flew at him but he was just so calm about it all. He told me if someone asked to be withdrawn then he would do it and there was no going back. He wouldn't play games. He told me Paradise was lethal and it was impossible to come off it but as long as I took it when he offered it, as long as I did as I was told, I would be just fine. Of course that meant doing exactly what he wanted." Danny's head was held low as he listened and Alessi was running his hand thoughtfully over the lower half of his face.

"Ruby, that's a very sad story and I'm incredibly sorry for your loss," he began. "Marlon lied to you. He could have saved Sammy by giving her the next dose when it was due. He let her die and he did it to ensure that you'd conform. He needed you more than he needed her. You're incredibly feisty,

Ruby, and witnessing the horrible death of your friend was intended to scare you into behaving. It is possible to come off Paradise, if you do it carefully..."

"No!" she protested fervently. "I don't want to come off it, Alessi! I want to stay on. You said you had enough. I thought you had enough..." She was starting to panic now. What had she done?

"Ruby, we have enough," he reassured her softly. "It was just an idea that's all. We will talk about it later, when you're ready, OK? You're home now and I think you should just go to bed. You're clearly very tired and you've been extremely ill today." She calmed slightly and nodded. She was going to do as she was told this time round.

Danny took her upstairs where she changed into pink pyjama bottoms and a vest top. He tucked her into bed and then kissed her gently on the head before leaving and grabbing the room next door. He usually went back to his apartment or dozed on the sofa in front of the television but, on her first night back, he wanted to be close, just in case there was trouble...and *boy* was there going to be trouble!

9
Let the fun and games commence

Danny woke a few hours later to the sound of knocking. He rolled off the bed, still fully clothed and with the addition of creases. He hadn't meant to fall asleep, but after collapsing face down on the quilt he was soon dreaming. He opened the door and peered out into the hallway sleepily, surprised to see Ruby at Alessi's bedroom door.

"Alessi, wake up I need to talk to you," she whispered angrily, still knocking.

"Ruby, what are you doing, it's 3am?" he asked her softly. "Alessi's asleep, honey, what's wrong?" She looked at Danny briefly and then looked away again without acknowledging him. She had bigger things on her mind and she didn't have time for Danny. She needed to take her concerns up with the man in charge, the man who called the shots - the Paradise shots.

"Alessi! I know you're in there so just answer the bloody door! I'm not going away so wake up and talk to me!" she demanded more loudly now. The door unlocked and opened and Alessi supported his weight casually against the frame. He leaned out and glanced down the hallway to wave at his bewildered son.

"Morning, Danny," he greeted cheerfully, checking on his watch. He then looked Ruby over slowly, a whirlwind of rage dressed in pink pyjamas. "Not sure I need to ask you this but what do you want, Ruby?" he queried. She folded her arms, satisfied that she wouldn't need to be knocking any more.

"I want to see the stock of Paradise that you *say* you have. I have needs you know, Alessi!"

"So I've been told," he informed her raising his eyebrows. She tutted like it wasn't funny.

"I need to have 5mls at 7am and 5mls at 7pm, EVERY day - do you understand me?" She was pointing at him now and he nodded and smiled like she was ever so slightly funny. "I'm not sure you do because earlier you said something about coming off it and I don't think that's such a good idea. Maybe you said that because you don't really have enough. If that's the case then maybe it would be better if I went back to Marlon. It really wasn't that bad there and he knew how to manage the doses really well. I never felt like I needed it and that's how I want it to be."

"I have enough, Ruby. I can satisfy your need."

"I *want* to be on it, Alessi! That's what I *want!*" she demanded seriously.

"Hmmm well wanting is not quite the same as needing but, yes, I understand," he nodded. "You will get all you need I can assure you. I'm not going to put you in any dang..."

"No, Alessi! You don't understand, wanting and needing are the same bloody thing! I don't even know why they have two separate words for it. It's an abuse of the English language! I shouldn't have to want it if you do your job properly." She stepped forward and jabbed her finger at his chest. He frowned at her, she was pushing her luck now but what could he do with a girl in pink pyjamas? Had it been Marlon he'd have knocked him out or, better still, shot him. "Why don't you just let me be in charge of administering it?" she asked him simply.

"Errr no, Ruby, if you take too much you'll kill yourself. I am more than capable of giving you your morning and evening dose. Go back to bed and sleep."

"I can't sleep!" she shouted back in frustration. He was being completely unreasonable. "I can't sleep until you show me that you have enough! Prove it, Alessi!"

"And that would mean showing you where I keep it - no way, Ruby! Trust me and go back to bed. You are not due a dose until 7am, that's hours away..."

"But what if you go to work and realise you haven't given it to me, what then?"

"That will never happen."

"Well...what if you oversleep?"

"That's more likely to happen, especially if you keep waking me up to tell me what I already know. Go to bed, Ruby," he told her firmly. "I have set my alarm, not that I usually need it, and I will be up at 6am. I will give you a shot at 7am *before* I leave for work." She looked at him desperately and he sighed. "Look this is completely normal, Ruby, and you're just worried about the change in where the Paradise is coming from. Just you remember, if anyone's likely to play with your life, and just because he can, it's Marlon...not me. Go to bed." He looked back down the hallway and tilted his head towards Ruby as he spoke. "Danny, put her to bed please," he requested, before turning his back on her and locking the door.

She screamed at him and banged her fists against the wood, yanking furiously at the handle and trying to get in. Danny nipped up the hallway and tried to encourage her to come with him.

"Get your hands off me, Danny Glover, else...else...I'll use your head to break Alessi's door down!" she threatened. She stormed off towards her room but then suddenly stopped and turned back. She approached him again, her face still fierce but her movement slow and calculating. Once within touching distance she ran her hands over his chest, confusing the hell out of him. He moved back in response and she kept him walking until he was up against Alessi's bedroom door. "Danny, do you know where he keeps the Paradise?" she asked in a soft purr. Alessi, guessing he may well be needed again, was standing on the other side shaking his head. She was a living nightmare!

"No, Ruby, I'm sorry. He's unlikely to give me access to it and I think that's probably...whoa Ruby...the safest...don't do that...option. I can't help you get your hands on it. Please don't do that, Ruby, because I'm not so sure I can...stop!" he demanded. "I can't get you a dose so pack it in. You are not going to bribe me!" he told her sternly. He peeled her hands off him but she took him by surprise with a sudden and hard kick to the shin.

"You're rubbish do you know that!" she snarled like a vicious little animal. "What kind of bloke can't get his girlfriend the drugs she needs?"

He frowned at a logic that only she could truly understand as she spun away and went back to her bedroom, slamming the door three times just to make sure everyone knew that she wasn't happy.

At 6am Alessi and Danny descended the stairs together. Alessi was whispering about Ruby's disturbing behaviour. He didn't want to wake her but he did want to explain that her outbursts were to be expected and they were set to get much worse. They stopped before reaching the foot of the stairs, seeing a small figure propped uncomfortably against the front door. Alessi shook his head as they made their way over to her. She jolted forward, trying to resist sleep but failing miserably. Hearing them approach she looked up, her face exhausted.

"Hello, Ruby, what are you doing here?" Alessi asked her and she rubbed her eyes sleepily, trying to straighten herself into a sitting position. Her muscles were tight and painful and she groaned.

"I just wanted to make sure you didn't leave for work without giving me my morning dose," she explained and he nodded as if he understood.

"Yes and that will be at 7am." He glanced at his watch. "You have another forty-five minutes until I need to give it to you. I'm on it, Ruby," he told her confidently, tapping his head like his brain was in. "Why don't you go up to bed and I will come and see you up there shortly?" He turned away and headed for the dining room and she called after him, fed up now.

"7am, Alessi! That's when my next dose is due. You've only got forty-five minutes so don't go getting bogged down in anything. I need you, Alessi!" He turned and grunted at her in acknowledgement before addressing his son.

"Danny, the Rossi appeal kicks off in just a few hours so I'm going to go and make some preparations. You might want to join me?" he encouraged, making it sound more like an order than a suggestion. He glanced at Ruby one more time and sighed before turning and shutting the door on the both of them.

She clenched her teeth like she could kill him and then noticed that Danny was still standing and looking at her. She tilted her head back and closed her eyes. She was going nowhere and she felt really guilty for kicking him too. When she opened them again he was gone and she frowned, feeling dejected. She worried that he must hate her for being so horrible, be ashamed of her for being so desperate and disgusted at how ugly she felt she had become, with the dark circles under her eyes, dry painful lips and pale face. She closed her eyes again as tears touched the corners. She felt so vulnerable, so dependent, so helpless, and the last person she wanted to be any of those things in front of, was Danny.

"Hey, don't cry," someone soothed and she looked up in surprise. He was back and smiling down at her handsomely. He held a cup in both hands and plump cushions were wedged under his arms. He placed the cups of coffee on the floor and slipped a cushion behind her back. He tossed the other on the floor beside her so he could slide in close. "As you seem to be persisting with the draft excluder thing, is it OK if I keep you company?" he asked, nudging her and catching her tears on his finger. She nodded sadly.

"Danny, I'm so sorry for being horrible to you...and for kicking you. I just lost it. I never meant to..."

"Shhh," he interrupted, placing his fingers over her mouth gently. "All I want to know is: were you planning on using my head as a battering ram to break Alessi's door down or as a key to unlock it? The first would have hurt a lot and the second, well, I'm pretty sure the second is impossible, Ruby, even for you." She managed a giggle and nudged him back.

"Seriously, Danny, you don't have to do this. You always try and make me laugh but I've been awful to you. I don't deserve you and I've been such a bitch!"

"Ruby, you can be a bitch as much as you want, I'm going nowhere. We are doing this together, you got me? We're a team, remember? Now drink your coffee," he ordered and she remembered the cup on the floor. She scooped it up, warming her fingers and sipping at the hot, brown liquid.

"Are you working today?" she asked and he nodded.

"It's the first day of the Rossi trial, remember? But Bardo will be here with you.

"I'll miss you, Danny. I wish you could stay. Did Alessi get someone to replace me?"

"No that would be impossible," he smiled widening his eyes teasingly. "He did get someone to come in and do some copying and filing and stuff, but what she definitely isn't doing is replacing you."

"What's she like? Is she young? Is she pretty? Is she clever and sexy? I bet she's all over your desk isn't she?" she grumbled and he laughed.

"You've just described yourself and we've already established you can't be replaced so, no, none of those things. If she was I wouldn't have noticed anyway, I've been too busy missing you. It's not the same without you."

"Does Alessi really like her? Has she hit it off with him? I bet she mastered everything on the first day and he wishes he replaced me sooner." Danny shook his head at her in disbelief.

"Ruby, you do feisty like no other. You do angry with a cherry on the top. You do happy in a way that excites me and you do sexy like I really can't handle or deserve but, Ruby, what you don't do is insecure. It's just not you, do you hear me? You don't need to be. It's a waste of your time because there's not a girl that exists that can come close to matching you. You are way too good to be insecure," he told her proudly and she grinned and snuggled up to him as he put his arm around her.

Eventually Alessi came back and clapped his hands to declare the hideous waiting game over. "Come on, my little Ruby, let's go get you...hmmm...well...let's go, shall we?" he laughed uncomfortably."

"Do you need to go get the Paradise and measure it out, 5mls remember?" she enquired, sounding much more upbeat and positive now. She was attentive, like a little puppy, and it reminded Danny of how she'd reacted that first afternoon when he'd visited her at Marlon's. He'd been jealous then, but now he realised it was simply because she was due her next highly addictive shot. She was desperate and Marlon was pulling her strings, messing with her feelings and toying with her life.

Danny watched in fascination at how she studied Alessi so intently. She was wondering whether she could follow him and work out where he kept the drug, but he'd already predicted that she might want to do that.

"I have it here in my inside pocket ready and waiting and, yes, I do know that you are expecting a 5ml dose, my little ray of sunshine," he smiled. He seemed much nicer now and she wondered whether he was trying to condition her into not pestering him between doses. That wouldn't work!

"You've already prepared it? So you had it on you the whole time?" she asked sounding suspiciously like she might be preparing an ambush. He laughed.

"I think I'd better watch my back, it's a dangerous job being Marlon's proxy feeder," he exclaimed. Danny felt sorry for her.

"Perhaps we could share the responsibility, you know, between you, me and Bardo? That might help a bit, like placing a ping pong ball under one of three cups instead of under the one and only cup" he suggested and Alessi nodded.

"I think that sounds like a good plan, Danny," he agreed. "It also means Ruby can stop worrying about me getting held up because there will always be someone who can give it to her. Nice one, Danny. Do you really think you can handle it?" he asked and now Ruby was staring expectantly at him too. He smiled and brushed the hair from her weary looking face. "I can handle it, Alessi," he confirmed.

"In that case you'd better come see this."

She jumped up immediately and made a beeline for her room, the most obedient Ruby had *ever* been. She slipped up onto the bed and lay down. Alessi looked slightly uncomfortable while Danny looked a little pale.

"Right, Rubes, where do you want it?" Alessi asked her, trying to sound confident. She rolled onto her front, pushing down her pyjama bottoms slightly to indicate that she wanted it where Danny had seen the other puncture marks. Danny fidgeted. He hated that she'd spent time in Marlon's clutches and he couldn't get over how vulnerable and defenceless she would have been there. It seemed Alessi was thinking along the same lines as he hovered over her hesitantly and whispered. "Ruby, did Marlon ever...you know...touch you?"

"No," she muffled, her face still buried in the pillows. He leaned in closer as he revealed the cluster of needle marks.

"Would you tell me if he had?" he asked, concerned. She huffed and lifted her head to glance at her watch.

"Alessi, it's like 7am already! Can we just get on with it please?" she ordered, slamming her face back into the pillows again."

"Well, if you decide that he did and you'd like to talk to me..."

"ALESSI!" she screamed out making them both jump. He was holding the needle and was responsible for getting it in her, her anxious outbursts were not helping.

"OK. OK. Let's get it over with then shall we?" he asked, more to himself than to anyone else. Taking a deep breath first, he jabbed the needle into her and she yelped out. He forced himself to push the illegal substance into her body, though it mentally hurt him to do it. He was actively drugging the girl he'd promised to look after. While he battled with his conscience Ruby went from being painfully tense to completely relaxed. It had been a long and stressful wait for her first dose with Alessi and the relief was clear.

As it coursed through her veins she groaned and gripped at the bedding, pulling it all into the middle of the bed and rolling up in it. She rolled back out again and arched her back as she clenched her teeth and tried to keep from screaming. Pushing her fingers into her hair she let out a long low moan and Danny raised his eyebrows, now completely disbelieving that Marlon would have kept his hands off her. He looked over at Alessi who frowned back.

"Just give her time, she'll tell us everything when she's good and ready. You never know...maybe she's telling the truth," he smiled. "Are you OK?"

Danny nodded and watched as she settled and fell asleep. "Can I stay here with her, Alessi? I know work is busy and the Rossi appeal starts today, but I'll work all night if I have to. You could just bring stuff back here and I'll do it in the dining room. We've got a team of barristers representing Rossi, do you really need me as well?"

"I think our clients will be expecting to see you there, Danny. Johnny Giavani will be expecting to see a united front on our part and we've waited for this appeal for five years. It's a big deal, Rossi was his right hand man remember. He's as good as family" He'd folded his arms across his chest, his expression formal. He was now in work mode.

"I appreciate all that, Alessi, but I've only just got Ruby back and I don't want to be away from her, not just yet. I know Johnny Giavani will want us to show our loyalty but what about Ruby? Johnny has said many times that Ruby is the granddaughter he never had. Well where's our loyalty to her? If it wasn't for her protecting the Rossi file in the first place there wouldn't even be an appeal." Alessi ran a hand over his mouth and chin as he nodded thoughtfully. He had a good point. "She needs us here, Alessi. Well, at least one of us anyway. It's her first day back and I'm only talking about a few days, tops," he negotiated. Alessi continued to contemplate his son's request in silence, giving nothing away. "Marlon will know where she is now and I'm guessing he won't be too happy to have lost his little object of entertainment. If he comes I want to be here. I don't want a phone call telling me she's gone again. It would kill me."

"OK, Danny," he conceded softly. "I'll go in for a couple of hours, give Faye some jobs to do and then I'll go on to court from there. I'll bring back some work with me." Danny let out a long breath and Alessi could see how deeply troubled he was. "I'm sure she'll appreciate having you here with her but please just remember, she'll try anything to get what she wants, Danny. More than ever, *now* is the time to exercise self control. She doesn't know what she's doing."

"Oh, god, I know!" he exclaimed.

Alessi turned the young man round to face him and pulled him in to give him a strong hug. "Good boy, Danny, you're a good boy do you know that?" Danny smiled and gave an awkward nod. "I'm very proud of you. The thought of having to get you through something like this is awful. Having one of your own children fall into a life of drug addiction is a parent's worst nightmare. The thought that you could be this controlled, this helpless, and then have to be looked after by three strangers and not me..." He trailed off for a few moments. "This is going to be an incredibly scary journey for her. She has three men here, one of whom betrayed us all and then took her to Mickey, unsure of exactly what would happen to her. She's living in my home and I killed her father and she's head over heels in love with you, someone who also has control over the Paradise. You need to be careful that she doesn't draw you in and catch you off guard."

"Are you saying that she's a threat?"

"Danny, when we lower the doses she's going to think we're trying to kill her and when she's forced to decide between her own life and ours...she'll choose hers. She's likely to feel most betrayed by you so watch your back, Danny, please," he implored his son to understand with a squeeze to his shoulder. He then ruffled his hair affectionately and turned to leave for work, and a very long day in court.

10
Keeping busy

When she woke it was after seven hours of deep sleep. She had been exhausted by the sickness the day before and the trauma of not knowing if Alessi would actually go through with giving her the 7am dose. She slowly got her bearings and spotted Danny lying across the bed. He was reading through one of her girly magazines and she yelped and disappeared back under the quilts, pulling them over her face tightly. He grinned as he slung the glossy magazine to one side, moving down on to the floor so that he could slip the top half of his body under the covers and seek her out in her cosy, warm little hiding place. She closed her eyes, wishing he wasn't there.

"Hey, don't be shy. It's only me," he told her, clearly amused.

"Oh god...you saw me...like that!" she shuddered and he laughed again.

"I can handle it if you can, Ruby. It wasn't that bad really, just a bit of writhing around and groaning, you know, the usual stuff girls do when I'm in their bedroom," he laughed cheekily. "Though I have to say I'm not usually with Alessi at the time!" She cringed before breaking into laughter, the sound so beautiful he could listen to it forever. She rolled away, unable to look him in the eye.

"You are so bad, Mr Glover!" she scolded and he caught her before she could escape out of the other side of the bed. He rolled her back again, scooping her into a cuddle. She let herself be hugged. It felt so nice and safe.

"Are you OK?" he asked, stroking the hair away from her face so he could see her. His deep brown eyes took in every minute detail in an adoring graze as he sighed, truly grateful to have her back at last. She knew she looked unwell but he took hold of her face so she couldn't avoid him, forcing her to look back into his eyes. "I've missed you so much. You have no idea how good it feels to have you here...trapped beneath me," he pointed out with a grin, making his eyes grow wide. She squirmed and giggled as her face flushed slightly. Colour looked good on her, better than the ghostly shade of white that Paradise had left her with. He edged closer and her racing heart felt like it might just explode. "I really do think, all things considering, this is definitely the safest place for you," he continued to tease and she continued to try and fight the amusement pulling at her mouth. He was so cute and funny too, the perfect combination. "I might run it by Alessi, I'm pretty sure he'll go for it. What do you reckon?" he whispered. The smile on his face was so big now and so beautiful all she wanted to do was kiss him. Almost as if reading her mind, he touched his lips to hers gently. She could feel herself slipping away, sliding at breakneck speed into an abyss of warm pleasure...until the front door slammed hard making them both jump. It sounded like a gun echoing through the reception area at the bottom of the stairs and it brought back terrible memories of Mickey's siege on Alessi's place. "Shut the door, Bardo." Danny joked in a sarcastic whisper, giving Ruby a reassuring squeeze as he leaned in to tease her again. He brushed her nose playfully with his lips and then finally put her out of her eager suspense by pressing his mouth to hers, a perfect fit.

"Put her down please, Danny!" Alessi ordered stepping into Ruby's bedroom. She groaned and Danny let her go, begrudgingly. "I'm sure you two do it just to annoy me," he complained. "I even shut the door loud enough to warn you I was on my way, but still, I step into Ruby's bedroom and here you are...making out!"

"I thought it was Bardo," Danny grumbled moving to sit at the foot of the bed.

"Is that supposed to be an excuse?"Alessi sounded exasperated. Neither of them said anything, choosing to concentrate on the pink flower scattered quilt rather than face Alessi and his temper. He sighed, moving into the room. "So, anyway, how are you feeling now, young lady?" he asked assessing Ruby from the foot of the bed.

"Hmmm, yeah, OK...but are you sure you gave me the right amount? It was supposed to be 5ml. What's the time? Is it nearly 7pm?" Both Alessi and Danny shook their heads but said nothing. "It's just that it feels like it's nearly time," she went on, looking at her watch and frowning. "I feel disorientated. I know I've been asleep but...but it definitely feels like it's later than it says it is. Can you check your watch, Danny, I think mines stopped," she told him tapping the glass and holding it to her ear.

"No it hasn't stopped, Ruby, it's 2pm honey," he told her softly. "It must be because you had a stressful day yesterday," he soothed and Alessi nodded.

"Yes that's right, things will settle down soon," he reassured but she didn't feel reassured. She felt ever so slightly deceived...by both of them.

"How much did you give me this morning?" she asked, watching Alessi for cracks. He scratched his chin as he spoke.

"Enough," he told her, but she wasn't stupid. She knew there was a difference between a straight '5mls like I was supposed to give you, Ruby' and 'Enough.' She wasn't being fobbed off that easily!

"Alessi, how much did you give me?" She was firm now. "Please don't experiment with me, I've watched a girl die and I don't want to go that way!" She dropped her shoulders and sighed like she didn't have the fight in her anymore. She tried to be nicer. "Alessi, please. I know I haven't had enough I can feel it. I feel...like I need something...like...I'm empty."

"Maybe you're hungry?" Danny suggested and took her hand to take her straight down to the kitchen. He made her some toast and she took a couple of mouthfuls before shaking her head slowly and thoughtfully.

"No it's not that," she confirmed.

"Perhaps a drink then, maybe you're thirsty," he persisted but after a glass of water she still wasn't satisfied.

"No, it's not that either." She held the empty glass against her lips "No, it's definitely the Paradise. Alessi hasn't given me enough!" she concluded. She was beginning to panic and slung her glass into the sink as she passed. She was headed straight for the dining room and a not very surprised, Mr Alessi.

She stormed in, throwing open the double doors to find that he'd taken a seat at the head of the table. He was looking way too calm for her liking. "Alessi, you haven't given me enough. How much did you give me?" He remained quiet. "You're bloody weaning me off aren't you? How could you? This is my life, Alessi, not yours! Stop bloody playing with it! You promised you wouldn't. You promised I could trust you and now you're withholding the one thing I came back here for!" She shoved a pile of files off the desk and onto the floor in a temper. He refused to react, though she knew it would have bothered him. He liked clean and tidy and that was blatantly clear from his immaculately organised files and home. He leaned back in his chair casually.

"Not the only reason surely, Ruby?" he dared to question. She glanced back over her shoulder to see Danny standing behind her, looking slightly hurt.

"Ugh! How dare you play games with me, Alessi - this is serious! It's not just about Danny, this is about whether I live or die. What's the point of coming back here to be with Danny if you're going to do exactly what Marlon was going to do to me there? I'd rather a complete stranger watched me die than the people who say they care!"

"We do care," he told her simply.

"Right that's it! I'll just find the god damn stuff myself!" she threatened, leaving the room and running up the stairs to Alessi's bedroom. The door was unlocked and she let herself in, pulling his quilts off the bed, just to be annoying. She emptied all of his drawers into a pile in the middle of the floor and then moved her search to the en-suite.

"Someone's a bit cross," Bardo observed as he joined Alessi and Danny in the dining room. He grinned and raised his eyebrows like Ruby was slightly amusing but Alessi shook his head like he was tired already. They all continued to listen as Ruby left Alessi's bedroom and went into the main bathroom to search the medicine cabinet. Glass bottles smashed into the sink and she screamed out Alessi's name, along with quite a few obscenities. "Her French is pretty good too," Bardo joked and Danny collapsed into a chair with a deep sigh to wait it out. She came back down and made her way to Alessi's home office.

"Oh great you need a bloody code to get in!" she complained, resorting to kicking and punching the door and then shouting a bit more. "I CAN'T

TAKE THIS, ALESSI!" She screamed out before making her way back to the dining room. "Oh good, the three musketeers, all present and correct. One for all and all for bloody one!" she barked at them rudely as they watched on like she was some crazy sideshow. She made her way straight over to Alessi, he was public enemy number one. Dropping to her knees behind his chair she started to rifle through the blazer hanging on the back. He let her rummage unchallenged. She sat back onto the floor, defeated at last. "Alessi, please," she begged desperately and he turned in his seat to look at her.

"Ruby," he spoke calmly, "This morning I gave you a 4.5ml dose and your body is feeling it. You're missing that half ml. It is hard going, yes, but you are not dying, you are just wanting. You're craving, Ruby, and it's easy for me to say because I'm not the one going through it, but I know what I'm doing. I went into work before court this morning and spent my entire time speaking at length to health professionals and all the people I could think of who might have had dealings with Paradise. They all say that reducing the dose gradually, although very stressful, can lead to getting clean. I refuse to leave you on that disgusting stuff, Ruby, stuff that you would do anything for. That stuff makes you vulnerable, dependent and dangerous. That's not you, Ruby, and it would be kinder for me to shoot you now than watch you live your life like this."

"So shoot me then!" she declared seriously. "I'd rather that. You have no idea how this feels, Alessi. If you did you wouldn't do it to me! You have a gun on you don't you?" He shook his head slowly and she couldn't be sure if that was a, 'No I won't do it', or a, 'No I don't have a gun on me right now.' She was hoping for the latter because there was an easy way around that. "You could just use Bardo's." She looked at the largest of the three men now. "He'll have one on him, Bardo always carries a gun. Do you have yours, Bardo?" she asked from her position on the floor and he nodded by accident. "Can we borrow it? Or you just do it. I'm not bothered who really...but send Danny out," she decided suddenly. 'I don't want to hurt anyone's feelings, I just want to die. Do it quickly, that's all I ask," she informed him scrunching her eyes shut and waiting. Bardo's eyes had grown wide, he wasn't finding her funny anymore. She'd really lost it. She peeked at him and then huffed impatiently, turning back to Alessi. "You did it to my dad what's the problem? Come on, Federico!" She used his first name just to toy with him. Nobody ever used his first name but, unfortunately for him, she'd discovered it while ranting at him in front of his father and big mafia boss, Johnny Giavani. His father had addressed him using his first name and this was the first time that she'd dared to bug him with it. He'd wondered how long it would be before she plucked up the courage to go there. "Just send his trashy little daughter the same way," she pushed. He didn't respond. "Please, Alessi, I'm begging you now. This whole thing can be sorted so easily and it's the kindest thing to do, you said so yourself."

Danny was horrified, she'd only been weaned by 0.5ml and she was acting like death was better. Alessi was hoping to wean her off the remaining 4.5ml as quickly as her body would allow, she would be a suicide risk!

"Stop it, Ruby. Trust me and be strong like I know you can be. It's going to get worse before it gets better but we will get you there and you will be so glad when we do. It just doesn't seem that way right now. I'm not going to shoot you and nor is anyone else. We're not going to give up on you either...no matter how much of a pain in the backside you make yourself. Now, what you need to do is occupy your mind. You have four hours until your next dose, which will take the edge off." She hung her head and cried pitifully.

"Please, Alessi, don't do this to me. I'll run away I swear." She raised her knees and sobbed into them, rocking back and forth. Danny moved, desperately wanting to comfort her, but Alessi smiled and raised his hand to stop him silently. He did as he was told, though it broke his heart to see her so unhappy.

"If you run, Ruby, where are you going to go?" Alessi asked her gently. "Do you know the street value of Paradise?" She shook her head, she hadn't needed to know and nobody had told her. "Believe me it's more than you can afford. Are you planning on going back to Marlon?" he asked and she seemed unsure. "You say he never touched you but after walking out on him like you did his motives might well have changed. You didn't keep to the deal so why should he, Ruby? His word no longer stands for anything. You've made yourself a couple of pretty big enemies in Killen and Marlon. Do you want to be Marlon's?" he queried.

"No," she sobbed into her knees, shaking her head. She definitely didn't want to be Marlon's.

"Good, I don't want you to be Marlon's either so get yourself up off the floor and go and get showered and dressed. I want your hair clean, your make-up done and you looking as irresistible as I know you can be. It will make you feel better when you look in the mirror and it will also pass some time. Go get on with it please and then come back. I want to see you again," he ordered. She immediately stood and left the room without another word or complaint. Danny and Bardo were stunned at how well he'd handled her, how he'd managed to channel her frustration. "It's about keeping her occupied," he confirmed confidently, looking down to continue adding up a client's bill on his calculator.

An hour later Ruby came back and walked straight up to Alessi. Her face was hard, not happy, but not challenging either.

"Come here, let me see you," he beckoned and she stood before him in her short tartan skirt, flip flops and white fitted shirt. Her hair hung long, dark and shiny and she'd even curled the ends. She wore a touch of blush, a subtle pink on her lips and eyelids and he could even smell perfume. "You look fantastic, it would make Marlon sick," he told her with a satisfied smile. "Ruby, do you have nail varnish?" he asked and she nodded, seeming confused. "Good, go put some on your fingers and toes and then come back and show me." She spun round, rolled her eyes and walked away. "Ruby, don't get it on the carpets please - it won't come out!" he called after her and Danny smiled.

"Are you accessorising her now, Alessi? She's not a poodle you know. She told me that herself."

"Just keeping her busy and out of trouble, Danny. She can't be a nuisance when she's concentrating on her nails now can she?" Half an hour later she came back and held her hands out for him to see and wiggled her toes at him making her flip flops, flip flop. He held a red file out for her to place her hands on so he could study whether she'd done a good job. He nodded, seeming impressed. "Do you have pink?" he asked her and she gritted her teeth like she might just hit him, but bravely took a deep breath and nodded. "Hmmm, well, I think this is a bit too bright, pink would suit you better. Do you have nail varnish remover?"

"Yes," she responded flatly, dearly wishing she didn't have nail varnish remover.

"I'll see you in half an hour then, shall I?" he dismissed her. Danny looked away as she approached, feeling uncomfortable at watching her being ordered around. She reached over, lifted the file next to him and hit him round the head with it before slinging it at Bardo, who was chuckling on the other side of the table. It slammed Bardo hard in the chest, a lesson for daring to laugh at her. At 5pm she came back wearing pink on her nails and Alessi was finally pleased.

"What now?" she asked, like a teenager who'd been told to do the washing up. He glanced at his watch.

"Right, you can go upstairs and put my bedroom back together and then clear up the mess in the bathroom please. Oh and don't go cutting yourself. You lose blood, you lose the precious Paradise coursing around your body. You'll find bin bags under the sink in the kitchen and all that should take you...hmmm...about an hour I expect. Then I suggest you give the place a good vacuum upstairs and downstairs." He glanced at his watch. "That should just about get you there."

"So I'm your slave then?" she asked tersely and he narrowed his eyes at her.

"No, cleaning up your own mess does not make you a slave, Ruby Palmer. It's called taking responsibility for your actions and your *very* bad temper. Actually I should really make you wash your mouth out with soap while you're at it. As for the vacuuming, what else are you going to do to occupy your time? You need to think of things to keep you busy, to entertain yourself with."

"So give me my job back then," she told him bossily, like it was obvious.

"Oh, Ruby, do you know arguing has passed quite a bit of time already? Probably about half an hour so...well done!" he congratulated sarcastically, but then sighed sadly. "I can't give you your job back, sorry. I'm afraid I've given it to someone else." She looked totally dejected. Her mouth dropped open but no words came. She felt winded and hurt and he let her stew for just a few more seconds before smacking her gently on the hip with a file. "Just kidding, that was for hitting my son over the head. Clearly he's too soft to hit you back. I was teasing, that's all. You can have your job back when all this Marlon stuff has blown over and settled down. I can't have you working on files just yet and definitely not while you're under the influence of Paradise. For now it's cleaning...oh and cooking," he sounded upbeat. "You could make tomorrow's dinner. Now there's an idea." She left the room before he could chain her to the kitchen sink, which was the last place she wanted to be, well, after Marlon's place anyway.

11
Crossing boundaries

She didn't come back after vacuuming, just in case Alessi made her cook! While the three men worked on the Rossi appeal in the dining room, dreading her return, she went out into the garden and started cutting the grass with a pair of scissors. She ignored the perfectly good sit-on lawnmower parked in the garage, that would allow her too much thinking time.

At 6.30pm she made her way back into the house feeling an insatiable thirst. She went to the kitchen and grabbed herself a glass of water and a biscuit before wandering through the living room towards Alessi's study. She didn't have a plan - she was just passing time, but was startled suddenly when Alessi came out of his office. He was holding a vial of clear liquid and a syringe. Both stopped abruptly and looked into each other's eyes. A smile ever so slightly crept onto Ruby's face and Alessi closed his eyes, knowing he'd been well and truly busted. She struggled to keep from showing how pleased she was with herself. Setting her glass down on a side table, which housed a big purple plant and a black and white picture of a young boy, she raised her eyebrows at him cockily.

"So, you keep it in your office then?"

"Yes, well, you might have identified the source, Ruby, but it's always locked so..."

"Oh yeah the six digit PIN, but how hard could that be to find? Does Danny know what it is?" she asked and he broke into an uncomfortable smile.

"Leave Danny out of this, young lady, he has no idea what the PIN is. The most you're going to get out of him for your efforts is a few minutes of weakness and a lifetime of guilt."

"So why don't *you* just tell me then or, better still, show me?" she whispered seductively before biting down on her bottom lip. He shook his head and she just about caught the unsuccessful cover up of a sigh. He was tiring now and she was making him uncomfortable; the situation was perfect. She stepped forward and slipped her hands into his hair, raising herself on her tiptoes to kiss him softly on the mouth. The move was very intimate, crossing every single boundary in the book, but he was stubborn and refused to give her the benefit of freaking out.

"I think you should go upstairs to your bedroom NOW, Ruby," he told her quietly and firmly. Her next dose was due in fifteen minutes.

"Are you coming with me, Federico?" she asked, running her fingers down the buttons on his shirt as she looked up into his eyes sweetly and pulled on his tie. He smiled at her.

"Ruby, I'm old enough to be your father..."

"Hmmm, no, you're breathing way too much to be *my* father," she reminded him, cutting him off. He snorted, placing his hands on her shoulders to turn and step her back against the wall.

"Lucky for you I'm not the kind of man that, one, deals in bribery and, two, takes advantage of young girls. It's a good job because I'm pretty sure that after you've had your next dose you're going to wish that you hadn't just pulled this stunt."

"Is that a threat, Alessi?" she laughed.

"Take it as you wish, Ruby."

"I *will* get the PIN," she told him boldly and he nodded.

"I do believe you will, wherever I hide it, but I'll cross that bridge when I come to it," he informed her coolly. She hated it when he was so composed. She placed her hands over the top of his hands, her back still firmly pressed against the wall, and then she slid her fingers between his. She was playing games with him, trying to make him prickly. He gritted his teeth at her, wishing she came with a button that he could just switch off sometimes.

"Do you want your next dose or not, Ruby Palmer?" he scowled and she was finally surprised.

"You are threatening me, aren't you?" she exclaimed. "If you're trying to suggest that you will withhold my next dose if I don't behave how you want me to, then that makes you just as bad as Marlon!" she accused. He grinned and moved in close to her ear. Wisps of her hair tickled his face and she felt his breath on her neck; now she was the one feeling uncomfortable.

"You just upped the ante, Ruby. I'd say pretty much all rules are out the window right now so, yes, that's exactly what I'm saying. I am in charge of when, where and how much you get of this stuff, so you'd better tone it down else I'm going to have to do some barrier crossing of my own. Do you understand me?" he snapped at her softly. His tone was aggressive and she felt truly frightened by him; he'd never got so close and stern with her before. She was feeling the withdrawal bad now and, strangely, the fear was kind of exciting too, like a mini buzz before the big buzz. She closed her eyes and turned her mouth towards his as she breathed as naughtily as she dared to push.

"I love a challenge, Mr Alessi, but I wonder who will break first?" Her lips skimmed against the stubble on his jaw line and she smiled feeling the weight of his hands press more firmly against her shoulders. He wanted to snap big time and she knew it. "Oh and by the way, I think you're right - finding something to do is really helping. I feel properly entertained right now."

He slipped his fingers out of hers, looking much less cool than usual, and took the pressure off her shoulders. She smiled up at him and then slipped out of the gap he'd created, heading for the stairs. After pausing to get himself together, and running his hands through his hair and over the back of his neck, he followed her, calling out to Danny to come and give her the next dose.

Danny arrived a few minutes later already looking hot under the collar and a little bit stressed. He noted that Alessi looked stressed too. Ruby was already in position on the bed, waiting as patiently as she could manage. This time she was wearing a skirt, which made it a little easier to get to her. Alessi explained very slowly how it worked, taking the opportunity to make her sweat for it. Any delay, no matter how small, made the wait unbearable and he knew it. He then summarised cruelly.

"So, Danny, basically you stab her with it as hard as you possibly can, give her half and then chuck the other half out of the window. Or you could give her even less than half or, if you don't feel like it today, we could all just go on strike and lock her in her room till she agrees to behave herself." She refused to bite and stayed still, waiting for the prick of the needle, yearning for the prick of the needle.

"OK, Alessi, you're making me really nervous now. Am I going to hurt her when I do this because I really don't want to?" Danny asked him looking ready to back out.

"Why not? I think you should." Alessi told him.

"Come on, man, do I do it slowly or quickly, which hurts less?" Ruby slammed her fists into the pillow. It was already 7.20pm thanks to Alessi's little payback and she was so desperate she was starting to feel sick.

"Oh god, Danny, I don't give a crap whether it's slow or fast just as long as you do it and do it, like, NOW!" she yelled at him. He flustered, hesitated, and then jabbed it into her. Clenching his eyes tightly shut he forced himself to push the plunger down until it wouldn't move any further. He pulled his hand away and stood, feeling unwell and dizzy.

"What was all that about, Alessi?" he asked, wiping his forehead on his shirt sleeve. Ruby had started to writhe about and so he reached out and flipped the quilt over her, he didn't want to see. Alessi frowned at the bundle in front of him. He didn't want to stay and watch the girl who had just thrown herself at him roll around either. He was already feeling completely overwhelmed. He had planned on Ruby trying to seduce Danny to get what she wanted; he was the easy and obvious target, but he certainly hadn't planned on her doing it to him.

"I think things are going to get much more complicated much sooner than we thought, Danny. We might have to think of a different way of handling Ruby," he informed him bluntly before walking out and leaving Danny to it.

She woke at 5am to see Danny asleep in the chair. She had slept most of the last dose off but she still had two hours to go and now her tummy and chest felt empty, but her head felt full. She slipped out of bed and approached Danny, crawling up onto his lap. His head had been tilted back against the headrest but he was only dozing. He narrowed his eyes sexily at her.

"Hey," she greeted sleepily leaning in to kiss him. He allowed the kiss to happen. It was a sweet little kiss, nothing too heavy.

"How you feeling?" he asked her with a stretch, and she cringed.

"Dissatisfied," she told him and he looked like he was about to say something but then changed his mind. "Do you remember when you accused me of hitting on you at work when I hadn't been with the firm long?" she asked him and he grinned and laughed.

"Yes I remember it very well. You told me I was too old, you cheeky little madam. I'm not old," he protested. She giggled and snuggled her head into the crook of his neck, like a kitten trying to encourage some affection. He stroked her hair and then her face.

"But you are, what, three years older than me?" she asked and he nodded.

"Yep always three years, Ruby, that never changes."

"So if I was born in 1993 then you must have been born in, 1990?" she asked scrunching her nose like the calculation was awkward.

"Very good, Ruby, you've managed to subtract three from ninety-three, well done you. Your teachers were so wrong," he teased. "Anyway, you've woken up and suddenly you have an interest in what year I was born - what's that all about?" he asked her, squeezing her round the middle to make her squirm and giggle. She was very ticklish and it was an easy and obvious way to get Ruby to crumble.

"I've just never really thought about it before and it jumped into my head," she told him, grasping his hands to stop his fingers from moving. "Anyway, Alessi said to keep busy and we have just under two hours until my next dose soooooo...do you fancy keeping me busy?" she asked innocently, playing with the top buttons on her shirt. He clenched his jaw like she was the most demanding person he had ever come across, before reaching out and slipping the first few buttons through their holes. He paused, thought about it, and then continued right down to the middle. He ran the back of his fingers over the skin on her chest, looking her over and fighting the burning temptation that she always fired up in him. He sighed deeply before looking back up into her eyes.

"Ruby, I don't think this is really what Alessi had in mind when he said 'keep busy' do you?" She shrugged, unbuttoning the rest of her shirt and wriggling out of it. He placed his hands safely on her hips, squeezing her tightly to keep from doing anything else with them. "Ruby, are you hitting on me because you love me and want me...or because Alessi turned you down earlier?" he asked calmly and her eyes widened. She looked utterly mortified.

"Oh my god, Danny, how do you...He told you!" she exclaimed, sounding like Alessi had cheated on her. He sighed deeply, lifting her up on his lap and lowering her back down again to get comfortable.

"He never told...I saw...all of it. I knew Alessi had gone to get the Paradise and so I went to go and get you. I wanted to break it to you that your excruciating wait was finally over but it seemed you were already occupying yourself...in other ways." She placed her hands over Danny's, wishing he wasn't holding her quite so tightly. She wanted to get away but he was keeping her there. She had no choice but to face him. She burst into tears and tried to move again. "Where are you going, Ruby?" he asked her softly.

"Anywhere but here! I hate myself, Danny, and you must hate me too. I'm so, so sorry. Please let me go," she pleaded but he wouldn't, he just carried on holding her tightly.

"I don't hate you, Ruby. I hate Marlon. I hate Paradise and I hate how it makes you behave. Sometimes it's almost funny watching you, but watching you kiss Alessi, that was so not funny. Also, might I add, it is so not you. I can separate what is you and what is the Paradise. I'm perfectly capable of doing that. I'm just relieved to see that the 'No bedding Ruby' rule applies to Alessi too and not just me," he smirked slightly, though his eyes still showed pain.

"Please don't joke, Danny, stop it! You don't have to joke all the time! You don't have to make me feel better about being such a complete bitch. I wasn't hitting on you to get anything - I just wanted you, like I've always wanted you. God, I can't believe you saw. I'm so sorry...and then you gave me my next dose like nothing happened. You didn't even want to hurt me..."

"Why would I want to hurt you?" he frowned. He just didn't seem to get how her mind worked.

"Surely you must have wanted revenge, surely you'd have got some satisfaction from getting at least a yelp out of me...but you didn't. You were so gentle. I'd just kissed your father but you just pushed it to one side and looked after me. I love you so much, just about as much as I despise myself! I need my shirt, where's my shirt!" she panicked. "I need to put it on, I need to go. I need to get some air." She was crying and desperate and she couldn't even manage to look him in the eye. He was calm when he next spoke, his demeanour both controlled and soothing.

"Don't go...and...don't put your shirt on," he ordered cheekily. That got her attention and she looked tearfully back at him, trying to work him out. "It's a very nice view from where I'm sitting, Ruby, don't spoil it by getting all huffy and dressy on me," he grinned at her.

"Huffy, Danny? You caught me with Alessi! I invited him up to my bedroom just to annoy him. I've seriously pissed him off and he threatened not to give me any more Paradise..."

"Did he?" he asked, the shock making him sound slightly amused by the revelation.

"Yes and I'm pretty sure he meant it too. He hates me now. I bet he won't come near me. I didn't plan it, I swear, my instincts just took over. He was there, I was there, he was holding exactly what I wanted and I wanted a share in the control too. He had it all and I wanted to sway him, distract him, win at least one bloody battle for a change, because all I'm doing right now is losing!"

"No, that's not all you're doing right now," he corrected with a very sexy grin. "You're also looking pretty damn hot too," he told her, pulling her closer into his lap.

"Are you serious? Do you actually still like me?" She was frowning in disbelief and he cupped her face and kissed her gently for what felt like an eternity of bliss. He pulled her to him and slid his hand up her bare back, losing his fingers in her soft dark hair and pressing his chest against her body. "I've...promised...not to...touch you," he confessed through long, deep kisses. "But..." He parted lips with her to explain more easily. "But I want you to know I'm only not touching you because of the Paradise. As soon as you're off it you can have whatever you want from me, Ruby. I nearly lost you to Marlon and I had no idea where you were so I'm not waiting any longer than I have to for you. If you want me you can have me, but all I ask is you get off the Paradise first. I will be by your side, Ruby. I won't let you do this alone. I know you can't promise me anything while you're on it because your mind isn't really your own, but try and be strong, baby. Try and resist the urges whenever you can and whenever you can't, well, trust that we will keep you from yourself. "

He hugged her tightly and snuggled her across his lap so she could relax and be kissed. He played with her hair and caressed her face, her lips, her arms and neck, intertwining his fingers with hers and occupying the next two hours in the most amazingly comforting way.

"This certainly beats vacuuming and cutting the grass with scissors!" she told him sleepily, as he cocooned her safely in his arms.

12
Quiet before the storm

At 6.45am they woke up, startled, and still curled up in the chair. Alessi was standing in the doorway with Ruby's next dose of Paradise. She felt groggy and her eyes were bleary. She couldn't focus properly and all she wanted to do was to go back to sleep.

"My, you get around, Ruby Palmer," he commented dryly and she suddenly remembered that she wasn't wearing her shirt. She sat up to grab it and hide herself but as soon as she did she felt too rough to care. Her head was thumping and it had started to spin. She rested it in her hands delicately. "So, did he have the PIN?" he asked her, taking in her half dressed state. Danny shook his head, unimpressed.

"I swear that's not all I wanted from you, Danny," she groaned, hating Alessi for wanting to ruin everything. "Leave me alone, Alessi. I'm not feeling well," she complained and Danny was immediately attentive. Alessi stayed put, in no hurry to get close to Ruby again.

"What's wrong?" she heard Danny ask as he fussed over her. "Do you feel sick?" She shrugged away from him feeling hot and sweaty. Raising herself on unsteady legs she went to the balcony doors to get some air. She still hadn't bothered with her shirt and she slid down onto the floor feeling faint. "What's wrong with her, Alessi? He exclaimed. "Did you drop the dose too quickly? Is this punishment? She said you threatened to withhold the dose? You wouldn't do that...would you?" Alessi laughed like he'd said something ironic.

"Did she tell you *why* I threatened to withhold the dose?" he enquired, like that would make a difference.

"She didn't need to, I saw! I know what happened yesterday and I don't care. If I can handle it then so can you! You're not telling me you've never been hit on before. So it was Ruby, so what, she's not well. She can't help what her body is making her do, what her brain is telling her. You're a grown man and she's still so young and, right now, she's desperate too. Did you drop the dose too quickly?" he demanded furiously. Alessi stepped into the room and approached them.

"Of course I didn't," he mumbled regretfully. "I was winding her up." Now he felt guilty.

"Well you shouldn't have. When she feels bad she's going to think you're doing it to get back at her, that you're doing it on purpose to watch her suffer. You've gone and made things so much harder. How much was in the dose I gave her?"

"Enough," Alessi argued.

"Well if I gave her enough then what's wrong with her now?" he spread his hands wide, right over her laid out body. "She was OK at 5am, Alessi!"

"Yeah I can see that," he snorted.

"She's my girlfriend! I've agreed not to sleep with her but I can still touch her, right?" Danny was getting seriously angry now. "I can tell her and show her that I love her, surely? She wanted affection and attention and I gave it to her. I didn't hurt her or take advantage of her. She was fine, then, so why is she like this now?"

"What's up?" Bardo asked craning his head around the door fame. "I heard arguing. Is Ruby kicking off already?" He looked from Alessi to Danny and then spotted Ruby on the floor between them. "Jeez, what's happened?" he asked rushing in and moving her onto her back to check her over. Danny began to explain how she was fine at 5am but that she'd just woken up and keeled over. "Ruby, can you hear me?" Bardo asked her. "Ruby, it's me. It's Bardo. Can you open your eyes, sweetheart? Can you tell me what's wrong?" He frowned and put his head to her chest, then held his fingers to the pulse in her wrist while he looked at his watch. "Why's she half dressed?" he asked frowning up at Alessi.

"That's how fine she was at 5am this morning, Bardo," Alessi informed him dryly. Bardo looked from him to Danny and grinned.

Danny was quick to defend himself. "It's impossible to live your life in this house, do you know that? Nothing! Happened!"

88

"And you expect me to believe that Danny Glover, Alessi's son, spent the early hours in a girl's bedroom and nothing happened?" Bardo laughed. "I'm afraid your reputation precedes you, Danny. I'm definitely not buying it!"

"What's wrong with her, Bardo?" Danny asked, moving his attention to Ruby's condition and agitated at being teased.

"She's suffering from..." Bardo scooped her up into his arms effortlessly and carried her to the bed before continuing, "withdrawal, Danny. How much did you give in her last shot, Alessi?"

"4mls," he responded. "Danny gave it to her."

"She was fine all night - she just slept..." Danny chipped in.

"And took her shirt off and climbed all over Danny," Alessi added. Danny looked back at him seriously and Alessi held his hands up in surrender. Bardo laughed out loud, a long roll of thunderous mirth.

"Right so she's just had..." he paused as his head tried to catch up with it all. "What, another 4ml or did you drop it again? Has she had 3.5ml this time?" he enquired, putting his ear to her chest again. Ruby started to stir and realised Bardo was over her. She panicked and hit out.

"Bardo, no!" she protested, kicking and screaming at him. "Get off me! Leave me alone!" she begged, bursting into tears.

"She's fine, Danny, try not to worry," Bardo reassured. "She's just feeling it now, that's all. It's to be expected I'm afraid..." he trailed off with a frown and shook his head as if something wasn't adding up. "Her heart isn't beating as fast as I'd expect it to be after a shot. It doesn't make sense." He checked his watch. "It's 7.30am so, technically, I'd be expecting her to be rolling around still or at least her heart to be going ten to the dozen."

"Is it 7.30 already?" Alessi asked, astonished. "She hasn't had this morning's shot, Bardo. She came over funny and collapsed and then you came in. It's here. Her last shot was last night, 4mls, like I said. She's due a 3.5ml dose...like...half an hour ago. I'm so sorry guys," he apologised pulling it from his top pocket and passing it to Bardo, who was trying to keep her contained against her will. She was determined to get away from him so he sat on her. She hit out in desperation, so spooked she hadn't even registered that Danny and Alessi were in the room. In her Paradise fogged mind Bardo had come in, found her in bed and jumped on her. She was fighting for her life now and screaming out for Alessi and Danny to come and help her but they didn't seem to hear. As far as she was concerned, the only people in the room were her and the huge and intimidating Bardo. She didn't stand a chance and her arms were weakening against his more powerful ones. He put the needle between his teeth and caught her left arm in one hand, pushing it securely under his knee. He then caught hold of the other arm and pulled it straight, taking the syringe from his mouth so he could speak.

"Ruby, listen, I'm going to give you this next shot intravenously, it will work quicker. It's late and I want to get you more comfortable as soon as possible. You need to hold still, I won't hurt you," he told her. She gritted her teeth and sobbed, feeling completely helpless under Bardo's weight. She was exhausted from fighting him and she felt hot and unwell too. He ran a finger over the vein in the crook of her arm and then pushed the needle in slowly and confidently before releasing the liquid into her body. The effect was almost immediate, like eight to ten seconds rather than minutes. She stopped fighting and crying and began her usual performance.

Bardo quickly climbed off her and Danny grabbed a blanket and threw it over her so she couldn't be watched by any of them. He hated how exposed she always was, how raw her feelings and desires were and how vulnerable and desperate they made her. He scowled at Alessi, disbelieving he had given her enough. He was sure this was punishment for throwing herself at him - one of his harsh lessons. Danny had been so nervous about giving her a dose for the first time that he hadn't even thought to check it was 4mls. He could have given her anything, naively going on the word of his father who, until now, he had trusted implicitly. After threatening to withhold the doses Danny would be double checking each one.

He looked up at Bardo. "So do we need to give it to her like that now?" he asked wearily.

"No, Danny, don't worry. We'll stick to the usual place, it's relatively well hidden but it takes a bit longer injecting into muscle than it does into the vein. I only did it because she was so distressed and I was worried her heart was too slow. I gave it a kick start by getting the nasty stuff into her quicker. It was more about my sanity really. I didn't want to take any chances waiting a few minutes when I could get the results I wanted within seconds.

"How do you know so much about Paradise? Where did you learn to do what you just did?" Danny asked him, impressed with the careful administration.

"It's my job, Danny. I've had dealings with Paradise before and I wanted to know how to deal with it if I needed to. It's what Mickey threatened my family with during the siege on this place. It's proper nasty stuff and I didn't want Mickey controlling my family like Marlon's been controlling Ruby. I've been in the drugs business a long, long, time and I know a thing or two...let's just say that," he smiled and gave Danny a reassuring pat on the back. "Don't worry, she's in safe hands and she'll be absolutely fine. We'll get her back soon."

A few hours later Ruby woke. Initially she felt well rested, warm and cosy but soon she was feeling that gnawing, nagging hunger again. She groaned and rolled onto her back as a knock came at her bedroom door.

"Yes!" she shouted out, feeling agitated already. Bardo pushed it open and peeked in. He never came into her room she noticed. He always hung about outside.

"How you feeling now?" he asked her.

"Now?" she queried slowly, squinting at him suspiciously.

"Yeah you got a bit sick earlier, passed out, don't you remember?"

"No." She shook her head not liking the fact that she'd obviously lost a chunk of her memory. Anything could have happened. "What's the time?" she asked him, sounding stroppy. "Have I even had my shot yet?" He smiled at her cautiously. He didn't want to tell her the time. She might freak knowing she had so long to wait until the next dose. From now on the levels were barely going to take the edge off and the between times were going to be hell, for everyone! He changed the subject.

"Alessi and Danny have popped to the office, they won't be long. They left early, right after your last dose. They've got a meeting with Johnny Giavani about the Rossi case. Court doesn't reconvene until 10.00am and Alessi is taking the morning off. He said they'd only be a few hours. Why don't you get some breakfast and get dressed? I'm sure they'd like to see you up and about when they get back," he suggested kindly and she scoffed at him.

"Yeah and maybe I'd like to see more of what Alessi promised me! He's a liar and a murderer, although it seems he only shoots people who *aren't* begging him to do it. Because of him I'm suffering so, to be perfectly honest with you, Bardo, I couldn't give a toss what he wants to see. You can tell him that from me!" She pulled the covers over her head and waited until she heard the door close again. She felt so narked, so on edge and ready to snap that if someone so much as looked at her the wrong way she would kill them.

Her legs were jumpy and her hands were shaking so she climbed out of bed and took a shower, changing into a short black skirt and a black vest top. She was feeling depressed and black was the only colour that seemed right. She slipped on some flip flops, also black, and then brushed her teeth and combed her hair. She felt tired, she looked tired and she was determined to make herself look and feel better. There was just one thing she needed and it wasn't more sleep like her body told her, and it wasn't more food or water like Danny told her.

She made her way to Alessi's office, sneaking past the dining room and being careful not to be spotted by Bardo. He was reading through a file with his feet on the table. Alessi would kill him if he saw. They ate at that table! She tried the door, but it was locked. She ran her finger over the keypad, feeling the raised cold silver numbers. Six digits she needed and she'd already guessed what they might be. She typed in 151090, Danny's birthday, but the door wouldn't open. She felt deflated and close to tears, or tantrum, she wasn't quite sure. She stepped backwards and leaned against the wall, sliding down and sitting on the cool floor. Suddenly she scooped herself back up, her finger poised over the keypad once again. She typed in 101590 instead, changing the month and the day around, and then turned the handle. This time it clicked and opened and she almost hyperventilated, she was so close! After a quick check back over her shoulder she slipped through the gap and closed the door softly behind her.

The place was stacked neatly with files, papers, photographs and equipment. There was a huge writing desk, a big fat leather chair, a telephone, a fax, copier and even a sofa. Alessi's private room had everything an office could possibly wish for. Did he even need to go in to work, she wondered!

She found the cooler box in a cabinet drawer and lifted the lid. Stacked inside were vials upon vials of Paradise. She scooped a handful out and a syringe. She would take some now and stash the rest for later. Alessi would never know and she could top herself up while he thought he was weaning her off.

Suddenly her heart jolted in her chest; there was someone outside the room. The handle turned and the office door opened as Alessi made his way in, closely followed by Bardo and Danny. She was trapped! She was also in *big* trouble!

13
Commit the crime and you'll do the time

She dived for the desk, hiding beneath it while she frantically slipped the vials of Paradise into her top and the syringe into the waistband of her skirt. The door closed quietly and she huddled in a tight ball preparing to wait it out. She hoped they would have a private conversation and then go but, strangely, they hadn't said a word since entering the room. She watched as Alessi's shoes passed along one side of the desk and out of her view. She breathed out shakily, that was close! The next thing she was aware of was a sudden scream exploding from her lungs as she was pulled out from her hiding place and held tightly in Alessi's arms. She struggled as he grasped her arms behind her back so she couldn't lash out at him.

"Danny, check her over please," he ordered. Danny rolled his eyes at her. He didn't want to search her but she was the reason he was having to. He stepped forward and begrudgingly frisked her. He found the drug down her top and then ran his hand around her waist and removed the syringe. He sighed at her for making things harder. Alessi wasn't going to stand for it and he was seriously worried for her now.

"What have we got?" Alessi asked him and he wished he could hide what he'd found and cover up for her, but he knew that he couldn't. He held the drug paraphernalia up for them to see.

"She found it," he declared sadly and Alessi nodded and turned to Bardo.

"Right I think we need to contain her. She's a danger to herself. If she were to actually take what she's just hidden she would kill herself. She doesn't know what she's doing and I can't watch her all the time. I can't manage the pressure of wondering what she's going to do next."

"Got it, Boss. What do you want me to do?" Bardo asked helpfully, both talking as if she wasn't even there. Alessi thought hard while they all waited in agonising silence. He sighed deeply.

"Go to the viewing room and remove anything that doesn't need to be in there. Leave her a bin in case she gets sick and throw her bedding in there too. I'll bring her along in ten."

Bardo nodded and left the room, closing the door behind him. Once it was safely shut Alessi let Ruby go and she backed away from him.

"What are you doing, Alessi?" Danny asked him anxiously.

"She's going to stay in the viewing room until she's better and I think me and Bardo should administer the shots because you have no idea how dangerous she is. You're too close to see it. Why don't you go back to your apartment and I will let you know when she's clean? You can visit her then," he suggested. Ruby was mortified.

"What? No, Alessi! I'm sorry, OK. I just felt desperate. I won't do it again, I swear. I wasn't going to take the lot! I was just going to use it to top myself back up. I'm not stupid! I wasn't going to take more than I need. I was happy on 5mls and that's what I was going to make my shots up to after you left, that's all. Please don't send Danny away! Please don't shut me anywhere. I'll go mad, Alessi, please!" She begged and sobbed but he was hard now. He had no intention of caving in to her.

"Ruby, it's not forever but I was naive. I thought I could help you and things could stay pretty normal but you still have days left and you're already like this. I'm sorry but you have to be somewhere we can watch you twenty-four hours a day, somewhere we can monitor you and somewhere that you won't be a danger to yourself or to others."

The tears streamed down her face and she looked at Danny hopefully, but Alessi got in there first. "Danny, I could really do with your support on this. It's the safest option and you know it. It's not nice but it's not forever either and then you can have Ruby back in all her monstrous glory." Danny looked unsure as he reasoned it through in his head. Ruby could see he was undecided and dropped to her knees in a desperate attempt to get him on her side, grabbing at his hands and holding them in hers.

"Danny, please, I swear I will try harder. I will stay in my room but please don't shut me in the viewing room. There are no windows in there, there's no air! It will kill me! He's mad at me, Danny, that's why he's doing this," she told him, attempting to chip away at his confidence and drive a wedge between him and his father. She needed Danny to be with her not against her. Bardo and Alessi would support each other on everything but they needed Danny's support as well and she was the only one who could stop that happening.

"Ruby, please get up. Don't kneel down like that - I don't like it," he told her uncomfortably but she shook her head as she sobbed.

"Danny, please, I will do anything you ask. He's punishing me. I...I heard him tell Bardo he was going to stop the doses because he's mad at me. He hates me because I threw myself at him. He wants me dead, I heard him. Bardo's agreed to help. That's why they're putting me in the viewing room, Danny!"

He looked from her to Alessi but Alessi shook his head slowly. He held his hands out, a gesture that it was clear as day she was lying. He wasn't about to protest his innocence over such an absurd allegation. Danny looked her in the eye.

"GET. UP!" he ordered more sternly than he'd ever been with her before. She immediately did as she was told, frightened of his tone.

"It's true, Danny, I heard him. That's why he told you to go home. They're going to torture me and then stop the Paradise completely. I will have a heart attack and they will tell you it all went wrong. He's always hated me! I've never been good enough! I've always disgusted him. He doesn't like girls!" she suddenly declared and Danny looked amused for a second and slightly surprised before turning to look at Alessi.

"Will the room be ready?" he asked in a whisper and Alessi nodded. That was all he needed to know as he stooped and put her over his shoulder. "Let's get this over and done with then shall we?"

She beat at his back and clawed at his shirt but he wouldn't put her down. He held her tightly all the way to the viewing room while she screamed about how much she hated him. Bardo was waiting, holding the door open, and Danny took her inside and lowered her down onto a pile of quilts. She beat her fists relentlessly against his chest.

"I despise you, Danny Glover! I wish you were dead. You've made my life hell and I will never, ever, forgive you for doing this to me. I hate you. You make me sick!" she screamed at him. She stopped, suddenly noticing her surroundings. The room was empty, save for the quilts on the floor and the metal bin. There was a big mirror along one wall, which she knew they could watch her through, and the desk and chairs had been removed for everyone's safety. This was to be her home now. This was where she would eat, sleep, get sick and suffer, all in front of the big glass mirror; all in front of them. She brought her attention back to the only man she had ever loved, raised her hand and slapped him hard across the face. He caught hold of her wrists and pushed her back down, towering over her. She felt so helpless, so turned upon by all the people she thought she could trust. She was sure he was going to hurt her but to her surprise he spoke softly.

"Ruby, I love you. You can do what you like to me but I will still love you - that is why you're here, that is why I've brought you here and that is why I'm leaving you here now. You won't be alone, I will be here too. There will always be someone looking out for you and I will stay right in here with you as much as I can. That's not going to be possible when you're losing it. When you're asleep and when you're calm I will be in here too. Do you understand me? I have something I need to do and then I'll be back. You're not due another dose for quite a few hours but I will get you a clock so you at least have some concept of time. It might help. I love you, Ruby," he told her again and then, just like that, he was gone.

He'd moved quickly, before she could attack him again, and she watched in dismay as the door shut securely behind him. She heard the key turn on the other side and then rolled onto her front, screaming into the quilts until her voice was harsh and broken.

"I hate you, Alessi! I hate you!" she shouted, but her throat was sore and she couldn't continue. She rolled onto her side, her back to the mirror, and sobbed bitterly. Danny pressed his palms up against the glass on the other side wishing he could comfort her, while Alessi moved to place his hand on his shoulder.

"Are you OK?" he asked, genuinely concerned. "She will be fine you know. I promise we'll get her through this." He tried to support him but Danny looked at him briefly and then turned to leave the room.

When Danny arrived back at the viewing room a short time later he'd showered and changed and was feeling much more composed. He brought in four hot drinks and Bardo suggested that Ruby's should wait until it was cool enough not to hurt anyone. He nodded sadly and placed the cup on the side. Bardo grabbed a paper cup from the water cooler and poured the hot drink into it.

"China cups hurt when they're launched at your head," he informed him and Danny half laughed.

"Yeah, I guess. I didn't think of that either," he confessed. Bardo smiled kindly.

"If it helps she's just been apologising for the last hour for hitting you. I think she's sorry, mate."

Danny smiled back and rubbed his cheek. "She should play golf - she's got a really good right swing on her, Bardo. I'll be watching out for that in future!"

Bardo gave a low rumbling laugh. "But worth it?" he asked, already knowing the answer.

"Definitely worth it," Danny nodded with certainty.

"We'll get there," Bardo assured him. "She'll stop hitting you soon," he joked and Danny laughed it off, leaning back in his chair and stretching his arms out above his head. He placed his hands on his neck and groaned wearily.

"Ugh, even just leaving her in there a few days feels like a lifetime! Can I go in and see her? I won't disturb her if she's asleep."

"Are you mad?" Alessi asked, astonished.

"Yeah I think I am a bit," he confessed. "Look I don't care, Alessi, she's hardly going to kill me is she!"

"Hmmm," Alessi mumbled like he wasn't too sure.

"Look, I just want her to have some company, that's all," he reasoned.

"Go for it...oh and take this," Bardo told him, handing him her coffee. Danny thanked him and took the paper cup before letting himself in. He made his way cautiously towards the bundle on the floor and soon realised she wasn't sleeping at all, she was counting. He put the cup down on the floor and called out to her softly, so she wouldn't be alarmed.

"Ruby, it's Danny. Why are you counting, honey?"

"Time," she whispered. "I'm counting the seconds till 7pm." She rolled over and sat up and he scooped her into his arms, rocking her and cuddling her tightly. She buried her head into his chest and begged him to forgive her, which he assured her he already had. She was like a different person now, sweet, soft and much, much, calmer. Maybe they'd been a bit hasty in locking her up. It had only been a blip, they could manage her on the outside a little while longer, surely. He tilted her face up and kissed her in the way that only Danny ever had. It was long, slow and gentle and she let her fingers play in his hair. He kissed her like that over and over and she felt herself relax, carried away from the awful box she was trapped in. She closed her eyes pretending she was anywhere else with Danny, anywhere but stuck in a room with no window. "Is Alessi watching?" she eventually asked him and he narrowed his eyes at her suspiciously.

"Yes, yes he is, but please don't go trying to bug him, Ruby. I just want to be with you. If you don't behave I'm going to have to wait on the other side of the mirror," he warned her and she looked hurt.

"I wasn't going to do anything," she told him adamantly. "I just wanted to know if he was still here, that's all." Danny felt bad but with Ruby now it was impossible to tell when she was lying and when she was telling the truth. If she tried to rip his clothes off, or heaven forbid her own, Alessi would chuck him out of the house and not let him back in until she was sane. "You think I'm easy don't you?" she accused, sitting up straight in his lap and looking ever so slightly like she might be about to lose it.

"No, but I do think you want to get your own back on Alessi. Knowing he's watching is probably getting the cogs turning in that calculating mind of yours," he told her. Her eyes were cold now and she looked ready to snap. He felt the change in her temperament and shifted her off his lap. "I think I might give you a bit of space. I'll be back in a bit," he told her, standing to leave.

"Danny," she called after him and he turned back. She had stood up too and was holding the paper cup. "I'd rather something stronger!" she told him, throwing the contents in his face. Now he knew what Alessi had meant - she was completely unpredictable. She was twisted and vengeful and he guessed that she would have done the same thing had the coffee still been hot. He felt slightly hurt but, strangely, he didn't feel as furious as he thought he would be. Had she done it in the office, just being Ruby in a strop, he would have done the same back to her, but right now all he wanted to do was tell her that it was OK. The drug was like a demon possessing her mind and he could see that behind all of the nasty, bitchy behaviour, Ruby was stuck and desperately wanting to come back. She couldn't control herself and she was doing things that upset her as much as they upset him. He took the paper cup coolly out of her hand, wiping his face on the sleeve of his shirt.

"I'll make sure it's got two spoons of coffee in next time then," he told her with a handsome smile, leaving her baffled as to why he wasn't pinning her up against the wall with his hands around her throat. He crushed the cup, grateful now that it wasn't made of china. "I love you, Ruby," he told her simply and then turned away to leave the room.

She stood there completely stunned for the next ten minutes while Danny stood on the other side of the glass watching her. He dried his face on the hand towel that Alessi passed him.

"Another coffee anyone?" Bardo asked with a grin, breaking the silence. Danny looked at him slowly, his shirt stained and his hair still wet and sticky. Bardo couldn't contain his laughter.

"Yeah and I vote you take the next one in to her," Danny suggested with a smile.

"I'll second that," Alessi grinned, ruffling his son's matted hair.

On the other side of the mirror Ruby sat down quietly, turned her back on them all and began to count, again.

3mls and still counting

Danny offered to take the next dose in at 7pm but Bardo insisted he should do it. He wanted to check her over after her collapse earlier that day. He pocketed the stethoscope to listen to her heart and drew 3mls into a syringe before letting himself in. Ruby spun round, pushed herself up off the ground and backed away from him looking scared.

"What's in the syringe, water?" she asked sarcastically. He laughed.

"No, Ruby, it's 3mls of Paradise, honey."

"Huh!" she scoffed, raising her eyebrows cockily. She still kept moving along the wall though, like she was worried about him getting too close. "Only 2mls less than originally agreed then," she pointed out.

"Yep and only 3mls away from being clean like you were promised," he reminded. She was now in a corner and had to accept that it was time to stop, there was nowhere else to go.

"It hurts, Bardo," she pleaded, trying to hold back the tears and he felt terrible for her. "My whole body hurts, everything hurts," she whimpered. "Can't you just...help me?" she begged him pitifully. He felt her pain. The suffering was visibly clear and her face was exhausted.

"I'm trying, sweetheart, but sometimes you just have to be cruel to be kind."

"That's what they say about animals, Bardo!" she snapped. "I'm not an animal, I'm a human being, and you've shut me in here like this! I'm in pain and I feel sick. It would be kinder to kill me. I know you can do it. It wouldn't be the first time you've pulled a trigger, right?" He shook his head at her.

"Ruby, I'm trying to save you - I'm not about to kill you. Come on, let's get this next shot done and then I can check you over. "

"Check me over?" Her eyes scanned the room, desperate for an escape route. "Marlon and his so called 'doctor' checked me over and look how I've ended up!"

"No, Ruby," he stopped her before the paranoia got out of hand. "I checked you over this morning when you collapsed. I never hurt you then and I'm not about to hurt you now. I just need to keep a note of your pulse and your heart rate and make sure it's safe to continue reducing the dose at the rate we have been. If it's not we will have to do it more gradually which will take much longer. We want you back as soon as possible because we miss you, Ruby. We've done it so quickly it's almost cruel, but Alessi insisted he wanted it done as fast as it was possibly safe to do. He's desperate to get you clean. It's not nice for you, I know, but there is no nice way of coming off Paradise. We may as well hit the detox hard and get it over and done with eh?" She didn't respond but just stared at him coldly. "This way, if your heart can take it, you will only suffer for a few days."

"Only!" she exclaimed looking like he'd just clicked his fingers in her face.

"As opposed to weeks," he clarified. "That's got to be better, right? Come on, Rubes, let's not do this the hard way." She'd backed herself up to the big mirror and now Alessi and Danny were only a thin sheet of clever glass away as she turned, placed her hands against the cool surface and bowed her head. She clenched her eyes tightly shut and Bardo pushed the needle into her thigh, sending 3mls into her body. She gritted her teeth bravely and as she weakened he scooped her off her feet and looked into the mirror. "Sorry, guys, I hadn't realised where she was."

He carried her back to the pile of quilts where the drug kicked in. She began her usual display, which wasn't lasting as long as it had when she was on the full 5mls, and ended up on her front gripping the quilts like her life depended on it. Bardo gently felt for the pulse in her wrist and timed it. He rolled her slightly so he could reach her chest with the stethoscope and then he gave the thumbs up. Danny saw him take a deep breath and sigh as he sat back on his haunches and placed a reassuring hand on Ruby's hip. He looked like he felt sorry for her, giving her an affectionate and reassuring pat before standing and backing towards the door.

The night was long and tiring, with Ruby screaming out every hour or so for someone to help her. Danny spent some time with her but she would go from being passive and lovely to accusing him of trying to kill or attack her. He held her when he could and when she was fighting and mad he left her to it, figuring staying would just make her worse. By sunrise she had started to see things again, like she had when Danny first found her in the bathroom at Marlon's place. She kept moving around the room, trying to hide and wrapping herself in quilts to keep the creepy crawlies off.

At 7am Danny took 2.5mls in to her and she watched him approach from the corner of the room. There was no recognition in her now very dark eyes, and her breathing was shallow and quick. Her face was streaked with droplets of sweat and she looked barely able to go on. Though he desperately wanted to hug her she looked too delicate to even hold.

"Hey, baby, I have your next dose," he whispered, dropping to his knees a short distance from her so she wouldn't feel threatened. She looked at the syringe vacantly and then back to him.

"Thank you," she whispered helplessly. He wasn't expecting that! "Will it help, Danny? I don't know if I want out or in now. I don't know if on is worse than off or if off is worse than on." She seemed slightly delirious and he tried not to appear too confused.

"In is good, it's the only way to get out," he told her confidently. "We give you this a few more times and then you'll get better. You need just enough that your heart can adjust but as little as possible so we can get you off the evil stuff as soon as possible, OK? You only feel so bad because what we're doing here is working - feeling bad is kind of good," he tried to reassure her, scrunching his nose sympathetically while she continued to stare at him.

"Why are you here?" she asked and he looked at the syringe and then back to her.

"I've come to give you this," he told her, his eyes squinting slowly.

"What is it?" she frowned.

"Paradise," he answered suspiciously, unsure what was going on now.

"So you haven't come to measure me then?"

"No, I definitely haven't come to do that. Why would I measure you?" he smiled, feeling slightly amused.

"The man sat over there, the one dressed in black, he said you'd come to measure me...for a coffin." Danny glanced over his shoulder at the other side of the room and then up at the viewing room window. He knew Bardo was watching and listening in.

"Ruby, the man in black is a lying bastard and you can tell him that from me. There will be no coffin for you, just a shot of medicine that will make you feel a little bit better." She nodded and curled up so he could get to her. He gave her the shot and then covered her over with the quilt so she could wriggle around with some degree of privacy.

He stayed put until she fell asleep and then he left the room to join Bardo. "Did you hear that?" he asked him, taking a deep breath and blowing it out slowly. Bardo nodded.

"I don't know who invited him but the man in black really isn't helping is he?" he observed falling back into his chair. "Oh and by the way, Alessi said he wants you to go into work today, he has clients or something. He's gone to get ready...that sounds like him coming back now."

Danny sighed; the last place he wanted to go was to work. As Alessi let himself into the room Danny swung his chair round to face him. "Why do you need me at work?" he asked boldly. "Can't it wait? Can't I deal with it from here?"

Alessi shook his head. "No can do I'm afraid. I've already taken on someone else and she needs a bit of support else I risk losing her."

"You've employed someone else? You never told me!" Danny exclaimed.

"I just did."

"You kept that pretty quiet. What about Faye?"

"Faye's good, in so much as she does as she's told, but she *needs* telling. Neither of us have really been there and she just can't seem to think for herself. Last week she was in tears because she didn't know how to handle the filing and so I asked Mrs Hughes to advertise and select the best five for me to interview. I interviewed the other morning and gave Tabitha the job on the spot."

"Tabitha?" Danny asked with a grin. "On the spot," he echoed, making Bardo laugh.

"Is she a tabby cat?" Bardo teased.

"Or a sexy little Kitty Kat?" Danny joined him.

"Grow up you two - she's a very nice young woman and she performed very well in the interview."

"So she performed for you, did she?" Danny laughed looking thoroughly delighted. "Tell us, Alessi, did you actually ask her any questions or just check to see how good she looked next to your desk?" he dared to push, standing to check on Ruby through the window. She was still sleeping so he sat back down again.

"Danny, you did not just say that. I don't want to be taken to a tribunal over sexist comments from you so shut it and go and get smartened up. You're coming in to meet her and you need to get some work done too."

"But..." Danny protested gesturing towards the glass window.

"But nothing! Bardo is more than capable of looking after Ruby and I need you at work." Danny huffed, mumbled something incoherent, and then left the room.

15
Bad girls

When they arrived at work Danny immediately disappeared for forty-five minutes, in true Danny fashion, and Alessi couldn't find him anywhere. By the time he made his way wearily up the stairs to the office, looking like he'd been out drinking all night, Faye was already sat at Ruby's desk. He didn't like her sitting there but smiled at her anyway, just to be polite.

"Hi, Faye, how's it going? Not given up on law yet then?" he asked her, deeply wishing she would. Ruby would kill Faye for sitting at her desk. She would also hate the fact that Faye was an incredible flirt who didn't care who knew it.

"Hey Danny," she cooed at him and he smiled, unable to look anything but sexy and tired. "My, what have you been up to? You look all partied out, you gorgeous thing you," she teased. He shook his head at her and took his seat, keeping an eye on her for just a second and wondering how he was going to find the energy. She blushed and giggled, taking his attention as interest.

"I haven't been clubbing - I've been looking after Ruby," he told her as he searched his drawers and reacquainted himself with his desk. "She's been quite sick, Faye." He could tell from the fake smile that had crept onto her face that she didn't like that. She looked jealous but she continued with the facade anyway.

"Ohhh you poor thing! That must be so hard, having to look after your girlfriend. She's been sick for ages hasn't she? Someone said she ran away - is she a bit of a tearaway, Danny? Do you like bad girls?" she asked, sounding thrilled.

"Hmmm, I quite like them, yes," he told her distantly, paying no attention as he read through his telephone messages. They had been taken by Amanda on reception, which meant they were both vague *and* rude. To top that, there were loads of them!

"So must be frustrating then... if you know what I mean? I mean if you like bad girls and your girlfriend is, how would you put it, out of action, it must be *really* hard?" she giggled. He looked up at her as she chewed on her gum seductively. He narrowed his eyes, a move that was meant to be disapproving but looked very much to her like a come on to her.

"Yeah, I think I know what you mean, Faye, but I can't say as I'm frustrated. Tired, yes, but not frustrated. I miss having her around, especially around here. And she's not out of action thanks...you make her sound like an old military aeroplane." He frowned at her and went back to his messages while she sauntered around the room trying to get his attention. He picked up the phone and made some calls. While on hold he whispered to get her attention. "Faye, what's Tabitha like?" She leaned back in her chair, performing an exaggerated stretch and crossing her legs, but only so she could uncross and cross them again. He smiled at her, she was indeed trying.

"Hmmm, well, she's cute and she's actually really nice too. I thought she might be like some old dragon that Mr Alessi had employed just to boss me about, but she's not. She's really helpful. She's in there with him now."

"What! She's in there?" he asked, stunned. "With Mr Alessi?" Faye nodded, checking to make sure her cleavage was still there. Something just wasn't working on him! He grinned and at last she caught him looking too, which he hadn't meant to do. She smiled, happy at last, and he was flustered. "Faye...I never meant to...oh, yes, hello...I...erm...sorry...someone was just...erm..." He coughed and tried to compose himself. "I just wondered if you could check the court record for me? Thanks. Can you tell me when case number NB245634 is listed for trial?" He waited a second and then nodded. "Brilliant. Thanks very much. Yep. Bye." He hung up quickly and closed his eyes feeling mortified.

"Hey, Danny, they look better close up," she invited and he pointed at her sternly with his pen.

"I wasn't looking...I mean you made me look...by you looking first...you drew attention...oh you know what I mean. Get on with opening bloody files, Faye! No wonder it takes you so long!"

"Ugh men are *so* gross, it's like all they ever notice are your breasts," she complained.

"Oh give it a break, Faye, you've been..."

"Ahhh, Danny!" he was interrupted mid rant. "I wondered whether we were going to see you at your desk this morning." It was Alessi. "I heard voices and guessed you'd made an appearance...at last." He gestured for him to come in. Danny stood and as he did he noticed that Faye had the audacity to try the cleavage thing out on Alessi too. He just frowned at her like she was mad and then opened the window and put the fan on high, throwing her cardigan at her. "I suggest you put this on, Faye, because the office is about to get much colder."

Danny couldn't help but laugh. If there was one thing Alessi could do well it was take the wind out of someone's sails. Faye grumbled in response, pulling her arms through her cardigan and shuddering as the fan blew cold air at her.

Danny stepped into Alessi's office where Tabitha was seated in one of his client chairs, perched on the edge like she wouldn't be staying. The first thing he noticed was the long dark hair framing her pretty little face. It had been scooped back loosely and clipped up like she'd been under pressure when she did it. No doubt she was feeling the strain of Mr Alessi's strict and fairly tight ship. He smiled as she pushed the fallen strands behind her ears shyly. Clearly she felt awkward so he quickly made the first move, holding out his hand to greet her.

"Hi, I'm Danny. It's very nice to meet you, Tabitha. Mr Alessi has told me a lot about you. Apparently you outshined everyone in the interview," he grinned. "I'm sure you will fit in very well." She smiled like she was relieved.

"Thank you, Danny, that's really nice to hear. I've heard a lot about you too," she replied and he kept hold of her hand but stopped shaking it.

"What have you heard?" he asked her, sounding intrigued, and she squirmed and looked to Alessi and then back to him like she wasn't quite sure what to say. "Didn't happen to be gossip from the secretaries downstairs did it?" he guessed. She looked uncomfortable and nervous as she slipped her hand free of his.

"I never meant...I shouldn't have said...yes, it might have been," she confessed.

"Oh, Danny, and I'd love to tell her none of it is true," Alessi sighed.

Danny squinted at her playfully. "It was just a phase," he defended poorly and she giggled sweetly, crossing her arms to keep him from trying to shake her hand again.

"Right, well, I just wanted you two to meet. Tabitha is also helping out in accounts because she's very good with figures. A couple of days a week that's where she'll be," he updated Danny. "Actually, Tabitha, would you mind just grabbing the records I'm waiting for on the Sanderson file please?" he asked her and she nodded keenly as she smoothed her skirt towards her knees.

"Would you mind?" Danny teased and she stopped mid stand to look at him, her big blue eyes seeming thoroughly bewildered. "I'm sorry, Tabitha, it's just that Mr Alessi doesn't usually talk to staff like that. He usually says 'Get me the figures and do it now!'" He raised his eyebrows and her face flushed.

"That's enough, Danny, don't you have some work to do...*now?*" Alessi growled.

"See, I rest my case!" he shrugged and she stood, brushing between the two men, eager to escape the both of them.

"Danny!" Alessi snapped at him as soon as the door was closed.

"What?" he asked innocently, falling into the chair that their newest little recruit had just slipped out of. "Mmmm, nice perfume," he observed, running his hands up and down the armrests. "Oh come on, don't tell me you haven't noticed how cute she is? How old is she?"

"How would I bloody know? I'm just her boss? Why would I be interested in her age?"

"How old is she, Alessi?" Danny asked again, the grin spreading wider. Alessi shrugged.

"I don't know, thirty-four...nearly thirty-five...in November," he added with more certainty. Danny laughed out loud before standing and leaving the room.

A short while later Tabitha arrived back upstairs with the figures, slipping passed Danny's desk to knock on the office door. He seemed engrossed as his pen scrawled across a piece of paper, so she was thrown when he acknowledged her.

"Hello again, Tabitha," he smiled like he knew something, his eyes still fixed on his paperwork. "Nice perfume."

She gave him a frown, that he didn't see, and then took the figures in to Mr Alessi.

While she was there he spent some time showing her around the computer system, inviting her to sit down in his chair. Danny was right, she did smell good. He leaned over her shoulder to move the mouse as he navigated around the network, showing her where all the most important documents and files might be hiding.

"It's all here, somewhere," he confirmed softly. "It's not as clear or as logical as I'd like it to be but sometimes, when people are stressed, they seem to save things under random headings. She giggled and he seemed in no hurry to get rid of her.

She'd initially been worried about Mr Alessi. Amanda on reception had been eager to tell her all about how awful he was. Apparently he regularly made employees cry. Tabitha was yet to be convinced that he was a monster, though he definitely had a presence about him. He didn't seem to smile as much as Danny and whenever she was in his company she felt like he was analysing her. He hadn't been around as much as she thought he would be but, when he had been around, he had been nothing but lovely to her.

"Thanks so much," she smiled gratefully when his whistle-stop tour was finally concluded. "If you ever want me to go though and resave things more logically just let me know. I'd be very happy to help."

"A woman after my own heart," he told her and she turned to look at him, slightly taken aback. He was very close. His green eyes grazed over her face and she quickly looked away again, it seemed she wasn't one for eye contact. He turned the chair away from the screen, with her still in it. "I

110

must evict you now I'm afraid, Tabitha. I have to make an abusive phone call and I don't want you to hear it."

She slipped out of his chair obediently and made straight for the door, closing it softly behind her. Save for her perfume it was like she'd never been there. This time she had Danny's full attention as she emerged.

"You OK?" he asked her with a cheeky grin and she nodded, looking anything but. "You look a little flustered, Tabitha, I do hope our Mr Alessi is being nice to you." He opened his eyes wide, as though making a point, and she smiled wearily back at him but didn't bother to answer. Mr Alessi was being *very* nice to her and suddenly she wasn't so sure she could handle it. Things had just got more than a little bit complicated.

16
A visit from Sammy

Danny and Alessi left work early and made their way straight home. Alessi wanted them to make an appearance in court but Danny insisted that they should go home first. After making some calls, and being reassured that the Rossi appeal was coming along nicely, Alessi finally conceded. Danny was clearly missing Ruby and when they'd left that morning she had been deteriorating like they knew she would. Fortunately, there had been no phone call to say that she'd got worse or that Death, sitting in the room with her, had tried to take her away.

As soon as they got in Danny threw his blazer on the sofa and made his way to the viewing room. Alessi picked up after his messy son and then followed him. When they joined Bardo he was at the viewing glass looking stressed and tired.

"What is it?" Danny asked following his line of vision. Ruby was being sick and he immediately began rolling up his sleeves. "What's wrong with her? How long has she been ill?" He was understandably concerned but Bardo just sighed.

"All day, Danny, I'm sorry. It's just another symptom I'm afraid. The drug is leaving her body and it's taking its toll."

"Why didn't you call me? Have you been in there with her?" Bardo shook his head, he'd tried but she hadn't trusted him. "She needs company. I don't want her to be sick on her own. She'll be scared, Bardo!"

Danny grabbed some water from the cooler and soaked the handkerchief that he'd pulled from Alessi's blazer pocket without asking first. He went in and pulled Ruby's hair away from her face, wiping it over with the wet handkerchief. She sat back on her knees for a few seconds and managed a brief smile in thanks but then lunged forward again to be violently ill.

"Make it go away, Danny," she begged, too exhausted and hurting even to cry. He mopped her face again and encouraged her to take some water. She immediately threw up and he repeated the process. She was sweating and cold and her top and skirt were soaked through. He left her side to put his head round the door.

"Can someone grab me a bunch of clean quilt covers, a couple of towels, a flannel, a change of clothes, a bowl of warm water and some cream. Don't worry, Alessi, I'm not talking squirty cream, I mean hand and face type cream. Oh and a couple of bottles of water. If we've got any, bring some sweets too. We're going to get her cleaned up."

They immediately set about doing as they'd been asked and a short time later they joined him in the viewing room where he nodded at them gratefully. "I'd appreciate it if she could have some privacy for just a few minutes," he asked and Alessi and Bardo were both eager to help out. Alessi managed to conduct a telephone conference with the barristers working on the Rossi appeal as he wedged his phone between his chin and his shoulder. Turning away, to give Ruby some privacy, they blocked the door for safety while they changed all of the sheets and covers for fresh ones. Alessi had to apologise quite a few times as he quite unsuccessfully juggled the call and stuffed quilts into their pretty pink covers but, from the gist of it, Bardo gathered that the penultimate day in court had gone very well indeed.

Danny removed Ruby's top and washed her face, neck, back and hands. He plaited her hair in one long braid and pulled a clean top over her head. He then removed her skirt and washed her legs and feet before drying her off and slipping on another skirt. The whole thing took him two hours, with her needing to be sick every fifteen minutes, but then he encouraged her to suck on a sweet for the energy and she eventually agreed. The sugar seemed to lift her slightly and the sickness subsided. He got her to sip water and made her comfy on the clean bedding, while he put cream on her face and lips. He then rubbed it into her hands and feet, massaging gently to help with the debilitating aches and pains. She complained that her legs hurt and so he massaged cream into those too. By the time her next dose was due she looked like a different girl, still very unwell, but much more cared for.

Bardo brought in the 2mls and the stethoscope and let Danny listen to her heart. He then showed him how to check her pulse. "A healthy pulse should be about sixty to one hundred beats per minute. Count how many you feel and time it using the second hand on your watch. Ruby's pulse is much higher but that's because of the increase in her heart rate due to the Paradise. That will regulate as she comes off. What we don't want is the rate to skip, slow or suddenly increase. If she's having 125 beats in one minute and over the next few minutes they are pretty much the same then that's fine. But, if they are very different from one minute to the next, we need to do something about it." Danny gave it a go and then listened to her speeding heart using the stethoscope. He administered the 2mls and covered her over while the drug kicked in, before crashing out next to her. He woke up five hours later, at midnight. Thankfully she was restful so he kissed her head and left the room. Alessi came in with coffee and Danny yawned.

"I'm not coming in to work tomorrow," he confirmed boldly. "Ruby was really ill today and I wasn't here for her. I'm not doing it again," he told him. Alessi smiled and nodded.

"Fair enough, Danny. I need you but she needs you too and things are just going to have to wait for a bit. When she's better you're going to be putting in some serious hours to catch up, son" he forewarned. Danny nodded.

"Yeah of course. You took that remarkably well!" Alessi shrugged and passed him his coffee. "It wouldn't have anything to do with Tabitha would it?" Danny grinned. Alessi told him to shut up but Bardo wanted to know what the new woman was like. Danny filled him in. Alessi took himself off to bed, refusing to get caught up in the conversation, much to the other two men's amusement and frustration.

Danny finished his coffee and rested his head on the table. He woke a short time later to the sound of screaming. Ruby was pulling at her hair and trying to cover the mirror with sheets and quilts but, of course, it was a totally useless exercise.

"Stop looking at me! What do you want? Leave me alone! I don't like how you look at me!" She was thoroughly disturbed and both men watched on in bewildered silence.

"I don't think she likes that we're watching her. I don't know what spooked her but for no apparent reason she stood up slowly, in the middle of the room, looked towards the mirror and then properly lost it," Bardo whispered, looking strangely pale in the dim light. They watched for a while longer as she tried over and over to cover the glass and then Danny shook his head.

"No, I don't think it's because we're watching her, Bardo. I think it's her reflection. She doesn't recognise herself. It's the mirror that's freaking her out. She can't tell what's real and what's not." He made for the door but Bardo warned him that he needed to be careful. "I can't leave her when she's like that, it's not fair. She must be petrified that someone is in there with her."

He pushed open the door and she spun her head to look at him, while simultaneously managing to stay rooted to the spot. Her face was deathly white and etched with fear. Long strands of hair hung from her fingers and her eyes were huge. He stopped just inside the door. "Ruby, it's me, do you recognise me?" he asked her, but she didn't reply and now he wasn't so sure if he should approach her. He swallowed hard and took a deep breath, moving ever so slightly closer. "Ruby, baby, what's frightened you?" he asked, edging forward again. "What do you see?" She looked to the mirror, squealed and then looked back to him again as her legs began to shake. "Ruby, sit on the floor - it's just a mirror. If you sit on the floor you won't see anything." She stayed rooted, her eyes fixed on him as he inched towards her, trying not to freak her out any more than she already was. Now he was within touching distance and he held out his hand to her but she made no attempt to move. "Ruby, what do you see?" he asked her softly.

"Sammy!" she cried out, her body convulsing at the sound of the dead girl's name. "The man in black dyed her hair. He likes black, it's not blonde anymore. She's dead and she's standing over there." She pointed towards the mirror but she didn't dare to look again. "She's come to take me back with her but I don't want to go, Danny. She keeps screaming at me and ripping her hair out. She doesn't want black hair she wants blonde hair, blonde is beautiful and she wants to be famous. She doesn't want to be dead, she wants to be alive. I don't want to go with her, Danny, please make her go away. Make her go away like you made the man in black go away."

"I'll make her go away for you, Ruby, but to do that you have to sit down with me. Don't look at her and she won't look at you. Just sit down and she will know that you want to stay here, with me. She will go back to wherever she came from then," he assured her, taking her hands in his. She was cold and he pulled her down gently. Her legs buckled and she dropped to her knees. She looked back to where she'd seen Sammy but, just like Danny had told her, Sammy was gone. She'd left the room.

"She's not there," she whispered, relieved but still worried she might hear her. She looked down at her hands. Danny was trying to brush away the black strands of hair twisted around her fingers but it was too late, she'd seen them. She shook them out violently like they were contaminated. "It's her hair, it's all over me!" she panicked. In Ruby's eyes it wasn't just a few strands it was a whole head of hair, and she kicked back trying to escape across the floor.

Danny brushed at her legs and gathered it all up as quickly as he could. She was sobbing and shaking and he pulled her up close to his body and wrapped a quilt tightly around them both so she'd feel safe. The shaking continued to wrack at her small frame in unforgiving waves as she drifted in and out of a delirious sleep. Danny didn't sleep at all and his energy was wearing dangerously thin.

"Hey," Alessi whispered when he came in at 7am ready for work. "Bardo told me what happened last night. Are you OK?" Danny felt rough and he looked rough too. "Get some sleep today please. I'm worried about you and I don't want you getting sick. Ruby is going to want you around when she's better. There's no point getting her through this and then being too ill to enjoy having her back," he told him sternly.

"I promised she wouldn't do it alone. She's been really brave and the least I can do is be there for her during the worst of it."

"I have 1.5mls," Alessi showed his exhausted son. "Do you want to give it to her?" he asked kindly. Danny was snuggled up to Ruby and he felt so tired he couldn't be sure he wouldn't mess it up so he asked Alessi to do it for him. Alessi took her pulse and listened to her heart while she slept and then quickly and smoothly administered the small dose. "It's the last day of the appeal today. I'll let you know as soon as we have a verdict," he smiled sympathetically

Danny nodded and sighed deeply, preparing to go another day with Ruby's withdrawal.

17
A friend

It was very early when Tabitha entered Alessi's office and gasped out in shock, dropping the files she was holding all over the floor. She quickly stooped to collect them up again, evidently rattled to see Mr Alessi.

"I'm so sorry I had no idea you were here already. If I'd known I'd have knocked, I didn't mean to...I was just going to get some filing done...for Faye...she's been struggling,," she explained. Alessi lifted his head from his hands and then rubbed them over the slight stubble on his chin.

"I got in early. It's the last day of a big trial for us today and I needed to get some work done before court. Please, Tabitha..."

"You can call me Tabby if you like...I mean you don't have to...I'm just saying..."

"Tabby," he interrupted her and she shut up instantly. He laughed. "It's fine - breathe," he ordered, worried she'd collapse if she didn't. For the first time in years he was utterly captivated. For the first time in his life he was captivated by a woman who worked in his building, one that he'd employed and *that* made things slightly more complicated. Women caught his eye all the time, he wasn't blind, but they didn't manage to do it to quite the same extent as Tabitha, and she wasn't even trying. He'd realised when he sat at his desk and hung his head in his hands first thing that morning, he was actually looking forward to seeing her and was glad that he'd taken her on. He leaned back and studied her with interest.

"Erm..." she dithered. "Can I do anything for you?"

"You already do," he answered in amusement and then mentally kicked himself. That was not meant to be out loud! She looked confused. "Ignore that. I'm fine, thank you."

"How about a coffee then? Have you eaten?" she asked, but he didn't answer her. He just sat, taking in how sweet she was. "I don't mind getting you something. You should eat you know. Both you and Danny looked tired yesterday and there's some rumour that Ruby's sick. If there's anything I can do, anything at all."

"Yes," he nodded. "Ruby's quite sick. She has been for a while."

"Is she your daughter?" she asked but he shook his head.

"No not really but she is like a daughter...to me. She's very special and she has Danny well and truly hooked. He's taking a few days off to be with her."

"Ahhh that's good. It sounds like she's being well looked after."

"Yes. Yes she is," he confirmed distantly. "He's got nerves of steel that boy."

She smiled and went to place the files by the cabinet. "I'll go grab you a coffee then. Food?" she asked and he shook his head, smiling as she disappeared out of the door.

By the time she brought the coffee back he'd forced himself to start working, to get his mind on the job and off her. There was a spread of papers all over his desk, a mission to get something done before 10am. She struggled to find a place to put his drink down and he shoved the mess about until a gap appeared. She placed the cup down and went to remove her hand but her finger caught in the handle, pulling it over. Hot coffee spilled across the table and, just like that, she crumbled. Gasping out in horror she desperately tried to collect up as much of his paperwork as she could, before suddenly realising that he wasn't shouting at her. He was calm and when she looked up he was studying her intently. He made her nervous and both of them knew it.

"Tabby, please, don't worry. It's just coffee." He swivelled his chair smoothly and grabbed a roll of blue paper towel from the shelf behind him, ripping some off for her and some for him. They proceeded to mop up the mess together.

"I'm so sorry. It's everywhere!" She was close to tears now.

"It's fine - look, as long as it's not on...where is it?"

"Where's what?"

"A court order. I had it here somewhere - that's the only thing that really matters. As long as it's not on that we're...oh..." he declared, pulling out the document he was looking for and letting the coffee drip from the bottom.

He looked up and her eyes were so sad he couldn't be mad at her even if he'd wanted to be. "Hmmm, well, you can still read it...I guess," he joked hanging it over the radiator to dry. "It will be fine, don't worry."

She crossed her arms and then gave up trying to contain herself and ran her hands through her hair. "Was it something I said?" he asked her and she frowned, emotional, anxious and now well and truly confused too. "Well, it's not the first time a woman's thrown coffee. In fact, Danny had coffee thrown at him only the other day but I know what he'd done to deserve it. I was just wondering what I'd done to deserve it?"

She managed a giggle and then took a deep breath. "Can I get you another?" she asked hopefully and he laughed out loud.

"Call me old fashioned, Tabby, but can I have the next one in a cup please?" She cringed and left the room, feeling mortified. Making another drink was a good excuse to get away.

Alessi got home at 7pm just as Ruby was receiving her 1ml dose. Danny and Bardo emerged, slightly ruffled, after fighting with her to get the job done. Danny looked tired and Ruby looked terrible. The three men gathered at the viewing window to watch her quieten down while Alessi updated them on the success of the trial. Rossi was in the clear, the outcome they'd all been working so hard to achieve. Alessi filled them in on all that they had missed. It had been a very good day for the firm.

A huge weight finally lifted from their shoulders, Alessi happily relieved Bardo of his duties and told him to go get some rest. He then ordered pizza and they kept some aside for when he returned. Ruby had point blank refused to eat and then cried herself to sleep. She had made life hell all afternoon, screaming that she hated them all, that they were killing her and then she rolled around on the floor completely bored out of her mind. Danny tried to keep her company but she was horrible and violent towards him, so he left her to it and dozed with his head on the desk while she shouted out that he was a pervert. She insisted that he was only keeping her locked up so he could film her and she banned all of them from ever touching her again, threatening to break the arm off the next person who tried to inject her. Consequently, it had taken both Bardo and Danny to administer the 7pm dose. She fought them savagely and accused them of trying to take her clothes off. They got it over and done with as quickly as possible and Danny covered her up before getting out.

It had been a long day and it was nice to finally have someone else to talk to. Danny took advantage of the opportunity for some gossip as he nudged Alessi. "So, how's Tabitha doing?" Alessi put his feet up on the ledge, choosing to ignore him. "Oh come on I'm bored, Alessi! This place is doing my head in."

"No, Danny, I won't 'come on.' She's a member of staff. I've employed her..."

"So what?"

"*So*, it's not appropriate to gossip about members of staff with *other* members of staff..."

"But I'm not just a member of staff," he reminded him. "I'm your son."

"What exactly do you want me to say, Danny?"

"I don't know. What she's like."

"She's young."

"And so are you!" he interjected but Alessi rolled his eyes at him. He certainly didn't feel young. "Come on, Alessi, you're hardly old! Most of the women at work think you're seriously fit. You forget that they tell me stuff. When I go visiting for a chat they tell me *all* about it! You have a little fan base, Mr Alessi. Actually it's quite a big fan base," he frowned suddenly, like he was slightly jealous. Alessi laughed and then sighed.

"Danny, I don't need a woman in my life, it's complicated enough."

"Liar! You just don't like getting attached to things because you figure if you don't get attached then you suffer no losses. That's a bit cowardly, don't you think?"

"Cowardly?" he cringed, passing Danny a beer and opening one for himself.

"Yeah, I mean, mum moved on."

"Danny, your mum moved on while we were still together," he protested and Danny scowled.

"Don't say stuff about my mum, Alessi, it's disrespectful. The point is she moved on and you never did. You stayed alone because you were too scared of being hurt again. That's a waste and it *is* cowardly. If Ruby knew she would have you shredding perfectly good copier paper just to prove what a waste it really is." Danny downed half his can and placed it on the floor while Alessi pondered his words quietly.

"How is your mother?" he asked him. Danny nearly choked.

"You want to know how my mum is?"

"No, not really. If I know Lilliana she will be doing great, looking great, you name it she'll be doing it...better than everyone else." Danny smiled and nudged him.

"I bet Tabitha's pretty great too. She looks great and she seems really lovely. Faye even managed to stop hitting on me yesterday for long enough to give our little Kitty Kat a glowing reference."

"Her name is Tabitha not bloody Kitty Kat!" he erupted. He rolled his eyes. "And, yes, she is very nice," he conceded more calmly. "She's kind and gentle...and I like her..."

"BINGO!" Danny shouted out, making Alessi spill his beer.

At midnight Bardo came back in, bringing his pizza and a drink with him. He pulled up a chair next to Alessi just as Ruby began to stir and whimper like she was in pain. She called out for Danny and he went in to keep her company. She told him that she wanted a cuddle and he pulled her in close and held her tightly. She settled and they both drifted off, but not for long. A couple of hours later Ruby was screaming and trying to escape him.

"What, Ruby? What is it?" he asked her in a daze. She was fighting and sobbing.

"I want Danny!" she shouted desperately. "I don't want you, I want Danny!"

"I am Danny. Ruby, it's me. Baby, I'm here."

"You're not Danny. I know who you are! He sent you didn't he? The man in black, he sent you. First he sent Sammy and now he's sent you. You deserve to be dead so go back to where you came from!"

"Ruby, I don't understand." He rolled her and tried to look into her eyes but she protected her face and head with her arms and hands, begging him to leave her alone. She looked like she thought he would hit her.

"Why don't you ever stop drinking? I can smell it. All the time I can smell it. You get close to me and I don't like it, it's all over you. You're breathing it all over me!" she cried furiously. He tried to peel her hands away from her face.

"Ruby, come on look. It's me."

"Don't hit me! Don't beat me, please, don't beat me - it hurts. Just go to bed, go to sleep and get out of my room!" she shrieked at him as she slid herself back from under him and tried to kick him away with her feet. "Alessi shot you, you're not supposed to be here anymore. You're dead and that's where you should be." Danny followed her on his hands and knees as she continued to push herself backwards.

"Ruby, you think I'm your father?" He was stunned by just how extreme and cruel the hallucinations could get. "Ruby, he's gone, baby, it's just me. It's Danny."

"I smell alcohol; it's everywhere. You've been drinking!" she accused bitterly.

"Yeah, I'm sorry, I did have a couple but I'm definitely not drunk. I promise."

"No you're not Danny! Please someone send in Danny!" she begged, wrapping herself up in the covers and crying. "Please don't come near me, don't hurt me. I've been good. I haven't done anything wrong, don't hit me again, please, don't hit me!" He had to accept that his being there was just making her worse. He had been drinking and she could smell the alcohol, there was nothing that could be done about it. As much as she wanted him there, and he wanted to stay with her, it was making her frightened so he left the room. She continued to beg them to send Danny in but every time he tried to join her she screamed the place down. She could instantly detect the alcohol on his breath, even after he'd had mints and gum. He felt awful because that night, although he was there for her, she truly believed she was alone.

At 7am he and Bardo checked her heart rate and blood pressure and gave her a shot of 0.5mls. Alessi came in to wish them all luck before he went off to work.

"Danny, I know you said that you didn't want to come back in until Ruby was up and about but I have a double booked appointment at 9.30 this morning. Amanda's fault, not mine," he defended, holding up his hands. "Would you mind? You could come in and see Mrs Karbul while I see Mr Shayla, and then you can go off again. You could be back here before lunch and Ruby's sleeping now. What do you say? For your old man?" Danny rolled his eyes and shook his head at him.

"You're hardly an old man, Alessi! In fact I really think there should be a law against a father being as popular as his son," he grumbled. Alessi shrugged it off.

"What can I say, we have good genes!" he laughed. "So is that a yes?" he asked hopefully.

"Oh, go on then...but just one appointment and then I'm leaving. If Ruby stays asleep I'm going to get some too. I've hardly slept in days and Mrs Karbul is going to think I'm a drunken idiot, especially when I'm too brain dead to answer any of her questions."

"Just nod and look meaningful, Danny, you're really good at that," Bardo laughed.

18
Temptation

Danny turned up at 9.25 just in time to walk straight in, grab Mrs Karbul from reception and take her to the meeting room. He wasn't staying long, he'd promised himself. He wasn't going to get drawn into anything, by anyone. He was just going to be in and out by 10.30, Ruby would be peaceful and he would go to bed and wake up feeling great. That was his plan. What he didn't yet know was that Alessi's client *hadn't* turned up so he didn't even need to be there. Mr Shayla had been taken into custody the night before for breaching a harassment order so there would be no 9.30am meeting in the office for him. Alessi had arranged to see him at the police station later and was now trying to work out what was going on with the case. He was on the phone, leaning back in his chair, slicing pieces of folded paper with his letter opener like he was bored.

"Yes, well, that's your job and I'm not doing it for you. Unless you're planning on sharing your pay cheque with me at the end of this month I suggest you speak to your client and sort it out yourself." He put the phone down hard and Tabitha tried to pretend that she wasn't listening. He was silent now, no more slicing. She wondered if he was working on a file; she couldn't hear any papers shuffling and she prayed that he wasn't looking at her. "Tabitha," he called out and she looked up, her arms full of the files that she'd just grabbed up off the floor.

"Yes," she answered nervously. He was studying her and something told her that he had been since he put the phone down.

"Come here for a minute please?" he beckoned. She dithered, looking from the files to him.

"What do you want me to do with these?"

"Do what you like with them, Tabitha, chuck them on the floor for all I care," he told her, turning his mouth down at the sides like he really didn't care.

"Oh...OK," she smirked, placing the files back down carefully. They slid, as files do, and she began to try and neaten them.

125

"Oh, Tabitha, just leave the files will you and come here," he bossed. She let them slide and made her way over to his desk

"Did you want me to sit?" she asked, starting to fret that she'd done something wrong. She'd be devastated if he sacked her.

"No I didn't. I wanted you to come here," he told her. She frowned and made her way round to his side of the desk, positioning herself so she could stand with her back to his paperwork. The solid surface just about helped to support her shaking legs. He smiled.

"Relax," he told her, and she tried to breathe.

"I'm not sure I understand..." she began, feeling a strange mix of emotions about his behaviour.

"Oh I think you do, Tabitha," he challenged, giving her a very handsome smile. He didn't smile often she noticed, but when he did it felt special.

"Tell me something about yourself?" he asked and she clammed right up. For someone who prided himself on reading body language the change in her posture was strikingly obvious.

"I'm not sure there's much to tell..." she began but he wasn't buying it.

"Hmmm...I bet that's not true. Have you ever been married, Tabitha?" he asked her and she clenched her jaw.

"A very long time ago," she confirmed stiffly.

"And things went bad?" he guessed, raising his eyebrows, keen to know more. She laughed sardonically.

"No, I wouldn't say that. That makes it sound like things started off good when actually they started off bad...and just got worse," she shrugged.

"Why, what happened?" He was picking at her defences and she didn't like it. Nobody had ever asked her about her past; nobody had ever cared and she'd certainly never had the urge to confide. She felt put on the spot and anxious, and it manifested itself as annoyance.

"So we're asking questions now are we?" she demanded curtly. He smiled but didn't reply. "In that case, Mr Alessi, were you ever married?" she fired back at him and he nodded and laughed. She was actually quite feisty when pushed, a seriously suppressed emotion.

126

"So it looks like we're both asking questions then," he grinned, taking it on the chin. "OK, Tabitha, let's see...in answer to your question, yes, I was married, once."

"And things went bad?" She used his question against him. He smiled.

"Yes they went a bit bad," he confessed uncomfortably, closing one of his eyes like the 'bit' that went bad had just poked him in it.

"A bit?" she asked "So which bit? What happened?" She was eager now and clearly trying to keep the attention away from herself. Very clever.

"The bit where we had a huge argument, I went out and got very drunk and then accidentally spent the night with someone else. That bit," he told her truthfully. She was surprised and immediately went from defensive to utterly shocked.

"Oh my god, Mr Alessi, you...you cheated?" she declared. He shook his head, finding her quite amusing.

"No I said 'spent the night' I never said I slept with anyone," he told her smoothly.

"So your wife divorced you because you 'spent the night' with someone?" she clarified. He smiled that handsome and rare smile again.

"No I divorced her because *she* slept with someone. She always liked to go one better than me. A very strong minded woman, my ex-wife. We were both a bit too similar I think; neither of us wanted to be the one to back down or seem weak...or say sorry," he sighed, like maybe one of them should have. "Anyway, we had an exciting yet unpredictable marriage where one of us constantly risked either being loved or murdered, depending on the general mood of the day."

"Oh my...I'm so sorry I didn't know she cheated on you. I guess I just assumed...I'm sorry." She seemed awkward and moved to leave.

"Erm where do you think you're going?" he asked her playfully and she couldn't help but smile, desperately trying not to be flattered by his level of attention. She'd seen him in action around the building and usually he passed people without speaking at all. Sometimes he shared a word or two, but only very occasionally did he stop and chat. When he did it was never anything about himself. She bit furiously on her bottom lip and moved back

127

into position to wait and see what he would say next. "That's better," he told her, acting at being stern. "Right, I lose track, but I definitely think you got more answers than me and that's not really fair is it?" he asked her and she turned away to hide the smile that had crept onto her face. She took a deep breath, composed herself and looked back again.

"What?" she asked him firmly, trying to contain the cute grin that was threatening to give her away. He didn't answer, making her wait it out agonisingly. He was staring at her, searching again with those amazing eyes of his. She wasn't surprised that she was the first to give in. "What answers do you want, Mr Alessi?"

"Truthful ones," he confirmed coolly, leaning back in his chair. "What did you mean by 'it started bad and just got worse'?"

"Ohhhh, Mr Ale..." she began to moan, but he interrupted her.

"Drop the Mr it's too formal," he ordered. She paused, looking over his features, his strong jaw, slight stubble, green eyes and very dark hair. He was older than her but that just made him even better. He was very good looking and, most annoyingly, *very* hard to resist. She imagined that she would probably do anything he told her, but then that was her problem. History had shown her she was way too easy to manipulate, submissive...and never going there again.

"Alessi," she began, and he nodded like that made him happier. "I was very young and he was much older than me. I was nearly seventeen when I married and completely naive. I hadn't had a nice upbringing and I was desperate to get out. He took me in at the age of fifteen but then he manipulated me. He was horrible."

"Actually I think I'd prefer it if you called me Federico," he told her softly and she took a breath and whispered his name.

"Federico."

He smiled, liking how it sounded on her lips. "Perhaps we should keep that between you and me," he squinted wickedly and she couldn't help but feel flattered by the informality. "So, Tabby, what kind of horrible are we talking here?"

"I'm sorry," she was lost...somewhere quite beautiful and a little bit scary.

"Your charming husband," he reminded her. "You said he was horrible to you. In what way?"

"Oh...yes..." She took a steadying pause and looked down at her hands awkwardly. "He hurt me, Alessi..."

"Federico," he corrected.

"I was scared of him, Federico. He controlled me and he punished me. I was sixteen when he proposed and he even did it to me on our honeymoon." She stopped and he watched her, waiting for her to continue. She sighed and fidgeted.

"Tell me?" he spoke softly, his eyes grazing over her face slowly as he ran his thumb over his mouth.

"One day he beat me...and then..."

"And then?" he nodded. She clenched her jaw and pursed her lips.

"And then he attacked me," she confessed shakily. Alessi frowned.

"Attacked you? How is one different from the other?"

"He had found and confiscated my contraceptive pill a few days before. I never wanted children with him, Alessi. I made a promise to myself on our honeymoon that I would *never* have children with a monster like him. I didn't want children. I just wanted my life to be easier...not harder. I was only a child myself...but..."

"But?" he encouraged concerned that she might be about to clam up on him. Now he knew this much he definitely wanted to know more.

"But...I was pregnant. The baby came early because of the stress and the abuse. It was tiny and helpless but I didn't feel any connection with it. There was no immediate love or bond like people talk of. I never experienced 'the rush'. I just felt sick. I was depressed and I couldn't think straight. All the other mums on the ward knew what to do. They fussed over their babies and their families and partners fussed over their babies, but I couldn't even bring myself to look at mine. She was beautiful, Alessi, don't get me wrong, but I felt like a stranger holding someone else's child. My husband made me feel like I couldn't do anything right. He took over all the time, telling me he could do much better. He was very confident with her and he always seemed to know what to do."

"That must have made you feel quite incompetent as a mother?" he guessed and she nodded, seeming ashamed. He could almost feel her pain.

"He said that she didn't love me and that I would end up hurting her. Then, just weeks after she was born, a man whistled at me from a car and he took me home and did it again. He hadn't touched me throughout the pregnancy, well, not like that anyway. I was petrified that I would fall pregnant again so when he went to bed I walked. I left there with nothing, no phone, no money, no ID, no keys, no change of clothes, nothing...not even my baby. I couldn't, she was in the same room as him. I was seventeen and homeless," she confessed bitterly. Alessi ran his right hand over the bottom half of his face and cupped his left hand around her hip to slide her along the desk so she was now in front of him. He didn't want her escaping.

"Where did you go? What did you do for money?" he asked her. She looked out of the window at the rooftops across the road.

"What do you think I did?" she responded with a sigh. "I needed places to stay the night and I had nobody else to go to. I stayed with strangers. One man wanted to know how old I was. He was recently married, a police officer would you believe..."

"Yes I would," Alessi told her simply, not seeming shocked in the slightest.

"He sorted me out a flat and gave me money for the rent. I could have carried on like that, living in the flat he'd arranged, paying for the rent with the money he gave me, in return for...erm..."

"Spending time with him?" he asked and she managed a smile of appreciation and a nod.

"But I didn't want to carry on like that. I hated it...and him. He was scary and he always carried a gun. He refused to remove it...ever! I dared to go looking for other types of jobs and offered to work a few days for free at a small local supermarket, just stacking shelves out the back. I wanted to prove that I could make myself useful and they gave me a job. I worked there every day and at night he visited me. He wouldn't let me see anyone else - I was his. I never told him about the day job and I kept my savings secret too. As soon as I had enough I did a bunk and moved out of the area. I never stayed with strangers again and I never dared to go back home either. I left all of it behind, including my baby. That's so awful isn't it? Not only did I leave her but I left her with him. I didn't know what else to do and he would never have let me take her with me. I just prayed that he would be different with her...he seemed different with her." She battled with the tears admirably, refusing to give in and cry.

"What was her name?" he asked running his hand from her waist down the outside of her leg to her knee. Her legs were trembling.

"I don't know...she never had one. You get a few weeks to register the birth and we hadn't decided on a name. He would have taken her. I'm not even sure if my name would be on the birth certificate."

"Perhaps she's never seen it," he suggested. "So where did you move from originally, where was your home?"

"Here," she responded. Alessi looked confused. "We lived here, this is where I ran from," she explained.

"So you've come back?" he asked, astonished. "Don't you worry you might bump into your husband?"

"He died. The police informed me as his next of kin. I'm on the marriage certificate. I never filed for a divorce because that would have meant making contact with him. I've lived my life constantly looking over my shoulder, until I knew I could come home again. I don't know what happened to our little girl. I went to the house but it was boarded up. I don't know where she is and I don't know how to find her either. I don't even know if I want to. She has every right to hate me for what I did. I mean, what if he tortured her like he did me? What if not only did he beat her, but he attacked her too? God, the guilt is immense. I feel like it's crushing me sometimes."

"Yes I bet you do," he agreed distantly, his mind elsewhere. "I'm sure she's fine now. You landed on your feet and she probably takes after you, strong and determined to break free."

"Yes, but at what cost?"

"You were a child, Tabitha, don't forget that," he berated her. "Try not to be so hard on yourself. I can see that you're a good person. I like you," he told her. She smiled back nervously. "Has there been anyone since him?"

"Not really. A couple of guys tried to persevere with me, they wouldn't get the message, but I was never brave enough to get involved. Eventually they gave up on me."

"Isn't that lonely?"

"You tell me?" she retorted. "Are you lonely?"

"Not lonely, I have a lot going on, but it's not quite the same thing as sharing your life with someone is it?"

"I wouldn't know - maybe love's not all it's cracked up to be. Maybe love was something made up by men to lure women in, just a clever and manipulative trap. Maybe love doesn't really exist. Maybe it's just a word and not an actual *thing*. I've honestly never felt it so I couldn't really say."

"Maybe you just need to learn to trust someone and then maybe you will find out," he suggested.

"Maybe I'm not that desperate to know, not if love means going down that painful road again."

"Maybe..." he stood and placed both his hands either side of her. "Maybe..." he tilted his head down towards her face and she tilted hers to make it more difficult for him. He persisted while she continued to shy away. "Maybe you should let me try and convince you that it does exist and it's not always painful, Tabitha" he whispered finding her mouth with his and kissing her gently and slowly. It was the first kiss that had ever felt kind and delicate. The first kiss that had ever made her feel beautiful rather than ravaged and she gave in, enjoying the moment like she never thought in a million years that she would.

He broke free briefly and gently to look into her eyes. "How did he die?" he asked and she frowned. He had scrambled her mind, left her legs feeling like jelly and now he was asking her questions! "Your husband, Tabitha, you said he died," he reminded her.

"He was shot."

"Oh," he grimaced. "That must be pretty rare. Was he on drugs?"

"I don't know, the police didn't tell me, but..." she began to explain as he ran a delicate finger down her perfectly shaped nose and tilted her chin so he could kiss her again. It was a mind blowing cocktail of desire and Alessi had to accept that, for once, Ruby was right, wanting and needing were indeed *exactly* the same thing. "He was found at home, our matrimonial home," she panted when he eventually allowed her time for air. He nodded, the man was clearly mixed up with the wrong people. Alessi had no care for a man that beat and forced his wife. All he cared about was how many more times he could kiss Tabitha before he had to get on with his work. "An intruder shot him," she went on. "Upstairs, while he was drunk and unconscious. Apparently he wouldn't have known a thing." Alessi pulled back and looked at her like she had said something totally inappropriate.

"What, Federico?" she sounded concerned. "What is it?"

"I just need a moment...to process things," he explained, his mind in turmoil. She sat back and waited patiently, wondering what she could possibly have said or done that was so wrong. He shook his head. "This isn't good," he murmured and now she was upset, pushing herself away from his desk to leave. "No, wait," he blocked her. Kissing Tabitha had felt so right and he didn't want to lose that. "I just mean...you have this ability to make me want to...kiss you..." he stumbled over his words, desperately trying to think on his feet.

"And that's not good?" she whispered, sounding hurt.

"No, it's not good...because you work here, I'm your boss and you have every right *not* to make out with me on my desk," he smiled "But you're just so tempting, Tabitha Andollina, and I just can't seem to help myself." He stepped close and slipped his hands onto her lower back, letting them follow up her spine towards her neck. He lost his fingers in her hair and she finally let go of his desk to push hers into his, creating partings and dark shiny waves as he kissed her again. His back and neck were strong and she gripped his shoulders underneath his suit. The door suddenly knocked once and swung open. They both let each other go instantly to see Danny standing in the doorway, slightly mortified, mouth open, eyes roaming over the scene before him.

"Well, well, well, Mr Alessi! I do hope you've given Tabitha a good talking to about self respect before trying to have her on your desk. Sorry to interrupt, I'm just going to go and...erm...huh," he laughed uncomfortably. "Think of a suitably random punishment to enforce a point that I don't intend to follow myself." He backed out of the door, putting his pen between his teeth so he could reach out and close it firmly. Tabitha hung her head and rested it against Alessi's chest, unable to look at him.

"I'm really sorry, Tabitha, I didn't think about the door. I got totally caught up with you. Please don't worry, I'll speak to Danny and make sure he..."

"Why does he call you Mr Alessi?" she asked, braving a glance at his face.

"Because that's my name," he smirked, straightening his collar and tie.

"No, I mean, why does he call you Mr Alessi if you're his dad?" she asked, bringing her eyes up to meet his.

"What makes you say that? I've not told you he's my son," he frowned, wondering whether he'd been caught off guard, whether she was working for someone else. She could quite easily be some kind of sweet mafia honey trap, employed by another organised crime group to find out about him and his most private of clients.

"Am I really the only one who's noticed?" she asked, unconvinced, and also slowly starting to feel angry at herself for giving in to his advances. Regret was a feeling she didn't handle well. Men were dangerous, no matter how good looking. She had slipped, made a big mistake and now she felt stupid too. "He's your son and he's absolutely right," she breathed, sounding cross with herself. "What kind of self respecting woman behaves likes this with the man who pays her wages?"

"Tabitha, this isn't just some..."

"No, Mr Alessi," she stopped him short and reverted back to his formal title. It stung like a slap to the face. She was panicking and backing right off, dropping him in the process. "This isn't what I want," she told him determinedly as she wriggled out from between him and his desk. "I'll go and collect the files from downstairs and carry on with my job, if that's okay with you?" He nodded but stayed silent, the last thing he wanted to do was pressure her. "I'm sorry, Mr Alessi, please forgive me. It won't happen again."

And just like that she was gone.

19
A breach of confidence

She walked passed Danny's desk feeling like an attraction at a parade. If she'd felt awkward around him before, this was positively agonising. She done something drastically wrong, jeopardised a good job and a nice, easy, platonic relationship with her boss. Now she was on the defensive.

"Has he sent you to shred a few boxes of paper to pay penance?" Danny asked her. "A punishment he once gave Ruby for underage drinking." She narrowed her eyes and something about the look stirred something inside him, fear, exhilaration, familiarity...recognition!

"Don't push it, Danny Glover!" she warned him. "Nobody tells me what to do, not any more. If Alessi wants paper shredding he can shred it his god damn self!" She left the room and disappeared down the stairs. He leaned back trying to calm himself, but his head was racing. Pushing his chair out, he stood and stormed into Alessi's room.

"Knock, Danny, for god sake!

"Who is she?" he asked, ignoring Alessi's little rant. "Alessi what have you gone and done?" he growled.

"I haven't *done* anything...and I don't know what you're talking about," he argued, trying to dismiss him, but Danny was furious and he had no intention of going anywhere.

"*She* just looked at me..." he told him, pointing towards Alessi's office door.

"Well she won't be the only woman who's done that, I'm sure." He was trying to concentrate on the file in front of him until Danny walked up and ripped it out from under his hands, slinging it across the room.

"You know who she is don't you?" he shouted at him. "Do you know what this is going to do to Ruby?"

"It's not going to do anything to Ruby - Danny, try and calm down."

"She's her bloody mother!" he exclaimed. "Ruby said she wanted nothing to do with her. She made her feelings clear about that! What the hell have you done?"

"We don't know that for sure and I certainly didn't know that when I took her on," he lowered his voice, trying to get Danny to quieten down too. "How was I supposed to know that she might be her sodding mother? She was just a young woman going by the name of Tabitha Andollina when she came in here for an interview. Andollina I'm assuming *may* be Ruby's mother's maiden name. I only just had the same realisation myself, so I'm only about fifteen minutes wiser than you."

"Right, so the big fat penny dropped, you worked out that she is the woman responsible for bringing Ruby into this world..."

"We don't actually know that for sure. It's just a possibility and..."

"Yes, Alessi, she is! I'd put money on it. She left Ruby to handle that bully of a father all by herself and you thought now was as good a time as any to get her in your office for a bit of fun? Do you not care about Ruby's feelings at all?"

"Of course I do, Danny, but it's not that simple."

"Don't you care what kind of woman she is? Damn it she walked out on her child, Alessi!" he ranted. Alessi suddenly closed his eyes and hung his head as if defeated and Danny turned to see that Tabitha had come back in. She shot him a glare as she walked across the room to place the files by Alessi's cabinet. Alessi was the first to break the agonising silence.

"Tabitha, please let me explain," he tried but she blanked him and dumped the files loudly onto the floor. "Danny, look, it's not what you think. It wasn't like that and anyway it's none of your business."

"Oh, sorry, but yes it is my business. My sex life has been your business right from the age I was legal so, as far as I'm concerned, if you've got the right to interfere with mine I have the right to interfere with yours! You take this moral high ground where everything I do or want to do is hedonistic and selfish, disrespectful and deceitful but, when nobody's looking, there you are being all of those things with some bitch of a woman who abandoned her baby!" Tabitha looked devastated, believing that Alessi had told her story to Danny as soon as her back was turned, his way of getting even with her for turning him down. Typical! Her eyes quickly filled with tears; her trust had been betrayed and she made for the door but

Danny swung it shut so she couldn't leave and stood in front of it, trapping her.

"Danny, I *will* talk to you about it," Alessi told him calmly, "but not like this, not with the shouting and hollering and not with Tabitha being cornered and bullied." He turned to Tabitha who now looked frightened enough to make for the window. He held up the flats of his hands. "Tabby, I never told Danny what you told me, I swear."

"You liar!" she cried out. "How else would he know? Nobody knows. I never told anybody but you!"

"Not proud of yourself eh?" Danny remarked raising his eyebrows.

"What do you know, Danny! It must be nice to be a man, to bully and judge and never have to worry about what someone has planned for you. You lot get to live your life free!"

"Oh I'd say you've been pretty free for the last eighteen years! How much freedom do you want, Tabitha?"

"Danny, pack it in! I won't have you talking to her like that!" Alessi jumped in to defend her. Danny turned to look at the woman in front of him, who was looking more like Ruby by the second. Until now she had worn her hair up but Alessi had let it free when he kissed her, keen to see it down. It was long, black, and shiny and it even had the same little signature curl that Ruby sometimes tried to straighten out of it. Her eyes were bright blue and her frame was small. Her face was very pretty and she looked young, too young to be Ruby's mother, but the fire he had seen in her eyes was all the evidence he needed to convince himself that she was. *She* was the woman who had given birth to his precious Ruby and then dumped her like a bag of rubbish. It was all her fault.

"You asked me what I know," he prompted and Alessi tried to stop him.

"No, Danny, please just let me handle it."

"Let *you* handle it," he laughed. "And you're doing so well at handling it at the moment, Alessi," he told him sarcastically. "So what's the plan - you sleep with her and then break the news? Tabitha, you asked what I know..."

"What, Danny? What do you know?" she practically screamed at him.

"I know that all Ruby has wanted since she was old enough to want was for her mum to come home and save her from her bully of a dad. I know that now someone's done us all a favour and shot him dead she doesn't need *you* anymore. So, Tabitha, you may as well keep your arse off my father's desk and take it someplace else because you're not needed and you're sure as hell not wanted around here!" She looked at him like he'd hit her; her mouth opened and then closed but no words came. She was stunned. She looked to Alessi and he seemed unsure what to do. She looked back at Danny as the tears rolled down her face. He looked away. As much as he hated her, she looked too much like Ruby to enjoy watching her cry.

"Ruby?" she whispered finally. "Her father was shot? Oh my god, my husband was shot...I mean what are the chances of that? Alessi, are you saying that Ruby...your Ruby...she might be..."

"Your Ruby," he concluded softly. Her heart rocketed and she put her hand to her chest, struggling to keep it together. "I can't breathe...I need air... I don't feel well..." She dropped to her knees and Alessi moved to comfort her. "So she's OK, Alessi? She's being looked after by you?" She began to plead for information between gasps and sobs. The shock was like a punch to the stomach and she'd had plenty of those.

"Tabitha, I didn't know when I took you on here, I swear. I only just realised and we don't know for sure yet but, yes, after you declaring that your husband was shot too, it definitely sounds like she might be your daughter. I know it's an unexpected blow and Danny should not have told you the way he did." He looked up and glared at him like he was not his son.

"Are you serious? Are you really trying to make her feel better?" he exclaimed, hating his father with a passion. "Are you really telling me that you would choose to be with the woman who destroyed Ruby's childhood, and nearly her whole life, just because she's pretty and cute and willing to do more than just your filing?"

"Danny!" he stopped him fiercely. "For your information she was a child herself," he snapped back through gritted teeth, wishing he would just shut up and stop being so cruel. "She was only seventeen when she had Ruby, younger than Ruby is now, and he beat her regularly."

"Yeah well he beat Ruby too but she never got to run away did she? She just counted herself lucky if she got her hands over her face in time and he kept his off her. What kind of excuse is that supposed to be anyway, accusing him of making her life unbearable but then happily leaving Ruby with him?" He turned to look at her with not an ounce of pity, "So he beat you, Tabitha, and you thought having a baby would...what...bring you closer together?" he asked dryly.

"He hurt her?" she cried, turning to Alessi who was now desperate to ease her pain.

"He raised his hands to her but he didn't do anything else," he explained, trying to swipe some of the wetness from her cheeks. "Damn it, he forced himself on her, Danny, can you just pack it in now. She was Ruby's age and he beat and forced her. He made her pregnant against her will and then only weeks after she'd given birth, while she was suffering from post natal depression and seriously vulnerable, he forced her again. She snapped and that's why she walked. She was petrified of him and he made her feel like they didn't need her so, yes, I do want to make her feel better because none of this was her fault. She was a victim too."

Danny took his hand off the door, covered his mouth with his other one and closed his eyes tightly, trying to comprehend what he'd just learnt.

"Is it true? Tabitha, is it true? Did he do that to you? Is that how Ruby came about?" He was thinking out loud now, his brain trying to process this new and quite sickening information. "Oh my god, that's going to kill her! We can't tell her who you are, we can't!" Alessi stood and put his hand on Danny's chest in an attempt to protect the woman on the floor from anymore trauma.

"This isn't just about Ruby, Danny," he told him firmly.

"She was the product of rape!" he snapped back furiously. "Who else could it possibly be about? She's going to feel even less worthy than she does already, even more of an outcast. Think about it, Alessi!"

"Yes, and I get that, but Tabitha was the one that it happened to," he pointed out. "I know you're mad but it could quite easily have been Ruby and Matthew. *You* think about it, Danny. He manipulated and bullied her, she had nowhere else to go and she was trapped. Either way Tabitha would have suffered...she still is!" It slammed Danny in the face. It could have been Ruby. When she had come to their firm on the last day of school it was after being hounded by Matthew, a boy on her estate, with a list of sexual conquests and a stubborn desire to have Ruby's name on there too. He used her, made her feel like she was stupid and capable of nothing more than the sorry life she had been born into. Imagining Ruby in a relationship like that at such a young age, and having a baby she never wanted, broke his heart. He dropped to his knees at Tabitha's side and reached through her hair to touch her chin and raise her face. She was distraught, traumatised, and all Danny could see in her now was a more battered and bruised version of Ruby.

He leaned forward and cupped her face gently. "I'm so sorry, Tabitha," he whispered. "I've been a complete...god there's not even a word that exists for what I've just been."

"Yes there is," she corrected painfully, pushing his hand away as another wave of tears hit. He ignored her attempt at rejection and pulled her forwards and into his arms.

"I was in shock. I should never have spoken to you the way I did - you didn't deserve that. It's just that I love Ruby so much and I can't bear to think of her being hurt...but I shouldn't have overlooked how hurt you must be too. This is just such a mess. What do we do now? What do you want to do, Tabitha? Do you want Ruby to know?" he asked, releasing her slightly so she could look up at him. At least now he was involving her like she was a human being, with feelings.

"No, please, don't tell her. She will hate me. She has every right to hate me but I don't want to see it in her eyes. I don't want to be slapped by my own daughter, Danny. I know it's an impossible thing to ask of you but, please, not yet. I'm not ready." Both of them were looking at him, eager for his understanding and co-operation.

"Oh jeez, man, this is a nightmare. She's going to kill someone when she finds out we've been keeping this from her. I don't want to see you having to run and hide, Tabitha, but you being here right under Ruby's nose, well, it feels like deception of the worst kind. I know it's not your fault," he sighed, biting on his nails. He looked up at Alessi and shook his head slowly. "When Ruby finds out about you and Tabitha she's going to kick your arse. I wouldn't want to be you, Alessi. She's going to feel like you've stabbed her in the back...like we all have."

He stood and left the room, grabbing his car keys from his top drawer and taking himself somewhere far away. He didn't want to face anyone, not Alessi, not Tabitha and definitely not Ruby.

20
A desperate bid

Danny arrived home after 6.30pm and immediately went to the viewing room. He struggled to look Alessi in the eye as he greeted Bardo, apologising for leaving him with Ruby all day. Bardo was fine with it and said she'd slept mostly. She had got upset and tearful at times but nothing that wasn't to be expected. Danny guessed it hadn't been quite that easy, but Bardo was sparing his feelings. She was now sitting in the middle of the room staring at the clock, waiting for her next dose. What she didn't realise, and what none of them wanted to tell her, was that there wouldn't be a 'next dose'. Tonight she would be going cold turkey. Danny still hadn't slept and he was now dead on his feet, but offered to be the one to break it to her. As they expected she took it badly.

"Why are you trying to kill me? What have I ever done to you? And why didn't you come see me all night and all day? You're getting bored of me aren't you? You're going to forget about me and one day no one will come. I'll be alone and dying!"

"I was here last night, Ruby, but you thought I was someone else and I scared you. I was here. I never left you. I just didn't want to frighten you and you're NOT going to die."

"Lies! Why would I think you were someone else? Why do you lie to me?" she screamed at him.

"I don't lie to you, I'm not..." he trailed off realising that he was lying to her by not telling her who Tabitha, their new employee, really was. He looked guilty and she pounced on it.

"Yes you do lie - I see it in your eyes, and I bet you cheat too! Where have you been all day? Where's been more important than here? Looks like you're dressed for work, have you had a good time with Faye?" she accused, and he rolled his eyes at her.

"NO! And I don't cheat...not on you."

"Oh good I am privileged. How strange, I don't feel it!" she told him sarcastically. "Perhaps that's because I never expected my boyfriend to shut me in a room for weeks on end while he withholds what I need to keep me alive..."

"It hasn't even been a week, Ruby, it's been days," he corrected but she wasn't listening.

"And then, to top that special treatment, he breaks it to me that tonight he's not giving me anything and I'm going to die right here in front of him, just like Sammy died in front of me!"

"You're not going to die," he told her again.

"Oh that's a relief, the man who lifted me over his shoulder, threw me in a room with no windows or air, continuously reduced the dose that he promised me until I became desperate and sick, tells me I won't die. Thanks, Danny, but I'm not sure I trust you or your meaningless words anymore." She was mad at him and he was tired.

"OK then, Ruby, I'll go and have a shower and get changed and see you in a bit." He stood to leave but she suddenly changed tack, moving fast so she could slip herself between him and the viewing room door. Her eyes had turned all damsel in distress and they'd lost the, 'I could kill you with my little finger' glint he'd just been subjected to. She was breathless from her sudden sprint as she spoke.

"I'm sorry, Danny, I'm just really lonely that's all. Don't go. Stay with me...all night." She reached forward and began to loosen his tie. He kept his hands on his hips as he watched her play with him and his emotions. "I just miss you. I get jealous imagining you with Faye."

"I'm not with Faye. I'm with you, most of the day and all of the night. I wouldn't have the time or the energy for someone else even if I wanted to, WHICH. I. DON'T!" he told her firmly and she giggled at how cross he got with her. It was cute. She started to unbutton his shirt all the way down and he never stopped her. She was getting somewhere and the thought of swaying him, manipulating him, and getting what she wanted and needed spurred her on. "Ruby, what do you think this is going to achieve?" he asked her.

"A girl can touch her boyfriend can't she?" she asked innocently, running her hands inside his shirt and over his skin. It felt good. Her hands were so soft and gentle and he closed his eyes and imagined they were on their own, anywhere other than the damn viewing room...and without two very intrigued spectators. He opened his eyes as she reached for his belt.

"Whoa, Ruby, no way! You'll be better by morning and once you're up on your feet you can have whatever you want, but I'm not doing this while Bardo and Alessi are watching, and not while you're sick either," he told her, trying to stop her hands from wandering. She was quick and everywhere, and he was now struggling to control her, but she was also too close to the viewing room door for him to escape.

"Just tell them to look the other way," she whispered, and he suddenly realised that she was fixated on his neck tie. He was stunned and angry.

"Why, so you can try and strangle me?" he asked her and she glared at him - he'd foiled her plan. He grabbed her wrists and took her back into the middle of the room, rolling her so tightly in a quilt she couldn't escape quick enough to get to the door before him.

Alessi and Bardo said nothing as he passed them, shoving a chair out of his way furiously as he disappeared off for a shower.

He made some pasta and left a big pan half full for Alessi and Bardo. He took his bowl outside to eat in the garden. Leaning back in a patio chair with his foot on the dwarf wall, he watched as Alessi's precious cherub peed into the huge pool. He finished his food and felt much better, grabbing four hot drinks to take to the others on his way back to the viewing room. As he placed the cups down on the side he noticed that Ruby was looking uncomfortable. She was sweating and lying back on the quilts looking up at the ceiling.

"Hey, there's pasta out there if anyone's hungry," he whispered.

"Nice one. Well done," Bardo told him squeezing his shoulder firmly. "I'm starving."

"How's she doing?"

"She's feeling it," Alessi told him and Danny's eyes managed a brief sweep of his face before feeling unable to contain the embarrassment at seeing him with Tabitha, his hurting her feelings so badly she cried and then finding out the truth behind her disappearance. On top of that he had agreed to keep it all from the young woman he loved. The betrayal was going to kill her...and him.

"But that's normal, right?" he asked, looking back to the window as she shuffled awkwardly and wiped her arm over her moist forehead.

"I'm hot!" she called out. "I just need a window, that's all I want. Please just find me a room with a window and I will be good I promise. Alessi, please," she begged, getting up and walking around. She pulled at her top like it was stuck to her and wafted her skirt to try and get some air against her legs. "I'm so hot, it's not normal. I feel like I'm burning up. Can I have a fan? Is Danny there? Tell him I'm really sorry and I want him to come back. I'll be good this time, I swear." She dropped back down onto the floor and sat cross legged, her hair beginning to dampen around her face. She scooped it up and held it on top of her head so the back of her neck was exposed. "Ugh someone. Bloody anyone!" she called out, frustrated now that nobody was listening to her. She threw herself back onto the quilts arching her back like she'd been given a shot of Paradise, trying to escape the heat emanating from her body.

"It's normal. It's good," Bardo told Danny. "Hopefully a bad night will be followed by a good morning. This is going to be the longest so far. I'm afraid she's going to be seriously disorientated and suspicious about what we've been up to when she looks at where she's been kept, through clean eyes. Do you get what I'm saying?"

Danny shook his head. "Clean eyes?"

"Yes," Bardo confirmed. "Right now she would believe, accept, or do, anything for the drug but by morning, if it's out of her system fully, then she won't. She won't believe that we needed to contain her like this. She won't believe that she was such a danger to herself or others and she might think that we really have been trying to trap her. She might be fine but...then again...she might not. We'll have to wait and see." Danny frowned and looked back through the glass. She'd sat back up and was hanging her head forward so her hair could dangle away from her. He could see the gleam of moisture covering the skin at the nape of her neck and a

146

droplet ran down over the bumps in her spine. It made him feel uncomfortable just watching.

"Can we put the air conditioning on, Alessi, would that help?" he asked and Alessi nodded keenly.

"That's a great idea, Danny, go for it," he told him after he'd swallowed the hot mouthful of coffee he'd just taken. When Danny came back from messing with the controls they were very pleased to see him.

"Ahh, Danny, she's just threatened to take her clothes off - any suggestions on how to keep them on?" Alessi asked him.

Bardo laughed. "I think Danny's better at getting them off," he teased and Alessi pretended he hadn't heard. He was certainly in no place to lecture. Danny smirked, shaking his head at Bardo in mock disapproval before disappearing off to go gather some things. When he returned he let himself into the viewing room and Ruby propped herself up on her elbows to watch him approach.

"I thought you didn't love me anymore," she told him insecurely, and he gave her a very handsome smile.

"I promise to love you if you promise not to try and get my trousers off in front of my father again," he bargained, raising his eyebrows at her. She groaned and fell back again, complaining of being too hot. He placed a bowl of cool water on the floor and soaked a sponge. "I've put the air conditioning on so you should feel more comfortable very soon," he soothed, dipping the sponge into the bowl and dabbing at her skin. He moved from her feet to her knees and then squeezed so that the droplets of cool water ran down her legs on both sides.

"I'm so thirsty," she whispered with her eyes closed, and he fetched her some cold water and a straw. She threw the straw behind her and downed five cups in one go. She then told him to carry on with the sponge because she liked it. He sponged her face and neck and then she sat and held her hair up so he could sponge the back of her neck. He then sponged her chest, squeezing so the water would run down her top. She rolled her eyes at him wearily while he tried not to laugh.

"Danny, you tell me to behave and then you encourage me," she pointed out and he agreed to stop. He dribbled water into her hair instead so it would rest damp against her back.

"I really want a shot. Just a little one, please," she whispered, rising up onto her knees and moving towards him. He had finished sponging her down and was now sat on the floor with his legs bent and his weight leaning back on his hands. She climbed onto his lap so she could look into his eyes and he smiled gingerly, gripping her thighs so he could move her back slightly and maintain some distance between them.

"Ruby, remember what I said," he told her cautiously. "I really want to stay in here with you." She pressed her lips against his and kissed him.

"Just a little bit, Danny?" she asked again, softly and sweetly, as she placed another gentle kiss on his mouth. "5mls?" she suggested, and he shook his head slowly.

"I can't," he told her, sliding her back again to keep the space, as well as the peace.

"4mls?" she pushed, so softly he wouldn't have heard if it hadn't been for the fact that her lips were now touching his ear.

"I can't, I'm sorry," he apologised, suddenly feeling very tense.

"What about 4.5mls?" she asked hopefully, and he frowned.

"Ruby, that's more than 4mls!" She ran her hands up his neck and into his hair.

"Oops, silly me," she giggled. "OK let's just make it 4mls then," she agreed, and he leaned his head back and laughed.

"You are a serious game player, Ruby,"

"Oh god, bloody 3mls then! What's 3mls? It's nothing! Can't you just get me that? Alessi will never know and nor will Bardo. Just slip it to me...under the quilts," she told him, suddenly getting excited at the prospect. He slapped her on the thigh and slid her off of his lap completely. She hit the quilts with bump.

"No can do, Ruby. I'm this close to getting you back," he told her pinching his fingers so they almost touched. "No amount of that crappy stuff is going to make it longer for either of us. I want you back and if that means no Paradise when you're desperate, then it's no Paradise when you're desperate. You feel a bit cooler to me. I'll give you half hour to get your head straight and then I'll be back," he confirmed before standing and leaving her opened mouthed on the floor.

When he arrived back with Alessi and Bardo she was still sitting where he'd left her, looking stunned.

"Well, well, well, Ruby got cooler and Danny definitely got hotter," Bardo laughed. Danny told him to shut up. "What was she saying? She spoke so quietly even the microphone didn't pick it up," he asked, still chuckling to himself.

"She wanted a dose of Paradise, tried to negotiate a lesser amount and asked me to slip it to her right under your noses."

"Hmmm, how will we know when Ruby's back - both are underhand and seriously sneaky?" Alessi commented accidentally. Danny frowned at him.

"Do you mind?" he asked, feeling both offended and very protective. Alessi cringed.

"Sorry that just slipped out!"

21

Bodies, bodies, everywhere

Danny grabbed a chair and rested his head on the table. He was so exhausted that he drifted in and out of sleep to the sound of Alessi and Bardo speaking and occasionally laughing softly. When he came round they were both stood up watching Ruby intently.

"What's up?" he mumbled sleepily.

"She's shaking. I think she's cold," Bardo told him. "She's not settled at all but we thought we'd let you sleep rather than bother you. She keeps saying she feels sick too." Danny stood quickly and made his way to the glass.

"Has anyone been in to keep her company? How long was I out?" he asked feeling disorientated.

"No we haven't been in," Bardo confessed. "Sorry, Danny, but it might be best if we don't now. It's only a few hours till morning. A few hours of suffering and then we can go in. She could do anything, it's just too risky." Danny squinted trying to check his watch in the dim light.

"It's seven hours till her next dose would have been due, that's too long. We can't just leave her to do all of this on her own. I know she's a bit pushy and disturbing but seriously, what's she going to do? The worst she's going to do is strip, right? Or make a pass, but she's small, she's hardly going to rape any of us!"

"Danny..." Alessi began but Danny was unhappy.

"No, I'm not leaving her. It's not fair. She's had the rough end of the stick all her life and she's done it alone. Well she's not doing it alone now. If you're too scared to go anywhere near her then *I* will," he snapped, grabbing a cup of water for himself and then filling one for her before letting himself back in.

She was huddled near the bin shaking uncontrollably. She lifted her head to watch him approach.

"Hey, are you sick?" he asked her softly, and she nodded and began to cry. Almost as if asking her was all the permission she'd been waiting for, she began to vomit and moved onto her knees to lean over the bin. He held her hair out of the way but it was only the water from earlier that came back up. That didn't stop her continuing to vomit fluid for the next three hours. Eventually she lay on the floor doubled up in pain, rocking and screaming out. She wouldn't let him touch her, telling him every time he did it burnt her skin. Alessi joined them and Danny looked surprised to see him.

"Well while she's happy to keep people at arm's length I thought I'd pluck up the courage to pay her a little visit," he confessed guiltily. "I'm so sorry, Danny. You've been the one shouldering most of this. You've been the one getting stuck in, always putting her needs first, even when you're clearly shattered. You've never faltered once. She slaps you, screams at you, loves you and then hates you but you've never turned your back on her."

"I love her, Alessi. I always have. Even from the first time I set eyes on her at school, I knew that Ruby was the girl for me."

"Hmmm, well, she is very much like your mother," he mumbled and Danny frowned.

"What's that supposed to mean?"

"The long dark hair, the pretty eyes and beautiful mouth the monstrous temper and savage determination...*your* mother!" he exclaimed, like just thinking about her exhausted him.

"You say it like it's a bad thing. I like strong women who aren't afraid to stand up against people who are bigger than them. And, funnily enough, Ruby also looks very much like Tabitha, what with the dark hair, eyes and mouth. So, it seems, you also go for women like my mother!"

"About that, Danny, I'm really sorry that you've been asked to keep such a big secret. I'm also sorry that you saw me...like that...earlier. It was unprofessional and weak and..."

"And exactly the kind of thing you'd bawl me out for," Danny concluded for him. He nodded, taking it on the chin.

"Yes I know and I know I've messed up big time with Ruby too. It won't be for long, just until Tabitha can work out what she wants to do.

She might just want to move on. It must be pretty hard to deal with," he told him distantly and Danny sighed, feeling bad.

"It is good to see you with someone after all this time. I know there have been other women but none important enough for you to risk being caught with. I mean Faye could have walked in on you and you know what crap she talks! You must really like Tabitha...I guess?" Alessi nodded but it seemed he wasn't about to share his feelings; or the fact that she'd made it clear that she didn't want anything like that with him. Ruby stirred and groaned and Alessi called to her.

"Ruby, you're doing really well, honey. You're nearly there. It won't be much longer now and then you'll feel so much better," he soothed. She sat cross legged and looked at him distantly. She didn't seem to recognise him. "It's Alessi," he clarified for her and she wrapped her arms around her body as another wave of shivering took a hold.

"Alessi, are you ever going to let me go?" she asked in a whisper. "My dad's expecting me home and he'll punish me if I'm late. You've kept me here for months..."

"Days," he corrected quickly.

"I'm going to be in so much trouble and I'm frightened. Can I please go home now? I want to go home. I want my bedroom and my patchwork quilt. I want my lamp that makes things look so warm even when it's freezing. It's always freezing and the heating's never on. It's not on now and I'm cold. I want my things back, Alessi. I want my home back. And I want my dad. He told me that he missed me and I think he's really sorry this time. I think I should give him another chance. Maybe he's changed. He'll stop drinking one day, I know he will. He said so. Alessi, can I go home...please?" He looked into her eyes. They were dark in the dim light, like hollowed out holes against her ash white skin. She looked like she was dying and her pleas brought a lump to his throat. He couldn't very well tell her that her home was gone, just like her dad, so, feeling like the worst person in the world, he changed the subject.

"Are you looking forward to seeing your friends?" he asked her and she glanced at Danny suddenly as if she were frightened of him. She edged a little closer to Alessi as she answered.

"Yeah...maybe." She was watching Danny like he might pounce on her. She worked her way around Alessi so she could hide behind his back.

"Ruby, what's wrong?" he asked over his shoulder as she snuggled up behind him and buried her face into his shirt.

"It's Mickey," she whispered like someone might overhear. "He's come to get me. He said they're all waiting - him and his men. Don't let him take me." He could feel her shivering against his body and turned to put his arms around her. She curled herself into his lap and hid her face against his chest, chanting relentlessly as she rocked.

"He's coming. They're coming to get me. He's coming. They're coming to get me."

Danny sighed. Once again he was the bad guy and this time his girl was seeking comfort from another man. He rolled his eyes and Alessi cringed for him.

An hour later she jumped up from Alessi's lap and tried to get away but she tripped and fell right onto Danny who had been sleeping stretched out on the floor. She began to scramble, trying to escape and telling Alessi that he was dead. Danny sat up and took hold of her arms as he tried to reassure her but she kicked and fought him.

"I don't want to go with you. Alessi, get him off of me - he's going to take me to Mickey. Danny, please leave me alone. Get your hands off me!" Every time Danny tried to reason with her or reach out, she saw a dead man coming and she was petrified. He was talking to her, telling her to calm down but it was impossible, how could she calm down when he wanted to take her six feet under? Then the quilts on the floor began to move and she pulled at them one by one. Underneath lay body upon body, all with their eyes still open. They were all looking at her. She tried to run but she kept stepping on people, on their hands, their fingers and their faces. She found a corner and cowered in it, sobbing and begging for them to go away, but they wouldn't. They reached out and touched her, they called her name, they tugged at her clothes and she fought them - all of them.

She had definitely lost it now and Alessi practically pulled Danny from the room and locked the door on her. When they looked back through the glass she was still hiding and hitting out at things they couldn't see. The look of sheer terror on her face told them that this was the worst hallucination by far. After skirting the room as if she were balanced on a precipice, she banged on the viewing room window and pleaded for them to let her out. She looked back over her shoulder at the monsters constantly moving in on her. She ripped at her clothes and scratched at her skin as creatures started to run from their dead bodies, out through their eyes, ears, noses and mouths and straight for her. They covered her until there was not an inch of skin to be seen and she beat at herself and tried to pull her hair out.

She yanked her top off and shook it, trying to get the creepy crawlies and maggots out of it. Flies kept landing on her and buzzing around her ears and mouth. She tried to brush them off. She felt a tug on her skirt and looked down to see a huge tarantula clinging to it. She tried to shake it off gently but it stayed put, weighing heavily on the pleated fabric. She unhooked the clasp on the waistband and carefully, so not to disturb it, lowered her skirt to the ground and stepped out. Danny wanted to go in, but Bardo told him their being in there seemed to be making matters worse. Her hallucinations were very real. He was forced to stand and watch helplessly as his girlfriend took refuge in a corner. She looked so traumatised and damaged. She was so delicate and vulnerable and her body looked thin and bruised from beating at herself. He held his hands over his face, listening to her incessant screaming. It sounded like she was being attacked, she looked like she was being attacked and all he could do was watch the horror unfold right in front of him.

By 4am she'd thankfully passed out from exhaustion and Bardo nipped in to check her pulse and heart rate. He gave them the thumbs up and then backed out of the room silently. She settled and drifted into a deep sleep on her front, where she remained until 6am. Feeling dazed, she stretched out like she was in bed but then she frowned and looked about her. She sat up quickly, seeming confused at her surroundings and then she looked down to see that she was in her underwear. Terror flooded her face as she searched for the door and gathered the loose sheets around her body. It was obvious she had no idea what was going on.

"Alessi," she whispered into the room, her voice hoarse and painful. "Danny. Bardo. Is anyone there?" Danny moved to enter the room but Bardo warned him that she needed time to recall what was going on. She would be feeling caged right now and vulnerable. She stayed on the floor looking tiny. "Why am I here? Why have you put me in here? Where are my clothes? Why did you take my clothes?" she cried and to all three it was a heartbreaking sight. Danny tried to get past Bardo but he wouldn't let him and he refused to give up the key, which he'd placed in his pocket at 4am. He knew that Danny would want to go in as soon as she woke looking vaguely normal. "Oh my god I thought I could trust you and especially you, Danny, but you let them take my clothes. You let them leave me here. You helped them!" She was distraught and noticing her skirt and top she crawled into the middle of the room, trying to keep herself covered with the sheets. She clearly felt exposed right in front of the huge mirror. "What do you want with me? What are you going to do to me?" she begged in desperation, knowing they were watching her. What made the horrifying experience worse was that she didn't know if they'd invited others to enjoy her suffering and containment too.

She picked up her things and moved back to the corner of the room, turning away so she could dress in relative privacy. She then buried herself into the quilts and went back to sleep.

At 7am Bardo let Danny have the key so he could go and check her pulse and heart rate. "If all sounds normal and regular then you can take her back to her bedroom if you want," he told him. Danny was desperate to get the checks over and done with. He just wanted to get her out of there. He made his way silently to her side and placed the stethoscope to her chest, listening for a while so he could compare the rate minute on minute. He then placed the stethoscope around his neck and put his fingers to the pulse in her wrist and timed. She seemed fine and everything sounded normal so he turned to look at the mirror and give the nod. As he did so, her eyes opened wide. Bardo spotted it and desperately tried to engage the microphone to warn him but it was too late, she'd jumped up and crossed her arms over Danny's head. Gripping the two ends of the stethoscope she pulled hard using it as a garrotte. He was taken by surprise and tried to get his fingers underneath but she'd made sure not to leave any slack.

"I'm warning you, Danny Glover, if you so much as try and escape I'm going to pull so tight I'll cut your head right off and don't think I won't because I bloody will!" she threatened ferociously. He automatically tried to twist and she was true to her word, yanking so hard he went dizzy. He couldn't breathe but she wouldn't let up. "Alessi! Bardo! If you don't want me to strangle him completely I suggest you get in here right now!" They came to the door and she told them to move to the far corner. Alessi knew her intention was to back up to the exit, drop Danny and lock them in, but he wasn't going to let her run out into the street in the state she was in. She'd be likely to run right back into the eager and destroying hands of Marlon.

She could see Alessi had stopped. "Don't try anything, Alessi, I'm warning you." Her voice sounded panicked this time. She didn't want to be confronted by Alessi and she didn't want to hurt Danny either, but there was no way she was going to spend another minute longer than she had to in a room with no windows or daylight. She had woken up in just her underwear and right now she couldn't remember a thing, other than being carried there over Danny's shoulder. None of them could be trusted and it was them or her now. "I mean it Alessi!" Alessi began to move towards her, so she pulled tighter pushing Danny almost to the verge of unconsciousness. She was so busy watching Alessi that she hadn't noticed Bardo come up behind her. He pushed her forwards over Danny's shoulders and onto the floor. Bardo lunged forward before she could scramble up and escape and held her still while Alessi plunged a needle into her leg and pushed down steadily. Her fighting slowed and then she stopped screaming. Danny rubbed his neck and coughed painfully.

"What did you give her?" he demanded, worried that she'd been given another shot of Paradise. He couldn't do it all again!

"Sleeper, Danny. Don't worry, your shy and retiring girlfriend, who very nearly killed you, is just taking a power nap. We gave her a sedative, that's all."

"So I can take her back to her bedroom then?" he asked and Alessi and Bardo looked at each other, unsure. "Look, I'll stay with her the whole time. She's less likely to kick off if she wakes in her own room. She's going mad and I just want to get her out of here." Alessi moved forward and checked the marks on his neck.

"I don't know, Danny, maybe just a couple more hours. She just turned on you."

"Because I was the one who brought her in here - I don't blame her for turning on me. Now, if nobody is planning on actually stopping me, I'm taking her to bed." He scooped her up off the floor and with nobody attempting to stop him, he did exactly that.

He washed her face over and plaited her hair before tucking her in to her own big, cosy bed. He then opened the windows wide so she would have lots of the one thing, other than Paradise, she'd been so desperate for. The cool air blew in gusts against his face and he smiled; they'd got her back at last. After locking the bedroom door, he hid the key and settled into the armchair, where he drifted off for some much needed sleep.

22

All clean

When Danny woke up Ruby's bed was empty; the sheet, quilt and bedspread had been pushed back and there was no sign of her.

"Oh god, Ruby, no!" he called out, rushing for the window and scanning the garden. "No, no, no! Please don't have done what I think you've gone and done," he panicked. There was no doubt that Marlon would be watching the place and waiting to hook her again. Next time he might kill her.

"What do you think I've done?" he heard a voice from behind him and spun round. "Danny, that was a myth that I flew like a bird from the window to escape Mickey," she smiled looking amused. "I actually hid in the base of the bed...remember?" He beamed at her in relief as she leaned against the doorway to the en-suite looking *much* better.

"Damn, Ruby, you scared the life out of me. Just as I was about to get you back I thought you were gone again. I was starting to think I'd never keep you."

"Sorry," she cringed. "I woke up and you were zonked so I thought I would check to see if I looked as bad as I felt."

"And?" he asked hopefully.

"Well, someone's plaited my hair and washed my face and these aren't the clothes I was wearing when you cruelly hoisted me over your shoulder and threw me in the viewing room so...I look a little bit better, I guess. What's with the braid, Danny? Do they teach *that* at law school?" she teased and he grinned, looking embarrassed.

"My mum taught me. She has long hair, like yours, and I wanted to know how to plait it like she does. I was six by the way - it wasn't recent or anything freaky like that," he defended sweetly, and she giggled.

"That's so cute. And you're actually very good - this is *really* neat!" she told him, holding out the long twisted rope of hair and admiring it. I have also brushed my teeth...a lot!" she confessed and he grinned at her.

"Yeah that's something you can't really do for someone else, sorry."

She shuddered. "So, anyway, enough about my breath, what have I missed? I feel like I've been away for years."

"Well, unfortunately, you missed all the action. Come to think of it so did we! Despite Carlito, Sergio and Mickey trying to sabotage our appeal on the Rossi case..."

"And blowing to bits all those relentless months of photocopying Alessi made me do to get the evidence files ready in time," Ruby reminded him and he snorted in amusement.

"And that, yes, baby. All before shooting you and scaring the life out of me!" he added on and she squinted painfully at the memory. "Well, the appeal went ahead as rescheduled. We had barristers taking care of everything. The judge and jury were given all the evidence we'd collected and we argued that the initial verdict was unsafe because the jury had been nobbled."

"Which is the term used for bullying the jury to get the results you want, right?" she recalled.

"Yeah that's right, honey. It's not breaking someone's ankles like you originally thought," he chuckled, and she punched him on the arm playfully.

"Shut up, Mr Clever Clogs!"

He rubbed his arm like it really hurt and then flashed her a handsome smile as he continued. "We showed that Officer Killen's men had put pressure on the jury and threatened them for a unanimous guilty verdict that saw Rossi, an innocent man, go down for five years. With someone like Killen breathing down your neck the last thing you're going to do is be the only one of twelve jury members voting the other way."

"Yeah I can see how staying alive might be an incentive," Ruby joked. "So, basically, they'd sent Rossi down because they were scared of Officer Killen," she concluded simply, and he nodded and sighed.

"Yep. I suppose the way they saw it, they could either choose Rossi's life, a man they didn't even know, or their own. Not a difficult choice eh? Killen always gets what he wants, Ruby, he's a nasty piece of work."

"Yeah and don't I know it," she sighed still feeling traumatised by her Paradise ordeal. "God, it must have been so awful for the jury."

"And the victim," Danny pointed out. "The officer tortured and then thrown from a cliff in the boot of a car. With friends like Killen who needs enemies eh?" he whistled, and Ruby frowned.

"What do you mean, friends?"

"Well there was evidence to suggest that the victim, the tortured officer, had close links with Killen right up until his little 'cliff accident'. Basically his statement wasn't worth the paper it was written on. They'd had a fall out over some business deal, so when Killen needed a victim he went through his little list of 'people who'd pissed him off recently' and came up with his fellow colleague. Being an officer just made it all the better, just made someone like Rossi, with links to an organised crime network, seem all the more guilty."

"Wow!" Ruby's head was spinning.

"We have a couple of witnesses, jury members, who are now under police protection for speaking up against Killen. We managed to talk them into giving statements and that's exactly what we needed to get Rossi cleared. Johnny Giavani intends for you to meet Rossi as soon as possible. He's told him all about you and how you kept the file in our hands, even when your life depended on it. He's very proud of his little unofficially adopted granddaughter." She smiled seeming embarrassed and Danny moved to whisper into her ear. "Between you and me, the way he's been going on about you, I think Johnny might actually be broody!" Ruby giggled and Danny straightened up to lean against the other side of the doorframe. "Seriously, Rubes, without that file, Rossi would still be in prison for a crime he didn't commit." Danny looked her over and then shook his head. "If you thought Carlito and his brother were scary you wait till you meet Rossi!" Ruby paled slightly.

"Is he likely to want to kill me like Carlito and his brother?" She was being sarcastic but still sounded worried as she reached up and slipped her hand under the strap of her vest top to her shoulder. She let her fingers roam over the deep scar left behind by the bullet Carlito's brother, Sergio, had put in her. "I'm not in any hurry to meet Rossi, Danny," she confessed. "You can tell your grandfather, Johnny Giavani, I appreciate the offer, but an email will do just fine." Danny chuckled again and gave her a cuddle, pushing aside the strap of her top so he could kiss the scar on her shoulder gently.

"I'm so glad you're still here, Ruby, please don't ever get yourself killed again," he pleaded, recalling how it felt when she'd slipped away in his arms and then, thankfully, returned to scream the place down. He looked into her eyes while cupping her face in his warm soft hand and she smiled back at him.

"I'll try my hardest," she promised, caving into a giggle. "So, what now?"

"Well Rossi is back with Johnny and has taken the place of Carlito and Mickey, his last two right hand men. Rossi is scary but he's genuine, like Bardo. I think you'll like him better than the last two," he joked. "Killen is now preparing to stand trial for the torture of his fellow officer, the crime that Rossi was originally imprisoned for. He can add to that list, perverting the course of justice, intimidation, false imprisonment and GBH. He's going down for a very long time. Killen's such a nice chap - I bet his mother's so proud," Danny joked, but Ruby looked uncomfortable.

"Yeah and I'll bet he's going to hate us for helping to put him there too!" She wrapped her arms around her body, suddenly feeling nervous and sick. "A man capable of all that and we're on the wrong side of him, brilliant!"

"And from all of that to all of this!" Danny exclaimed looking exasperated with her. "Does trouble follow you around would you say, Ruby?" he grinned and she rolled her eyes at him.

"You're not the first person who's said that, Danny. You know my mate, Sasha?" He nodded. "Well her older brother, Mario, he was always saying that to me. I'm beginning to wonder if he was right now." She fell silent for a few moments and then she looked into Danny's eyes. "Oh it was so horrible. I was so scared of everything. I'm not sure I'll ever get over the Paradise ordeal," she confessed, and he pulled her into his arms.

161

"Well how about I try and help with that a little bit," he told her, finding her mouth with his briefly, before stopping to look into her eyes. "That's if you still want me of course?" he asked her, and she looked taken aback.

"Are you kidding me? I distinctly remember you promising I could have whatever I wanted if I stopped the Paradise and here I am, look, Paradise stopped!" she told him innocently, holding her hands out to display just how stopped the Paradise really was. He laughed and pulled her in for another kiss and cuddle. *She* stopped the kiss this time. "So I suppose the question is do you still want me? I wouldn't blame you for going off me..." He used one hand to hold the back of her head and put the other over her mouth roughly, making her laugh.

"Shut up, Ruby Palmer," he told her. "I haven't got you back so you can get all insecure on me. You're feisty and I want you, and don't you forget it! Got it?" He scooped her up and carried her to the bed, throwing her down like a savage. He then dropped himself over the top of her, holding himself on strong muscular arms to keep from crushing her. His eyes were menacing and she looked back into the black pupils and dark brown irises, but he couldn't keep up the pretence. Breaking into an incredibly sexy grin he shrugged. "I think this is where I'm supposed to say 'ugg ugg' or something...oh and then ravage you," he explained and she nodded like she now felt adequately updated.

"Oh I see...OK...I'm ready to be ravaged," she declared throwing her head back at exactly the same time as the door knocked. She groaned and Danny looked back over his shoulder feeling torn. She placed her hands either side of his face and pulled him back round to look at her. "Just ignore it and they'll go away," she told him eagerly and he grinned.

"I can't because it's obviously Alessi and he knows we're in. He will be worried about you. Chill, Ruby, I'm not going anywhere. There will be plenty of time to get yourself ravaged later," he promised with a wink. She huffed and threw her head back so she was flat out again. After standing and straightening himself, Danny unlocked the door.

The first thing Alessi saw when he entered the room was Ruby, who had stubbornly refused to get up off the bed and look like nothing had been going on.

"Ruby, I...take it...you're feeling...better?" he asked, tilting his head to get a clearer view of what she might look like upright.

"Much better thank you, Alessi," she confirmed sitting up. "You know I'm quite hungry now," she turned and grinned at Danny cheekily and his eyes widened. "I think I could definitely do with something, I'm getting a bit desperate here." Danny couldn't help but laugh and Alessi narrowed his eyes at her.

"Paradise or no Paradise, you're still in big trouble, Ruby Palmer, do you know that?"

She nodded with the cutest smile and he turned to look Danny up and down. "Go get showered and changed - you look like a homeless person," he ordered. Holding out his hand he then reached to pull Ruby up from the bed, gently. He looked her over slowly, making her feel self conscious. He was still holding onto one of her hands and she looked over at Danny nervously, unsure what to do. "It's really good to have you back. I've really missed having you stropping about the place. Don't you ever go near Marlon again, do you hear me?" he demanded, accidentally squeezing her hand too tight. She yelped out, looking shocked. He immediately lessened his hold, but he still didn't let go. He wasn't ready to let go; she could have died...right in front of them.

"I...Alessi...I   wouldn't...ever...I'm   so   sorry," she   apologised, stammering awkwardly. Just as she thought she couldn't take any more, he pulled her towards him and hugged her tightly. He cupped her head with his hand as he held it securely against his shoulder.

"I love you, Ruby. I want you to always know that," he told her and she remained quiet, unsure what to say or do. This was a vulnerable side of Alessi that he *never* showed. He might deny getting attached to things but they both knew differently. He was attached to them. He let her go suddenly and resorted back to Alessi mode. "Go get showered, not with Danny please, and then both come down for breakfast. We've got things to do - work is seriously behind and we need to catch up." He turned to walk out of the door and Ruby slumped back onto the bed, deflated.

"Are you serious? I've just been really sick and you want me to come in and work?" she protested.

"I couldn't care less whether you lift a finger, Ruby," he called back over his shoulder. "We have to go into work and I'm not letting you out of my sight until Marlon has been dealt with, so quit arguing for once in your life and go get dressed!"

23
First day back

They arrived at work, where Ruby was immediately bombarded with questions. Everyone seemed genuinely concerned, except for Amanda who just looked at her like she'd tasted something bad. Ruby had only stopped in at reception because Danny and Alessi needed to grab their huge piles of post.

"You're better then," Amanda forced herself to acknowledge. "You look a bit peaky to me, but then I suppose you do look rough after you've been ill, don't you?" Ruby ignored her but Alessi and Danny both heard her sigh. Amanda continued, "What was wrong with you anyway? I hear it was pretty nasty. It's probably those nightclubs you young ones spend all your time in, get all sorts in there?"

"What like a good looking bloke and a sexually transmitted disease?" Ruby asked her, glaring back furiously. Alessi immediately stopped playing with the fax, to guide her out of reception and up the stairs. Halfway up Tabitha was caught by surprise as she nipped out of accounts. She stopped and backed up, looking petrified.

"Morning, Tabitha," Alessi greeted professionally, and in the way that he greeted all of his members of staff. She smiled at him and caught a look at Ruby through a gap as she was bustled to the foot of the second flight. Ruby tried to check Tabitha out but Alessi seemed keen to keep her moving.

"Wait, Tabitha's new, shouldn't you be introducing us? I mean I know you said I don't have to work today, but I still have a job, don't I?" Alessi immediately stopped and turned.

"Yes of course, Ruby, you will always have a job here. I'm sorry. I don't know why I didn't think of it myself. Tabitha, Ruby. Ruby, Tabitha. Tabitha knows you've been off sick. She's doing some work for me, Ruby, and she's also helping out in accounts with Mrs Hughes. She's a very good all rounder."

"I'll say," Danny commented, completely by accident, and all three looked at him in surprise. His eyes were huge and he immediately shut up. Tabitha half smiled at him and then braced herself to face Ruby.

"It's really nice to meet you, Ruby. I've heard...a lot...about you," she told her cautiously.

"Hi," Ruby greeted her with a cute little wave. "Nice to meet you too." Alessi nodded, seeming relatively satisfied, and then started them walking again as he called over his shoulder.

"Come see me in my office as soon as you have a moment please, Tabitha, I need to run some things by you." She never answered but he knew she'd heard.

They got to the top of the stairs and Alessi threw Danny a sideways glance. They both wondered how Ruby would take to Faye, who they found sitting at Ruby's desk.

"And this is Faye," Alessi concluded like that's all the introduction needed, and now let's move into my office before someone lights the fuse. Ruby nodded and Danny saw her actually check the distance between the two desks to see if they'd been pushed any closer.

"Oh, Ruby, I've been soooooooo looking forward to meeting you. Are you feeling OK?" the new girl asked like Ruby was slightly old, slightly deaf and slightly stupid too. She was now ever so slightly annoyed.

"I'm fine...thank you," she managed with difficulty. Faye swung her long golden hair and fluttered her eyelashes at Danny.

"Would you like me to go get you a drink? Would you like your usual, Danny, or is there something else you'd like?"

Danny smiled uncomfortably and held his hand up like he was fine. "Perhaps you could just put the kettle on and we can sort out our own drinks thanks, Faye," he suggested and she jumped up like an obedient gangly puppy and skipped off in her little skirt, heeled shoes and tight top. Alessi put the fan on high and opened the windows before cranking up the air conditioning.

"That should see her dressed in the next ten minutes," he grumbled.

"How does she manage to make getting a drink sound like an offer of sex?" Ruby demanded, with no care for who might be listening. Alessi coughed uncomfortably and Danny burst into laughter. "No, I'm serious, you have to get rid of her, Alessi! And she's sat at my desk! Alessi, do something!" she ordered putting him on the spot as Faye walked back in. To make matters worse, the girl took to leaning sexily against the doorframe while she twiddled with her hair.

"I will, Ruby," Alessi agreed, trying to draw her attention away from the blonde bombshell who was checking Danny out again. "But for now Tom Marshall wanted to say hi...and I saw his car in the car park...so...why don't you pop down for a nice long chat. You can have a coffee with him if you like, but don't leave the building please," he told her, turning and shutting himself securely in his office like that would make it all go away.

Ruby looked Faye up and down as she blinked her big brown eyes innocently back at her. She was gorgeous and Ruby hated her, with her long tanned legs and immaculately tended nails with white tips. Ruby felt ugly. She'd been really sick right up until the early hours of the morning and, though she was much better, she still looked pale and worn. Her eyes were dark and her head hurt. She glared at Danny like he'd been cheating on her and pushed past Faye. Faye put on a distressed act for Danny's benefit but he just smiled before telling her it would be really useful if she would go and photocopy the entire Encarta English dictionary, which she did...eagerly!

When Ruby came back up to the office Faye was thankfully still tied up copying in the coffee room. Ruby sat in her chair, at her desk, to stare at *her* Danny, while he pretended to work. She knew he wasn't really working because he hadn't done a thing. He just kept looking at the same papers over and over again. She was making him nervous.

"What's Alessi doing?" she asked swivelling her chair back and forth like she was bored. He looked up at her like she'd said something shocking.

"Erm... Tabitha...I think," he informed her awkwardly and she narrowed her eyes at him and smiled widely.

"Is he now?" she asked, sounding delighted and he realised what he'd said, cringing painfully. Looking back to his papers he busily started to do nothing again, desperately wishing they could just swallow him up. "Hmmm, Tabitha you think, or Tabitha definitely?" she asked, wondering why he was being so cagey about it.

"Uh huh, Tabitha, definitely," he confirmed, sounding more sure now.

"How long's she been in there?" she pressed on and he put his pen down, like he was frustrated and forced to give her his full attention.

"About an hour or so, Ruby," he told her.

"Wow," she exclaimed sarcastically. "I think maybe Mr Alessi has found himself a cute little lady friend?" Danny half laughed and picked his pen back up.

"I'm not sure about that," he dismissed her observation, lowering his eyes to his desk and shuffling a pile of papers.

"He doesn't even spend that long with his clients, Danny. What do you think they're doing? I've a good mind to bug him and then make him stand while I recall all the gory details about what a naughty boy he's been. She's probably only after one thing. I wonder if he knows he can say no. Perhaps I should go tell him," she teased.

"God, Ruby, no! Don't do that...please don't do that," Danny begged her and she frowned back.

"He's seeing her isn't he?" her eyes were almost as wide as her mouth now. "Oh my god, Mr Alessi is having unprofessional relations with a member of staff! And a new member of staff might I add! How long did that take him?"

"Look, Ruby, I don't know if they are. They just seem to like each other's company, that's all. I don't want to get involved..."

"Don't tell me you were still hoping your mum and dad might get back together?" she teased and he threw his pen at her just as Faye walked in.

"Don't be mean, Ruby - I stopped wishing that when I was six," he told her seriously, and she caved in to his deep brown gaze.

"Ohhh, Danny, that's so sweet! I'm so sorry," she giggled, feeling really bad. Standing up she made her way over to his desk to comfort him, giving

Faye a quick 'back off' glare as she passed her. She wriggled herself onto his lap and looked into his eyes. "Perhaps I could make you feel better," she told him softly and he grinned, knowing exactly what she was up to." He caught a glimpse of Faye moving back into Ruby's chair. She occupied it like Ruby had never been there and he didn't like it one bit. Ruby was there first and he wanted her back there again, as soon as possible.

"Ruby, I can't wait to get you home," he told her, nuzzling into her neck and making her genuinely giggle. She gave him a big smile when he came up for air and then he gave her a lingering kiss on the lips. Feeling satisfied she slipped off his lap, the point well and truly made with his co-operation.

Danny territory sufficiently claimed, she turned to confront Faye for taking her seat but Alessi walked out of his office. Ruby spotted Tabitha through the gap in the doorway. She'd only just started filing so they'd obviously been up to something other than preparing his work and tidying his room. She grinned at him, unable to help herself, and he ruffled her hair and cupped her chin affectionately. Faye seemed slightly more shocked by Alessi's behaviour towards Ruby, than Danny's. He was usually so cool! Ruby felt slightly taken off guard too.

"Danny, can you stay late tonight please? I will take Ruby home and stay with her," he asked, trying to assess whether she was looking more or less unwell.

"Is she under house arrest?" Faye giggled and as Ruby pushed Alessi's hand away in frustration, they all turned their attention fiercely on the annoying blonde. She shut up instantly.

"I thought you could help me at home, Ruby?" Alessi told her and she nodded obediently. Danny was co-operating too.

"Yeah of course I'll stay," he agreed. He couldn't very well say no after all the time Alessi had let him have off, not to mention the cost of the Paradise that he had funded to get Ruby home and better.

"Oh goody I won't be alone then. I always get scared working here late," Faye chipped in. "Especially after the guys downstairs told me all about Ruby being shot here. How scary is that! Did you think you were going to die, Rubes? Did it hurt, babe?"

"It's Ruby to you, I'm not a babe and, yes, it hurt!"

"You are a babe?" Danny whispered from the safety of his desk, but she ignored him.

"What do you mean you're working late?" she demanded to know, looking Faye over and wishing her legs were two inches shorter and her skirt two inches longer.

"I go to college on a Friday morning and Mr Alessi lets me work late on a Wednesday night. It's so I can keep on top...if you know what I mean? Isn't that right, Danny?" Danny dropped his head to the desk and placed his hands over the back of it. Alessi spun round and went back to his room, closing the door firmly behind him and Ruby was at last left to do what she needed to do to put Faye in her place. She leaned over the desk, pinning the other girl with her ferocious glare.

"Let me tell you now, Faye, if you so much as touch Danny you will never need to worry about the expense of a manicure again because I will chop every last one of your fingers off! Do you understand me?" she hissed. Faye sat back, completely horrified, and Danny looked up sheepishly, checking his letter opener was still in his desk tidy. It had given him a nasty paper cut earlier in the day. In the hands of Ruby it was probably capable of so much more. The atmosphere was seriously tense and Faye nodded a fraction. It took all Ruby had not to slap the conceited little cow and, with her jaw clenched and her hands balled into fists at her sides, she left to go shut herself in the box room.

The last thing she wanted to do on her first day was explode in front of anyone. She hated the box room at the best of times and now it reminded her of the viewing room, with its lack of windows and air, but she wasn't allowed out of the building. The box room was the only place she knew she'd be alone as she slid down between the reams of copier paper and cried. As the rage slowly subsided she eventually fell asleep, her body and mind completely exhausted. A knock at the door a few hours later woke her - Alessi had finally come to take her home.

24
The birds and the bees

When they got back Alessi began preparing vegetables in the kitchen while Ruby wriggled up onto a stool and huffed. He turned and looked at her.

"What's up with you?" he asked as she kicked her feet back and forth like a child. "What is it, Ruby? I can't help if you don't tell me. You do know you can tell me anything?" he asked her and she smiled. Alessi could be so lovely when he wanted to be.

"It sounds stupid...it's just...I don't like...I don't feel...you and Tabitha...and Danny...and Faye!" she suddenly seemed like she might cry. He scrunched his hands into a tea towel before throwing it onto the side. Placing his hands on his hips he walked towards her and stopped to survey the sorry mess that was Ruby; the girl he'd 'apparently' rescued.

"Ruby Palmer, could you be jealous by any chance?" he teased and she rolled her eyes and shook her head at him like that would never happen.

"Yes! Yes I am!" she suddenly gave in and he grinned and pulled a stool up to face her, sighing like he wasn't quite sure what to do.

"Look, Faye is just Faye and there's nothing you can do about girls like that. She would steal your boyfriend in the blink of an eye and then smile sweetly to your face, but she could only do that if your boyfriend was willing to let her...and he's not, Ruby. Danny has been so worried about you. He's been here the whole time and he's never been scared to confront you, to take the abuse you hurled at him and resist the passes you made." She looked away, embarrassed, knowing that she had made a pass at him too. He guided her back into his line of vision with his hand beneath her chin. "Ruby, you were very sick. You can't help or change what's happened so please forget it...I have. As for Danny, he only has eyes for you and I'm so looking forward to my grandchildren. I want lots, Ruby," he told her seriously. She was astonished.

"What?"

"I can't wait to see you all *big* and *fat*. Of course your hips will change shape too and probably never go back quite the way you want them, but what does it matter when you have lots of babies to worry about? You'll be too tired to care about your appearance anyway, believe me!" He laughed like that was charming. "And I know that Danny will make a great dad. When he's not busy pursuing a successful career, he'll buy you cabbage leaves for your bra..."

"Cabbage leaves?" she repeated, "For my bra?" She scrunched her nose in disgust.

"Oh yes," he told her smoothly. "The smell is awful but it helps no end with the very painful effects of feeding. But that's what good mum's do, right?"

"Right," she nodded slowly, unsure.

"And he'll massage your swollen legs and ankles and pop out in the middle of the night to get cream for your piles..."

"Piles of what?"

"No just 'piles', also known as haemorrhoids."

"Ohhh," she exclaimed sadly.

"Yes but that doesn't last forever and, you know, when the time comes and you're in labour, Danny will help by telling you the hell will end soon. He'll be lying, of course, it lasts for like twelve hours...but you have to keep the spirits up!"

"Spirits. What, like wine?" she asked hopefully and he shook his head.

"NO! No alcohol for the duration of the pregnancy and then, if you breastfeed, for like the next year or so too. But alcohol isn't good for you and who wants a 21st birthday anyway?" She was looking at him like she might slip off the stool and run "And then, when the midwife, doctor, trainees and whoever else happens to be in the room watching, tell you that you're ready, the drama of labour begins!"

"Alessi! No! Stop!" she screamed out, making him jump. He'd been really getting into it. He tried desperately not to laugh at her and she frowned, working him out. "Alessi, you're winding me up aren't you? You're horrible! That's an awful thing to do to someone!" she shouted at him angrily. He was so amused by his little stunt that he was completely unprepared when she hit out at his shoulder with the palm of her hand. He nearly fell off his stool.

"Ruby, I'm just encouraging safe sex by highlighting the consequences of teenage pregnancy!" he reasoned, still smiling.

"So why can't you just say, 'Ruby, use a condom!'" she bellowed at him as he laughed.

"Ruby, you will always do the opposite of whatever I say, just to defy me. I figure if I tell you I want lots of grandchildren you will ensure I never have any," he chuckled.

"Oh brilliant! We haven't even done anything, Alessi!" she grumbled resentfully. "Apparently your son respects your wishes more than he respects mine!"

"Glad to hear it," he nodded back, looking pleased. "I just hope it stays that way." Ruby shook her head at him, unimpressed.

"Why do you hate sex so much?" she asked openly and he choked on a mouthful of coffee.

"Ruby! I don't hate sex, thank you very much, far from it! I just want you to be careful and I don't want you to get hurt." She didn't look convinced and he sighed. "Look," he seemed uncomfortable. "When my marriage broke down I lost all faith in the opposite sex. I was sure women were just out to cause pain and so, I'm very ashamed to admit it, but I wasn't very respectful for quite a time. I ended up hurting quite a few women"

"OMG! What did you do to them?" she squealed, looking scared, and he held his hands up quickly.

"Oh no, Ruby, I never hurt anybody physically," he defended. "No, I mean, I happily moved from one woman to the next without much care for their feelings. As far as I was concerned, if they were willing to give in to my advances, they were fair game."

"Jeez, Alessi, you were a...player?" she whispered, her expression one of sheer astonishment. "It's not that I don't think you have the looks for it but you just seem so...charming...and...straight."

"What's that supposed to mean?" he asked her, looking put out. "What, like, as opposed to kinky?" he smiled cautiously.

"Oh my god, Alessi, I don't want to know if you're kinky!" she protested, scrunching her eyes tightly shut. He reached up and grabbed her hands to pull them away from her ears.

"Ruby, I am *not* kinky!"

"Look whatever fetish stuff you get up to in your own time, that's your..."

"RUBY! Will you pack it in! How on earth did you get from me trying to convince you that I'm looking after your best interests to me being sexually deviant?"

"Oh no, Alessi, I've got images and everything now!" she squealed, covering her eyes and bringing her knees up to hide behind them. He sighed. She was such hard work sometimes.

"Ruby!" he called out, but she was still battling the pictures of him being very bad and predatory-like in his office with beautiful young women. "Ruby," he called her more softly and she lowered her hands and looked him in the eye, blushing heavily.

"Sorry," she apologised and he smiled, trying desperately not to laugh at her.

"Look, when I met Lilliana, Danny's mother, we were very young. We married early and we were only seventeen. Our families were very traditional and we were eager to get closer - marriage was the only way to do that. We had only ever been with each other and I loved Lilliana very much. I had a great amount of respect for her. We had Danny when I was twenty and we split up when he was just three. I wasn't much older than Danny is now when I went off the rails. As long as the girl was legal and willing I took her back to the office or to a hotel...or my car. Heck, if I'm being totally honest the only place I wouldn't take her was back to my place. Home is special, private, and it's always been my son's home too. Well, you know, while he was with me. I would never have brought a woman back here that I didn't intend to commit to, Ruby." He paused and the seconds felt like an eternity. "I've never brought a woman back here -

do you understand what I'm saying?" She nodded sadly. He had never found anyone special after his wife and now she felt terrible for him. That was so lonely. "If Danny was like I was back then you, Ruby Palmer, would have been spun the lines you desperately wanted to hear. You'd have been sucked right in, used for the fun of it and then spat right back out again. I can't bear to think of anybody doing that to you."

"But Danny wouldn't do that to me," she protested and he smiled a strained smile and nodded sympathetically at her.

"Any man could do that to you," he told her, moving off his stool and going back to the vegetables.

He slid the diced carrots into a pan and popped the lid on with an air of finality and then turned back to Ruby, who was still processing what he'd told her. "Right, anyway, from your little moan can I gather that you're also jealous of me and Tabitha?" he asked, changing one difficult subject onto another difficult subject. She nodded. "What's there to be jealous of, Ruby?"

She shrugged. "I'm not sure...are you seeing each other?"

"I like her, Ruby, but I'm not sure she feels the same way. Nothing's really happened...but if it had..."

"And when it does, which it will, you won't want me here anymore. I'll be out," she concluded resentfully.

"No, Ruby, why would you say that? I want you here for as long as you'll stay. You're like the daughter I always wanted. I know I'm not your dad and I can't replace that...that...blood line, but I would really like to try and give you what you would like a dad to be." She looked at him cautiously and he made his way back to the stool and sat opposite her again.

"Seriously?" she asked him, and he nodded.

"I didn't take your father away without a considerable amount of thought. That night when Danny was there and your father pinned you down, called you the most awful things and then beat you, that was the last straw. The first straw was hearing what your life was really like for the very first time, the night I bugged you because you'd seen my private

175

clients and looked at their file. He chucked you out of the house after hitting and grabbing you so hard he left bruises on your wrists and face. It made me feel sick listening to it and not being able to help you. You hid the marks very well, Ruby, a pro I imagine after years of putting up with it. He left you no choice but to wander the streets for three hours or go and find some willing person to take you in. Matthew was always willing wasn't he, for a price?" he asked her and she shook her head, stubbornly.

"We just mucked about - it wasn't anything serious, and I *never* did anything for money, Alessi!"

"That's not what I meant, though you did go to him for safety when it was cold and dark. He might not have got anything 'too serious' for his troubles but he certainly pushed for it and he definitely got enough as far as I'm concerned. You should never have been made to feel that way. You should never have been put in that kind of terrible dilemma and you never will be again, I promise. This is your home, Ruby, and that will never change."

25
New recruit

The following day Ruby woke in her bed, tucked in and feeling more well rested than she'd felt in weeks. She stretched out and then slowly got herself ready. Alessi had driven in to work early for an appointment, having decided to advertise for a trainee in accounts. The interviews were set to start first thing, before Tangle & Alessi opened for business.

Danny and Ruby made their way in together and Ruby filled him in about the conversation she'd had with Alessi the night before. He laughed in places, teased her and then went quiet when she talked about Tabitha and how he had never been close to anyone since Danny's mum. Ruby guessed he felt sorry for his father and she leaned in towards him and gave him a reassuring hug. Her sudden warmth and affection brought him round and he put his arm round her and kissed the top of her head. She felt warm, safe and free of the dreaded Paradise, but nothing could quite match the feeling that she was loved.

They got to the firm and Danny held the door open so Ruby could go first. She stepped inside but came to an abrupt halt causing Danny to bump right into her.

"Hey, Ruby, great to see you, it's been ages. How you doing?" a young man greeted her from the lobby. "I heard from Sasha that you've been ill." It was Matthew and Ruby felt more than a little uncomfortable, sandwiched between him and Danny. "You must be Danny, nice to meet you. I've heard a lot about you," he told him, reaching his hand past Ruby's waist and brushing against her as he did so. Danny took it and shook as Ruby continued to stand deadly still and awkward.

"What are you doing here?" she asked him sounding a bit ruder than she'd intended to be. He laughed at her as he looked her up and down, in the same way he always had.

"Job interview, pretty sure it went well," he told her, full of his usual arrogance.

"Job interview?" Ruby echoed. "You? Here? In accounts?" she exclaimed, and he laughed again.

"Yes, Ruby. Me. Here. In accounts. Nothing gets past you, does it?" he laughed and Danny immediately put his hands on her middle, not liking the suggestion that she wasn't clever.

"Shall we go, Ruby?" he asked, pushing her right towards Matthew so he had to step back out of the way. "Nice to meet you, Matthew, and good luck with the job...or finding another one."

"Thanks but I don't really need the luck, Danny, Mr Alessi just offered it to me on the spot. I start immediately. I'm just going out to put a longer car parking ticket on my car. I don't want to get into trouble on my first day do I?" he chuckled, winking at Ruby and grinning at Danny. They both stood and stared at him, speechless. "It will be nice working so closely with you, Ruby," he smirked, rolling his lips like he might just prey on her before extending his car parking ticket. Ruby felt Danny step forward slightly and she stepped back into him to keep him from reacting. As soon as the door closed and Matthew was out of sight, she turned and flew up the stairs. Destination: Alessi's office.

"What the hell do you mean you offered him the job on the spot? Why would you do that?"

"I've never actually met the guy, Ruby. I've only ever heard his voice and he never told me he knew you," Alessi defended. "I've already offered it to him now and he's accepted so it's a legally binding contract. I can't back out...well not easily anyway. Oh Ruby... just...just stay away from him," he advised tiresomely. "He probably won't last the three month probation period anyway, not now I know who he is. Look, the building is a fairly big place and there's no reason for him to be up here - he works in accounts, remember?"

She raised her eyebrows and scoffed at him. "So does she and she's up here all the bloody time!" she pointed out, gesturing towards Tabitha who was pulling files from the cabinet. Tabitha looked over briefly and then looked away again.

"Tabitha..." Alessi pointed out slowly, like Ruby should use her name rather than refer to her as 'she', "...also works for me and that's why she's up here a lot."

"Yeah and the rest," Ruby commented under her breath, and Alessi leaned forward and growled at her.

"Quit it, Ruby," he warned. "Matthew's hired and that's final. If he gives you any grief let me know. If you want me to have a word with him, I will, but just give it a chance."

"But why does he have to work here alongside me and Danny? It's like working with your boyfriend *and* your ex!"

"Unfortunately in life, Ruby, things get awkward sometimes. What matters is how you deal with it."

"Oh right it does, does it?" she asked him antagonistically. "Well you just see how I deal with this, Alessi!" She stormed off and he called after her but she didn't even bother to look back. He slumped back into his seat and rubbed his temples, wishing Tabitha hadn't witnessed any of it. When he dared a look in her direction she was gripping onto the cabinet drawer for support. He smiled and she finally found her voice.

"Are you sure, Alessi? She's so not like me at all...she's...she's scary!"

He laughed and called her over to sit down and recover.

Ruby slammed about in a strop until lunch time and then, after receiving a text message from her best friend, Sasha, suddenly cheered up quite a bit. She rapped on Alessi's office door and pushed it open before he had given her permission to come in. He looked up from his papers, his eyes dark and tired now.

"I didn't say you could come in," he pointed out.

"Yeah but you were about to..." she began and he held his hand up to stop her.

"Ruby, when do you think you and Danny will get the hang of how knocking works? There is no point to knocking if you don't intend on waiting to be invited in. It's about courtesy and PRIVACY," he told her angrily. Now he was in a strop. She shrugged.

179

"Yeah if you say so, anyway, what time are we leaving this evening because I've been invited to a fancy dress party at Sasha's house and I need to be home, changed, and at hers by 8pm."

"You're not going," he told her flatly just as Tabitha came up behind Ruby and slipped by to collect a box of closed files from beside Alessi's desk.

"She didn't knock," Ruby pointed out and Tabitha stopped what she was doing and hesitated. She didn't realise she had to. Alessi waved his hand at her to carry on and Ruby huffed, her mouth dropping open at his casual and unfair enforcement of the rules. Clearly he had favourites and now she was glaring at Tabitha, it was obvious why she was one of them. She snapped her accusing gaze back towards her boss.

"I am going," she nodded defiantly, but annoyingly he stayed calm.

"You're not going, Ruby, you're busy tonight...you have a tutor coming."

"No I don't!" she protested. "You never said anything about studying tonight!"

"Well that's because, until just now, you weren't going out. Obviously if you're feeling energetic and strong enough to go out partying with your friends you must be over the worst of your recent...ordeal..." he put it tactfully, glancing to make sure Tabitha wasn't clocking on to anything that she shouldn't be. "So, I shall be making arrangements for someone to come and teach you something useful, perhaps some manners?" he suggested.

"No way!" she argued. "I'm going out."

"We're staying late, you can't," he tried again and she glared at him.

"As if that's going to work, Mr Alessi, there's more than one way to get home you know."

"You are not to leave this building without me, Ruby Palmer!" he shouted after her as she stormed out of his room and started slamming around again.

At 5.40pm it suddenly dawned on him that the place was pretty quiet and he hadn't heard any screaming, swearing or arguing for quite a while.

That's when he realised that Ruby was no longer in the building. He called her mobile to be told that she was home safe and sound; she'd taken a taxi and Bardo was with her. Alessi was relieved to know she was safe and well, but also furious that she had made the journey between the two places by herself, a journey that could have seen her easily picked up by Marlon. He slammed his office phone down and shouted at Danny to hurry it up. After telling him they were staying late he was now telling him that they were leaving...early! He wanted to get home and straighten Ruby out before she snuck out against his strict instructions.

26

She shall go to the ball

"And what are you meant to be?" he frowned, hands resting on his hips. He'd just walked in, thrown his keys in the direction of the coffee table and started on her immediately. Ruby turned away from the mirror at the bottom of the stairs to glare at him briefly.

"*I* am a honey bee, thank you for noticing, Alessi," she quipped sarcastically, turning back to adjust her feeler headband.

"Wow, Ruby, you look awesome!" was the next and more favourable comment. She turned to smile at Danny who, unlike Alessi, had walked in and thrown his briefcase and blazer down on the sofa. Alessi scowled at him. "What?" he asked, oblivious to the two things that were most bugging his father; one being the blatant disrespect for coat hooks and the other how Ruby was dressed. Danny shrugged it off. "You look so hot. I might have known you'd dress up as a wasp, what with the nasty little sting you've got," he smirked. She placed her hands on her waist, just above her little black netted tutu skirt, and huffed at him.

"I'm a blinking honey bee, Danny!"

"No way, Ruby," he chuckled. "You're definitely a wasp!" he told her proudly.

"No, I'll tell you what she is," Alessi cut in. "She is about to go back upstairs and change into being a Ruby. Jeans, skirt, pyjamas, I don't care! As long as it doesn't involve knee high socks, corsets or netted belts..."

"It's a tutu!" she protested indignantly.

"Call it what you want, Ruby, it's totally unacceptable!" he boomed back at her. "Go get changed, NOW!" he ordered.

"No way!" she snapped back, her rock solid defiance kicking in.

"I think she looks cute," Danny defended and Alessi sighed.

"So will every other bloke, Danny," he urged him to understand and Danny smiled awkwardly.

"I trust her, Alessi."

"So do I...I just don't trust them."

"So I have to wear jeans else men might look at me?" she asked in disbelief. "Basically, if I dress like this and they can't control themselves then that's my fault is it?" He stayed silent. He hated it when she was right. "If I dress in a sack they still win, Alessi, because then they get to control my wardrobe, my life and my freedom of choice." She was pointing at herself now; the honey bee was angry. "No way. I will wear what I want to wear, when *I* want to wear it! It's a fancy dress party and *I* am going as a honey bee!"

"You are not leaving this house like that!" he told her firmly.

"Are you stopping me?" she asked him, her jaw angled defiantly. He wasn't about to get physical with her so he backed up a little, trying to gain at least some control of the situation.

"Of course I'm not...but just so long as you know...I'm not taking you," he confirmed, raising his eyebrows and subtly pointing out that she had no other way of getting into town...unless...unless...her eyes grew wide just as Alessi's closed wearily. He knew her inside out.

"Danny," she cooed turning on him and smiling sweetly. He melted just like Alessi knew he would. She moved to play with his tie, curling it around her fingers.

"They're bad news on that estate, Ruby," Alessi tried to get their attention.

"They are my friends. Sasha is my friend. She invited me to her fancy dress party and I'm going. On my very last day of school, right before I came looking for a job at your firm, I was so scared everybody would move on without me and that I'd be forgotten. I so badly didn't want to be on my own and for my friends to leave me, but it's been the other way round. I've moved on. I'm the one who left and I miss Sasha. I haven't seen her in ages, Alessi!" she protested, desperately wishing he would just understand for once.

"And why is that, Ruby?" he asked, reminding her that she had been out of action for quite a while and in no state to see anybody, let alone Sasha.

"Are you saying the Paradise thing is my fault? I didn't ask to be hooked on that stuff. Marlon injected me against my will!"

"Yes I know that but he wouldn't have been able to inject you against your will if you hadn't given him the opportunity to do so. He certainly wouldn't have injected you against your will while you were sat here on the sofa minding your own business. You walked into that situation of your own stubborn doing, Ruby Palmer. The situation was dangerous and risky, just like the situation you are planning on taking yourself into this evening."

"It's a party, Alessi, it's not the lion enclosure at London bloody Zoo!"

"Mind your language, young lady! It might only be a party but it's a party on a nasty estate on the edge of town, with a gang of trouble makers!"

"That nasty estate is where I come from. One of those 'trouble makers' is my best friend!"

"That estate is where you were dragged up; this is where you come from, Ruby," he told her, pointing towards the expensively tiled floor at her feet. "This is where you will grow into a fine young lawyer with prospects and influence and respect...not there!"

"You don't understand!" she huffed at him. "When I was being beaten every day, Alessi, where were you?" she didn't give him time to defend himself. "You were sat at a desk in your warm, comfortable office, that's where you were. Where was Danny? He was sat in the room next to yours being encouraged to do well, being given the support and love he needed and expected. I relied on Sasha and Matthew and his stupid little crew for love and support. I can't just pretend they don't mean anything to me. They took me in when I desperately didn't want to be on my own. Alessi, not everything is black and white, not everything is so easy to box up and chuck off a bridge when it's done with. Please, Alessi," she begged him, but he wasn't willing to back down.

"I will meet you halfway, Ruby. You go get changed and I will take you. I will wait for you outside and you can stay for an hour...just to say goodbye. Maybe if you say goodbye you will be able to move on. Oh, and just so you know, I will be taking my gun and if anyone so much as looks at you the wrong way I shall take him out...and that includes Matthew. I will just have to advertise for a new assistant in accounts."

"Ughhh!" she screamed at him in frustration and swung round to storm off. As she reached for the front door he spoke again.

"Walking out, Ruby?" He was so smug sometimes! "Just remember what happened the last time you did that and don't blame me when you get hurt again. Don't resent me when I have to be hard on you to put right the damage that's been caused. Just remember who will be left trying to pick up the pieces of your life and, while you're at it, also remember that some damage can't be fixed. You are the most pigheaded little girl I have ever known and maybe one day these hard lessons you are being faced with will actually do you some good. Maybe they might teach you something."

"So I deserve everything I get then?" she asked waiting for an answer, but none came. Painful tears stung at her eyes. She turned the handle and yanked the door open, slamming it hard behind her.

"Hey," she heard the soft familiar voice of Danny as he slipped alongside her, placing his arm around her shoulders to give her a warm, strong hug. She was sitting on the top step out front, her face buried in her knees, and she lifted her head to wipe her eyes and sniff. "Are you crying?" he asked, surprised. She shook her head but she wouldn't look at him either. "Hay fever then?" he asked with a cheeky grin and she nodded and giggled. "Here," he passed her purse and jacket to her and she frowned up at him, sniffing again.

"Why would I need these?" she asked feebly. He grinned and swung his car keys around his finger.

"Because Alessi isn't the only one with a car and I completely understand what you were saying in there. I'm not going to lie, Ruby, I hate that estate and I hate Matthew and his crew too. I think Sasha is OK but she's constantly led you into risky situations and encouraged you to get into vulnerable states in the name of fun. Then, when you're unable to look after yourself properly, she's nowhere to be found and you're left to handle the creeps you've attracted all on your own. I rescued you from a nightclub on your seventeenth birthday remember, right after you carried out her 'drink the first fit bloke under the table' mission. You were being harassed by some drunken idiot twice your age, Ruby, and she was too busy having fun with your so called 'friends' to notice. She didn't even know that I'd taken you from the club. Anything could have happened to you, Ruby."

"I know," she whispered regretfully and he sighed and smiled.

"Look, I've texted Mario and he's promised he'll be there all evening, and that he'll keep an eye on you. I'm pretty sure we can trust Sasha's big brother to do that. I've given strict instructions that I'm to be called to come and pick you up and you're not to be leaving or getting into cars with *anyone*. If you promise to be careful, Ruby, and to look after yourself and not be stupid then I will take you. But you have to promise that nothing will happen because I'd never forgive myself. Alessi would never forgive me either. He just cares about you, Rubes, that's all," he explained and she nodded and smiled.

"I know...and...I promise, Danny. I will be on my absolute best behaviour. Nothing will happen. I'll stay in the house and I won't even go upstairs!" she giggled.

He shook his head at her wearily. "Don't even joke about it, Ruby, my imagination is already working overtime here, all the possible things that could happen to my little honey bee. I'll kill anyone who messes with you, got it?" She nodded, wide eyed. He sounded serious. "You can tell Matthew to keep his grubby hands off your little netted belt too!"

"It's a tutu!" she argued, sounding exasperated. He grinned and cupped her face gently before kissing her softly on the lips.

The thirty minute drive was uneventful as she sat snuggled and warm in Danny's passenger seat. As they pulled onto the estate she took in the familiar hang out areas and the hooded figures loitering in bus shelters. Two girls pushed their prams over the zebra crossing in front of them and Danny turned and raised his eyebrows at Ruby as he waited patiently for them to get to the other side.

"Could have been you and Matthew," he told her romantically and she punched him in the arm and told him to shut up.

As they pulled into one of the many side roads Ruby was suddenly very quiet. They were passing her old home. It had never looked great, one in a row of houses that all looked exactly the same from the outside, but seeing it all run down, the creepers in the garden reaching right up and over the fence, the windows boarded and spray graffiti on the gate, made her sigh. The house looked sad, the end of an era and a very painful part of her life. Inside she felt a pang and it brought with it such horrible memories that her skin turned cold. Danny was watching her and he placed a reassuring hand on her knee.

"It's all in the past, baby," he smiled kindly, as if reading her mind. She took a deep breath and nodded as he turned the corner and parked up.

27

An uncomfortable conversation

Sasha opened her front door, dressed like a schoolgirl, and bounced up and down eagerly as she beckoned for Ruby to hurry up and get inside. Danny walked her up the path and Mario shoved Sasha to one side so he could get out onto the step to greet them. The two young men shook hands and then gave each other a jovial hug and a firm pat on the back. Ruby hadn't realised, until sharing her traumatic story about John Billingham's cruel bullying at school, that Danny had been in the same year as Mario and John. They had known each other very well.

"She's in safe hands, Danny, trust me," Mario reassured. "I'll watch over her like I'd watch over my own girl. I'm in all night so I'll be keeping it under control. Anyone kicks off and they'll have me to deal with. I won't take no crap, man."

"Cheers, Mario, I appreciate it...oh and no alcohol for Ruby," he requested. Ruby stared at him in wide eyed humiliation.

"Danny, do you mind?" she whispered angrily.

"I think you've had enough poison coursing through your body, Rubes - it could do with a bit of a break," he smiled at her stroppy little posture.

"What poison?" Mario was eager to know and Danny shook his head.

"Paradise, Mario, and we've been to hell and back getting her clean, so, no more substances please. Turning back to his honey bee he spoke to her sternly. "Rubes, honestly, you'll give yourself a heart attack...if you don't give me one first!"

"Ruby, Ruby, Ruby," Mario echoed, just like he always had and Ruby counted down in her head, as she waited for his usual line. "Trouble just seems to follow you about." There, it was out! "You're a naughty little wasp do you know that?" he chuckled.

"I'm a honey bee actually, Mario," she told him cheekily before pushing her way past and letting Sasha grab her hand to pull her into the kitchen. Mario grinned after her and then looked back to Danny.

"She's hot, mate. I can see why you're worried but you have my word, I'll look after her. I always have and I always will. Ruby's had it tough and I have a lot of time for her."

"Is Matthew here?" Danny asked him and Mario grinned again, reading his mind.

"Nah, mate, apparently he's staying at home tonight. My younger brother, Marcus, has gone round to play some new game with him. I tell you, I'm worried about my little bro. If Marcus don't sort himself out soon he'll still be playing X-Box when he's the same age as me! I'm hoping now Matthew's got himself a proper job at your firm Marcus will shape up and find himself one too. My mum and dad are going out of their minds worrying about him and this crew business. They've had some new members join and they've been getting into some serious trouble recently, making themselves a real pain in the arse on the estate - you know."

"Like what?"

"I'm not talking petty stuff, Danny, I'm talking intimidation, threats and basically making trouble for everyone. My dad hardly lets Sasha out these days. He keeps her working at his place all the time, answering phones, faxing, filing, you name it, he gets her to do it. She's knackered and desperately trying to find herself another job, bless her. My dad's worried that her only options are either working for him or hanging about on the estate late at night. Who knows what she'll get caught up in then! She's always followed Marcus about but now there's no Ruby so she's knocking about with some new girls, proper mouthy they are too. Not like Ruby. Ruby's mouthy but she's straight, you know, she don't go nicking stuff and doing people over. She's a good girl really." Danny nodded and shook Mario's hand again.

"Yes she is. Call me when it's all winding up yeah?"

"For sure," Mario reassured him, closing the door as Danny climbed back into his car. He sat wondering whether to wait it out or go home. He didn't feel comfortable. Something felt wrong, but he trusted Mario and he couldn't keep Ruby caged all her life; caging wild things was always wrong. Begrudgingly, and with an ache in his chest, he put the car into gear and made for his apartment to wait it out.

Mario made his way to the kitchen and quickly swapped the bottle of vodka Ruby had her hand rested on for a plastic bottle of Tizer. She rolled her eyes at him.

"Tizer? Are you serious, Mario?"

"Never been more serious, babe. Paradise is nasty stuff - how the hell did you get yourself hooked on that?"

"Long story...and I didn't do it on purpose either," she defended. "Someone forced it on me - I had no choice," she explained, pouring herself some of the red fizzy drink and giving it a sniff. When she looked up Mario was frowning at her.

"Are they looking after you properly, Rubes?" he asked, referring to Alessi and Danny and she smiled and nodded.

"Yes, Mario, but I don't think my life will ever be risk free...let's just say that. I think you're right - me and trouble, well, we kind of go hand in hand," she squinted playfully and Mario leaned onto the breakfast bar. He pushed some of the bottles aside to peer at her more closely. She fidgeted, wondering what to do and wishing Sasha would hurry up and find the CD she'd gone looking for in her bedroom.

"Hmmm, Matthew's going to kick himself for missing this party. I'd be so hacked off if I was told I'd missed a party where Ruby Palmer was dressed up as a naughty little honey bee," he teased.

"Just a honey bee, Mario," she corrected. "I'm being good so don't go getting any ideas...got it?" She was firm but he could tell she was nervous. He straightened himself and chuckled, holding up his hands submissively.

"Best behaviour, Ruby. The last person I want to piss off is Danny Glover, I like my limbs," he told her arching his brow. She nodded, wondering how much he knew about Danny.

"I'll just go and wait for Sasha in the living room then," she excused herself.

She was hoping to gain some relative safety in the darkness and heavy beats thrumming through from the open plan lounge/dining room but, unfortunately, she felt just as uncomfortable in there. But this was a different kind of discomfort, a much more sinister type. She could handle Mario and his flirtatious, harmless comments, but in the living room things were heavy. She immediately felt out of her depth. The sofa and two armchairs were almost hidden beneath a large group of young males. Some she recognised as part of Matthew's old crew and some were new faces. They looked her over and made comments between themselves. She turned to look into the dining room where music was playing and girls were dancing, drinking and smoking. Sasha's parents would flip if they saw them smoking in the house.

Ruby folded her arms and dug her phone from her purse, not quite sure why but liking the feel of it in her hands. It felt reassuring.

"Hey," one of the young men called to her and she looked back at them but said nothing. "Ruby Palmer isn't it?" a dark clothed figure in a peaked cap asked her. The peak was low and it was hard to see his face properly. She nodded. "I heard you deserted?" he asked her and her body immediately froze. She suddenly felt overwhelmingly sick and very hot. She looked away without saying a word and willed Sasha to come and save her. She would have gone looking for her but she'd promised Danny she would stay downstairs. "Hey," he called her again and she ignored him this time. He continued anyway. "You should never turn your back on your crew, do you know that? You don't know how lucky you were to be part of a family, to have brothers and sisters that looked out for you. Things could have been so much harder, Ruby Palmer," he told her like he knew it all and she spun round and glared at him.

"Harder? Do you have any idea what you're talking about?" she snapped and his friends laughed, jeered and clicked their fingers.

"Oooooh" he laughed. "I heard you were feisty, not one to take it lying down."

"Right, did you also hear that I never actually deserted then? My dad was shot in my own home you...you...idiot!" She was furious. "Where was

I supposed to go? I'd just turned seventeen and the council weren't about to give me the house were they? Even if they had, do you think I'd have stayed in the place my dad was murdered? Why don't you just shut up you stupid little boy!" she fumed and they heckled her, laughing and enjoying the entertainment.

"OK calm down, angry little bumble bee. I just thought you should know that you were wrong to turn your back on your roots, on your friends, on the people who've looked out for you. You're hot, little girl, and I heard you were never initiated. I think that's a bit unfair - being cute should never be enough to get you off the hook. Matthew had a soft spot for you, claimed you early on as his own and kept you from ever being set a task, didn't he?" he badgered, but she stayed quiet. It was true. She was the only one who hadn't had to do something disgusting or dangerous to be a part of the group; she was just part of it, simple as. "Now, if I'd been in charge, I'd have seen to it that you were put through your paces, bumble bee, proved how committed you really were. People who fail initiations are weak, Ruby, their hearts just aren't in it and then, when they get a better offer, they desert. When the pressures on, they talk. They grass, Ruby. People who aren't initiated can't be trusted. At the very least you should have been punished for turning your back."

She moved to lean against the wall and concentrate on the dining room again. She tried not to make eye contact with the girls, dressed in sexy little themed outfits. They seemed quite interested in her. She toyed with the phone in her hand and then unlocked it and messaged Danny, telling him she didn't like it and she wanted to come home. She then locked it again just as Sasha bounced up to her in a burst of excitement, giving her a hug and offering her a bottle of drink. Ruby passed on the alcohol and Sasha held up the CD.

"I'm just going to put this on it's got some absolute tunes on it! See if the guys want a drink, yeah," she ordered, turning to the lads and calling out. "This is Ruby, she's my best friend, so be nice to her. She'll get you all a drink," she offered before disappearing into the dining room.

Feeling like she was wading through treacle, Ruby turned back to look at the boys, who were all waiting to see what she'd do.

"What do you want?" she asked them resentfully.

"We'll all have a lager, bumble bee," the one in the peaked cap smirked and she moved to go into the kitchen. "They're in the back garden, keeping cold," he informed her and she stopped, turned, and placed her hands on her hips, desperately trying to feel brave.

"I'm not going outside," she told him firmly. "I promised I'd stay in the house. I'll get you something from the kitchen, but I'm not going in the garden." The one in the cap continued to check her out slowly.

"Worried someone might come get you?" he asked her, and she ignored him moving back into her position against the wall. Mario popped his head in.

"Hey, babe, I'm going upstairs to make a quick call to my girl. I can't hear a thing down here. I'll be fifteen minutes, tops. Can you keep yourself out of trouble for fifteen minutes do you think, Ruby?" he asked her with a chuckle and she smirked and nodded as he disappeared back through the doorway. Sasha came bounding back over, completely in love with the track she'd just put on.

"Hey, Rubes, come and dance, the boys will love it!" she exclaimed but Ruby shook her head and resisted the tug of Sasha's hand. The last thing she'd be doing at this party was dancing. The other girls were chatting between themselves and they were all still looking at her, between drinking, dancing and dragging on their cigarettes. She willed Danny to go faster.

"I tell you what we'd love more, Sasha," the lad in the peaked cap spoke up. "We'd like a bloody drink! What kind of party leaves its guests without a drink, Sasha?" he complained. She stopped and turned to look at Ruby, confused.

"But I thought..." she trailed off. Usually Ruby was friendly and more than happy to help out.

"She refused to go outside and get us all a can, Sasha. She thinks going out in the dark and cold is beneath her. She's moved on to better things,

193

remember," he laughed and his mates laughed too. Sasha looked hurt and Ruby tried to defend herself.

"I said I'd get them something from the kitchen, Sasha," she explained. "It's just that I promised Danny I wouldn't go upstairs and that I wouldn't leave the house either. You have no idea how hard it was to get here tonight. I had to compromise on some things to keep Danny and Alessi happy. I even fell out with Alessi over this!" she appealed to her friend desperately. Sasha thought about it, nodded, and then turned back to the boys.

"Don't be nasty to Ruby! We go a long way back and I love her. If she can't go outside then she can't go outside - don't be mean to her! She said she'd get you something from the kitchen. She doesn't think it's beneath her so shut up. If you're going to be like that then you can just leave - go round Matthew's house and have a go at him for not turning up tonight. We hardly ever see him anymore and this is supposed to be *his* god damn crew. Just leave Ruby alone - she's been through enough. If you want lager so badly and you're too bloody lazy to get it yourselves then I'll go," she snapped. "I'll be back in a minute, Ruby," she told her friend softly before disappearing off into the kitchen.

Ruby's face was burning and she could feel all eyes concentrated on her now. She wasn't sure how much longer she could take the pressure and she glanced at her phone, willing Danny to hurry up. It had been fifteen minutes since she'd texted him. Perhaps she should have rung - maybe he hadn't even seen the message! It only took twenty minutes by car from his place. She scrolled through her phone and found his number. Just as she was about to press 'call' and beg him to come and get her, the doorbell rang. The relief was immense and she made straight for the hallway without turning back. She grabbed at the handle in a panic. Danny would save her from it all, he would take her home and she would never go against his or Alessi's advice again. She swung the door wide, almost in tears, but there was nobody there.

28
Punishment

She leaned out to look left and then right but it was dark, cold and deserted; there was nobody in sight. She was confused and about to close the door and call Mario to come and stay with her, when suddenly a strip of tape was pressed over her mouth from behind and a sack was pulled over her head. She tried to struggle and scream but it was pointless, as she was slung over somebody's shoulder and taken out into the dark. She beat at the strong back but her arms were trapped inside the sack and she couldn't get at him properly.

Soon she could feel that they had stopped moving and she could hear whispers. She tried to work out what was being said and whether she recognised any of the voices, but then she was passed and slung over another shoulder. This one felt bigger, higher and stronger than the last and she squealed and cried. What the hell was happening to her? He spun around a couple of times and she quickly lost all bearings. When they started moving again she had no idea what direction they were headed in.

She heard the sound of an awkward gate and she knew then that she was being taken to somebody's house. A renewed wave of fighting started; she was so fierce that he nearly dropped her, and then she heard a door slam and she was inside. Her captor threw her to the ground and she fought her way out of the sack and grabbed at the tape on her mouth, ripping it off quickly and crying out when it hurt.

The place was in darkness, the floor cold and covered in splinters of glass, bottle tops and fag ends. It stunk and she couldn't see a thing other than a wall of mobile phone lights as people recorded what was happening to her. She shielded her eyes and tried to slip backwards but a large man dropped down over her and gripped her chin tightly. All she could make out was that he felt big when she shoved her hands up against his chest, trying to keep him at arm's length. He was wearing a balaclava so that only the whites of his eyes and the glint of his teeth showed in the darkness.

"Mmmm, Ruby Palmer, when I was told that you were set to get a punishment for deserting I was more than eager to step up to the job. It seems a shame to wipe out such a pretty little bumble bee but bumble bees are pests, Ruby."

"No," she whispered, as she heard the sound of girls in the background laughing. Someone turned a torch on and that's when Ruby saw what she was really dealing with. A group of six, including her attacker, all wearing masks, bandanas and balaclavas as they looked on, eager to see something gruesome, and even more eager to have it recorded on their phones. She looked about and then screamed out as the terrifying realisation set in. She was in her kitchen, her dad's kitchen. She was in the boarded up house - she was home!

Her attacker picked up a broken bottle neck and pushed it into the palm of her hand before squeezing her fist tightly shut, cutting her deeply. She felt it slice through her skin and she gritted her teeth against the searing pain.

"What do you want from me?" she asked him. "Who are you?" She was sure there was something about him, something familiar, but with only his eyes and mouth exposed it was impossible to tell. She noticed a couple of figures lower their phones and make their way towards the back door; now there were only three. Though Ruby was sure at least two of them were girls, that still left her seriously outnumbered. But this was her house and she had hidden in it for sixteen years, trying to escape her abusive dad. She reasoned that she must have a slight advantage over them.

She squeezed the bottle neck in her hand again, the pain spurring her on, reminding her that every day of her childhood she'd been through worse, much, much worse. She took a deep breath, and as he moved to kiss her, she slammed the broken glass into his forehead. He yelled out and fell back onto the floor. The others gasped out and quickly crowded him to see what the damage was. They turned their backs on her as they tried to remove his mask, not wanting to risk her seeing his face. The last thing they wanted was any of the group being identified.

She wasted no time and moved silently. Keeping low, she headed straight for the living room. Within seconds she was over the back of the sofa, her familiar hiding place, although now it stunk of urine and stale smoke. She had hidden in the exact same place while her father snored on the sofa loudly, having forgotten that he had a beating to finish off. He would finally be defeated by the alcohol he'd drunk so much of and she would stay in the small cramped place until morning, waiting it out. The sofa was almost flat against the wall, the gap behind it tiny, but Ruby had always been small too and she fitted perfectly. She huddled, wishing she had her phone which she'd dropped at Mario's front door. Danny wouldn't have a clue where she was and she still didn't even know if he'd received her message. She sat and waited to see what her fate would be.

Danny reached Sasha's house only a few minutes after Ruby had been thrown to the kitchen floor. Mario was waiting for him at the door, his face pale, his breathing deep and fast.

"I've looked everywhere but I can't find her. I'm so sorry," he explained. Danny's expression turned furious.

"What? She's gone? You've lost her? What do you mean you've looked everywhere? You said you'd watch her! Where the hell is she, Mario?" he yelled at him. "She sent me a message saying she wasn't happy, she didn't feel comfortable. What happened?" he demanded fiercely as Sasha came to the door.

"Danny, I didn't realise until it was too late but I think maybe the guys were picking on her. I didn't think it was anything serious but they said she thought all this was beneath her, like she'd moved on to better things. I argued with them, put them straight. Mario had popped upstairs..."

"You left her!" he snapped turning on Mario now, who held up his hands defensively and took a step back.

"Just to go to the toilet...and make a call. I was fifteen minutes, tops. I just wanted to speak to my girl..."

"Yeah and I'd quite like to speak to mine, Mario! Stupidly I thought she'd be safe with you! They could be doing anything to her!"

"They sent her out to get alcohol," Sasha whispered now, feeling scared.

"So she went outside!" he exclaimed but Sasha shook her head, quick to stick up for her friend.

"No, Danny, she said she'd promised she wouldn't go upstairs or outside. She refused to go so...I went...but that meant she was inside on her own. When I came back in she was gone, the front door was open and this was on the floor..." she held Ruby's mobile phone out and Danny took it gingerly, not wanting to see the last thing she'd said or done. He was ready to explode when the screen display showed that she was about to press 'call' on his number. He ran his hands over his face, resisting a desperate desire to run out in to the estate shouting her name over and over. The area was huge, she could be anywhere. She could have been bundled into a car, taken to a house, an alleyway, an abandoned garage. Anything could be happening to her and he looked about helplessly. He walked to the end of the path, desperately trying to think, and then he turned back to look at the blank and distraught faces of Mario and Sasha. He looked to his left towards the road he had driven down and caught a glimpse of Ruby's old house. Sasha's house was just around the corner from Ruby's but the row of rooftops could be seen from the very end of Sasha's front garden.

"They've taken her home," he suddenly guessed and Mario didn't hesitate in ordering Sasha to stay inside, lock up, and wait. He was running and at Danny's side in seconds.

They found her; a masked face peered over the back of the sofa and a girl grabbed Ruby by the hair and pulled hard. The other grabbed her clothes and helped to yank her out. She tried to escape them but they were all claws and name-calling as they tore into her viciously. She swung at one and knocked her right off her feet. Then, feeling a rage strong enough to kill somebody, she grabbed the other round the neck and walked her backwards so fast she fell, slamming her head against the wall. Ruby wanted to stay and finish her off but she could hear two male voices in the hallway. She thought quickly and grabbed the unconscious girl's feet, dragging her to the far side of the room. She left her next to her friend, who was holding her covered face as if her nose was broken. Ruby grabbed a fistful of balaclava and hair from the top of her head, making her squeal, and whispered into her ear.

"Say a word and I will come back for you. I know some very nasty people and they will make your life hell, do you hear me?" she threatened, and the girl nodded and stayed quietly sobbing on the floor. Ruby moved to crouch under the table near the door to the kitchen and stayed hidden in the shadows. The boys entered the room to find one of their friends crying and the other lifeless. They immediately rushed to their aid and, as they did, Ruby slipped out and grasped the handle of the back door. She was so nearly free and then it would all be over. She would run back to Sasha's house and Mario would keep her safe until Danny came. But the backdoor wouldn't open. It was locked from the inside. She pulled again and searched for the key in the lock and on the floor but it wasn't there. She turned and rushed for the hallway and the front door, but it was nailed shut and the small window at the foot of the stairs was covered with a metal grille. She spun round in desperation; she was trapped, and the one who had carried her there and thrown her to the floor was now filling the doorway to the kitchen, smiling.

"Looking for this?" he asked her, swinging the back door key between his bloody fingers. She turned and bolted up the stairs with the hooded monster right on her heels.

"The rest of you stay down here," he boomed out at them as he chased her. "I'm taking over. She's mine now!" As she neared the landing, gasping for air and crying, he grabbed at her and she ducked sideways into her old bedroom, skidding across the floor and then falling to her knees. Her bedroom was the last place in the world that she wanted to be, the room where her father had tortured her relentlessly, the room where he had finally been shot and killed by Alessi. She was shoved from behind and she struggled for her life. He was rough now as he pushed her face down and yanked something around her wrists, tying them tightly behind her back. He turned her over and gripped her face. "I'm going to have fun with you, Ruby, give you the initiation you should have had years ago!" he snapped, throwing her head back so it hit the floorboards. She felt dizzy and close to being sick. "Then, when I'm done, I'll dish out your punishment for deserting. I'm not sure which I'm going to enjoy more," he sniggered, grabbing at the front of her dress like he was about to rip it right off. She screamed and struggled, the tears streaming down the sides of her face.

A whistle sounded and he let go of her like she'd burnt him. She hit the floor again, hard. While she struggled not to black out completely he sat up straight and listened. Three more short whistles sounded and he snarled. "Damn it! Out of time..." he was thinking now, the dilemma clear. "We'll have to skip straight to the punishment, Ruby," he informed her, yanking her to her feet and then lifting her up onto a low stool. "Move and you die," he warned, so she stayed as still as she could, but the dizziness threatened to topple her. She didn't have a clue what was going on. He placed something over her head and pulled her hair free. She was oblivious to the significance of the stool until he pulled the thing around her neck tighter, a slip knot, she panicked. She was caught in a noose. She began to struggle but then quickly realised she had to stay on the stool to keep from being strangled. The whistle sounded from outside again and, placing his hands on her waist, he paused and sighed like he was disappointed. He was admiring her, running his hands around her middle as he moved behind to whisper into her ear.

"Without an education, Ruby, there's no hope, no prospects. Without hope and prospects it's only a matter of time before somebody gets into trouble. I blame you, Ruby Palmer!" he snarled, before kicking the stool away and leaving her hanging.

The rope pulled tight, stopping her from getting a breath. She kicked her feet, trying to find something, anything, to take her weight. The stool was on its side but one of the three splayed out legs was just in reach and she used the toes of her right foot to push against it. It was just enough to create some slack but not enough to keep her breathing fully. Her lungs were struggling and her head was spinning; she was close to passing out. She knew she had to stay calm. If she panicked or wriggled she would use up her energy and oxygen levels even quicker, common sense told her that.

She needed oxygen more than anything right now. She stopped fighting and concentrated on getting the toes of her other foot onto the stool. Then she heard something; it was Danny - he was calling her name. She wanted to shout out to him but she couldn't, and her attacker was nowhere to be seen. Her voice was choked off every time she tried to scream and the tears streamed down the sides of her face as she attempted to push herself up and stretch herself as tall as she could. Then she heard Danny talking in the hallway.

"I just had a feeling that's all." He sounded defeated and lost and she desperately wanted to let him know she was there. If he left now she would lose her strength and the rope would take her life, if her attacker didn't come back and cut her down to draw out his punishment and carry out that initiation he'd promised her. She couldn't let that happen. She pushed herself up again, this time she was going to get his attention. Even if it was her last and only breath she had to give it a go, but she pushed too hard and the stool toppled away from her. Her feet swung and the rope pulled tighter, crushing against her windpipe. She was hanging, with absolutely no hope in hell of getting out of it.

Her ears pounded with the sound of her blood as her veins were pushed to bursting and this was how her life was going to end. She'd survived being beaten, she survived being shot, she'd even survived a lethal drug but now a length of rope was all it would take to steal her from the world and the people she loved. She couldn't reach up and grab the rope because her wrists were tied, and she could feel a warm sticky flow coming from the deep cut in her hand.

White spots flashed in front of her eyes and her head felt like it was going to explode, and then everything went black. It was over.

29

Danny stopped at the back door and closed it again. He'd heard a noise from the floor above, like something had toppled over and he wasted no time in running for the stairs, climbing them two at a time.

"It's probably a cat, mate." Mario tried to prepare him for disappointment. The place was derelict; it looked liked nobody – other than vandals and squatters - had been there for years. Even so he stayed close behind Danny as he headed straight for Ruby's bedroom. As Mario reached the top of the stairs Danny had grabbed at a swinging, lifeless body, lifting to take the weight and calling out to his friend.

"Mario, cut the rope or create some slack. I'm not sure if she's breathing!" He sounded breathless and Maio could tell she was heavy, a dead weight in Danny's arms. It didn't look good. Using the stool to gain some height, Mario slid the knot back in the noose and passed the rope over her head so Danny could lower her to the floor. He put his ear to her chest and held her limp wrist between his fingers, praying for a pulse. She was breathing and her chest was rising and falling. As he monitored her, and willed her to stay with him, the faint pulse he'd found started to pick up and she came round. As soon as she could she pushed herself up and huddled into Danny's arms, shaking and petrified.

"Who was it, Ruby?" Danny tried to get her to answer, but she shook her head as she cried.

"I didn't see their faces, Danny, they wore masks," she barely managed to speak, her voice hoarse and painful.

"I'm going to kill Matthew," he threatened, but she stopped him.

"No, it wasn't Matthew. He wasn't even at the party. It was a group I didn't know. I didn't recognise them." She swallowed hard and clenched her eyes tightly shut against the raw drag at the back of her throat. "They trapped me in a sack and carried me out of the house. I was passed to someone else. I don't even know if it was the same gang or whether they just delivered me to another one. Danny..." she whispered and he wiped her face and held her tightly, just relieved to have her back in his arms.

"Yes, baby, I'm here. What is it?" he asked her, feeling her shudder. She was completely traumatised and now quickly slipping into a state of shock.

"I think I know the one who carried me in here, the one who pinned me down and cut my hand, the one who tried to hang me..." she trailed off, shaking so badly her teeth were chattering.

"Ruby, who was it?"

"There was something about him, he was familiar, but I can't get my head to work. He said he blamed me, like he knew me. The size of him, the look in his dark eyes, his fat ugly lips, the tone of his voice, the feel of his hands as they held me, I recognised it all but I just can't get a name."

"Ruby, baby, perhaps your mind isn't ready. Perhaps when we get you home safe and sound his name will come to you and then we can deal with him. Believe me, Ruby, we will be dealing with him," he promised her. She nodded; that made sense. Perhaps she wasn't ready to know; perhaps her brain would drip the shocking reality in, to keep her from being overwhelmed by it all. It felt awful that the person who attacked her so viciously might be someone she knew. The characteristics kept coming back to her: his mouth, his voice, his slow, grazing leer. Until the name came to her she would feel vulnerable; until a name came *everyone* would be a suspect.

Danny noticed she had fallen very quiet and he held her tighter, waiting for the right moment to move her. She heard a whisper; it was Mario.

"What the...Danny...have you seen this?" he asked in disbelief, but as Ruby tried to turn her head towards the light that Mario was flashing around the room, Danny grabbed her head and held it firmly against his body. He wouldn't let her see.

"I think we should go. Turn the torch off, Mario!" he ordered sharply and Mario immediately did as he was told, twisting the maglite on his keys so they were plummeted back into darkness.

"What...what is it?" Ruby demanded, getting to her feet unsteadily and grabbing in the direction of Mario's keys. He let her rip them from his hands and she turned the light back on, pointing it at the floor. She gasped as she walked backwards, stepping out of a chalked outline of a body, a body labelled in red letters with *her* name. She then shone the light over towards the bed which had been stripped, the bloody covers recovered by forensics after her father's death. She was morbidly drawn to where her father had lost his life and moved closer, recalling the horrible details of the night he died, the night she nearly died too.

She flashed the light upwards and that's when she saw the graffiti marking her bedroom walls.

RIP Ruby Palmer! D.O.D. 1ˢᵗ September!

The walls were covered in the same message, painted in bright red letters that had run before drying. She turned back to Mario and Danny.

"1ˢᵗ September...but...that's today." She struggled to stay calm and Danny nodded while Mario looked at the floor guiltily. "This was all planned. This was prepared and ready for me," she fell quiet "...Sasha," she whispered. Mario snapped his head up to look her, shaking it determinedly.

"No way, Ruby, none of us had any idea about this. My god, I would never do anything like this to you. I like you, Ruby, I *really* like you. Sasha thinks the world of you. We were set up too. Danny, come on, I'm serious, man!" He sounded scared as he looked between the two of them and Ruby nodded as if she believed him as she turned to look back at the walls. It was impossible to comprehend that complete strangers would hate her so much that they'd want her...wiped out. "I was meant to die tonight," she declared flatly, right before passing out and hitting the floor, hard.

When she came round she was in the back of Danny's car and they were pulling up outside Alessi's house. No sooner had the car come to a standstill then Alessi had the door open and was scooping her out and into his arms. He carried her to the sofa and glanced over her, assessing her injuries quickly.

"Right, Danny, we're going to need steri-strips, surgical glue, gauze, alcohol swabs and antibacterial cream. I could also do with some cool water and a cloth...and perhaps some blankets too," he suggested, seeing Ruby shiver. Danny immediately left. He had already started moving towards Alessi's study, even before Alessi had finished talking. They both always seemed to know just what to do to put her and each other back together again after they'd been hurt.

"Alessi, I'm so sorry," she coughed painfully and he dropped to his knees beside her and looked at her like she was mad. "You were right, I shouldn't have gone and this is all my fault," she admitted tearfully. Danny arrived back, juggling all the things, and then held her good hand while Alessi dipped the cloth in water and began to dab at her neck.

"Ruby, I should never have insinuated that any of what's happened to you is your fault. I was angry, I spoke out of turn and I shouldn't have. That was a cruel thing to say to you and you absolutely did not deserve this tonight, do you hear me?" he told her firmly.

"You just feel sorry for me and you shouldn't. I'm going to change because if this is where feisty gets you then I don't think I want to be it anymore. I'm going to grow up. I won't ever argue with you again. I'm going to try really hard now not to be a bother or a burden..."

"Ruby, please shut up," he frowned and she sucked in air as he swiped an alcohol wipe over her neck. "Perhaps some pain killers might be a good idea, son," he smiled at Danny, who obediently disappeared off to the kitchen.

Alessi was lovely to her for the rest of the night and he, Danny and Bardo all stayed in the living room while she slept off her trauma on the sofa, swaddled in quilts. Every time she stirred, or needed a drink, or suffered a nightmare, they were all there in an instant, ready to take her order, offer their assistance or just provide comfort. When she woke in the morning, her eyes heavy and her body aching like she'd gone ten rounds with the Incredible Hulk, she was surprised to see Alessi and Danny already smart and tidy and ready for work. She pushed herself up into a sitting position.

"Where are you going?" she croaked, sounding worried. Alessi smiled and moved to perch on the sofa beside her so she wouldn't have to raise her voice. He ran a gentle finger over the marks on her neck.

"We are going in to work and Bardo is going to look after you. Danny and I will pop back at lunchtime and I promise we will be home on time this evening. You rest," he whispered. Her eyes darted between the two of them. Even her eyes hurt to move them and she whimpered.

"But I want to come," she told them. "I've missed so much already. Faye will be at my desk, taking over my job and then there's...Matthew", she suddenly remembered. "What are you going to do to Matthew?"

"We are going to talk to him and ask him what he knows, Ruby, that's all," Danny told her coolly, straightening his tie in the mirror and smoothing his eyebrows.

"He wasn't there, I swear. Please," she begged. "I don't want any trouble." Danny leaned over the back of the sofa and kissed her.

"I'll be good," he smiled and then, before she could strap herself into the car and make herself into a human obstacle, they were out of the door and pulling away from the house. She took a deep breath and fell back into the five pillows they had plumped up behind her head. Bardo smiled at her like the grinning, towering giant that he was. She felt safe with Bardo.

Danny and Alessi arrived at the office and made their way into reception to check their messages and collect their post.

"Matthew here yet?" Danny asked Amanda, and she stopped banging and stomping behind her desk to check her watch and shake her head.

"No and you two are early so he's not late either," she defended; unusual for her. It seemed Amanda did have a soft spot for some people. "He's due in by 9am, like everyone else, so I'm sure he'll be here any minute," she advised. Danny had been preoccupied with swapping some of his misfiled correspondence with Alessi but suddenly he stopped, spotting an ideal opportunity to grab Matthew. If he was on his way in, he could get to him *before* he reached the office. Alessi reached out to take a hold of his arm.

"Just remember to keep it tidy," he warned. "No unnecessary risks, you don't know the truth yet," he reminded him. Danny clenched his jaw, nodded stiffly and slipped his arm away, before heading for the door.

Matthew was climbing backwards out of his car, having stuck his car park ticket to the inside of his windscreen. He straightened and reached to close his door when suddenly he was grabbed from behind and slammed up against it. A hand was round his throat, gripping tightly, the fingers pushed into his neck...Danny's fingers. Still shocked he grabbed at his wrist to try and hold his arm back but the guy was seriously strong.

"You hear what happened to Ruby?" he asked him, and he barely nodded.

"Yes," he tried, but it was strangled off.

"You know who did it?" he demanded and this time Matthew shook his head. "Did you arrange for her to be set on?" he snarled. Matthew looked frightened but couldn't speak. Danny reluctantly released him but he stayed close enough to take his feet out from under him if so much as tried to escape.

"Danny, I heard on the estate this morning," he confessed, running his hands round his neck and pushing his tie back into place. "People are talking about it but I have no idea who it was, I swear. I would never hurt Ruby. You don't get it do you? I love her."

"Oh yeah, you love her!" Danny laughed. "I remember now, Matthew. That's why all you've ever been after is getting her into your bed."

"That's not true!" he argued and Danny shrugged.

"What, so you planned on doing it in other places too?" he snorted. "You're not really fussy about how or where are you, Matthew, to be honest, as long as you get it from whichever girl you happen to be pressurising, right?" Matthew stayed quiet and wouldn't look him in the eye. Danny hated men that couldn't do that; they were shifty, untrustworthy and full of bloody crap! "You don't know the meaning of the word love, Matthew! You think love is using a young girl who needs your help? I have no time for you and if I had a choice you wouldn't be within two feet of

Ruby. I tolerate you because Mr Alessi has employed you and I respect his wishes as a boss, but I don't agree with his choice of employee. I'd rather he hired a monkey to crunch the numbers than a creep like you! You're bad news and if I find out you had anything to do with Ruby..."

"I don't...I didn't...I haven't done anything wrong!" he butted in, looking scared enough to cry. Danny shoved him hard up against the car. He didn't feel sorry for him in the slightest. He was sure Matthew had made Ruby cry plenty of times in the past. It was his turn now.

"If I hear you had anything to do with it I will break every window in your precious little boy racer, every light, every mirror and then..." he was seething, his breathing controlled, but with a great deal of stamina, "and then, Matthew, I will break every bit of you," he promised, shoving him aside, reaching into his car and yanking out his ticket. "I will make your life hell, Matthew," he told him, scrunching up the sticky bit of paper. "You better get yourself another parking ticket if you intend to stay here or you'll get a fine," he told him, dropping the screwed up ball down the drain.

"Oh man, that cost me £6.50!" he complained. Danny turned back and smiled at him.

"Not as much as it will cost you if I find you've been bullying Ruby. She's with me and she's never going to be with you, Matthew, so get over it. She prefers men to boys, blokes that treat her with respect, blokes with prospects, blokes who can offer her a damn sight more than you can. You're a joke and she knows it; she sees that now," he told him, keen to pierce a hole in his inflated ego. He was mad for all the times Matthew had made Ruby feel inadequate. "She doesn't love you and in fact she never has. You served a purpose Matthew, that's all. It seems you're not as popular as you thought, and you're going to be even less popular if you're late for work because Mr Alessi doesn't take kindly to people swan in whenever they feel like it. You can say goodbye to your probation period if you're not at your desk in the next...what?" he checked his watch. "Two minutes. Good luck with that, Matthew!" he smiled, patting him on the shoulder and leaving him standing in the car park with his hands and legs shaking.

Matthew felt scorched and his pride had been seriously dented. He loathed the young, trainee solicitor as much as he desired Ruby. The only thing standing in the way of him getting her was Danny, and he had just offered up a challenge he couldn't refuse. He was going to make Ruby hate him. *This* was war!

30

Painful secrets

A few days later Ruby was up to coming back into work and Alessi was keen to make her feel more needed. He felt deeply sorry for her and wanted her to find her feet in the firm again as quickly as possible. He couldn't expect her to be responsible if she didn't feel responsible. She needed something to get her teeth into, something more professionally demanding than photocopying. Danny had been called to attend the police station and Alessi had left to go home early. Tabitha had the day off and Faye had been sent, by Danny, to check every single file in storage had been numbered and filed correctly. It wasn't something that needed doing but he didn't want any fatalities while he was out. He figured getting rid of Faye would be the easiest option.

Ruby was finally alone and able to get some work done in peace. She was preparing a witness statement for a client that Alessi had let her interview that morning. It was the first she'd ever done and, although she just needed to get the facts down on paper - a chronological sequence of events - it was the first fee-earning type job Alessi had ever given her. She was really flattered.

Having made good progress she decided on a break, nipping to the coffee room across the landing to flick the kettle on. Grabbing a cup from the stand she rummaged through the cutlery and dug a spoon from the drawer. Humming to herself, she reached up to look for the new box of tea bags on the shelf and was shocked when a pair of hands squeezed her waist. She jumped and squealed, turning to see Matthew standing behind her. She was flustered and seriously glad Danny wasn't at his desk.

"Matthew," she breathed at him, trying to stay calm. "You scared the crap out of me - don't do that!" she told him off. He grinned at her and looked her over.

"You're looking seriously hot, Ruby. It's been way too long. I was beginning to think I'd never see you again now you're no longer on the estate. I liked having you...literally...just round the corner," he laughed. She sighed and shook her head at him. His jokes were still not funny. "Sorry about what happened at the party, I heard all about it from Mario and Sasha. You must have been really scared."

"You didn't have anything to do with it...did you?" she asked, sounding less sure than she had been when she'd protested his innocence to Alessi and Danny.

"Babe, it had nothing to do with me. I have no idea who was involved and nobody is talking either. I've asked around and I want them sorted, Rubes - that was bang out of order doing that to you. I could have saved you from all that," he told her.

"Whatever, Matthew, just forget it. What's done is done and I want to move on now," she tried to dismiss him, hoping he'd go back to his desk downstairs.

"Shame," he grinned. "Do you know I've still not completed my list? I have one more name to get."

"Oh god," she cringed like she'd just seen something disgusting. "Please, Matthew, the list was gross and you made that at school. I think it's time you grew up. Perhaps you could even get yourself a girlfriend while you're at it. A real life one and not something made of plastic. Chuck the list in the bin, Matthew!" she ordered and he chuckled at her and reached out to put his hands on her hips. "Matthew, I'm serious, pack it in." She slapped his hands away. "You've had this job all of a few days and if Alessi catches you messing with me you're fired...not to mention what Danny would do to you."

"So you are with him then, Mr Infidelity himself?" he asked her.

"What does that mean?" she scowled and Mathew smirked like she was stupid, exactly what he'd always thought she was and how he'd made her feel.

"Infidelity, Ruby, means unfaithful," he explained slowly, like she wouldn't keep up if he didn't. She suddenly felt hot; she didn't like the way the conversation was going.

"I know what it means, idiot, what I meant was why would you say that about Danny?" He could see her cheeks had flushed; she was bothered. He reached forward and brushed her hair out of her face and behind her ear.

"Don't you know?" he tormented, and she turned her face away feeling angry with his stupid games. He'd always played games with her.

"If I bloody knew then I wouldn't be asking would I?" she hissed at him. He pretended to bite his nails as if he were scared. "Oh just get lost, Matthew, I'm not interested!" She turned away and began to make tea, trying to ignore the fact that he was still very close behind and watching her every move. He ran his fingers down her back and tugged on her hair to try and get her attention. Eventually she caved in, swinging back round. "What? Why did you say he was unfaithful?" She'd wanted to play it cool but she also wanted to know what Danny had been up to. Now she'd turned to face him he was able to run his fingers down into the V neckline of her shirt and she knew the deal; there was always a deal with Matthew. If she wanted something from him she had to give him something in return. "What do you want?" she asked him and he pulled her shirt towards him slightly so he could look down it. She closed her eyes and tried not to shudder.

"You, Ruby, that's what I want. You were always meant to be mine, do you know that? God I persevered with you for years but what did I get? Not much more than this, a bit of a muck about. You're a real tease, do you know that?" She refused to answer and had already planned her counterattack if he tried to do anything heavy. She'd just made a hot drink and she knew exactly where it was going if he went anywhere near her skirt. "OK, Miss Stroppy Pants, how about a kiss in exchange for some information, and you really want to know this, Ruby," he told her seriously. The internal conflict showed on her face and he removed her need to answer by stepping closer and placing his hand against her hot cheek while he pressed his lips to hers. She let him kiss her and then pushed him away.

"Now tell!" she ordered, almost in tears. He smirked. She could see he wanted to go back for more but she kept her hand on his shoulder and he stayed at arm's length.

"Did you know that Danny has been with six different members of staff here?" Her mouth dropped open and she shook her head in disbelief.

"You liar," she whispered.

"No, I'm not. You ask Mr Alessi. Apparently they were all being played at the same time too. None of them knew about it until the girls started to talk, as girls do. They did a united walk out and Mr Alessi had to go to an agency to cover his work. He wasn't very happy by all accounts and Danny has been the topic of conversation ever since. Some girls apparently like that kind of thing. Do you like bad boys, Ruby?" he teased. She couldn't answer as she steadied herself with both hands, using the sink for support. "I have more," he teased and she shook her head.

"I don't want to know," she told him, so quietly it was obvious she was hurting. She felt winded and her stomach and heart ached.

"Are you sure?"

"Look I don't want to give you anything and I don't want to know!" she told him determinedly, vowing to have it out with Danny and Alessi as soon as she saw them.

"And you're absolutely sure about that?" he tormented. She clenched her jaw like she wouldn't be budged. "Even if it concerns Faye?" he tested, and instantly had her attention. "Hmmm, I thought so," he told her, sounding pleased with himself. He pushed her up against the sink hard enough to shove the air from her lungs and topple the stacked cups on the draining board. Threading his hands into her hair he kissed her more firmly. She gasped out and tried to push him away but he was too busy having fun running his hands over her. Between breaths she tried to protest and eventually managed to get him to back off. She was mad now, furious and burning with humiliation.

"I hate you, Matthew - do you know that?" she yelled at him, her cheeks flaming. He had always treated her like an object, his toy, only there for his amusement.

"Hey chill, Ruby, you'll get over it. It's not like I haven't done that to you before. You know me, right? I'm not some stranger. I'm an old friend."

"Huh and with friends like you..."

"Who needs enemies like Faye, eh?" he interrupted and she was suddenly thrown and interested again.

"What about her? You have to tell me now, you've had your fun!" she demanded.

"OK, well, Faye told me that she slept with him...while you were off sick. He stayed late on a Wednesday night and he looked really stressed and tired. She asked if everything was OK and he said you were really ill. He said it was all getting to him. She expected him to shrug her off when she walked round to the back of his chair to remove his blazer, but he didn't. She thought he would tell her to stop when she massaged his shoulders, but he let her. She didn't think he would want to join her for a glass of wine from the bottle she'd bought to have with her dinner that night, but he had two glasses. Then, while she was wondering whether to try and take it further, he suddenly scooped her up and made her staff member number seven in his little black book...or would that be eight? I suppose that depends whether you guys have done it already, which I'm assuming you have, given the fact that you've been together for ages?"

She felt like she'd been hit by something. She hadn't slept with him; apparently he respected her, and that made Faye number seven and her a big fat zero! She moved to leave but he blocked her way and tried to take advantage of her distress. She cried out at him, reaching to grab her slightly cooled coffee and throwing it in his direction. Most of it missed.

"Let me go, Matthew - I'm going to be sick!" she screamed at him.

"Nice try, Ruby," he snapped, tired of her fighting him all the time. He wasn't letting her go this time and she was trapped, trapped and running out of time. She dropped to her knees as she began to vomit and he got the bin in front of he just in time, rubbing her back and cringing as he spoke, "God, Ruby, you take things bad. You need to learn to be a bit more...easy. It doesn't hurt so much if you don't get too involved - believe me, I should know."

She leaned her head wearily against the cupboard while he rolled his eyes at her like she was such a drama queen and he hadn't just ruined her life. "Come on I suppose I'd better give you a lift home."

31

Who is she?

Matthew took her straight back to Alessi's and dropped her at the gates. He didn't mess with her again. He wasn't really interested while she was sick. She didn't want to go in but she didn't want to stay outside either. Just as she was unlocking the front door Danny pulled up and she blanked him, slamming the door behind her. She was surprised to find Alessi and Tabitha in the kitchen having coffee together - a woman...at home! She snorted and turned to walk straight back out again but Danny was right behind her now, all three wondering what had got into her. She was trapped.

"Hey, what's up? You shut the door on me?" he asked, his face suddenly turning pale when he looked over her shoulder to see Alessi and Tabitha together.

"Bad day I guess," she told him, wanting to hit him so hard his head would fall off.

"What's happened - you look fuming? Has Faye bugged you again?" he persisted, and she laughed at the irony and pushed passed him.

"I'm going to bed," she declared.

"But it's only 6pm. I thought we could all have dinner together," Alessi suggested and she spun round.

"Well you thought wrong...I think I'm sick," she backtracked as his face darkened.

"No, you're moody, and that's not the same thing at all. Go and get showered, changed, or whatever it's going to take to get you snapped out of it and get yourself back down here, Ruby. You're eating with us. You've not eaten properly for ages and tonight you sit and eat a decent meal. I've had enough of your attitude so knock it off for a couple of hours and be nice," he ordered. She knew when Alessi was deadly serious and it always sent a shiver up her spine. She turned away from him and continued in the direction of her bedroom.

Danny tried to follow her but she shouted at him to leave her alone and then slammed the door on him and locked it. Alessi took Tabitha's elbow and gently led her up the stairs so he could deal with the matter without her escaping while his back was turned. It had taken a lot to get her to even agree to come to the house. She hung about on the landing like a spare part and Danny kept looking at her, which made her feel worse. Alessi knocked on Ruby's door.

"Ruby, can you come out here please and talk to us like a grown up?"

"No!" she shouted back. "Leave me alone, Alessi!"

"How can I help you if you won't come out and talk to me?"

"It doesn't matter if I come out, it doesn't matter if I talk, because *you* can't help me!" she shrieked, hysterical and sobbing. "Send Danny home that would be a start!" she mumbled into her tear soaked pillow but they all caught it. Both Alessi and Tabitha looked to him for an explanation but he held his hands out and shrugged his shoulders.

"I haven't done anything! I've been out all day!" he defended sincerely. Alessi nodded and turned back to the door.

"Ruby, if you don't come out then I'm coming in," he warned her.

"It's locked so I don't think you are," she retorted cheekily.

"Do you really think I need a key to get through your door, Ruby? You have a choice - either you can come out now or..."

"Or what?" she shouted, sounding scared. "If you can't get someone to conform, to do it your way, then just make them, right? Go on then, Alessi, break the door down, just because you can, and then what? Make me talk? Make me eat dinner with you? What else are you going to *make* me do, Alessi?" He turned and looked at Tabitha, completely astonished at Ruby's outburst. She looked back at him sadly.

"The girl's got a point," she agreed, before turning away and going to wait downstairs.

Alessi tried to smooth things with Ruby and said she had some time to decide if she wanted to join them for dinner. He left her to it and went downstairs where Danny was eager to talk. He followed him around the kitchen anxiously while Alessi prepared meat and vegetables.

"What do you think you're doing?" he whispered angrily.

"Dinner."

"Obviously! What I mean is, why Tabitha? Are you hoping if you force it they'll like each other so much that Ruby will accept her with open arms? She won't!" he told him firmly. "She's going to hit the roof and all this is going to make it worse. You're making it impossible for me too because I have no say in this, no control, but I'm still going to look like the bad guy."

"You already are apparently," Alessi reminded him, while professionally chopping peppers, garlic and chilli. Danny ignored his comment. He hadn't done anything wrong. If he'd managed to upset Ruby it was in her head. This was a completely unrelated matter.

"Alessi, if she doesn't take it well you're going to have to make a choice, do you know that? It will be Tabitha or Ruby."

"I know...and of course...I will choose Ruby. Ruby needs me."

"I don't want to see either of you hurt - hell, I don't want to see any of you hurt - but you're setting yourself up for heartache."

"I just want them to get to know each other a little bit, that's all. Trust me, everything will be fine." Alessi seemed confident and ordered Danny to make coffee. He did as he was told and Tabitha came in and asked if she could help.

"It's fine, I've got it," Danny told her, sounding frustrated as he pulled open an eyelevel cupboard door to get some sugar. The door caught Tabitha on the head and she yelped out and grasped her temple. Blood began to pour from her wound and Danny suddenly crumbled, feeling terrible for hurting her, especially while he was mad. He took her by the shoulders, apologising over and over as he sat her down on a stool. Slipping his hands around her chin he tilted her head back to take a look. For a moment she'd looked petrified and had even cowered when he stepped towards her. He wanted to reassure her that he wasn't some monster as he pushed her dark hair away from the cut and behind her ear.

"I'm so, so sorry, Tabitha. Please forgive me," he begged. "It was an accident, I swear."

Alessi soaked a clean towel and brought it over to press against her head and both looked up at the same time to see Ruby standing in the kitchen doorway. She was watching Danny like he'd cheated on her. She turned without saying a word and left the room, making her way outside to get some air. Danny left Tabitha with Alessi, and one final apology, and ran outside to find Ruby.

"Ruby, I hit her with a cupboard door. I was just trying to look after her, that's all," he explained.

"I saw, Danny," she told him flatly. "I saw how you handled her, how you touched her. It was...personal...almost private," she cringed. "I felt like I was intruding. You're in love with her aren't you? You want her don't you? You and Alessi have your eye on the same woman!"

He raised his eyebrows at her. "No, Ruby, I really don't want anything like that with her..."

"Why not, is your list a bit busy?" she asked, looking him in the eye and he frowned, not understanding where that had come from. "I mean she's sexy, she's hot, she's got a great figure, she's got long dark hair, blue eyes and that sounds just like your type to me. If I am actually your type that is, Danny? Do all the women you fancy look the same or do you like a bit of variety? How about blondes?"

"You're my type, Ruby," he told her simply, "And I've never really been into blondes." He was completely baffled by her behaviour.

"In that case you should probably just find yourself some *big* Italian family then and go through all the daughters one by one, eventually making your way round to their...mother," she whispered, then stopped. Something looked like it registered. Something clicked into place and his inability to make eye contact with her stirred something uncomfortable deep inside her.

Her stomach twisted painfully. "Who is she, Danny?" He didn't answer but looked up at her like he was carrying the weight of the world on his shoulders. A guilty secret. "Oh my god," she began to panic. Her breathing was fast and she looked unsteady. "She is, isn't she? What has he done?" she despaired. "Why would he do that to me? He told me that he cared - he's a liar. He's playing with my life, Danny! First he takes away my dad and then he...he brings back my...her..." she almost screamed; she couldn't even bring herself to say the word. "And then, as if that's not enough, he sleeps with her! It's her isn't it?" she demanded to know and he nodded. He wasn't about to lie to her face when she'd asked him outright.

She turned around and stormed back into the house but before she burst into the kitchen she stopped and hung back. Danny kept his distance as he watched her sneaking a look at Alessi and Tabitha together. She looked like a child seeing something for the first time, both fascinated and intrigued. He was amazed, for he was sure she would go in guns blazing, in true Ruby style, but she didn't. She watched them for ages from her hiding place but as Danny approached and put his hands on her shoulders, she moved forward to get away from him and straight into the kitchen.

"Ruby, are you OK? Tabitha's fine - she just got a bit of a cut that's all. Did the blood make you sick?" Alessi asked, sounding concerned, and she shook her head.

"No, but the fact that you went against everything I said and brought her back from whatever hole she was hiding in, does." Ruby hit him with it straight. Tabitha's eyes widened. Alessi stayed frustratingly cool, his face not shocked in the slightest. It spurred her on; she wanted to hurt him, her... anyone. "Shall I tell you what else makes me sick? The fact that you said you wanted to be like a dad to me and then you go and sleep with the woman who gave birth to me..."

"We haven't..." Tabitha tried to set the record straight but Ruby glared at her and she shut up.

"Were you hoping to create some happy family despite my misery, despite what she did to me? Why would you want to be with someone like her?" she jabbed a finger in Tabitha's direction, ready to rip her hair out.

"Ruby, it's not that simple..." Alessi began, but she interrupted again.

"She's a whore did you know that?" Still no shock from Alessi, just the usual poker face and a slightly quieter tone to his words.

"No, Ruby, she's not..."

"Er, yes she is! My dad said she slept around and that she did it for money. I do believe that's the makings of a whore, a prostitute, a hooker, whatever you want to call it."

"Ruby..." Alessi began again, but she cut him off.

"No, Alessi!" She turned to face Tabitha now. "Is what my dad told me true or not?" she demanded to know and Tabitha dropped her head feeling totally humiliated. "Tabitha! Or whatever the bloody hell your name is, though it sure as hell ain't 'mum', answer the god damn question! I will rip it out of you if I have to, with my bare hands!"

"Ruby, please..." Tabitha began, and Ruby raised her eyebrows.

"Don't plead with me, you selfish bitch. I have no feelings for you other than hate. Now tell us what you really are and stop trying to hide from it! You've exposed yourself, so let's hear it...all about how you funded your new lifestyle while your bully of a husband raised your baby."

"OK, Ruby! OK! In the first few weeks after I walked out I had no money and nowhere to go..."

"So you did sleep with men for money then?" Ruby pressed. She wanted nothing more than to make Tabitha look bad in front of the two men she was twisting round her little finger with her good looks, butter wouldn't melt personality and perfect figure. Tabitha was stealing those men from her. She had them first! Tabitha nodded unable to look up. "How many are we talking here, Tabitha? A few weeks, a man every night, what's that? Get your calculator, Alessi, I think we might need to do some adding up!" The situation was volatile and Alessi wanted to comfort Tabitha but he knew full well if he did, or if he tried to comfort Ruby, she would blow up and cause some serious damage to someone or something. Tabitha finally found her voice, just wanting to get it over with.

"Enough, Ruby - even one was too many. I didn't want to do it..."

"Then why didn't you come back home? You had a choice. I don't feel sorry for you!" she snarled, feeling nothing but pure hatred for the woman. Alessi intervened.

"Ruby, it wasn't as easy as just opting to come home. Your father beat her. She was the same age you were when you came to my firm looking for a job."

"So what?" She really didn't care. "I'm sorry he beat you but that doesn't make it OK to walk out and leave me to handle him alone. I was younger than you were when he first raised his hands to me. I was younger than you when he called me all the names under the sun. I was younger than you when there wasn't enough to eat in the house, the water was cold and there was no heating. He hurt me from as young as I can remember so that excuse is just not good enough. I didn't get to walk. I had to stay!" she yelled at her. Tabitha held her hands over her mouth as Alessi began to talk again.

"Ruby, sweetheart, he forced himself on her. That's why she left." Ruby stepped back right into Danny, who had been near enough to comfort her but too worried to reach out. She shoved him away and shook her head.

"No, that's a lie! Why make something like that up? Why say things like that?" she demanded.

"Because it's true," Tabitha whispered after a long pause.

"So my dad was a monster? He was a predator? No! You lie! You were his wife!" she screamed out, feeling mortified.

"That doesn't always stop people like him, Rubes," Alessi told her softly, his eyes looking sad for her. Why was he sad for *her?* The woman was clearly lying. Ruby didn't need their pity, Tabitha did. What with her record for abandoning her husband and baby, sleeping around and then not being big enough to face up to it. She was the one that needed the pity. She was the bad guy. She shrugged off Alessi's gaze; it was making her feel icky, and she turned on Tabitha again.

"You had a baby with him, why would you do that if what you say is true?" There was a long silence before Alessi spoke up. Ruby felt narked. It was Tabitha she wanted to hear it from, not Alessi. She hated that Alessi was sticking up for the woman, that he knew so much already, that they had probably discussed all the details of Ruby's past while snuggled up in bed together just along the hallway from her! Ugh, that was totally gross. Alessi and her – her mum! She was still caught up in her sickening thoughts when Alessi's words reached her ears.

"That's why she had you, Ruby."

"That doesn't make sense," she half laughed. "What, she thought he'd stop raping her if she had children with him? Did she think having a baby girl and leaving her behind sounded like a good idea, because guess what, it

221

wasn't?" she informed them, shaking her head in disbelief. The look of sympathy on all their faces felt very, very, bad. She went back to Alessi's comment and mulled it over and then her hands suddenly flew up to cover her face and she screamed into them.

"No! No! No! Are you saying...? No! That makes me..." She couldn't say the words and Alessi continued.

"He made her pregnant, Ruby, and then, when you were only a few weeks old, he did it to her again. That's why she walked. She was too scared to go back. She was your age and she didn't know what to do. She was traumatised and suffering from depression. Ruby, baby, she wouldn't have left you otherwise, and that's why she's here now. That's why I've let her in because she's not the terrible person you think she is." There was a huge silence while Ruby's mouth was covered by her hands. If she let go she would scream until all her insides were outsides. She moved her fingers to cover her eyes, feeling humiliated. If she didn't look at any of them she could pretend they weren't all staring at her, waiting for her to do something, seeing her for all the disgusting freaky things she really was.

"No, no she's not," she agreed in a whisper, to all of their astonishments. They looked back at her, all eyes wide and disbelieving. "I understand why she left and why she didn't take me. Why would she stay? Why would she take me when every time she looked at me she saw *him?* How would you bond with a baby when it was half of the man who beat and raped you? Part of him is in my veins, part of him is my flesh. I have that monster's blood flowing inside me!"

She seemed to convulse right before pulling her cardigan off and throwing it on the floor. She yanked the band out of her hair and let it fall free around her face and waist. She turned her palms to look at them like they belonged to someone else, someone disgusting, and then she turned and ran for her bedroom. Shutting herself in the bathroom she reached into the tub and turned the shower to hot. She climbed in with all her clothes on and let the water burn the creepy feeling from her skin. The drumming gush from the showerhead helped to drown out the visions of her father who had

222

pinned her down so many times, who had called her a whore, who had done those same things to her mum and then gone on to do much worse...twice!

Then there were the memories of him lying to her about how her mother had run off with her pimp and how Ruby was set to go the same way. His hands had held her down and beaten her too. She had been petrified that one day he might take it further. He looked at her all wrong and threatened to show her who was boss. He likened her to her mother, the woman he attacked so viciously. She had always been thankful the abuse had remained physical and verbal but now she was realising it was only a matter of time, just like Alessi had said - the exact reason Alessi had shot him.

She was close to passing out as the water suddenly stopped. The silence was deafening. Strong arms caught her as she started to fall and carried her to the bedroom. She realised it was Alessi as he wrapped a quilt around her shivering body and held onto her tightly. She cried into his arms and told him that she didn't want to be around anymore, she couldn't cope with knowing who and what she was. When she heard Tabitha's voice every muscle in her body tightened. She couldn't look at her.

"Ruby, listen to me, please. I'm the only one who can tell you how it was," Tabitha tried to explain as she knelt down beside Alessi. "How I felt then and how I feel now. Please, will you listen?" Ruby nodded without bringing her ashamed face into view. She hated herself as much as she'd hated her mother. Tabitha twisted her hands in her lap uneasily, trying to work out exactly what she was going to say.

"You *can* help her," Alessi whispered, and she gave him a weak smile and began.

"When I walked out I hadn't bonded with you, Ruby, because I was sick. I spent the pregnancy frightened of how you would be when you were born. I got it into my head that you would be all wrong and that people would know somehow about my awful secret. But, Ruby, you were perfect and that is the honest truth. When I look into your eyes now I don't see anything of him, other than the pain we've both caused you. I don't even see me. I see a strong, independent woman that's defied everything. The odds have been stacked against you and yet you've come out braver and harder than I could ever have imagined and prayed for. You are nothing like I was then. I was shy and timid. I did as I was told and I never argued. I didn't even know how to. I wasn't streetwise like you are. I would never have stood up to someone like Alessi, let alone challenged him!" she laughed and dared to reach out and touch Ruby's cheek. It was a huge accomplishment and nothing stopped, the world just kept turning. She sighed with relief.

"I think I've just fallen in love with you," Alessi breathed into her ear softly and she was totally taken aback. That was the last thing she'd been expecting, especially considering her jaded past. She smiled back, still looking slightly startled by his declaration, and then continued.

"You're amazing, Ruby, and I'm fascinated by you. You said downstairs that I can't look at you, but I've done nothing but look at you since I found out who you were." She laughed sweetly. "I can't stop looking at you. You're so beautiful, you're captivating...no wonder you've got such a good looking young man like Danny hooked! I'll be honest, I do find it hard to make eye contact with you, but only because you're kind of scary. You're like a little wild cat and you're great to watch in action. I bet your dad had his work cut out with you. I bet he thought you'd be easy to bully like me, just because you were a girl. All bullies are cowards, Ruby, she told her."

"Especially men who abuse women," Danny mumbled distantly, sounding like he could kill him if he hadn't already been beaten to it.

"Exactly," Tabitha agreed. "I did everything to try and please him, but it never worked. I bet his beatings didn't stop you at all, Ruby?" she asked, and Ruby shook her head. "Did he...did he do anything else to you?" Tabitha asked cautiously and Ruby shook her head again. Tabitha's relief was immense as she leaned forward and breathed shakily into her hands. She straightened back up and forced herself to go on. "Ruby, I know things can't be undone and I will never seem like your mum. I would never expect you to treat me like one, but perhaps we could know each other...some other way? You make me so proud. Even though I never planned for it to be this way, it was my body that carried you almost full term, despite the abuse, and it was my body that delivered something so incredible."

Ruby stopped crying and snuffled as she leaned out of Alessi's grip. "Can I touch you?" she asked gingerly, fearing rejection. "It's OK...I'm sorry...I know that's weird, it doesn't matter..."

"Yes, Ruby, of course you can touch me," Tabitha agreed but Ruby shook her head and became withdrawn again.

"You'd say that anyway," she grumbled. "Even if I made your skin crawl you'd say yes, because you're that kind of person aren't you, Tabitha? You'd tolerate me just like you tolerated my dad." She sounded almost angry, but more at the situation than at Tabitha.

"No, Ruby, you couldn't possibly make my skin crawl. You are not him. He would make my skin crawl - just the thought of him makes me feel sick, but not you. You are you."

Tabitha leaned forward and put her arms around Ruby, pulling her away from Alessi gently and holding her tightly. "See, absolutely zero skin crawling," she smiled and Ruby dared to look at her.

"Stay a bit longer," she permitted uncomfortably. "I mean with Alessi because I'm going to bed. I've got a headache," she lied. "I'm sure Alessi would like it if you stayed." Tabitha's eyes filled with tears as she nodded sadly. They were a million miles away from being friends but it seemed she wasn't the only one on the wrong side of Ruby as she then turned a deathly stare on Danny.

"But you can go!" she told him firmly and he huffed at the injustice of it all.

"Ruby, what have I done?" he asked her, sounding desperate.

"What haven't you done, don't you mean?" she snapped at him, and he sighed and ran his hands over his face.

"I'm going to bed," he conceded wearily, it had been a long day.

"With anyone I know?" she asked maliciously.

"No, on my own!"

"Wow and I'll bet that's a first," she quipped dryly.

"Oh shut up, Ruby!" he mumbled under his breath as he closed the door behind him.

"What was that all about?" Alessi asked her and she shrugged.

"It seems I'm the only one left in the dark around here, always the last one to know!" she sobbed bitterly. Wiping her tear soaked face on the back of her hands she climbed into bed, still wet, and called out from under the covers. "Shut the door on your way out."

And just like that they'd been dismissed.

32
You're really bugging me now!

The following morning Ruby waited in her room until it was time to go to work; she didn't much feel like seeing anyone. She felt like Alessi would just want her to be OK and professional about it all and she had promised not to cause him any more bother. Danny was a cheating idiot who would try and talk her round, and Tabitha would pretend she liked her even though she actually made her want to vomit. Eventually Alessi called her down and said they were leaving, but when she got to the bottom of the stairs he asked if she and Danny would share a lift into the office together. He had something he needed to do before making his way in.

Ruby slipped outside straight away so she could sit in the back of Danny's car. She didn't want to sit next to him. When she caught him looking at her in the rear view mirror she changed sides so he couldn't see her as easily and he shook his head.

When they arrived at work Tabitha greeted them awkwardly on her way to the accounts department and Ruby and Danny made their way into reception. Danny grabbed his own post because he knew that, even though Ruby would be getting Alessi's, she definitely wouldn't be getting his. She was in and out like a shot, not even bothering to wind up Amanda, and Danny was hot on her heels. She made her way up the stairs to the noise of Faye giggling in Tom Marshall's office. Faye was scheduled to help him tidy his files all morning and so, for once, Ruby was able to sit at her desk without having to fight for the privilege. She immediately covered her space with paperwork and began to pour through the witness statement she hadn't got finished the day before because of Matthew. Alessi would demand to see it when he got in and she wanted to prove that she could manage the extra responsibility and workload.

She was struggling to concentrate as she rested her head against her right hand, letting her hair fall over her face so she wouldn't have to acknowledge Danny. She doodled with her left hand so she'd at least look busy. Danny made some phone calls and shuffled some papers and then she heard him lean back in his chair.

"Ruby, you're not fooling anyone you know. You're right handed so I'm not quite sure what you're doing with your left hand but it's definitely not writing, if that's the look you were hoping for." She ignored him and he sighed. "I really don't know what I've done," he continued. She said nothing. "Is that it then, Ruby, is it over? Just like that? I didn't think, after everything we've been through together, that you would just come home one evening and not speak to me ever again."

"Danny, did you mess about with six women from this firm?" she asked casually, without stopping the scribbling and without looking at him either. She was still hiding behind her hair.

"Who told you that?" he asked, her mood now becoming *a lot* clearer.

"Does it make a difference to the answer?" she asked him.

"It's true, yes, but..."

"And were you seeing them at the same time?" she continued. He leaned onto the desk with a groan.

"Ruby, I'm so sorry. I just didn't think it mattered at the time. They were all grown women. I never took advantage of anyone. It was clear from the start that it was a no strings thing. I'm not like that anymore. It was before you started here and that's one of the reasons Alessi was so determined to keep me away from you, because he didn't think I could be trusted."

"And with good reason I'd say," she pointed out, still doodling and hiding behind her dark curtain.

"I've never taken advantage of you, Ruby. I never tried to get you to go through with it when you came back here tipsy, after you had a fight with your dad. I never took you up on your offer in my car when you were completely out of your face and celebrating your seventeenth. I haven't used you, Ruby! I'm sorry about those other women but I can't change what I've done. I'm not proud of it," he defended, but she stood up smoothly and left the office without another word.

After lunch she came back to find that Faye had taken her cardigan off the back of the chair and moved it, along with all of her paperwork. She'd dumped the lot onto a stack of boxes. She'd then spread her own things out and was pretending to work while she tried to get Danny's attention by swinging her legs. Ruby had been evicted from her own desk, yet again, and she finally snapped. She grabbed all of Faye's things and threw them out of the door while Faye sat staring at her.

"Mr Alessi is so going to sack you for this and in front of Danny too. Poor Danny must wonder what kind of animal he's been dating...if you can even call it dating. You've been out of action for weeks and that's no fun at all is it, Danny?" He immediately stood to intervene, but as Ruby lifted a heavy file to bring it down on Faye's head Alessi pulled it out of her hands brusquely, having entered the office just in time.

"Ruby, my office please...*now*. Faye, get this mess tidied up," he ordered. She looked indignant as she huffed and leaned back into the chair. Alessi held the door open and Danny looked worried as he then closed it on the chaos firmly. Ruby stood by his desk, waiting for the inevitable grilling, but she was upset too and quick to defend herself.

"She deserved it!" she blurted out and Alessi nodded.

"Yes I know. Please sit down, Ruby, I need to talk to you," he told her. Her eyes grew sad and she looked like she might cry.

"You're going to sack me aren't you? You break it to me about Tabitha and then everyone turns against me. She gets to stay because she's been treated so badly and I get chucked out because I'm disgusting and nobody wants to be near me..."

"Ruby, that's not true. Now sit down," he told her again, taking one of the client chairs himself and pulling it round so he could sit opposite her. She slipped into the gap and sat. "Ruby, I've been really worried about losing you to Marlon again, worried that he's always somewhere close by waiting for you. The other day you were snatched and attacked so brutally by that gang that I panicked about how I was going to keep you safe. So...don't freak, OK?" he prepared her and she frowned.

"Why would I freak?" she whispered, wondering how this had anything to do with Faye.

"Because I planted a bug on you the night we put you back together. You had wounds around your neck that needed treating and that made planting a bug on you so easy, and the temptation impossible to resist. I decided yesterday I was going to remove it because you've been so careful, not taking risks and openly sharing how you feel. You've been through so much, Ruby, especially finding out about Tabitha last night and I am so very proud of you," he smiled but he didn't look happy. She didn't understand where he was going; he was making her confused. Where was the grilling? Where was the usual threat of dismissal? "Ruby, I decided you should have the freedom to take care of yourself for a bit. I need to be a little less...possessive. It was only because I was worried about you that I planted the bug in the first place but, Rubes, I never got round to removing it," he confessed, and she frowned at him.

"You're still bugging me?" she squinted at him. "Couldn't you have just said 'I'm worried about you, Ruby, do you mind if I track you for a while?' Why so sneaky, Alessi?" she asked. "Unless of course you don't trust me?" She was definitely feeling insecure and he felt very sorry for her.

"Ruby, I trust you implicitly. Anyway the why and how doesn't matter; what matters is that it's still on you. Do you know what that means?" She turned her mouth down at the sides. She hadn't done anything wrong and so hazarded a typically sarcastic guess to his question.

"You're rubbish at surveillance?"

He shook his head like it wasn't funny. "No, Ruby, it means that after your strange behaviour with Danny, the recording that I was going to ignore seemed quite intriguing. I wondered, after you took yourself off to bed and Tabitha went home, whether it could give some clue as to why you went from hot to cold with him in such a short space of time. I listened to it this morning, before I came in to work. Ruby, I heard everything that happened here last night."

She screeched out and hid her face in her hands. "No, Alessi, you can't have!"

"Ruby, I can have...and I did. Firstly, I would like to assure you that Faye's job is going to be terminated as of the end of this conversation. Secondly, I would like to clarify that Danny did not work late with her on *any* occasion. He spent most of his time at the house, watching over you and when he wasn't doing that he was with me. He was extremely protective of you and he cared about nothing else. He certainly wouldn't have had the energy or desire for anything Faye had to offer him." He took a deep breath. "The issue with the members of staff here, well, that's all true I'm afraid," he told her awkwardly. "I was not happy with him but, that being said, nobody was forced to do anything they didn't want to do and he wasn't in a relationship with any of them. A couple even had boyfriends of their own and they definitely didn't want a relationship either. The issue seemed to be that they didn't like that he'd managed to be with them all at around the same time. He worked a couple of very long shifts to pay penance for his disrespectful behaviour, and that just leaves Matthew." She folded her arms and fidgeted in her seat, refusing to look him in the eye.

"Are you going to tell Danny?" she whispered like she was devastated. She unfolded her arms, but only so she could bite on her nails anxiously.

"Let's work that out in a minute, shall we? First I want to know what happened."

"You heard what happened, Alessi, don't make me say it," she begged.

"Fair enough. It's clearly upsetting, yes?" he asked, and she nodded again, wiping at the tears. "It's very hard to tell from a recording, Ruby, but did he put his hands on you?"

"Not really, well, I suppose he did a little bit but nothing I couldn't handle. I just didn't like to think of Danny being with other girls. I knew he had been, I kind of guessed that. I mean he's older and he's gorgeous so that wasn't so much of a shock...but Faye! I just couldn't bear it, Alessi. She's been sitting in my chair, at my desk, smiling at me and sleeping with *him!*" she battled admirably with the tears and only a few escaped.

"It's not true, Ruby. He wouldn't do that because he's very much in love with you."

231

"Sweetheart, Danny will understand and we should tell him about this. He would want to know." Alessi tried to persuade her.

"No way, Alessi! I cheated to find out stuff about him. Matthew just made it sound like it was something I should know and I know what Matthew 's like. He would *never* have told me if I hadn't given him what he wanted. He would have walked around, day in day out, letting me stress over it. I was so hurt - I was devastated, Alessi!"

"You were assaulted in my building and I'm not willing to let that go," he confirmed, standing and walking around his desk. He pulled open one of his drawers and began setting up the recording equipment that he kept in there. It wasn't until he plugged in a set or earplugs that she realised what he was doing.

"Alessi, please, no, he'll flip!" she almost screamed, jumping up and pulling the earplugs back out. "He'll hate me. He'll never forgive me!"

"He *will* forgive you," he told her confidently, taking the earplugs off her and inserting them back into the machine. He put his hand on her shoulder to gently push her back down into her seat and then walked over to the door to call Danny into the office. He invited him to listen to the recording and Danny frowned, feeling puzzled, but inserted the earplugs anyway. He watched an upset looking Ruby suspiciously as he pressed play and then stood on Alessi's side of the desk, his hand wandering over his chin and messing with his tie. He faced her through the first few minutes of the recording, even through the kiss, which he only raised his eyebrows at. When it came to her sounding like she was in distress he turned away and leaned back against the surface to listen to the rest. He stopped it a couple of times and rewound to listen again before listening right up until the recording snapped off, making Ruby jump. He stayed where he was, strangely quiet and still.

Ruby began to shake in her chair feeling a cold dread pass through her bones. Alessi walked round to face his son and Danny removed the earplugs like he'd forgotten that they were there.

"We're getting rid of them, right?" he asked quietly and Alessi nodded.

"Of course we are, Danny. You can do what you want to him but just not in the firm, that's all I ask. He'll be sacked and asked to leave the building within the next hour and then it's up to you what you want to do about it." Ruby was shaking more visibly now and Alessi looked over at her.

"Ruby, are you OK?" he enquired kindly and Danny turned to look at her too; he looked surprised to see her still there. She was perched in the middle of the seat seeming small and vulnerable as she hugged her arms around her body. He pressed his lips into a hard line; he looked furious, and then he moved off the table to leave the room. Ruby's eyes filled with tears; he was walking out on her just like she knew he would. Everything was ruined because of her. She turned in her chair, choking on the grief that came with watching the only man she had ever loved walk out on her.

"Alessi, please!" she begged him to help but he put his finger to his lips, urging her to quieten down. She caught her breath and held it as she found herself listening to Danny right outside the door. He hadn't left and marched off down the stairs like she feared he would. He was at her desk, right in front of Faye, and now Ruby and Alessi could hear him speaking to her in a tone that was low, soft and utterly venomous.

"I would just like to tell you that you've just been fired and I have never been more pleased to see the back of someone. You, Faye, are a liar. You told Matthew that I slept with you, didn't you?" he demanded and she tried to protest.

"Danny I..."

"Save it," he cut her off. "Ruby is the only girl for me and I would *never* be tempted to stray away from her. It just wouldn't happen, not in a million years, and especially not with the likes of *you!*" Ruby looked at Alessi more hopefully, and he smiled warmly at her. She was sure she'd been dumped as soon as the recording clicked off. Faye burst into tears and grabbed her things and Danny yanked her coat off the back of the chair and threw it at her. "You've been squatting in Ruby's chair for too long. It's time to go, Faye!" he evicted harshly, giving her one last hateful look up and down. He then returned to the office and spoke to Alessi. "I suggest you go see Matthew else it could get messy."

As soon as Alessi had gone Danny approached Ruby and spun her chair so she'd look at him. She slid further back into the seat like she thought he might lash out and he could see the fear in her eyes, the same fear he'd seen in Tabitha's.

"Don't you *ever* keep something like that from me again, do you hear?" He was mad at her but only because she'd kept a secret. "You were going to dump me and never tell anyone what had happened to you? Ruby, I'm not going to hold something like this against you. He bribed and manipulated you. He's a nasty piece of work and he calls himself your friend," he laughed, though not amused in the slightest. "He has only one agenda, Ruby, and he's dangerous. He treats you like you're stupid and the scary thing is he makes you feel like you are too, doesn't he?"

She nodded. It was true; Matthew had this ability to make her feel small and pathetic. "He's just like your dad and he's had his claws in you for long enough. He always thought you'd be an easy target and that he'd get you in the end - he still does. I would never dream of telling you what to do, save for this one time: stay away from him, Ruby, he's bad news!"

Danny was fuming when he went back to his desk to try and engross himself in some work to keep from killing anyone. After pulling herself together, Ruby returned to their office too and slipped into her seat, wishing she wasn't there at all. She hung her head and tried to concentrate but she was dazed; she felt like she'd been hit by a truck load of exhaustion and everything was such an effort now. Danny was silent as he worked, only the sound of a furious pen scratching across paper gave any indication that he was still there. Suddenly his voice startled her.

"So, what did he have to say for himself?" he asked. She looked up with trepidation, fearing she would now have to fend off an interrogation. She couldn't handle it and she wasn't ready to confess the gory details of what a cheat she'd been. The lines of anxiety smoothed from her face when she realised that he wasn't talking to her at all. Alessi was in the doorway; he'd been gone for half an hour.

"He protested his innocence, just as I thought he would," he responded coolly, leaning against the white painted doorframe.

"What?" Ruby exclaimed. "He said I was lying?" She sounded hurt.

"Yes," Alessi told her simply. "Great mate you've got yourself there, Ruby."

"But I can't believe...he said I lied?" She tried to get her head round it.

"Actually he said you made the whole thing up because you're an attention seeking little bitch. He said that you were always trouble at school, lying and cheating, and that you're lying and cheating now."

"But how can he say that? You have evidence," she reminded him.

"Not as far as he's concerned I don't. As far as he's concerned I have your word against his. I couldn't tell him exactly how I know the truth now could I? I wasn't about to confess that I'd bugged and tracked one of my employees because I was worried they might be dragged off by a member of an organised crime group. He doesn't know that we work with the mafia, Ruby."

"So what did you tell him?" she asked slowly, panic starting to set in.

"I told him you told me, of course."

"So he'll think I'm a grass! So he'll think I came running to you because I couldn't handle it myself! Alessi, my friends will hate me!"

"Friends!" Danny scoffed in disbelief. "Anybody who would take his side over yours or judge you for asking for help is not a friend, Ruby."

"You don't understand, I've known these people all my life and that's not how we handle things on our estate."

"So how do you handle things on your estate, not that you live there anymore and not that it's *your* estate? You live with Alessi now," Danny pointed out. "Can you not just stop looking at that nasty hole where you grew up as your home and start looking at Alessi's place like that instead? It might actually solve some problems if you did," he complained.

"No, Danny, I can't because it's where I come from and it's all I've ever really known. Disputes get sorted out internally, you don't go to the police and you definitely don't grass! If they see me out on the street they will do me over - do you know that?"

"Well we'd better make sure they don't see you out on the street then," he told her simply. "All the more reason to stay off the estate, Ruby. Anyway, you work with the mafia - you really don't need to be scared of Matthew and his stupid little crew. If Sasha and her brothers are the friends you say they are, they will be there for you regardless. Mario said he would look out for you, didn't he?" She nodded at him. "Well there you go then. He will be on your side and no doubt Sasha will follow her big brother."

"No, no she won't, because she also has Marcus, and he's best friends with Matthew. Marcus will side with Matthew and Sasha will side with them. They will all be against me," she whined. "I know that Matthew is a creep and he overstepped the mark..."

"Understatement!" Danny blurted out furiously, and she huffed and slammed her hands on the table.

"Danny, he provided me with somewhere to go to get away from my dad. I owe him that at least. I can't be seen to be going around telling tales!"

"I think you've pretty much settled your debt with Matthew, Ruby," he told her. "Remember the day you walked out and straight into the hands of Marlon?" She didn't need to nod this time, they both knew she remembered all too well. "You told me that staying with Matthew for safety was always conditional. He got something out of it, Ruby, don't you worry about that. You owe him nothing. He's twisted you around his little finger and he's led you to believe that he looks out for you, protects you and cares about you when, in fact, all he actually wants to do is bed you," he concluded, leaning back in his chair to watch her. She sighed and wiped a couple of tears away, looking to Alessi in desperation. He gave nothing back; clearly he agreed.

"OK, so I know that's true, but it's just so hard to break all ties with my old life. I relied on being part of that group, crew, gang, whatever you want to call it. But now I'm outside of it and it's scary. When I was just living elsewhere that was one thing, but as far as they're concerned I've gone and done the one thing you never do, and that's desert. To top that, they will now think I'm a grass. Oh my god, they're going to find me and kill me. I'm scared, Danny! I'm frightened, Alessi! You saw what they did to me for deserting and now they think I've grassed - they won't think twice about taking me out and leaving me in some dirty alley!"

"Is he being tracked?" Danny asked, breaking eye contact with her to look at his father.

"Of course. Got him hooked up before he left. He hasn't got a clue."

"Tracked? What are you going to do?" she asked desperately, looking between the two men.

"I, Ruby, am going to sort it. Matthew won't be any more trouble and he won't be telling his crew members anything about you either. I will keep you from being targeted in punishment for being Matthew's little victim, though I'm not quite sure how you can pay twice for a wrong you never committed. I guess that's why I don't belong to a gang, Ruby. I don't like abusing and manipulating young vulnerable girls enough for that."

"Just leave it! You will make it worse," she protested, getting hysterical.

She stood, pushing her chair out and ran for the box room, locking herself inside. They stared at the closed door for a few silent moments and then Danny frowned.

"Right, suppose I'd better get to Matthew before he gets to anyone else."

Alessi nodded and checked his watch. "I'd be quick - I get the feeling he's a squealer."

"Oh he'll squeal alright," Danny promised, slipping on his jacket and grabbing his keys from the top drawer.

34

Torture by post

When Danny arrived back at the office at 5.25pm Ruby was still shut in the box room, refusing to come out. Alessi shook his head at him from behind his desk.

"I've tried persuading her every hour or so, between trying to get some work done," he told him hopelessly, spreading his hands wide over the mass of papers in front of him. "She seems really rattled about it."

Danny spun round, looking quite happy for a man whose girlfriend had spent the afternoon in hiding. He headed for the box room and banged on the door with the side of his fist three times. "Ruby, time to go! Everyone else is getting ready to leave the building, including me and Alessi, so if you're not out in half an hour you'll be here in the dark on your own." Twenty-five minutes later she unlocked the door and made sure she didn't get left behind.

When they arrived home, Ruby was first in the house; she was beat and ready for bed. She stooped and picked up the post, which was mostly junk mail, except for a brown envelope addressed to Mr Alessi. She noted that the address took up the whole of the front of the envelope as she handed it over and followed him into the dining room. He'd heightened her intrigue with his eagerness to get it out of her hands. He slumped down in a chair and looked at her.

"Can I help you, Ruby?" he asked teasingly, and she shrugged casually.

"No, just thought I'd hang about and keep you company." She was scared and feeling ever so slightly clingy.

"That's very nice of you," he smiled warmly. "Can you get me a glass of water please?" he asked her, and she frowned at him.

"What's in the envelope?"

"I'll let you know when I've had a chance to open it," he told her coolly.

She huffed and left the room, making her way to the kitchen to put the kettle on and fill a glass with water. She flicked through a magazine, only semi-interested, and then made her way back to the dining room with Alessi's cold drink. Danny and Bardo had joined him and Danny was holding a small selection of what looked like photographs in his hand, while they watched something on Alessi's laptop. She coughed to make her presence known and they were immediately flustered. She had never seen them so ruffled, so uncool. She made her way round the table to stand next to Alessi and look at the screen, but he clicked the toolbar and jumped to another document.

"What was that?" she demanded to know.

"Nothing," Alessi lied terribly. "It's just something I need to take care of, that's all."

"What was it?" she repeated, placing his glass on the table loudly. She looked over at Danny, "And what are those?"

He slipped them into his inside pocket and shook his head slowly. "Nothing," he told her.

"I'm not an idiot," she snapped leaning over Alessi to click the toolbar back again. It was a video and she clicked the screen to take it off pause, slapping Alessi's hand out of the way when he tried to stop her. She watched for all of two seconds before she knew exactly what she was looking at and slammed the lid down hard. Alessi held his hands up out of the way just in time. "Are they of me too?" she growled at Danny, practically climbing over Alessi to get to him. He let her pull them from his pocket and she screamed. "Marlon! No! How could he? How much did you watch? Are there other photos? How dare you look at these!" she yelled, scrunching the pictures in her hands and curling her fingers into fists."

"Ruby, we weren't looking at them for pleasure I can assure you." Alessi told her, leaning back in his chair and letting it swing from side to side gently. "Marlon sent them to me. He's mad that we took you away and that you messed up his deal with Killen. He's trying to wind us up by humiliating you." He handed her the scrawled note informing Alessi that he was considering putting the images on the internet for everyone to enjoy. Ruby wanted to throw up when she saw that he'd actually signed it 'The Puppet Master.'

"Alessi you have to stop him!" You can't let him do this to me!"

"I'll sort it, Ruby - just let me work out how we're going to go about it."

"Do you know what, don't bother, I'll sort it myself!" she suddenly announced furiously. "I don't need men fighting my battles for me. I hate men, they're all the same!" She turned and stormed from the dining room into the kitchen. She slammed about and came out with a heavy pasta pan which she took straight into the garden. Marching across the grass to the pool she started attacking Alessi's cherub with it. She hit it round the head until bits of stone flew off like missiles. One hit Bardo in the face and drew blood.

"Ruby, the cherub hasn't done anything to you. Can you please leave it alone?" Alessi asked her as he approached.

"Well, Alessi," she stopped to turn and look at him, tightening and loosening her grip on the handle, "it's the cherub or one of you," she announced, pointing the pan at each of them in turn. They all stayed quiet. "Yeah I thought so, men don't like it when the odds are less favourable do they?" She raised the pan again, bringing it down against the statue's abdomen and smashing his miniature peeing organ right off. The water glugged out and Danny couldn't help but smile. He hated the damn statue and it definitely looked better now. He had copied it when he was four and got into trouble for doing exactly what the cherub was doing. "Ruby, stop with the pan...and the cherub abuse...I will sort it!" Alessi ordered her, knowing that Matthew had a lot to do with how she was feeling.

"No you won't, I will!" she argued with him and he was quick to put her straight.

"Erm, you will do nothing of the sort. You will stay away from Marlon and let us sort it. He's messed you up enough already - now leave it alone...and my god damn cherub too!" he shouted at her. There would be nothing left of it and it had cost him a fortune! She wouldn't listen and slammed the pan down on its foot, causing its toes to snap off too. Alessi sighed in frustration; she wasn't going to stop. "Bardo, put her in the pool and get the pan off her please," he requested, before turning and walking back to the house. Danny's mouth dropped open.

240

"Alessi, you're kidding right? You can't do that!" he complained, but while his back was turned Bardo picked Ruby up and chucked her in the pool. She came up for air, gasping and coughing, and Danny rushed to fish her out. The water was cold and she was drenched. The stunt had definitely taken the wind out of her sails, and the air out of her lungs! She wiped her face on her arms and then glared at Danny, like it was all his fault, before storming off to the house to purposely drip all over Alessi's precious rugs and tiled floors.

After slamming around for the next two hours and then refusing to eat any dinner, Ruby stropped off to bed. She was seriously paranoid and checked under the bed, in the wardrobe, in the shower enclosure and behind the curtains, before locking her window and door to make sure nobody could get in to torture or kidnap her. She felt like the world was her enemy and that night she sobbed herself to sleep.

The following morning she was up and ready early. She was scared that Alessi and Danny might leave the house without her and Bardo might unusually take a day off. She would be all on her own in Alessi's big house and then Matthew might come and get her, or the gang...or Marlon. She wasn't hungry and she pushed her toast around on her plate and turned her cup on its saucer. At 6.30am Alessi came down in his crisp, white shirt and smart, dark tie and leaned back against the surface to watch the sorry little figure while he drank his coffee. A short time later Danny was in the doorway too. He coughed to get her attention, a cue it seemed for her to start arguing with him.

"You have no idea how serious this is! You might think working for the mafia is serious and, OK, you guys are pretty scary, but I have my own problems too, you know. Matthew and his group might only be small time but they can be really nasty and they've really hurt people in the past.

"I think we've seen that - they hanged you, Ruby," Danny reminded her.

"Exactly! You saw what they did to me and now I've made things worse for myself. I always stayed out of the nasty stuff. I was only really part of it because Matthew was nice to me and he took me in. I didn't hang around on the estate with them but I do know what they do to people who inform. Just before I left the estate to come here there was this girl who desperately wanted to be part of the group - she'd come from another part of the estate and she didn't want to be a loner. They told her she had to go through some kind of initiation because she was new in our area. The boys were like animals and what the girls made her do wasn't much better."

"Why does that not surprise me?" Alessi chipped in.

"She must have been really desperate because she did everything they told her, but then I heard she grassed and a few days later she was found with a knife wound to her leg. She'd been set upon and then left with no mobile phone. They'd even robbed her, Alessi! She nearly died and the authorities had to have her and her family relocated. She never said who did it, but I don't want any of that stuff to happen to me! I have enough to worry about with Marlon!" she gasped desperately, putting her face in her hands and shoving her plate aside with her elbow. The smell of cold toast was making her sick.

Danny frowned sadly. He hated seeing her so distraught, but he hoped that what he was about to share with her might be enough to make her feel a *little* better.

35
Fighting fire with fire

"Ruby, baby, do you trust me?" Danny asked her and she tried to nod but it quickly ended in tears. He came over to where she sat and placed a gentle hand on her back. "Come with me, I have someone who wants to talk to you."

Alessi came to take her arm and guide her outside into the garden. They followed Danny as he walked across the grass barefoot. He led them towards the covered well on the far side of the lawn and then he stopped to lean against it casually. "Right, Ruby, what do you fight fire with?" he asked her, glancing towards the well and raising his eyebrows like there was the clue to his question. She shrugged before replying tearily.

"I don't know...water?"

"Wrong! You fight fire with fire," he told her like it was obvious. "Right try not to freak, OK?" he prepared her and she nodded, taking a deep breath. "I know exactly what I'm doing and I need you to keep the tears under wraps. I need you to put a brave face on for me - in fact, the meanest face you've got, got it?" he smiled, and she just about managed a smile back and another nod. She was seriously confused. "Alessi, would you mind?" he asked politely, and Alessi grabbed one side of the wooden cover to help Danny slide it across. He then grasped the handle and turned it slowly to bring the bucket up, except it seemed way too heavy to be a bucket. The rope and wench creaked under the strain and it wasn't long before Ruby was looking at a pair of socked feet. She knew immediately who they belonged to.

"Oh my god! Danny! You put him in the well!" she whispered. Danny grinned like it had been great fun. "But what are you going to do with him now?" she asked, flinching and taking a step back when suddenly he started to wriggle and call out into the darkness.

"I, my precious little Ruby, will do whatever you want me to do," he told her. "Want me to cut the rope, I'll do it. Want me to drag him out and beat him to within an inch of his life...and then beat him again. I'll happily do that. For hurting you and trying to come between us, I would do anything to him. But, if all you want is for me to get rid of him...for good...I won't argue."

Her mouth was wide open and she'd started to shake; she couldn't believe what was happening. She looked to Alessi but he was busy checking through his phone idly, giving them some semi-private time to discuss Ruby's wishes. Ruby stayed quiet, unsure what to say or do, and then Alessi flipped his phone shut and looked between the both of them.

"Right, what are we doing with the dirty little sewer rat because I have an appointment in..." he checked his watch "...about an hour and I hate leaving jobs half done."

"Alessi, there's a man in your well!" she protested. "I'd expect you to be a little bit more bothered about that!"

"I knew already. Danny told me last night. Let's just say I wasn't surprised to see Matthew again."

"Oh my god he's been here all night!" she exclaimed, starting to panic now. This was serious!

"Ruby, you didn't want him to talk and I can assure you the only person he's been talking to, since he left our offices yesterday, is me. Well, when I say talking I mean mostly begging...and some crying too. I have his phone so he hasn't told a soul about you, and I have it on good authority that he won't be talking about you ever again, or even thinking about you ever again for that matter. You have no idea how happy that makes me," he squinted at her sexily. "Anyway, he has something he needs to say to you and he promised he'd be a good boy and do as he was told, so let's get him out shall we?"

Between them, Alessi and Danny hoisted Matthew out of the well and onto the grass. They both stood over him and Ruby hid behind Alessi, unaware that she was gripping onto his shirt. While Matthew's eyes struggled to adjust to the light Danny called out to her. "Sweetheart, you need to show him who the boss is around here and come and get your apology out of him. You can do what you like - nobody's going to stop you."

"Erm," Ruby struggled, unsure what to do, and Matthew tried to sit up. Danny pushed him back down onto the grass with his foot on his chest.

"I never said you could move and neither did Ruby. Maybe you need a little recap as to why you're here, Matthew. Yesterday we found out that you'd cornered and messed with her. You are no friend to Ruby, Matthew, and I'd like you to admit that to her face because you've led her to believe otherwise. You're not her friend are you?"

Matthew shook his head. "I did really like you, Ruby, I swear. I mean...I do...but I've used you to get what I want. A true friend would have been glad to see your dad dead and you relocated to somewhere better, but I wasn't. I'd have happily seen your dad hurt you again and again just so I could have you all to myself when you came running to me for safety. Your dad made getting my hands on you so easy. I'm sorry, Ruby, I've been the worst possible friend and I've taken advantage of you again and again. I've not cared one bit for your feelings."

"You were using me the whole time?" she asked, holding onto Alessi's arm now and stepping into view.

"I've used lots of girls, Ruby - it's what I do. You remember Candice on our estate, the girl who went through that initiation and then got cut?" Ruby nodded. "Well that was my fault."

"Your fault? How?" she asked sceptically.

"We got two caps. In one, all us lads put pieces of paper with our names on. In the other we put all the things we could get her to do to prove her loyalty. I picked four pieces of paper from each, first a name and then something she'd be expected to do with that person. The fourth name I picked out was mine, Ruby." Ruby shook her head and paled slightly.

"No, Matthew," she whispered. He closed his eyes so he wouldn't have to see the disgust on her face.

"She got attacked and hurt because, out of the four boys she was assigned obligations to, she turned down just one. Me. I could easily have lied, Ruby. Hell I lied constantly about doing it with you." Ruby's jaw clenched and Danny could see she was furious. "I could have told everyone she'd gone through with it and let her join our gang. I could have made sure she wasn't an outsider or a loner any more, but I felt rejected and annoyed so I refused her entry. I said she'd failed the initiation and then I told them that she'd grassed too, when she hadn't."

"*You* were the reason she was set upon, after everything she went through to try and be accepted?" Ruby couldn't believe it but to her horror he nodded.

"Yes, I'm sorry..." he began, but all she could see now was red; a glowing, pulsating red.

"Save it!" she seethed at him and then walked over to where he sat and dropped to her knees. "You're sick, Matthew Dean, and you make *me* sick too. I never want to see you or hear of you again, else I'll have you wiped out completely. I can do that you know. I have contacts who would do it just for the fun of it." She grabbed his chin so she could look into his eyes and then shoved his face away like he revolted her. He turned back to protest and apologise again but she struck him, hard. "That's for Candice," she snapped and then she struck him with the back of her other hand. "And that's for me!"

"Perhaps you might also like to take a little look at his mobile, Rubes? He has some pretty disturbing videos on it. I think your friend here has a little more explaining to do. We might even get some information out of him that we can use to our advantage."

"Like what?" she asked, standing and scowling down at Matthew. He shook his head to protest as she reached out and took the phone from Danny's hand. Matthew was groaning now and a couple of deep sobs left his body. She accessed his menu and then went to his media file and opened his videos. She pressed play on the latest one and there was Ruby pinned by a man much larger than her, wearing a black balaclava. She stopped the recording. "You were there," she whispered, the hate in her eyes as clear as the blue sky stretching out above her head.

"No, Ruby, I wasn't there. I stayed home that night, I swear! I didn't know what was going to happen to you. I knew there was a party and that you would be there but I also knew you were with Danny. I was insanely jealous and I knew if I saw you on your own I'd do everything I could to get you upstairs. For once in my life I was trying to do the right thing, Ruby. The recording on my phone was sent to me..." he blurted out and then suddenly stopped.

"By who?" she demanded but he shut down and refused to go on.

"If he won't talk then punish him. Punish him as if he were the one responsible. If his loyalties are that strong then he won't mind taking the heat for the person he's protecting, will he?" she ordered coldly and turned to walk away, but he struggled and called out.

"Ruby, it's not what you think. I'm not protecting that idiot who walks around in a baseball cap and thinks he owns the place. I've backed off from it all now, I swear. He's a nasty piece of work...I mean even nastier than I've been."

"Unlikely," she half laughed.

"No, Ruby, please, he thinks the crew belongs to him now and he goes around giving the orders. I couldn't control him. I don't want to go down for the stuff he does, Ruby. I just keep out of it now - I've stepped down. It's not my crew any more."

"So who sent you the recording?" she asked, turning back to look at him.

"I can't tell you - it's complicated, please..."

"Shut up, Matthew. I couldn't care less if you're scared of the payback, because god knows you've hurt enough people in your time! You deserve a taste of your own medicine!" she told him bitterly.

"No it's not that...that's not why I can't tell you...it's because..." He looked utterly torn, and then he started crying and she looked away. It was too pitiful to enjoy, but she wasn't about to back down either. "Ruby, the person who recorded it, they were there, the whole time...apart from upstairs. He didn't know what was planned for you upstairs, he promised me that."

"Who was it?" she demanded.

"Oh god, please, Ruby."

"Who was it?"

"It's impossible to say! Danny and Alessi will kill him and you don't want me to say his name, Ruby, really you don't."

"I will ask you one more time, Matthew. Who was it?"

"Marcus, Ruby! It was Sasha's brother, Marcus," he confessed, breaking into tears again. She was stunned. She stepped backwards, trying to keep it together. What had she done? Now it was out in the open; one of the people had been named and it was her best friend's brother! Alessi and Danny would kill him, just like Matthew had said.

"Why would Marcus do that to me? You lie!" she panicked. "He's a friend! Sasha never thought I should be initiated and nor did you. Are you saying that Marcus did? Why would you grass on your own best mate like that, on Sasha's and Mario's brother? He was at your house, Mario said so!"

"No I stayed in on my own...well...with my mum...you can ask her. I can tell you what I watched on TV and everything. Marcus didn't come round, not until the next day. He forwarded me the message first thing in the morning and then came straight round to speak to me. He wanted to tell me what he'd helped them do to you. He said he hadn't slept all night and that it had got seriously out of hand. It was supposed to be just girl on girl, two of theirs against you. The lads were just there to protect their own and to record it so they could humiliate you. He said the big bloke in charge seemed to have a personal score to settle with you though. He wanted you upstairs with him and he ordered everyone else to stay downstairs. Getting you up there on your own was all he seemed to care about."

"Why did he do it to me, Matthew?" she asked looking betrayed. "Because...oh god I swore I'd keep this to myself...because...he was jealous of you, Ruby."

"Jealous?" she frowned. "Why, did he want an abusive dad and a runaway mum too?"

"No, not like that. He was jealous of...you and me. Ruby, oh bloody hell, you're making this impossible for me."

"Oh I'm sorry, Matthew, do you want me to make it easier?" she exclaimed, astounded that he had the audacity to complain.

"I made a promise!" he shouted at her, getting angry now. "Unlike you, Ruby, I am loyal!" he snapped, wanting to hurt her out of desperation.

"Huh, get rid of him," she ordered, turning away. He gritted his teeth and tilted his head back against the grass.

"OK, I'm sorry! I never meant that!" he pleaded desperately. "Marcus is gay, Ruby," he declared suddenly. Danny was grasping a handful of his collar when she stopped and turned back.

"He's gay?" she echoed. He nodded as the tears ran down the sides of his face. Danny let him go but Ruby saw a flash of disappointment on his face as he did so.

"He told me the day he sent me the recording. He said that's why he did it to you..."

"Because he's gay?" she asked, unconvinced. "Being gay doesn't make people do things like that. It doesn't make people masochistic, Matthew." If he thought she was falling for that one he could think again.

"No but being out of your mind with envy does. Look, Ruby, he's in love with me." Now her eyes were wide, her eyebrows raised. "I know, OK, I was stunned too." She couldn't help but stare; for once she'd been shocked into silence. "I had no idea. I just thought he was a good mate, that's all. He never seemed bothered about girls either way, but then he just liked playing on computer games and hanging out with me and the lads all the time. But the whole time he was being eaten up with jealousy at seeing me constantly trying it on with you. He'd ask me to go out but I'd say no because you were round. I told him all the things I wanted to do to you, Ruby, and I was really graphic about it too." She shuddered and Danny and Alessi both scowled. "Sorry," he apologised to them, knowing that he wasn't doing himself any favours. If he didn't talk he was going to pay for it and if he did he was just going to piss them off even more! "I saved you from the initiation, Ruby, and then I spent every opportunity trying to make you mine, while he constantly hoped that I would notice him...like that. He heard you were coming to the party and he just wanted to scare you enough that you would stay away from the estate and never come back. He didn't really want you to be hurt and he certainly didn't want you to be hanged.

He said he thought that if you stayed away long enough it would give us a chance to...you know...but I put him straight on that. I mean I like girls, Ruby."

She frowned at him and then laughed at the fact that Matthew felt the need to admit that he liked girls. He had a stupid schoolboy list of conquests to prove it.

"To be fair, Matthew, you could like chimpanzees for all I care," she smiled. "So what about the big guy? Who was it who tried to hang me?"

"They will kill me if they know I've spoken out."

"And I will kill you if you don't," she pointed out simply.

"You stand more of a chance if you tell us," Danny advised. "It's pretty hard to intimidate someone after you've been dropped off a bridge."

"Who was it?" Ruby demanded, but Matthew pressed his mouth into an obstinate line. Alessi took a handkerchief from his pocket and then reached round to the back of his waistband and pulled his gun. Matthew watched, paralysed by fear, as he held it up to the light and then gave it a rub.

"This is new," he gloated. "I'm pretty keen to see if it lives up to the last one. I have it on good authority that it does the job," he smiled.

"Billingham, it was John Billingham," he practically screamed out. "He's in on it with that Ryan guy, the bloke with the cap who was hassling you at Sasha's house." Ruby forced her stomach to remain calm as he continued. "Billingham wanted to punish you and Ryan wanted a recording of it - they're both as sick as each other. Billingham hooked up with him when he got put in a young offender's institute for stealing, after he was chucked out of school. He met Ryan there and they realised they had something in common."

"Sticky fingers?" Danny asked but Matthew frowned and shook his head slowly.

"No, young girls, Danny," he whispered, glancing at Ruby. "They both have an unhealthy interest in young girls and intimidating women. Billingham told him some story about how he cornered Ruby in the sports shed at school." He noted that Ruby had paled considerably. "He said he had some unfinished business with you, Ruby. They intended to get rid of you but not until Billingham had finished off what he'd started all those years ago. They wanted it recorded so they'd have a little trophy, you know, to..."

"Right thanks, Matthew," Danny cut in, knowing Ruby had heard just about as much as she could take. "I think we've got enough to make sure they are properly seen to. So, Ruby, do you want me to drop him down the well now, honey?" he asked her. "Nobody knows he's here and as far as his family are concerned he was sacked yesterday for gross misconduct. They'll give up looking for him eventually and I'm pretty sure Mr Alessi's decommissioned well will be the last place they'd think to check. By that time he'll either be starved to death or bled to death from the fall. It's a pretty deep one and I'm not even sure if there's water in it. I reckon if we listen carefully, when I drop him, we should be able to tell." She couldn't help but smile. He was very good at the scary talk.

"Ruby, please, no! I swear I will just go away. I'll go back to the estate and say I went on a drinking binge after getting the sack. I swear I won't tell a soul about this, or about the coffee room thing, or about the fact that you grassed."

"I never actually grassed, Matthew," she informed him. "Alessi's firm has surveillance all over it and he managed to catch everything you said and did to me. You dropped yourself right in it, so don't blame me, Matthew. If anyone's a grass around here it's you, remember!"

"That's not what I meant. Oh god please, Ruby, just tell him to leave me alone and I swear you won't even know I'm still alive."

"I know where you live, Matthew, and I know where your family live too..."

"Ruby, you don't need to threaten them - I know that already. I won't talk, I swear, I've got too much to lose." She looked from Alessi to Danny, and Alessi checked his watch again.

"Thirty minutes till my first appointment and twenty minutes to get into the office. I have approximately ten minutes, but I'd hate for you to feel pressured, Rubes. If you're undecided, please, take your time and we will come back to Matthew later. Shall we pop him back in the well, Danny?"

251

he asked and Danny was quick to move and oblige. Matthew struggled as they lifted him and started to lower him head first back into the dark vertical tunnel. Ruby stopped them just as he began to sob.

"No, I'm decided. Let him go but have him tracked and bugged, Alessi. Don't tell him how, he'll never work it out - he's too thick. But if he does talk, to anyone, have him brought back here and I'll cut the rope myself! He might be useful alive for the time being. He knows Billingham and Ryan and he could get them in the same place at the same time - may as well make the most of him while he's here."

Swinging round on her heel, her beautiful long dark hair skimming at her hips, she strode back to the house to get her bag and jacket and to make a fresh piece of toast. The odds felt a little bit easier, the pressure that bit lighter, and now she was hungry!

36

Let the games commence!

Matthew was released and dropped off a few miles from home, just to make things even harder for him, and Ruby was pretty happy, all things considered. However, Marlon continued to send images and recordings to Alessi and each time Ruby reacted in the same way, getting angrier with each new humiliating episode. Alessi agreed to let her watch the recordings through, although it killed her to do it, but he also insisted on being present so he could at least hear what was being said. He was worried that Ruby might try and cover things up or meet Marlon's demands on her own. It wouldn't be the first time she'd considered it. While Ruby sat glued to the screen with tears in her eyes, crushing the cushions between her hands, Alessi sat behind the TV in an armchair, flicking through paperwork, pretending not to be listening.

She hated seeing herself so desperate for Paradise that she'd dance or wear whatever Marlon wanted while he took pictures of her. He'd also recorded her being given shots of the drug, including her first major and addicting dose of 10mls, apparently he loved to watch her getting high. He never touched her and he never let anyone else touch her either, but he used the drug to get his hands on the very influential footage and snaps. His letters always indicated that he would share them publically and widely and that she was already a massive hit. He made her skin crawl.

Danny, Alessi and Bardo watched her constantly and Alessi even brought in more men to help keep an eye on her and make sure she didn't run off and do anything stupid. She was dropped in the pool two more times until Danny went out one night and drained it. He then removed all of the pasta pans and put them in the loft along with the kitchen knives and, just in case she was feeling particularly brutal, the vegetable peeler and nutcracker too. He replaced them with a wide variety of takeaway menus.

It had been a week since Matthew had been released from the well. Every one of those days a new package arrived for Alessi, enclosing not just photos and recordings but also filthy threatening letters, written and signed by The Puppet Master. It was a Saturday morning and Danny was sitting back on the sofa reading through a newspaper when the doors to the dining room flew open and Ruby stormed out. She had endured yet another recording of herself begging for Paradise and then writhing around after getting it. Alessi had heard it all and his busy 'adding up an invoice' charade was wasted on her. She felt Danny's eyes as she walked in a strop through the living room. She was going to ignore him, in the same way she had done every day that week, but she felt a sudden pang of guilt and remorse. She stopped and pulled herself together, returning to sit next to him on the sofa. He smiled at her in the beautiful and handsome way he always did and she found it in herself, somewhere tangled up with the bitterness and fury, to smile back.

"Thank you, Danny, for everything you've done for me. I know I get mad at you sometimes and I take my temper out on you...a lot. You probably think that I don't appreciate you but really I do. You are always so kind and thoughtful. Danny, although my time coming off Paradise is still sketchy, I distinctly remember your arms around me making me feel secure. I remember you cleaning my face and giving me water. I remember you sponging me down and changing my clothes. I remember all of the soothing words you told me and I noticed that you were always the one that wrapped me up tightly after every dose so that I would have at least some privacy...unlike Marlon who used it as an opportunity to film me."

"He's one sick individual, Ruby, but you're safe now, honey," he reminded her, brushing a lock of hair behind her ear. She nodded.

"You stopped me feeling so exposed and I love you, Danny Glover, please don't ever think that I don't. I don't mean all of the things I say and do. I just struggle to keep it bottled sometimes, and I explode so badly I think I could kill someone. I want Marlon to pay for what he's done to me and I want him stopped. I want all of those DVD's back and I want them destroyed. I will do anything to make sure that happens." He listened quietly, his eyes drifting over her face, watching her mouth as she spoke. When she was definitely finished, he kissed her gently and nodded.

"I know all of those things, Ruby, but thank you for telling me."

She slipped off the sofa and left the room and he knew then that he would help her to get her own revenge. She needed it like he needed her.

Late that night, while the place was silent and sleeping, the alarm on Ruby's mobile phone vibrated through her pillow. She slipped her hand beneath and stopped it immediately. Danny, who had taken to keeping an all night vigil in the armchair in her room, was still fast asleep. She called him softly and he shuffled to get more comfortable, but stayed peaceful. She slipped her legs out of bed and pulled on some jeans, a fitted t-shirt and some slip-on shoes.

She grabbed a thin cardigan hanging from the wardrobe and slipped her arms in. She then pulled her dressing gown on, just in case she bumped into anyone, and made her way downstairs to Alessi's home office. She was relieved to find the code still the same and quickly began searching through Alessi's letters for one of Marlon's. She needed the address scrawled in the right hand corner. She had only ever travelled to his place and been brought back again by car and she wasn't quite sure of the route. Having located what she needed, she grabbed the Sat Nav from Alessi's top drawer and typed the address in. She would follow it by foot. Trying to take a car would cause a disturbance and Alessi would kill her. In his book it was ok to shoot someone but just don't underage drink, or drive without a licence! She snorted in amusement and then pushed everything else she needed into the pockets of her cardigan before leaving the office.

Her mind was racing, and the first most pressing issue was how she was going to escape the grounds when Alessi had stepped up security. She went from one room to another, checking through the windows to work out what men were posted where. She kept the lights off and moved silently and slowly to avoid suspicion. Her heart raced when she discovered that nobody was covering the downstairs toilet window. It had been deemed too small for them to bother with, but for her it was a perfect size. She wriggled through and dropped to her knees, keeping low. She made straight for the perimeter wall, and the trees that lined it, and called upon her years of stealing apples from her next door neighbour's tree, to get up off the ground. She pulled herself up quickly and effortlessly, trying hard not to bounce the branches and make them rustle. Once she was up high enough, she scaled the wall and dropped onto the path on the other side. The wall was high and the drop made her feet sting in her thin soled shoes.

She followed the directions on the Sat Nav until she reached Marlon's place over an hour later. It was now 3am and everywhere was deserted, making the walk both frightening and incredibly dangerous. The house was mostly in darkness and Marlon's men were inside, sure that nobody was either brave enough or stupid enough to attack *them*. Ruby wasn't sure which she was, as she reversed her escape strategy from Alessi's property to gain access into Marlon's.

She located a strong looking tree lining the street, one with branches that reached the wall that surrounded Marlon's land. She climbed the trunk, with difficulty, and then edged as far along the tree's arm as she dared, before making a lurch and a scrabble. Before too long she was unsafely on the other side and, once again, back on Marlon's turf. Her blood ran cold leaving her with a sudden urge to back out, but her determination to get things done and draw a line under the whole thing was pulling way too hard. She pushed reason and good judgement from her mind; it was trying to pick holes in her confidence. She had a job to do.

She knew she needed to be upstairs and she wasn't about to try and pass through the downstairs, where Marlon's men would be littered about. She climbed up onto the garage roof, using the drainpipe, and then used the window sills and a great amount of luck to get in through an open first floor window. It brought her into a bedroom where one of Marlon's men was sleeping. He was face down, hanging off the edge of the bed, his hand skimming the floor. She held her breath as she crept over him and through the room, her heart beating so hard she was sure it was loud enough to wake someone.

"Oi!" the man behind her suddenly shouted out, and she tried to keep from screaming, placing her hands over her mouth firmly and spinning around to face him. She wasn't ready to fight so soon. "I said I'd take the red one. Marlon will take the blue one," he rambled incoherently, and Ruby steadied her lungs; he was sleep talking. She placed a hand against the wall for support and it helped to ease the dizzying shock that was threatening to topple her.

As soon as she felt strong enough she cracked open the door and peeked out onto the landing. The upstairs was empty, just as she figured it would be. She worked her way right to the end of the corridor and through the unlocked double wooden doors that housed Marlon's self contained apartment. It was Marlon's suite, his wing, his own piece of mansion that he liked to call home. She made her way through the living area with the plump, purple cushions and leather sofas. A massive flat screen TV hung in front of a huge armchair, for maximum viewing pleasure. It made her feel sick and she guessed he'd probably played footage of her there too. The room flowed into another and there, exactly central, was a giant bed covered in deep purple satin sheets and quilts. It looked like an executive brothel.

She held her breath upon spotting a figure in the middle of the bed; it was Marlon. He was flat out, eyes closed, chest rising and falling deeply and slowly. She crept up closer and looked into his face; it was ugly and she despised it with a passion. She dug something from her pocket and then removed her cardigan, placing it in the chair. This was to be her payback, but as she loaded her choice of weapon, her fingers began to tremble and it dropped to the floor. She turned away from the bed and bent down to pick it up, spotting as she did so a red blinking light on a shelf in the corner. It was shining from between some books and she felt distracted for a few vital seconds. Before she could work out what was going on, a strong arm wrapped around her waist and she screamed out, trying to escape the vicelike clutches. Marlon wasn't asleep at all and he'd grabbed her so tightly she felt like her ribs might break. She dropped her weapon again and tried to reach out for it, but he lifted her effortlessly and threw her down onto the mattress, capturing her beneath him.

"Ahhh, Ruby, all I had to do was wait. I knew you'd be back for more," he crooned, holding her down and running his hands over her. "I promised

I wouldn't touch you didn't I?" he asked, and she nodded and gasped out. "Hmmm, but that was when you were doing as you were told - that was before you became trouble, ran away and caused me a whole lot of grief and disappointment. I could have had Danny just like that, but YOU!" She cringed and yelped as he grabbed her shoulders and shook her. It made her head hurt. "YOU ruined everything. So, baby, deals off. I was saving you for Danny but now, as far as I'm concerned, you're fair game like all the rest of them."

"Marlon, please don't," she begged, as he clawed at her top and yanked it over her head.

"Give me one good reason why not? You've cost me a lot of money in Paradise and I have nothing in return. A few hours with you should go a little way to settling your bill. But, Ruby, believe me, it won't settle it completely. I don't care how good you are, your debt's big...and I'm talking mega. Each of those shots I gave you has a value of £10,000. It was good clean stuff, not cut with anything like you get on the streets. You're first shot was double so that's £20,000 and, by my figures, you had eighteen shots in total. That makes a debt of £360,000, with interest, and I'm recalling it...starting now! You're never going to pay it off completely, Ruby, but you are going to spend the rest of your life trying."

37

She tried to push his face away as he kissed her. This was her worst nightmare come true. The whole time she had been under his roof she was worried Marlon would take it further, or let his men take it further, and now it seemed she was trapped and about to face the inevitable: becoming Marlon's. She was desperate and unsure what to do to help herself; the turmoil resulted in tears of desperation. He wasn't sorry for her; the crying only served to make him all the more brutal.

"I bet you owe Alessi quite a bit too, if he's been feeding you since you left me. The fact that you're still alive and well tells me he'll have invested quite a lot of money in you, young lady. You're not even related. How sweet - I wonder what he wants in return?" he sniggered.

"He cares, that's all!"

"Oh yeah of course he does, we all do, Ruby," he sympathised, whilst running the backs of his fingers over her mouth and tracing the shape of her lips.

"Marlon, I don't know what you want and I'm scared," she begged. He drew his hand away from her face and stopped, looking slightly amused.

"You don't know what I want? You do know how I intend for you to settle your bill?" he asked, rolling his lips over such a promising thought. She nodded between sobs.

"I know, but you said I'd be good at it, and I won't. I've never done it before, Marlon."

He grinned as the information slowly registered. "Perhaps I could knock a little bit more off your bill for that one," he chuckled.

"Marlon, I know this is punishment, but perhaps you could show me...how it should be. Danny wouldn't touch me and I don't know anything," she confessed with big, wide, innocent eyes.

"What about that evening in the bedroom?" he frowned, doubting her little story.

"I'm so sorry, Marlon, we set you up. I told Danny I'd been ordered to trap him. I grassed, Marlon. I was desperate and I'd tried, really I had, but Danny just wouldn't go through with it. I told you he was traditional. I even begged him. I told him it was a case of life or death, my death, but he still wouldn't do it! That's why I finished with him when I got back to Alessi's place. I felt let down by him. He said we should lie. It was his idea," she told him, dropping her so called 'boyfriend' right in it. Marlon smiled and looked her over.

"You want Marlon to show you?" he asked her, seeming keen. She nodded attentively. He liked that; it reminded him of when she hung on his every word and movement, eager for another shot of Paradise, desperate to keep him happy and amenable. He loved the power that administering the drug had given him over her.

"You know what you're doing, right?" she dared to ask, and he laughed at her blatant cheekiness.

"Oh yes I know exactly what to do with you," he told her, lowering himself and kissing her again. He'd been completely taken in by her. His defences were down, all sense out of the window, as he raised himself to undo his trousers. She took the opportunity to discreetly slip one of her legs between his and then she lifted her knee as hard as she could, slamming him with all her might. He yelled out loudly, making her freeze. She wondered what he would do but, fortunately, he did exactly what she hoped he would do. He rolled across the bed doubled up in agony, coughing and winded like she'd kicked him in the stomach.

She pushed herself up and when he lifted his face to look at her, his eyes furious, she rammed the palm of her hand right into his nose, breaking it instantly. It poured with blood and now he was stunned too. She threw herself over the edge of the bed and grabbed at the floor until her hands fell on what she had dropped earlier, a needle with 10mls of Paradise in it. She held it up with both hands as she straddled him, shaking in fear but mad with fury and revenge.

"I want the films and the photos, Marlon, where are they?" she demanded. He laughed deliriously at her.

"I'm not telling you!"

She brought the needle down and plunged the drug into him. She then extracted another vial and nervously drew another 10mls of liquid.

"Where are they?" she demanded. Now he was less defiant, his eyes wide, his body still. The drug had started its journey.

"The library downstairs - you'll find all the girls I've ever filmed down there." He told her stiffly. "Out of all of them you were the most popular, Ruby. You were constantly being loaned out," he smiled through gritted teeth. "The elusive Ruby Palmer, the one everyone wants to get their hands on."

"Button it, Marlon! You're not funny and you're not getting to me either. I don't care who's seen it. All I care about is that I get my hands on it...*now*. While I'm clearing you out of your little dirty rental collection I have a question for you, Marlon."

Looking into her blue eyes, he frowned; what could she want to know from him? She smiled so sweetly he couldn't help but smile back, lulled into a false sense of security and then, as she lowered herself towards his ear, she whispered; "Who's the Puppet Master now, Marlon?" His eyes grew wide as she sat back up and brought the needle down again. Within minutes he'd arched violently, throwing her backwards as he groaned and panted, the drug racing at high speed through his brain and body.

She shuffled to the foot of the bed to watch him; even her teeth were chattering as she witnessed him fall victim like she had. She snatched up the needle, petrified he might come at her again, and refilled it. But just as she finished draining the vial, an arm slid around her middle and held her tight. She snapped into action, struggling for her life again.

"Shhhhh, stay calm," a voice she recognised soothed, and she swung round and up onto her knees, throwing her arms out and hugging him tightly. "You were fine. I was here. I wouldn't have let him do anything to you," Danny promised, taking the needle from her hands and pushing a rubber stopper onto the end. He placed it on the table by the bed and came back to her.

"You watched?" she asked in disbelief. He smiled and checked her out; he looked impressed, and she rolled her eyes at him.

"You could handle it, Ruby. I contemplated cutting in, but you wouldn't have thanked me for it. This was your battle. I didn't want to take that away from you. I figured as long as your pants stayed on I'd keep from muscling in, and on they stayed," he observed, looking very pleased at just how sexy she was, kneeling in front of him partially dressed. "Damn, Ruby, you're good, I'll give you that. I worry about you so much but do I really need to? I'm not so sure. I think maybe you can handle yourself better than most...me included," he confessed begrudgingly, and she giggled at him.

"I was petrified. I messed up when I dropped the Paradise and he could have had me just like that. I guess I was lucky."

"Hmmm, so was he. Do me a favour, Rubes, if you ever need to teach me a lesson, can you take your clothes off and beg me to sleep with you first?" She slapped him around the shoulder and he laughed. "Bet you weren't planning on confronting Marlon in your underwear?" he asked her with a chuckle. "What a great way to die."

"Die?" she frowned. "I've only dosed him up with Paradise," she explained. "He's not dead!"

"He will be in a minute," he confirmed.

"What, why, what have I done wrong?" She was desperately thinking it over in her mind. 20mls, that was double what he had given her but it wouldn't be enough to kill him. Danny leaned over Marlon who was now still. He slid his hand beneath him and into his back pocket. He cringed. Rifling through Marlon's clothes with him still in them was utterly gross. As Ruby watched on he pulled his arm back out and with it a gun too. She gasped in shock; she hadn't realised Marlon was carrying a weapon; she hadn't even considered it. Guns scared the life out of her, especially given her own run in with one. She automatically reached up to her shoulder to the scar left by the bullet that had nearly taken her life. "He wouldn't have got that far," Danny confirmed, reading her thoughts. "He's not the only one with a gun but I don't intend on incriminating myself by using mine. I do believe that people do strange things when they're high, Ruby, and being found with their trousers round their ankles is a common one. Another is shooting themselves with their own gun."

"No!" she exclaimed. "I didn't come here to kill anyone I just wanted some revenge and the films and photos, that's all!"

"So you're happy to let him live after what he did to you?" He was casually checking out Marlon's weapon and getting to grips with it.

"Well, not happy as such but..." Suddenly Danny held the gun up towards her and she screamed and ducked out of the way. A shot rang out and she covered her ears and clenched her eyes tightly shut as she dropped flat to the mattress.

She screamed into the quilt and then sat up to shout at him hysterically. "What have you done! Oh my god, Danny, what have you done?" He moved to place Marlon's fingers around the trigger and then held it up before letting it go so the fall would look natural. He then turned to Ruby and placed his hands over hers, pulling them away from her ears so she could hear him.

"Ruby, he got you hooked on Paradise, he filmed you, took pictures of you and left you no choice but to try and get me to use you. He humiliated you by sending images of you through the post and he let his men enjoy them too. He drugged you in front of them because he got off on the power. He made you dance for him and he left you facing days of agonising detox. He let you be sick all day on your own, knowing you would think you were dying, and he killed Sammy right in front of you. He thought he was about to have you for himself and he was then going to make you do it again and again to cover the debt he got you into in the first place. Did you honestly think I was going to let him live?" She stared at him wide eyed, not sure what to say now he'd put it like that. "Ruby, this is what I do and who I am. I had every intention of taking him out but, though I was willing to hear your opinion on the matter first, he forced my hand a little sooner than I planned."

"What do you mean?" she frowned. He nodded towards the table next to Marlon's bed and she followed his direction. The needle wasn't there but the rubber stopper was. She was confused and frantically scanned the floor for the needle, only to spot it in Marlon's other hand.

"He was going to get you again, Ruby. A coward always takes their victim from behind. He's not the only bully who appears on my list of 'things to deal with' either. You will have to excuse me but I've been a little bit busy lately." He took a turn of the room to ensure nothing was there that shouldn't be, and collected up Ruby's top and cardigan before throwing them at her. She snapped out of her daze and immediately began putting them on.

"Who else, Danny, who else is on the list?" she demanded to know, struggling with her garments because her hands were shaking so much. "Not Matthew? I went to him when I needed help."

"Hmmm, and he took advantage and pushed his luck, Ruby," he argued.

"No, please, Danny, not Matthew!"

"I'll think about it, but you're definitely not getting me to change my mind on John Billingham. He's is so asking for it!"

"Oh Danny, no!" she protested

"You do remember what he did, right?" he asked, stopping to look at her incredulously before scouting the room again. She turned in circles on the bed, trying to keep an eye on him while he moved. Now he was cracking the curtains so he could check the grounds below for Marlon's men.

"Yes of course I remember...but..."

"He cornered you in the gym shed at school and made you pay for showing him up time and again over his failed attempts to bully you. I know you got your own back by getting him expelled but you never told me what he did, Ruby, and that has always bugged me."

"It's in the past, Danny!"

"Well his little initiation or punishment, or whatever you want to call it, that isn't in the past. As far as I'm concerned that's very much still up here," he told her, tapping his head. "I cut you down, Ruby. He let you swing! He deserves everything he gets and so much more. He's messed with the wrong girl this time."

"Come on, Danny," she pleaded desperately. "You don't need to. It's just so wrong and...and...I don't want you to go to prison. I'll be lonely."

"I'm not going to go to prison," he laughed, stopping to help her. "I know what I'm doing and I don't get caught." He grabbed her cardigan and tied it around her middle, making it so tight she sucked in a breath as he crossed the arms over again to make a double knot.

"You make it sound like you do this kind of thing all the time!" She sounded shocked and he laughed, but said nothing. "Danny?" she whined.

"Come, let's go find some DVD's with you on them," he told her, taking her hand in his and pulling her off of the bed.

38
A blast from the past

They made their way through Marlon's apartment and back out into the hallway. Taking the stairs down to the next level Ruby quickly took the lead. She'd lived with Marlon and she knew the layout of the building well. No sooner had they reached the bottom of the stairs Ruby stopped dead, ducking backwards and holding her hand out for Danny to stop too. There was a man stationed in the hallway and Ruby warned Danny to stay put. He began to argue but she stepped out into view before he could stop her.

"Hey, Hendrick," she whispered.

"Who's there?" he demanded, swinging round and trying to focus in the dim light.

"It's me, Ruby," she forced herself to reply. He pulled his gun on her and she tried not to collapse in fright. "Hendrick! Wait, I'm not a threat to you. Is that really necessary?" she exclaimed holding her hands up in front of her. He chuckled as he approached in a couple of long strides.

"Well, I've heard a lot, Ruby, and let's just say I wouldn't put anything past you. You say you're not a threat but I'd prefer to check that out for myself," he told her, pushing his gun into the back of his trousers. She shrugged, feeling a little cooler knowing the gun at least was out of his hands.

"I have nothing," she confirmed, holding her arms out. He smiled and looked her over.

"I'm thorough, I'd like to check myself," he grinned. "Face the wall." She turned at his order, not liking that she had her back to him but glad that Danny wasn't far away. He would never let anything happen to her...well...nothing that she couldn't handle, apparently. She took a deep breath. She had another two syringes full of Paradise in the pocket of the cardigan tied around her middle and she didn't want them in her. He stepped up behind and ran his hands over her back, playing with her hair and sweeping it to one side so he could reach her neck with his mouth.

"Hendrick, please," she whispered.

"Haven't you heard the 'keep your hands off Ruby' rule has been lifted? Marlon told us if you were to show your pretty face around here again he didn't care what happened to you, as long as we took you straight to him after. He turned her back round, looking down towards her feet and reaching for the button on her jeans. "I do believe that he told us the one who gets you, gets a reward for his bother. You're no bother, Ruby. In fact, I'm more than happy to be the one who gets you." He pulled at the arms of her cardigan, jerking her forward as he attempted to pull them loose, but Danny had pulled them *very* tight.

"Hendrick, I'll do it!" she told him sternly, grabbing at his beefy hands and pushing them away. "You don't have to rough me up too do you?" she complained, and he looked into her eyes for a long moment, sussing her out.

"No I don't have to rough you up...and I don't want to either. You do it," he told her, letting her untie the arms herself. He waited patiently to get his hands on her and she made a big deal out of trying to work out what bit went where. "Look, I know I said I don't have to be rough, but if you don't hurry it up..." he threatened, getting agitated. She slipped her hand into her cardigan pocket and pulled out the syringe, keeping it hidden in the material. She then pulled the thin garment away and threw it to the floor, moving her hand behind her back and out of view. The second the waist of her jeans was exposed his hands were there, trying to get them undone.

She suddenly realised that no part of his body was exposed and there would be nowhere to stick the needle. He was wearing jeans and a leather jacket and she was quickly running out of time and options. His neck was the only place and she reached her arm up and back and plunged it in, gritting her teeth at how repulsive it felt. He took a step back in shock and reached for the gun in his waistband, the needle still protruding from his neck. She covered her eyes and waited for it all to be over. She was ready for the deafening crack, the searing hot pain, the delirious hallucinations, the sound of her screams, but what she wasn't expecting was to feel Danny's hands on her shoulders. She dared a look through her fingers and Hendrick was already on the floor.

"What happened?" she asked in a shaky whisper while Danny did her back up.

"I think you must have got him intravenously. If you inject into the muscle it takes minutes to work if you inject into a vein it takes seconds - Bardo told me that. Looks like luck was on your side - he didn't even have time to get a hold of his weapon. Technically I should take him out too," he informed her, bending down and taking the gun from Hendrick's hand.

"Please, Danny, no!" she begged, grabbing at his arm to get his attention. "Look I have a plan and he'll be part of it. You don't need to shoot anyone," she told him, reaching down to scoop up her cardigan and letting him secure it around her waist, again! They were close, his head bowed while he concentrated on putting her back together. She could smell the soapy scent of his hair and the dark soft strands tickled at her face. When he looked up it was straight into her eyes, setting her pulse soaring. He moved his hands from the knot he'd just made to her sides and squeezed firmly, pulling her to him. His smile was so sexy, a wolfish grin that lit up his eyes. He stepped forward, walking her back until she was up against the wall and as far as she could go. She was up to her neck in trouble, standing on Marlon's turf with a dead body on her hands, armed to the hilt with a lethal drug - which she intended to use whenever the need arose - knowing if one of Marlon's men didn't kill her Alessi certainly would. But, despite all of that, all she could think of and care about was Danny. He found her mouth with his and kissed her, leaving her in no doubt as to how much he wanted her. He pulled away ever so slightly, their lips still just touching.

"Have I ever told you that I love you, Ruby?" he whispered.

"Uh huh," was all she could manage as she trembled in the little space he'd created for her.

"I think we make a pretty good team, don't you?"

"Uh huh." She wanted him so bad. He was a living nightmare! The way he made her heart pound, her adrenalin pump and how he caused her to sweat and shiver all at once, just about blew her mind. He evoked all the agonising symptoms of a night terror but with one crucial difference; she never *ever* wanted to wake up.

"I believe if you find something perfect, you hold onto it with all your might. You keep it safe, you honour and respect it and," he kissed her again, more slowly this time, "you give it all the attention it deserves and needs." She giggled as he dug his fingers into her sides playfully, knowing it would make her squirm. "I will always be yours, Ruby, for as long as you'll have me...which I hope is forever," he added with a sexy little squint.

"Forever it is," she agreed, smiling cutely. "To the library?" she asked him and he dithered, unsure what to do. He wanted to take her straight from the building and keep her safe, but he of all people knew that life wasn't really like that. He could keep her in a box, immaculate and treasured, but then he would be stealing her opportunity to live the way she wanted to - Ruby's way. He nodded in acceptance. They were in it now for the duration, regardless of the consequences, and so he let her take his hand and guide him towards the library.

As they approached the end of the hallway Danny slowed and reached for Ruby's arm to get her attention.

"Hey, what's down here?" he whispered, checking out a dimly lit stairwell.

"It's the back entrance to Marlon's dirty little basement club," she shuddered. "It's where he brings his girls and gets them to dance for him and his men. It's so gross!"

"Did he get you..." he began, but she put her hand up to stop him from going there.

"Only for him, Danny, but that was bad enough."

"Listen, I think I just heard something at the end of the hall. You stay here while I go and check it out," he ordered. "Here, take this." He handed her Hendrick's gun and she held her hand out flat. He frowned at her, hesitated and then laid it on her palm. She looked at it like it was a decomposing animal before looking up into his eyes.

"Why would I need this? I don't want it," she told him, holding it away from her. He smirked.

"Just do me a favour and take it. Point it away from you at all times and not at me, please," he told her, directing it away from his chest. "Be careful and you won't be able to hurt yourself with it. Sometimes pointing it at someone is all you need to do to get them to do as they're told, got it?" he asked her. She nodded and cringed. "Hold it properly, Ruby - you can't threaten people with it like that. They'll just take it from you," he told her tiresomely, shaking his head. She tried not to feel offended and plucked up the courage to gingerly lift it and turn it so that it rested in her hand as it should, or as she had seen others do it, with her finger on the trigger. "Very good," he commended. "It will just make me feel better knowing you have something. If you need to use it, Ruby, just do it - I don't want to lose you." She nodded obediently and held it out in front of her, trying it out. He smiled, "Lara Croft eat your heart out," he nodded proudly. "You are so sexy, Ruby Palmer." He pushed the outstretched arm to one side and pressed his lips to hers. "Don't shoot me," he whispered into her ear, making her laugh. "Just a few minutes, OK, and then I'll be right back. Wait *right* here." With that he turned and left her to hang about at the top of the basement staircase.

She soon became aware of music playing from the club below and checked her watch, 4am! How late did they make these girls work! She was suddenly intrigued. She'd promised she would stay put, but one little check wouldn't hurt, surely. Briefly glancing down the hall both ways first, to make sure she was alone, she made her way down the stairs towards the club door. She put her ear to it, music was definitely playing. She cracked the door slightly and tiptoed through the large dressing room towards the raised stage. She had been here before and she knew that on the other side of the heavy burgundy curtain was a runway surrounded by tables, chairs and cushioned booths. Girls would change backstage, where she was loitering, and then they would make their way back out to the front and onto the podiums, cages, club floor, wherever Marlon's men wanted to see them.

Ruby heard laughing and heckling coming from the club and dared to create a gap in the curtain, just big enough to peek through. To her horror she was faced with two men that she recognised: Ryan and John Billingham! She closed the curtains quickly and held onto them tightly, desperately hoping that they hadn't seen her. The air had been sucked from the room and the lights were dim and growing dimmer by the second, until she realised that she'd actually stopped breathing.

She was close to passing out, but she felt the weight of the gun in her hand and drew courage from having it on her. She wasn't so vulnerable this time; she was at least able to protect herself and the last thing she would allow herself to do was pass out and let them have her so easily. She wanted to see the girls that were entertaining them and another peek confirmed her suspicions, two females, both barely seventeen, dancing around poles in tiny little dresses that left little to the imagination. As she watched on in disgust, Billingham beckoned one of the girls over and she smiled amiably and made her way towards him. He ran his hands over her and it made Ruby feel sick, recalling that she'd once had them on her too. He rolled a bank note and slipped it into her top, laughing as he did so, and then he then spun her, struck her across the bottom and boomed out loudly.

"I demand a costume change!

The girls said nothing as they obediently and sexily slunk off in Ruby's direction. They were there to give whatever sordid little fantasy was requested of them; it was that or the streets and probably a habit too expensive for them to afford. The only thing that Ruby was happy about was that the young men seemed to be alone, a private viewing no doubt set up by Marlon in return for finding and grooming young girls from the estate. She wasn't sure how she was going to achieve it, but she definitely wasn't going to let them get away with it. Ruby moved to perch confidently on one of the dressing tables in front of the huge mirrors and begrudgingly hid the gun in the waistband of her jeans. Even though feeling the cold of the metal against her skin made her blood run cold, the last thing she wanted to do was frighten the girls away or have them scream the place down.

"Hey," she greeted them and they seemed uneasy, unsure whether to approach her. "My name's Ruby. Ruby Palmer," she smiled and they nodded back like they'd heard of her before. She knew the last thing Marlon would have done was let any of his girls know that Ruby had escaped his clutches; that would be bad for business. She was pretty sure she could win the girls' trust. "Marlon has a job for you. He said if you do it, and you can get out of the building without getting yourselves shot, then you're free to go. He won't come looking for you and he's wiped your slate clean. You owe him nothing," she coaxed, dangling a carrot she was pretty sure they'd go for. They looked between each other warily but, to Ruby's relief, they also seemed slightly hopeful. She guessed that he would have threatened them with the kind of impossible debt he'd threatened her with. She was relieved, but not surprised, to see that they were keen on severing the ties binding them to Marlon.

"What does he want us to do that he hasn't got us to do already?" one of them asked, the one that had been struck by Billingham. Ruby tried not to show the sympathy that she felt for her. Close up, she could be even younger than Ruby first thought.

"OK," she began. "Those guys out there, well they've apparently stolen a truck load of Paradise from Marlon and he's seriously pissed about it. He wants them taken care of..."

"By us?" the other girl asked seeming mortified. "I don't take people out - I've never done anything like that!" She looked like she might cry, but Ruby had seen her in action. She might be scared but she was also confident. She handled herself well.

"No, I'm to do that bit," she reassured them both, pulling the gun and trying not to seem petrified of it.

"Whoa!" the girls cooed together, just as a bellow came from out front. It grabbed all three's attention.

"How long does it take to get two school uniforms on?" Ryan shouted out.

"Not as long as it takes to get them off again!" Billingham called back, and then there was laughing and jeering. Ruby shuddered.

"OK, we don't have much time, but if we're going to do this I need you to do your part good. If they see me, or even know I'm here, they will flip and kill me and you two will stay Marlon's...probably forever. I need to know that by the time I make an appearance they will be secure."

"Secure?" the girl who'd been struck repeated.

"I need you two to get dressed up, get out there and tie them up. Can you do that?" Ruby asked them, and they looked at each other again and then turned back to her and grinned. "Now there's something we definitely *can* do!" they giggled. They immediately set to looking the part, no better incentive than the smell of freedom. They hooked handcuffs to their belts and Ruby looked them up and down. "You look good," she told them proudly. "Now go show them who's boss... and, you know, be careful," she tacked on all motherly.

She snuck up to the curtain again and watched. The boys were in for a good show and for guys who usually liked to be in control they were more than eager to sit back and be taken care of. The young women wasted no time and the two men were soon desperate and completely oblivious to just how vulnerable they were. Finally happy with their handiwork, the girls turned on their heels and made their way back to a very anxious Ruby. They arrived at exactly the same time as Danny stepped through the backstage door looking very frustrated.

"I told you to stay put!" he ranted and Ruby pulled a face at him, warning him to shut up.

"I know...but something came up," she whispered back, impatiently. "I need you to take these girls to the safest escape point, can you do that?" she asked him, and he gritted his teeth at her and took her arm gently, guiding her out of earshot.

"Ruby! We don't have time to go saving everyone..."

"Either you take them or I will. I have some business to sort out and if you're going to make me do both jobs then it's going to take me twice as long. So, what's it going to be?" she asked him stubbornly, just as another furious yell came from the front. Danny frowned at her slowly and suspiciously and then made his way to peek through the curtain.

"Ruby, what the hell are you playing at?" he snapped. She slipped alongside him so she could speak softly into his ear.

"Please, Danny, let me deal with them. I don't have much time and those two girls just did the most amazing job of getting them tied up like a couple of roast turkeys. The least we can do is make sure they get out of here...*alive*." He thought about it and then nodded.

"And you have the gun, right?"

"Of course."

"And you promise me you won't go soft or mad and start untying them or anything. They will properly hurt you, Ruby."

"Do you think I'm nuts!"

"Yes I do!"

"Look, you have my word," she promised. He sighed and ran his hand through his hair while he thought about what she was suggesting. Leaning in to stroke his finger down her cheek lovingly he then turned away and led the girls out of the dressing room and up the back stairs.

Ruby swallowed down the bile in her throat and took a deep breath, before pushing open the curtain and allowing herself to be seen.

She needed an act, just like the girls had done, to slip into a character of her own making that would help her to feel more confident and in control. She would pretend she was in the court room, she had seen enough of how that went down. She could be barrister, lawyer, judge and jury. This was her arena now, her rules, her laws, and right here was where she would see justice finally done.

"What the..." Ryan trailed off and Bilingham tried to stand but was restricted. Thankfully he hadn't seen the hesitation in Ruby's approach when she feared he might just get up and grab her. The way he slumped back into his seat made it pretty obvious he was going nowhere, fast.

"So, we meet again," she greeted them. "Ryan. Billingham. I'd like to say it's a pleasure but, of course, I'd be lying my arse off."

"If you're about to strip for us, Ruby Palmer, I'd say things couldn't get much better," Ryan sniggered and Billingham joined him.

"I got a little look at her once, Ryan, and I can confirm that Ruby has definitely got better with age. You were in your little gym kit when we first got cosy, isn't that right, Ruby?" he asked her, and she knew he was trying to pick at her defences. She wouldn't let that happen.

"Oh you mean the time you made me physically sick at the thought of having your dirty, sweaty hands on me?" she smiled. "The same day I opted to wash my body in a scalding hot school shower just to try and burn the feeling of you and your breath from my skin?" His jaw flexed, she was getting to him. "Or are you talking about the time I played you for a fool and showed you up for the pervert you really are? You know, when I got you expelled?" she laughed.

"You bitch! You deserved everything you got and you know it!" he seethed. "Strutting around like you owned the place, mouthing off, getting into trouble, getting too big for your boots. You were gagging for it in the sports shed and I told everyone that too."

"And by everyone, do you mean your one and only pervert friend, Ryan? I didn't want it, hence the reason I was begging you to stop, hence the reason I cried and hence the reason I refused to do as you said, and threatened you. Did you tell Ryan that you flaked under the pressure? Bet you didn't," she smiled coolly. "Bet you didn't tell him you couldn't go through with it. A fourteen year old girl scared the hell out of you didn't she, Billingham?"

"I got enough," he snarled. "I got my hands ALL over you!"

"And that very sad confession is probably the biggest achievement of your life," she sighed, like she pitied him and now he was mad. He tried to get up again and she accidentally stepped back; big mistake to show fear like that around the likes of him.

"I'm going to get out of this and then I'm going to give you that initiation you should have had all those years ago. Ryan here is going to help me punish you. You've messed with the wrong people, Ruby Palmer!" he fumed at her, just as she noticed that their hands were not cuffed, they were only tied. Her eyes drifted to Ryan, who had remained remarkably quiet for what was meant to be a gang ringleader, to see that he was almost out of his restraints.

She dithered - a fatal error. She wasn't sure what to do and suddenly he was reaching for his ankles and pulling the ties away.

He came at her fast and shoved her up against the podium. She reached behind to her back; it felt like it had snapped on impact and she was nauseous and winded. Her hand touched on the gun but she couldn't reach it in time before he'd slammed her up against the wall, banging her head and making her dizzy. He held her hands above her, crushing her under his weight, as he hooked the loops of the rope that had been tied at his ankles around her wrists. He then threw the length over a beam above their heads and pulled hard until she could only just touch the floor on her tiptoes. He secured it with a knot.

"What did I ever do to you?" she cried out at him, and he held her steady with his hands on her hips.

"You did plenty," he told her and she shook her head at him.

"You're a liar! I've done nothing to either of you and anything I've done to Billingham he deserved, and some! I'd never even met you before Sasha's party and suddenly you want me punished and killed! What's it to you if I deserted? What's it to you if I was never initiated in the first place?" she panicked, feeling the heat of his hands against the exposed skin at her waist.

"You remember Candice?" he asked her and she nodded.

"Yes, of course, I remember her but..."

"I should think you do, Ruby. Your little crew nearly took her out completely. So why was it OK to punish and initiate her when you got off scot-free?"

"What?" She desperately tried to piece together what she was hearing.

"Ruby, you were Matthew's girl - he kept you like a little princess by all accounts, keeping you from being anyone else's, keeping you from being set tasks to show your loyalty and then taking you home for the night. It made some members jealous how he went on about how eager you were, how easy you were...for him," he sneered. "Is that how you played it, Ruby? You're one clever girl I'll give you that, manipulating the leader and then seeing that anyone new, like Candice, had to be put through her paces. You know what she had to do, right?"

"Yes," Ruby nodded and whispered. "But..."

"You were happy to see her cut, robbed and dumped in some old garage like a dirty, used mattress, after everything she'd done to be accepted. Just because she'd refused your man, right?" he raged. She could feel the fury in his hands as he squeezed her tighter. He wanted to crush her to death, crush the life out of her, like Billingham nearly had when he let her swing.

"I don't under...I never..." she stammered out, but he held his hand over her mouth to stop her. She could taste the salt on his warm palms as she tried to shake her face away.

"Candice is my girl, Ruby, and she's told me all about what you did to her."

"She said I did it?" she exclaimed as frightened tears rolled down her face. This was a vendetta! "Candice gave you *my* name?"

"No, but she didn't have to. You were part of the crew and I'm guessing the slutty little ring leader's girlfriend was happy to play a part, just as long as it wasn't her own backside feeling the heat. That's how it works isn't it, Ruby?"

"No!" she protested. "I wasn't there! I didn't know about it! I stayed out of it all..."

"Just in case someone noticed it was your turn, yeah?" he laughed, looking her up and down like she was nothing more than scum.

"No I mean I wasn't even part of the crew...not really..."

"I'd say sleeping with the leader makes you part of the crew, Ruby."

"But I wasn't sleeping with him!" she shouted back, furiously. "How dare he tell you that I was! He's a liar, always has been, always will be. He offered me protection, yes, from my dad! My dad beat me every day of my life and I had nowhere else to go. Matthew took me in. He gave me somewhere to stay for a few hours, Ryan, not over night! All I wanted was a friend, someone who would take me in and save me for a little while. He was always trying it on but I didn't want that with him. I didn't want to be part of the gang, but that's who he was and what he was mixed up in. He

278

took advantage of my situation but I never slept with him, not once! I've never slept with anyone!" she defended desperately. She had no hope, and her only bargaining tool was the truth. Ryan had been concentrating on her middle when he suddenly looked up into her eyes.

"What?" he asked flatly and she dithered, unsure what he wanted her to say.

"I don't understand," she sobbed. He was frowning at her now. He glanced towards Billingham who was making good progress with his restraints and back to her again.

"I had no intention of touching you, Ruby. I'm with Candice and I'm loyal to her. I'll admit you're hot and if I were single, well, that might be another matter. When I met Billingham it seemed we had something in common..."

"A sick interest in little girls!" she spat out but he shook his head.

"No way, I'm not into all of that. Yeah, I'll admit that I've pretended that I was to get what I wanted. No, Ruby, the thing we had in common was that we both wanted revenge...on you. It was so easy. I needed you punished to get at Matthew. I took over his crew, saw that he became the underdog and then I enlisted Billingham here to see that you were put through your paces, give you a taste of your own medicine..."

"But I didn't do anything wrong," she whispered helplessly. "All I've been doing my whole life is trying to stay out of trouble, trying to prove everyone wrong and keep my head above water. I've had to fight every day of my life against people like Billingham, my dad, Matthew Dean, Marlon, you!" she choked out bitterly.

"But you were never even his...Matthew's?" he clarified, and she shook her head.

"No. He was always pestering me, telling me I should, I had to, it was about time I did. He accused me of being frigid, cold, a tease, but all I wanted was a friend, someone who would help me out and put a roof over my head whenever I was homeless! He used me - that's all he's ever done, and the other day he grassed on the both of you!" She hated Matthew more than ever now. She was taking the flack for his wrongdoings and it was just so typical of him.

"So you've never been with...anyone?" he asked her, looking slightly sceptical, and she tilted her head back and groaned.

"Don't tell me, that's a dream come true and you can't wait to do something about it," she guessed.

"Well I'm definitely going to," Billingham shot back, and she looked at him, petrified. How long was Danny going to take! She looked back at Ryan and his expression had changed.

"No, Ruby," he whispered, getting so close she could feel his breath on her ear. "It's not a dream come true for me, but I am going to do something about it."

She tried to fight the restraints in a panic but he caught her tightly and held her still. "Calm down or you'll just make things harder. I'm letting you go." He reached up and struggled with the knot. Something caught her eye and she glanced in Billingham's direction to see the ties finally fall from his ankles.

"Hurry, Ryan, he's coming!" she squealed out and he shot a look over his shoulder and then turned back to concentrate on her, pushing the end of the rope through a loop and yanking on it. "I have a gun in my waistband," she whispered and he stopped to let that register for a fraction of a second and then continued with the rope. "Ryan!" she screamed, as Billingham approached with his hands clasped above his head. He brought them down on top of Ryan, hitting him full force, and the young man grunted and then collapsed to the floor at Ruby's feet. Billingham crouched down to check he was unconscious. Now she was on her own...with Billingham. She couldn't let that happen. She pushed herself up on her toes and yanked until the knot slackened and the rope hung loose over the beam above her head. She curled her hands into it and gripped on tight so she could pull her feet up off the floor as Billingham stood, kicking him full force in the face. He fell backwards, hitting the ground hard and she dropped straight onto Ryan by accident. She felt his hands run around her waist pushing her forwards as he growled out at her.

"Run, Ruby, or he'll get you."

She pelted it as fast as she could, but Billingham lunged and grabbed her ankle, toppling her. She kicked him away and kept moving into the shadows but when she turned she could no longer see him. The lights dimmed; he must have found the switch, and now she could barely see. He cranked the music up and it vibrated right through the thin soles of her shoes.

"Hey, Ruby," he called out, and she spun to face the direction from which his voice had come but she couldn't see a thing.

"Damn it," she whispered to herself and then more loudly she spoke to him. "Once a coward always a coward, eh Billingham? That's what bullies are - that's why they need the lights out and force to get a girl. To be fair, you're not getting one any other way," she jibbed.

"To be fair," he echoed. "You're not doing yourself any favours, Ruby Palmer, but then you never did know when to shut your face, did you? I might just have to gag you when I catch you. I don't want to listen to any of your mouthy crap while I finish you off."

"I have a gun, John, and I'm not afraid to use it," she told him boldly, and he laughed back at her.

"Yeah, but being fearless isn't enough to shoot someone, Ruby, you need to be able to aim too. You're a girl and everyone knows that girls can't shoot." He had a point in one respect; she hadn't a clue how to shoot and she reached to her waistband to retrieve her weapon and give it a go, but the gun wasn't there! She gasped out, trying to work out where it could have gone. She'd lost her only means of protection! If he reached out from somewhere and grabbed her now she would only be equipped to give up and drop dead.

"Why me, Billingham?" she yelled, trying to buy herself some thinking time and keep track of him by keeping him talking. He chuckled out of the darkness. "Why have you come back for me, after all these years?"

"Because you were the one that got away," he informed her from right behind her ear and she screamed and swung round only to be grabbed and pushed to the floor. He wasted no time securing her under his weight. "You

281

won't get away from me this time. This time I get more than a lingering feel of your body while you sob beneath me, Ruby. This time it won't be my hands doing all the work either but, be brave, it won't hurt for long," he cooed sickeningly. His weight was pressing the air from her lungs and she fought and clawed at him but she didn't stand a chance. A crack rang out, deafening Ruby, and she screamed and clasped at her ears. Almost immediately she was aware of Billingham being hoisted off her and she watched as he hit the podium and collapsed to the floor. She could hear a voice, but it sounded as if she were under water. She shook her head, it cleared, and then she heard the words again.

"Ruby, get up and get the gun!" Danny ordered, and she wasted no time in doing as she was told. Danny was laying into John and though he tried to put up a good fight, Billingham's attempt at self defence was feeble in comparison. She looked about for the gun, the lights were back on now and she hadn't even noticed when that had happened. Glancing across the floor she saw Ryan still where he'd collapsed, blood pouring from his head. He was holding her weapon as he watched her and she stayed still now, too afraid to move.

He cringed painfully, putting his other hand to his head and then, to her surprise, he placed the gun on the ground and kicked it towards her. She moved to pick it up; it was back in her hands...at last! She felt a little safer now.

"I grabbed it when you landed on me. I was going to help you," he explained, pressing his hand to his head again and bringing it round to check the amount of blood on it. "You told me it was there and I figured you wanted me to use it, but after I pushed you up and told you to run I blacked out. I came round but I still couldn't stand. I could hear you but I couldn't see you and the lights were out. When the lights came back on he had you on the floor so I shot out but missed. I'm sorry, I tried," he gasped.

"Are you OK?"She edged a little closer, still cautious of him. He shook his head and the resulting agony was clear.

"I don't know what he had in his hand but he's cut me pretty bad. It's deep. I'd get moving but I keep passing out. I can't even stand. Go help

Danny," he told her. "Get out of here while you can, Ruby, you deserve better than all of this. I didn't realise - I made a huge mistake and I judged you. I believed everything I was told, and I made assumptions about who you were and where you came from. You know what, you're OK, Ruby Palmer," he smiled, before leaning against the wall and slowly passing out again. Ruby dithered and then turned to see Danny grabbing the other man around the throat.

"Not so good when it comes to fighting men are you?" he goaded, lifting him from the floor effortlessly and pinning him into the chair that he'd escaped from. He slapped him hard across the face with the back of his hand and then he turned to look at Ruby, now couched at Ryan's side. "Ruby, the girls realised they'd forgotten the cuffs; they're in my back pocket," he told her. She stood and made her way over, slipping the cuffs out and pulling Billingham's arms behind the chair back, securing his wrists so that *this time* he wouldn't escape.

"I just want to get the footage," Ruby confessed, wiping her teary face on the back of her hands. "I'm not so sure how much more I can take of this, Danny. Can we come back for them?" she asked and Danny nodded.

"Of course, sweetheart," he soothed, giving her a strong hug and telling her how much he loved her. She snuggled up close, wishing she were home, safe and warm, and then suddenly he covered her ear and held her to his chest firmly as he reached out and shot Billingham right in the foot. Billingham roared with pain but the music drowned it out and Ruby stared, mouth open, in complete shock. Danny smiled at his old classmate. "Don't worry, be brave, Billingham, it won't hurt for long...only until I come and finish you off."

No smoke without fire

After a steadying breath Ruby took the lead again and directed them up the stairs and towards the library. Once safely inside they spotted their first obstacle, a man asleep in the armchair, the television in front of him now fuzzy. He had a remote on his knee and two bottles of vodka at his feet. Ruby pulled the last syringe from her pocket.

"If he tries to undo your jeans or has the nerve to frisk you I'm just going to shoot him outright!" Danny declared, like he was tired now. She nodded, she was tired too.

She crept over to the armchair and loitered for a second. The man was snoring loudly and she figured he was drunk and probably unable to feel very much. With a great deal of care, and nerves of steel, she pushed the needle into the crook of his arm. He stayed still, only his breathing was interrupted for a second. She slowly pushed the fluid in and then she nearly jumped right out of her skin when he instantly jolted forwards. Sliding from the chair he hit the floor and began writhing around. She ran to the television and ejected the disk that had been playing. She read the title on the front.

"Oh god, that's so gross! I hate Marlon!" she exclaimed bitterly.

"Hated," Danny corrected coolly. "Past tense, remember? Is it you, on the disk?" he asked, growing annoyed, and she looked from his troubled gaze to the man rolling around on the floor and decided to lie.

"No, someone else." She made her way straight to the shelves and Marlon's DVD collection.

"Let me see then," he demanded. "If it's not you then you won't mind if I check, will you?" he tested but she snapped it up in front of him and pushed the pieces into the back pockets of her jeans. He huffed and pushed the man on the floor with his foot.

"Danny, just leave him! I want all the DVDs with me on them, right, so find them...now!"

"Sir! Yes sir!" he saluted with a grin, and then helped her locate what she was looking for. Ruby pulled them all from the shelves and removed every single disk before replacing the sleeves. She collected them all together and slid them into the back of her jeans.

"Anyone else trying to get into those tonight might get a nice little surprise," he joked, pulling on one of her belt loops gently. "How cool is that, you come with your very own collection of..." She scowled at him and he stopped. "Sorry," he whispered awkwardly. "Right, so, what's the plan?" he diverted sensibly.

"Erm..." she thought hard, biting down on her lip.

"Ruby, you said you had a plan!" he told her off.

"I do have a plan. It's..." she thought as fast as she could. "We torch the place."

"What?"

"Yeah, you know, it makes sense. Marlon looks like he shot himself while high. The bloke in the hallway was using and so is the bloke in here. They all still have the needles..."

"Yes they do," he agreed slowly. "Although in your neck in a hallway isn't the most conventional way of doing it." He raised his eyebrows at her and she giggled and shrugged.

"Do you think the police really care? This bloke here looks pretty legit and alcohol is very flammable," she reminded him lifting the bottles and putting them on the table. "You need to be especially careful when you're smoking at the same time. It's not very responsible, Danny." She picked up the packet of cigarettes and the lighter from the table and put one in her mouth, lighting it and taking a drag. Danny watched her, knowing exactly what was coming next.

"You do realise Alessi is going to have you rolling tea leaves into post-it notes by the morning for that little number don't you?" he told her, and she coughed deeply. It hurt her chest, tasted foul and she didn't like it one bit. She nearly gagged.

"Ugh that's so gross," she told him, blowing the smoke purposely in his face.

"These are very bad for your health," he told her, taking the cigarette from between her fingers and putting it to his own mouth. He took a long drag before blowing the smoke in her face; payback. She wafted it away, coughing again, and took it back off him to rest it in the ashtray. She unscrewed the lid from the vodka and spilt it around and over the armchair. Danny shook his head at her.

"We're still in the building, Ruby," he warned.

"Then we'll just have to make sure we get out again, won't we?" she told him simply, flicking the burning cigarette at the floor and watching as it burst into flames right in front of them. They were mesmerised for a few seconds and then the armchair suddenly went up too, licking flames as high as the ceiling. Danny grabbed Ruby's arm.

"Time to go me thinks!" he declared eagerly. They slipped out into the hallway and stepped over Hendrick's body. He was snoring.

When they reached the next floor they made their way back to the room they had come in through. There was a distinct smell of smoke now, but not strong just yet. As they reached the door to the bedroom Ruby suddenly looked back towards Marlon's suite and squealed.

"Oh god, of course, I've forgotten something! Danny, wait for me!"

"You can't go back for Ryan and Billingham, Ruby," he exclaimed. "Come on, let's go!" he told her sternly.

"I'll be two minutes, " she argued stubbornly, and before he realised what was happening she'd darted off down the hallway. He watched, defeated, as she passed the stairs they had come up. The girl was uncontrollable. He shook his head in despair and moved to go after her but to his surprise and frustration someone stepped out from the stairwell and pulled a gun on him. He stepped back, watching as smoke followed the gunman onto the landing, billowing black clouds into the hallway. Now he couldn't see properly and Ruby was lost from sight. He held his hands up, as if surrendering as he backed ever so slightly towards the door they had originally come through. When he reached it he dived for the handle, falling into the bedroom and hitting the floor. In seconds the man who had been asleep in there was on his feet and pointing his gun too.

"Oh great! RUBY!" he shouted out, praying she'd call back but there was no reply. The smoke was filling the room and it sat heavy like a dark, thick smog waist deep. Struggling to breathe, Danny stood up, showing the flats of his hands to the gunman. Then he slowly pulled his top off and pressed it to his face. The other man looked about him at the choking black smog, trying to work out what was going on. He took Danny's lead and swiftly started to remove his own top to do the same. As soon as his face disappeared inside his grimy looking shirt Danny dropped to the floor and kept flat. The smoke burnt his lungs but it was at least keeping him hidden.

"What the...where the hell are you? Show yourself!" he heard the rasp of the other gunman. The man in the hallway picked up his pursuit. He knew exactly where Danny was and it was going to be so easy to take him out. He stepped into the doorway to find a large figure in front of him, a fog of smoke obscuring his face. He soon registered that an outstretched arm was carrying a weapon, a gun, and it was pointed right at him. A double crack rang out and then the thud of two bodies as both men hit the floor. Danny stood and gasped for air, moving quickly to open the window fully.

Marlon's men had shot out in a blind panic and that left Danny just a jump away from freedom, but Ruby hadn't come back. He tried to retrace his steps, but he only got as far as the hallway before the heat hit him. He always believed that a burning fire wouldn't keep him from saving those he loved, but try as he might, he couldn't move past the crackling sparks and blistering inferno.

"Ruby! Ruby!" he called out, coughing hard, but he couldn't hear anything other than the crashing of debris and hunks of ceiling plaster as they fell to the floor. He was forced to turn back and leave, though it nearly killed him to do it. He climbed down onto the garage roof and then down to the ground. He called her again, over and over, but the place seemed dead. It was now just a burning tornado of twisting flames reaching high up into the dark sky. He had no idea where she'd gone and no clue where to even start looking.

He neared the building looking for any way in, but the windows had started to smash and huge, lethal shards of glass splintered down to the ground. Sickeningly, like a falling pack of cards, the roof started to cave in on itself. A creaking, thundering noise combined with the snap of red hot sparks as burning wood disintegrated and split into pieces. Danny walked backwards, quite some way from the hellish heat, and then fell onto the grass gasping for air and coughing painfully. His loss was so great, he felt desolate, destroyed and beyond repair, just like Marlon's property. He lifted his knees and sank his head into them, his hands clasped tightly to the back of his neck, as he rocked back and forth. She was gone; he'd finally lost his free spirit by letting her be just that - free. Was he wrong to give her so much slack, to let her make her own decisions, to let her fight her own battles? If he had done it Matthew's way she would never have been out of his bed, let alone tearing through a building looking for revenge. If he had done it Alessi's way she would be tucked up in her own bed, while everyone else dealt with her problems for her...albeit in their own time and in their own way. But he had done it his way, which was to give her the freedom to do it her way, to let her dictate her own life. That had resulted in him losing the one and only girl he had ever loved.

The noise of the fire raged on furiously and his thoughts were only of Ruby, so small and helpless inside a place so fierce and unforgiving. He wondered if she was trapped and screaming; there was no way she would get out now. He knew when hope was verging on a miracle, and now it would take a miracle for her to come out alive. He found himself praying she was already dead, the agony at least over for her. He looked up to see how much of the building was left: not much. The deep sound of idling engines thrummed at the locked front gates, unable to gain entry, and their sirens pealed out loudly into the darkness. They were too late as well. If the fire hadn't killed her the smoke definitely would have by now. There wasn't much left, nothing worth saving and she was gone. As if in confirmation, the first floor and roof completely collapsed into the ground floor. Marlon's house was obliterated.

He watched as the gates were taken down and four fire engines pulled up alongside each other at the other end of the vast gardens. The crew grouped together before pulling hoses and connecting to hydrants. What was the point in trying? Danny looked back to the corner of the building he had left through. A figure was walking towards him. It was dark and the thick smoke was being blown straight across the grass by the wind. One minute the figure was engulfed and the next the air had cleared and they were a little closer, but still quite far away. He watched as they were swallowed up once again but this time, when the smoke finally cleared, they were gone. He straightened himself. How was that possible? The most bizarre questions bombarded his mind. Did ghosts exist after all? Could spirits of good people be seen as they left their dying bodies? Had Ruby come to say goodbye, knowing how heartbroken he would be at losing her? He knew he must be delirious now, or desperate; he had never been a spiritual person, but he was genuinely considering the possibility of celestial visions. He moved to stand and then noticed the figure hadn't disappeared at all; they were on their hands and knees.

He got to his feet and made his way towards them; interest had been forced out of him and now he wanted to know more. If someone had walked out of the building alive, then that still left hope for Ruby. As he neared he quickly realised that the figure was small enough to be a girl. He broke into a run, pleading out loud for it to be her. She was coughing hard and it rasped painfully in her chest, in his Ruby's chest, where her heart was still alive...and beating. He threw himself down in front of her and pulled her into his arms. She was disorientated but allowed herself to be grabbed and held without even knowing who it was.

For a fleeting second she looked up into his eyes blankly. She didn't recognise him; her mind was playing cruel games on her and she wouldn't believe it was true. The pain of losing him all over again would be just too much for her to bear.

He smiled and shook her slightly, raising her chin and wanting her to snap out of the daze; he needed to hear her voice, for her to tell him she was alive and really there in his arms.

"Danny," she croaked. "I thought you were dead! There were so many bodies everywhere, I was treading on them but I couldn't see. I kept thinking one of them might be you but the lights wouldn't work, the place was pitch black." The tears smeared black tracks down her face and he smudged them with his sooty thumbs and kissed her anywhere he could find flesh. She fell back onto the grass, exhausted, and he straddled her.

"My god, Ruby, I would never have believed you would make it out of there alive. I'm so sorry I couldn't stay. I tried but it was impossible - I just kept getting beaten back." She closed her eyes and shook her head from side to side slowly. The cool grass was soothing.

"It's OK...I know," she panted for air. "I was trying to find you and I had to leave the building...thinking you were still in there too. I was trying to find another way in...on the other side...but the flames kept beating me back. It was so awful! I wanted to die if you were gone but it was impossible to make myself stay and let the fire take me - it was too hot. I felt so bad leaving you, Danny," she cried, and he leaned down and kissed her once, gently. She smiled with her eyes still closed and raised her arms above her head, stretching out and trying to fill her lungs with clean air.

"Why the hell did you go back when we we're nearly out?" he demanded "What on earth were you thinking!" He was just about keeping a lid on it but she could tell he was furious for what she'd just put him through. She bit down on her lip before leaning up onto her elbows to grin at him.

"I needed to get this," she told him digging into the pocket of her cardigan and pulling out a small camcorder, Marlon's camcorder. "It's what Marlon was recording me on when he attacked me this evening. I noticed the light but didn't figure it out until we were nearly out. He must have known I was coming somehow, set up the camcorder and then lay in wait for me...or maybe he just liked to record himself sleeping," she shrugged, turning it in her hands. "The recording light was definitely on and it would have caught everything that happened. I couldn't leave it. I mean there's nothing left of the building now, but there could have been, and then forensics would have found it for sure. If it had just been me being attacked and drugging him, I'd have taken my chances but you, Danny, *you* shot him! I just couldn't risk losing you."

"You did it to save me?" he asked her, holding her waist between his strong hands. He made her feel both safe and weak all at the same time. "Thank you, Ruby," he told her gratefully, as he leaned down and kissed her for longer, a lingering smoky kiss. He broke away gently and smiled at her with his seriously handsome grin.

"It wasn't a completely selfless act, Danny, I have to confess," she giggled, and he narrowed his eyes seeming intrigued. "I mean, look at you! You look great in your clothes, all those smart suits that fit you so well, it's criminal. But that's nothing in comparison to just how great you look out of them," she told him, reddening, and he looked down at his chest and cringed. He clearly worked out, though when she wasn't quite sure! The square shape of his chest, chiselled to perfection, and the stomach that bore the creases of a set of well toned abdominal muscles didn't happen all by itself. That took commitment and she was impressed. His arms were strong and he had a couple of scars on him. She was determined to find out later what had caused them. She gingerly placed her fingers on his collarbone and worked them down slowly over his skin to his bellybutton, which was seriously cute. He coughed, but this time it wasn't because of the smoke.

"We really ought to get going before people start asking questions," he advised, trying to be responsible, but she lost her fingers in his hair and reached up to kiss him again.

"Come on, Danny," she whispered. "What could be more romantic than in the garden, under the stars?"

"Next to a burning building with Marlon and his men still in it!" he added with a laugh.

"Yeah but it's dark and no one will know."

"Apart from the odd optimistic fireman who might get a bit of a shock."

"Oh, Danny, do you know waiting for you is driving me wild? You're so hot right now I could toast bloody marshmallows on you!" she snapped at him and he grinned, moving towards her ear as it turned into a really sexy chuckle. He nuzzled her neck and she coughed to get his attention. He pulled away and looked at her; she looked mad. "If you're working me up here with no intention of putting me out of my misery then you're going to wish you'd stayed in there and burnt to a crisp!" she threatened, jabbing a finger at his chest. "We agreed to wait until I was eighteen, just to keep Alessi happy, remember?" He nodded and she mellowed slightly. He wasn't arguing for once.

"And?" he smiled at her cheekily. "Your point is?"

"My point is that it's my birthday next week and what's seven days between lovers?" she giggled.

He licked his lips like he was hungry and she was dinner. The prospect excited her; she wanted to be all his. He stood and hoisted her to her feet, pausing for a moment before stooping to put her over his shoulder. "You are nothing but trouble, Ruby Palmer," he told her as he carried her effortlessly into the relative safety of the borders that surrounded the grounds. He lowered her back down gently and she felt the twisted trunk of a blossom tree against her back as he grasped the button on her jeans and teased it through the hole. "It's been all about getting your jeans off tonight," he told her with a wicked smile. "Looks like I'm the lucky man, unless of course you have any more shots of Paradise you intend to use...on me?" He looked slightly serious, even waiting for an answer, and she wondered whether he really didn't trust her.

"No more Paradise," she confirmed as he shaped his body to the contours of hers, sliding his hand around to her back.

"Are you sure this is what you want, Ruby?" he asked her and she huffed at him and scowled, making him grin. He loved her feisty side; it was *so* hot.

"Tonight I thought you were definitely dead, Mr Glover." She toyed with his name and he tried desperately not to laugh. It was impossible to do formal covered in soot. "We can't say for certain how long we have together and I don't know about you, but if my life's going to flash before my eyes, again, then I definitely want making love with you to be up here," she told him, tapping against her head. "If you don't want to, Danny, that's fine I'll just..."

"Shut up, Ruby," he told her, pulling her to him so he could create a memory with her that would burn to their minds like a recording to a disk. Only complete destruction could ever take it away from them.

For as long as they lived so too would that precious, thankful and doting night under the stars, fuelled by a desperate longing to be together...a desperate longing that went against *all* of Alessi's wishes.